SUNSHINE AND SHADOWS

KATIE FLYNN

SUNSHINE AND SHADOWS

arrow books

Published by Arrow Books 2008

2 4 6 8 10 9 7 5 3 1

Copyright © Katie Flynn 2008

First published in Great Britain in 2008 by
Arrow Books
The Random House Group Limited
20 Vauxhall Bridge Road, London SW1V 2SA

www.rbooks.co.uk

Addresses for companies within The Random House Group Limited
can be found at: www.randomhouse.co.uk/offices.htm

The Random House Group Limited Reg. No. 954009

A CIP catalogue record for this book
is available from the British Library

ISBN 9780434016235

The Random House Group Limited makes every effort to ensure that the
papers used in its books are made from trees that have been legally sourced
from well-managed and credibly certified forests. Our paper procurement
policy can be found at: www.rbooks.co.uk/environment

Typeset in Palatino by Palimpsest Book Production Limited,
Grangemouth, Stirlingshire
Printed and bound in Great Britain by
Printed in the UK by CPI Mackays, Chatham ME5 8TD

For Dot Shears, who loves a good story – let's
hope you enjoy this one, Dot!

Chapter One

Spring 1929

'Daisy Kildare, just what do you think you're doin'? Why, if Mam could see you now she'd skelp you, so she would! And the only half-decent skirt you own is bound to be wet, and not a jacket to your back, though the wind is comin' straight from the North Pole! Get up, you bad child, and don't tell me you've already picked the mussels because I can see the bucket's as empty as it was when you left the croft!'

Daisy, who had been sitting on the edge of the cliff and swinging her short legs over the twenty-foot drop, jumped guiltily at the sound of her elder sister's voice, and very nearly slid down the sheer face of the cliff on to the beach below. She looked down at her ancient blue blouse and skimpy grey skirt, thinking that Amanda must be joking. Despite the fact that it was a chilly spring day with a threat of rain on the gusting wind she had not felt cold, so why should she bother with a jacket? None of the Kildare children ever thought about the weather. Why should they? They had all been born and bred on the west coast of Ireland and took both rain and wind in their stride. Indeed they laughed at their mother, who was English born, when she said that if it wasn't raining in Connemara it was blowing up a gale, and if it wasn't blowing up a gale – or raining – the high moors and the Twelve Bens behind them would be a foot deep in snow.

Now, however, Daisy got to her feet and turned to glare at her older sister before bending to pick up the bucket. 'You near on made me jump out of me skin, so you did,' she said reproachfully. 'If I'd fallen and been kilt on the rocks, what would you have told Mammy, eh? She's upset enough about the work Daddy's got to do on his boat, wit'out you makin' it worse by nigh on killin' me.'

Amanda gave a contemptuous snort. 'Killin' you, indeed! You've as many lives as a cat and never a one have you lost yet, for all you're as wicked a spalpeen as any I've known and always into trouble or mischief. Oh aye, if you'd fell over that cliff you'd have landed on your feet right enough. But you've not answered me question. Why haven't you picked the mussels our mammy sent you out to collect? You know right well that there'll be no fish on our table until the *Mary Ellen*'s fit to go to sea again. It isn't even as though we can put out shore lines because we've not got any until Daddy or Brendan goes into Clifden again and buys some. Mammy will want the mussels cooked and some soda bread baked by the time Daddy comes in for his dinner. Oh, Daisy, you're only a kid and I dare say you don't mean to be naughty, but . . .'

Daisy spun on her heel and pointed to the beach below. 'And how should I pick the mussels when they're still under the water?' she enquired belligerently. 'Am I a mermaid, or an otter, that I can pick mussels when the sea surge is a foot or more above the rocks? Oh, I suppose clever, know-all Amanda, the most beautiful colleen in all Connemara, knows how to do such a t'ing, but as you say, I'm only a kid, and . . .'

'I'll give you a clack if you call me names,' Amanda hissed. 'Why, you wretched little worm, it was your turn to clean up after breakfast and what did you do? You cleared off, same as always, and if Mammy hadn't spotted you and yelled to you to pick mussels, you'd not even ha' done that. I've been up to me eyes in bakin' all mornin' and Brendan's gone off wit' Daddy to see if he can find a tree what he can cut down and trim up for a mast; even little Finn has been helpin', keepin' an eye on Dermot while Mammy's cookin'.'

The *Mary Ellen* was a sturdy black-tarred fishing boat, the pride and joy of Colm Kildare's heart. However, on the previous day, Colm and Brendan had been returning to the little cove where they kept the boat, delighted with their catch, when a sudden gale had sprung up. Colm had leapt to reef the sail, meaning to lie out the storm, as they had done on many another occasion, but whilst he was lowering the stiff rust-red canvas a strong gust had torn the material from his hands, ripping it to shreds and snapping the mast off short, a mere foot above the deck. It would be a costly business replacing sail, mast and sheets but, as Colm had pointed out, it could have been a great deal worse; if the sail and mast had not gone, then the *Mary Ellen* might well have turned turtle, and had that happened she would doubtless have been wrecked on the rocks that ran down from the shore into deep water.

'Sorry, sorry, sorry,' Daisy mumbled, because the thought of the awful accident which would put the *Mary Ellen* out of commission, her father had said, for as much as a fortnight, made her ashamed to admit that she had indeed hoped to escape from the cottage before her mother saw her. 'I forgot it were my turn to do the dishes. I expect Annabel did 'em, so I'll take her turn tomorrow. I'll go down and start pickin' the mussels as soon as the tide turns, or do you want to lecture me some more?'

She was watching Amanda's face a trifle anxiously, for her sister was quick on her feet and if she chose to hand out a few sharp slaps there was little Daisy could do to prevent her, but to her secret relief she saw amusement in the quirk of Amanda's mouth and knew she was safe, for the time being at least. 'I don't want to lecture anyone, but you know we won't be gettin' any fish until the *Mary Ellen*'s able to go to sea again. We'll probably all be pickin' mussels an' diggin' cockles for a week or two.'

'Yes, and Aunt Jane's coming soon,' Daisy

reminded her sister. 'That'll mean spring cleaning the cottage from top to bottom and even more cooking than you and Mammy have done today. I wish we could write and put her off because of the boat being broke, but Mammy says there's no time and anyway she says Aunt Jane is a big help and won't mind if Daddy spends most of his time refitting the *Mary Ellen*.'

'It 'ud be grand if the *Mary Ellen* was afloat by the time Aunt Jane comes,' Amanda agreed. 'But it's not likely; the mast may not cost us but you don't find sails or ropes growing on the moors, worse luck. And now I'd best be on my way. I'm walking into the village to buy a bit of dried fruit; Mammy wants to make brack and we've run out of currants. Now off wit' you, alanna, and get the mussels back to Mammy just as quick as you can.'

The older girl turned away as she spoke and Daisy stood for a moment, gazing after her, admiring her sister's slender figure, and the long wheat-gold hair which fell almost to her waist. Aunt Jane had said that Amanda looked just like her mother at a similar age and Daisy thought that must be true, for mother and daughter were alike still. Amanda was fifteen, six whole years older than Daisy herself, and though Daisy considered her far too bossy and quick to correct the younger ones with a clack, she still thought her the prettiest girl she had ever seen.

Now, she turned back towards the shore, bucket in hand, and headed for the stony little path which led down to the beach, thinking as she did so how strange it was that her sweet and gentle mother should have a sister who was just the opposite. Jane Dalton was a tartar, strict and demanding and not slow to hand out a slap either, if a child were rude or disobedient, and Daisy, who disliked her aunt, was frequently both. She knew she was not alone in disliking Aunt Jane. None of the older children had any time for their mother's sister, because she disapproved of them and was so strict, and also because she despised their whole way of life. She was fond of reminding the family that Colm had had a good job in Liverpool, working for the railways, when he and Maggie had first married. And though she never actually said he had done wrong to return to Connemara and the hard life of a fisherman, the implication was there.

There was also the fact that she sometimes referred, almost wistfully, to those early days when Maggie Dalton had been the belle, according to their aunt, of half Liverpool. 'There was a butcher on Leece Street and the feller your mother worked for in the insurance office, and I dare say a dozen others who would have been proud to take your mammy to wife. And they were all what we call warm men, which means they were well off financially,' she had told them. 'But then Colm appeared on the scene and there's no denying he were the best-lookin' young feller for miles around; well, you know that, for he's still a grand-lookin' chap. Your mammy was only a foolish girl and before

6

you could say knife, they were promised.' She had heaved a sigh. 'Ah well, I dare say Maggie has no regrets, but I sometimes wish things had turned out different.'

Amanda, Brendan, Daisy and Annabel had been shelling peas, sitting in a row on the dry stone wall whilst Finn and Dermot played with a pile of pebbles. It had been the previous summer and thirteen-year-old Brendan, who believed in speaking his mind, had said frankly that he was relieved, so he was, that Mammy had took to Daddy instead of one of them other fellers. 'For I'm sure there's no place better'n Connemara in the whole world and no cottage nicer'n this one,' he had said roundly. 'Of course I don't know nothin' about Liverpool but I've heard tell it's bigger'n Clifden, an' I couldn't live in Clifden, not if you were to pay me a hundred pounds.'

Fortunately, this remark had taken Aunt Jane's mind off her sister's choice of husband. She had given an indignant snort, her cheeks reddening. 'Liverpool bigger'n Clifden! Ah well, you're only a lad and know nothin'. But Liverpool's the biggest city in England and though they say London's even bigger, I don't reckon much to it meself. Why, there's shops in Liverpool near on as big as the whole of Clifden Main Street, and you can meet folk from all over the world shopping in Paddy's Market or St John's. You think your home is a grand place, and so you should, but that's because you've never walked down the Scottie on a sunny morning and seen the wonderful shops and the seamen, black, white, yellow and coffee-coloured, wi' their arms full of bargains what they're takin' back to their ships. An' then there's the Overhead Railway, what runs alongside the docks . . .'

'We know all about railways; there's a grand railway at Clifden,' Amanda had put in, flushing as she did so, for she always tried to avoid an argument with her aunt.

In fact, Daisy thought now as she crossed the sand, their family could be divided neatly into the good and not so good, simply going by their colouring. She and Brendan, both dark-eyed and dark-haired, were the only Kildares who ever stood up to their aunt. They were like their father in looks, though not in temperament, for he was as easy-going and good-tempered as his wife. But there was no doubt about it, Amanda, Finn and Dermot, all with hair the colour of wheat, were the quiet and biddable ones, leaving Daisy and Brendan to argue, complain and insist on being listened to, should the need arise. But her theory fell down when she remembered Annabel, who was almost as dark as Daisy herself but was quiet and obedient, always doing as she was told and never getting into scrapes. Folk often thought Annabel was older than Daisy, though this was not the case, as Annabel was ten months the younger.

At this point in her musing, however, Daisy reached the surf. She had to wade into the water to get to the first of the great black mussel-encrusted rocks and she reflected, as she began to pick, that she and Brendan, both hot-tempered and prone to speak their minds, would have to bite their tongues for a while. Until the *Mary Ellen* was back at the fishing, things would be hard enough for the Kildares, without a strained atmosphere prevailing between the family and their no doubt well-meaning but critical aunt.

But perhaps Aunt Jane isn't all bad, Daisy told herself as she scrambled back up the cliff path, her bare toes digging into the rough surface, for the now filled bucket was heavy and needed both her hands. Mam always tells us how her sister Jane took care of her when she was a kid, even though she was only six years older – the same age gap as there is between Amanda and me. I must think about that, then it will be easier to be nice to her.

Reaching the top of the cliff, she stood the bucket down for a moment to get her breath, and looked about her. What had begun as a chilly day had turned into a nice one, she saw with satisfaction. The sun shone, fluffy white clouds chased each other across a pale blue sky, and when she presently reached the deep little lane which led to their croft she saw that the hazel catkins were yellow with pollen, and she chirruped to a bright-eyed thrush searching for snails in a patch of mossy dry stone wall. It was tempting to put her bucket down for another rest so that she might pick a bunch of catkins, but even as she contemplated doing so she remembered Amanda's words and glanced at the position of the sun in the sky overhead. She had best hurry, for the mussels must be scrubbed clean before they were put in the pot and Daisy guessed that Mam would want the kitchen cleared of all signs of baking before Colm and Brendan arrived home for the midday meal.

As she walked, swapping the bucket from hand to hand to ease her burden, she wondered whether her father had taken the donkey cart, for she knew that the nearest woods were a good seven miles away and guessed that if they did manage to find a young pine of the right size, then bringing it home strapped to the cart would be considerably easier than trying to carry it between them. Brendan was a good deal shorter than his father, which would make carrying even a young tree for such a distance extremely difficult. On the other hand she had gathered, from a conversation between her parents the previous evening, that Colm felt a little diffident about the taking of a tree without anyone's permission. The copse he had in mind was almost certainly part of a large country estate whose owner lived for most of the year in Dublin. But he had an agent who would doubtless object to the removal of even one tree if he knew of it. Maggie had suggested that her husband should ask permission and offer to pay for the tree, but, knowing the agent as he did, Colm was sure such a request would be refused.

Better to mark the pine down and cut and cart it away unobserved if possible. If not, the two Kildares would return after dark and spirit the tree away then.

Thinking of the donkey cart made Daisy think about Tina, with her velvet muzzle, enormous pricked ears and gentle brown eyes. The little donkey was much loved by the whole Kildare family and most years she produced a foal, as pretty as herself, which was sold at the Clifden horse fair and made a nice profit which Colm spent on improvements to the cottage or extending the croft.

Maggie Kildare and Amanda would take the donkey cart as near the shore as they could get it, fill the big plaited straw baskets with as much of the *Mary Ellen*'s catch as they could hold, and drive to the surrounding villages, or even as far as Clifden, to sell the fish. Dad had crab and lobster pots too, but without a boat to row out to the pots there would be no shellfish either for a while. Daisy knew that this stretch of coast was a particularly dangerous one because the long reefs of rock caused swirling currents in which the unwary might easily perish. Then there were the sea caves in which her father put down most of his crab and lobster pots. There, a man and boat could enter at low tide, but once the tide had turned he had to move quickly if he was to escape into open water again. That was why Brendan's offer to try to clamber out to the caves at low tide had been turned down as too dangerous. Men had been drowned in those caves and boats lost in the currents caused by the reefs of rock, impossible to see at high tide, and even dangerous at low tide, when a boat could be wrecked and her crew drowned in a matter of minutes.

Which was why the *Mary Ellen* was the only craft to sail from here. Most fishermen preferred to keep their boats either in Roundstone harbour or in Cleggan, but the Kildare family had fished from the little cove, not a quarter of a mile from their croft, for as long as anyone could remember and Colm was not the man to break with tradition if he could possibly help it.

Halfway along the lane, a tiny brook bubbled its way down to the sea and here Daisy stopped for a moment, knelt down and cupped her hands to catch a drink of the fresh water. There was a well in the back yard of the cottage but in dry weather the water was sometimes brackish and the Kildares preferred to collect water from the brook for drinking. Wedged against the bank was an ancient bucket and normally Daisy would have filled this and carried it back to her mother, but today she could not do so for the mussels were as much as she could manage.

Having slaked her thirst, she heaved up her bucket once more and set off in the direction of home, wishing that the donkey cart would arrive right now so that she might get a lift, if not for herself, at least for her burden. She glanced hopefully behind her but the deep little lane was empty, so she gritted her teeth and walked on. She did wonder whether she might dump half the mussels and come back for them later, because with every step she took the bucket banged against her shins. However, she was rather proud of the quantity of mussels she had picked, so continued on her way.

Having thought about the donkey, however, she remembered that there had been talk the previous evening concerning that selfsame animal. Tina was a solemn, good-tempered little hinny and she was in foal now, yet Mam had actually suggested that both Tina and the cart should be sold. 'They'll bring in a decent bit of money which can go towards refitting the *Mary Ellen*,' she had said, and Daisy could only be thankful that their father had vetoed the idea.

'Mercy, and what would I do with me catch when the herrin' are runnin' and we've more fish than we could eat in a month?' he had asked. 'Do you expect me to harness Shep to an orange box and drive him all the way to Clifden? Or maybe you t'ink I should strap a creel to me back and sell the fish from that, like a pedlar or a tinker?'

He had looked so comical when he had made the suggestion that Mammy had burst out laughing and then jumped up from her chair and gone over to give her husband a hug. 'Oh, Col, there's still hope while you can make a joke of it and I can laugh,' she had said. 'But I'd rather anything than see the children starve or grow weak from eatin' nothin' but spuds and a few skinny cabbages.'

Colm had pulled his wife on to his lap and tickled her while the children had surrounded them, wanting to join in the fun. 'Maggie, oh Maggie, what sort of a feller d'you t'ink I am?' he had said plaintively. 'I'm not sayin' there's much work around because I know there ain't, but I can turn me hand to most t'ings. No Kildare will starve while I'm alive to prevent it.'

Brendan had immediately exclaimed that he would go to Roundstone, or even to Galway itself, and earn money at the fishing for a couple of weeks, for he didn't reckon much to school.

'I could help as well, so I could,' Daisy had chimed in eagerly. 'If Brendan goes to Roundstone for the fishing, I could help at the farm in his place.'

Amanda had scoffed at her sister's suggestion. 'You'd soon grow tired of it, same as you grow tired of helpin' Brendan on the croft, or sellin' fish from the donkey cart,' she had said. 'Why, the number of times Mammy has sent you to get potatoes from the clamp and when you've not returned, she's gone to find out what's happened to you and there you are, sittin' on the ground wit' a bit of stick, drawin' faces on the taties like a kid of three.'

Everyone had laughed except Daisy, who ruffled up indignantly. 'I hate you, Amanda Kildare,' she had said wrathfully. 'I were only five when I done that . . .'

'Ah, but in the years which have passed since

14

then you've done all manner of similar things,' her mother had reminded her. 'Any little task I set you either gets done by Amanda, or is half done by your good self. And you're such a dreamer, alanna; I don't see you stickin' to any sort of job for longer'n five minutes.'

'Oh well, yes, but that were before Daddy couldn't go fishin' and needed money for repairs,' Daisy had said eagerly. 'I've changed, Mammy, truly I have, and I am strong; when the Clancys began to bully Annabel and lie in wait for her after school, I nigh on kilt 'em; ain't that so, Annabel? And Paddy Clancy is two years older'n me and even Cait is big for her age.'

'But it's not fightin' we're talkin' about, alanna, but working,' her father had said gently. 'However, I'm not expectin' you to work for wages just yet; only give your mammy a hand when she needs help and have a wee bit more patience wit' Finn and little Dermot when you're asked to look after them. Remember the cuttlefish eggs?'

Daisy had felt the hot blood rush into her cheeks. The cuttlefish episode had clearly not been forgotten, though she had done her best to persuade her family that it had not truly been her fault. She had meant to be helpful, it was just that time had passed so quickly . . . and anyway, how could she have guessed that Finn and Dermot would be so naughty, would not heed her command to stay just where they were and do nothing until her return?

15

The truth was that she had been sent to mind the two little ones on a hot summer day and had taken them down to the shore whilst her mother and elder sister drove the donkey cart into Clifden to sell a quantity of fine codling and a dozen large and very angry lobsters. At first she had minded the two little boys diligently – that is to say she had played with them at digging in the sand and paddling in the pools – but then she had grown bored, and also thirsty. Bidding them to stay just where they were and do nothing naughty for ten minutes or so, she had climbed up the cliff path and gone to the brook for a drink of water. Only when she had got there she had decided to dam the stream, since it was a mere trickle and, besides, damming a stream was better fun than chasing after Finn when he wandered off or preventing Dermot from rubbing sand into his own eyes. And later, when she was told to fetch water, it would be a far easier task to scoop it from the fine pool she would make than to wait and wait, holding the bucket, whilst the water trickled slowly in.

Industriously, she had built a fine wall across the brook with big pebbles and lumps of slippery clay and when, more than an hour later, she had returned to the beach, feeling virtuously that she had done a good job, it was to find Brendan trying to persuade Finn to spit out something unpleasant which he appeared to be eating with every sign of enjoyment whilst the baby lay over Brendan's shoulder, screaming and dribbling and looking like an animated sandcastle. Brendan had been furiously angry with her, for when he had first seen his little brothers Finn had been almost choking upon a large half-eaten cuttlefish egg and the baby, sand in his ears, hair, nostrils and mouth, had been wailing dolorously and vomiting seawater.

When their mother heard what had happened she had given Daisy the only beating she had ever received, for neither of the Kildare parents believed in hitting their children. 'But some kids need the wickedness beating out of 'em,' Maggie Kildare had said breathlessly, slapping Daisy as hard as she could and then confining her to the girls' bedroom when school finished every afternoon for a whole week. Daisy would infinitely have preferred another beating, and despite knowing how very bad she had been, despite loving her little brothers, she had slid out of the narrow little bedroom window several times to sneak off down to the shore or up to the moors, feeling like a condemned prisoner escaping from her cell.

But that had been ages ago . . . months, in fact. I'm a changed person so I am, Daisy told herself as the cottage came into view. I'll show them! I'll help, and be good, and work harder even than Amanda and Brendan. I'll do anything, anything at all, to see my daddy gets his boat mended and back to sea!

Reaching home, she hurried up the short path

17

and let herself into the kitchen, then stopped short. The room was full of people and the table, instead of being spread with Mammy's baking, was covered in papers. Daisy stared, almost unable to believe her eyes. Amanda, Brendan and her parents were ranged on one side of the table whilst three strange men, in stranger clothes, faced them across it. One of the men was thin, old and white-haired, and when he turned his head Daisy saw that he wore a tiny pair of gold-rimmed spectacles clipped to his long thin nose. He was looking worried and uncomfortable, but a glance at his companions showed them to be very different. One reminded Daisy of Farmer Vaughan's bull, for as she sidled round the table, wanting to get a good look at the strangers, she saw that he was fat, his face white as lard and crowned by reddish curls. His expression was both aggressive and bad-tempered, and Daisy disliked him at first glance. She could just imagine that the curls hid budding horns and thought him a dangerous, even a fright-ening, person.

The third man wore a dark suit and what Daisy knew to be a trilby hat. He was sturdily built, and his dark eyes were heavily lidded, giving him a secretive look. His skin was coffee-coloured, and when he saw her staring he smiled with a flash of very white teeth. Daisy thought his smile even more frightening than the fat man's scowl, and tried to shrink behind Amanda, clutching her sister's hand convulsively as she did so.

'What's happenin'?' she whispered. 'Where's Annie and the kids?'

'She's took 'em down to the shore to play,' Amanda whispered back. 'Hush! I dunno what's goin' on meself, but . . .'

She stopped because the fat man had leaned forward and banged his hand down on the table, hitting the wooden surface so hard that the papers spread out on it jumped. 'I guess this is noos to youse folks,' he said in a strange accent. His voice was coarse and unpleasant, as unpleasant as his appearance, Daisy thought. 'I'm kinda sorry if it's a shock, but I wrote weeks back, tellin' you I was comin' over to claim my rights. Only you say you ain't never had my letter, and . . .'

The tall, thin man cleared his throat. 'You said you despatched a letter by the same post to my own law firm,' he said quietly, and Daisy had no difficulty in recognising his English accent. 'But I was as shocked as Mr Kildare when you turned up in my office yesterday because I, too, knew nothing of this matter. If I may say so, Mr Kildare . . .'

The man with the trilby snatched it off, revealing a thatch of black and oily hair above his coffee-coloured face with its spreading, squashy-looking nose. 'I hope you ain't suggestin', Mr Prescott, that this feller' – he jerked a big square thumb at Colm – 'is thinkin' of contestin' my client's right to this property, because if so, we'll fight him every inch of the way, and we've got documentary proof

19

of ownership, while all he can do is protest.' He turned so that he was facing the English lawyer. 'Can that hick read? If not, you'd best start readin' to him because there's a deal o' evidence and it'll take a while to get through.'

Daisy glanced sideways at her father and saw a dark flush creep up his neck and invade his face. A quick look at her mother showed Maggie's cheeks pink and her eyes bright with indignation. How dared the man suggest that Daddy could not read, and what was a hick, anyway? Something rude, by the look on Amanda's usually gentle face, but Daddy was speaking, his voice low and level.

'My whole family can read, Mr – Mr . . .'

Before he could finish the sentence, however, the fat man with the reddish curls interrupted. 'I'm Paddy Kildare; that's my moniker and mebbe you'd best call me Paddy to save confusion. And you're Colin, that right?'

'Colm, C-o-l-m, his name's Colm. It's an Irish name,' Maggie said quietly, but for some reason the remark brought the hot colour surging into the fat man's cheeks.

'Are you thinkin' I'm not Irish meself?' he said angrily. 'Well I'm as Irish as any of youse, ask any member of the Noo York police department. I've walked the beat for twenty years and there's no man more respected in Brooklyn than Paddy Kildare.'

'Yeah, mebbe we should introdooce ourselves,' the coffee-coloured one said in a low growl. 'I'm

20

Paddy Kildare's attorney, Mitch Mitchell, here to see fair play for my client.' He turned his flat malevolent gaze directly on to Colm. 'And I'm not the guy to be trifled with. If you're thinking of starting any funny business, you want to remember my arm is long and you've a wife and kids who don't want to end up as bait for the fishes.'

The thin man looked shocked, and Daisy felt her heart begin to beat at twice its normal speed. Did that horrible man mean what she thought he meant? Surely not! Neither Daddy nor his family had done anything wrong, so why should this nasty person make evil-sounding threats? But the thin man was speaking and suddenly he no longer sounded anxious or frightened. His voice was firm and cold, and the coffee-coloured one actually looked taken aback. 'I don't know very much about the United States of America, Mr Mitchell; nor, from what you have told me, do I want to. But you are in Ireland now, and a remark such as the one you have just voiced would be enough to land you in court with a charge of threatening behaviour hanging over your head.'

'Gee, I'm shakin' in my shoes,' the coffee-coloured one said, but he said it so quietly that Daisy thought she was the only one who heard. Aloud he said: 'All right already; read the goddamn papers, then we can start talkin' turkey.'

Colm hesitated, then began to pull the papers together and sort them into some kind of order.

When he had them in a neat bundle, he walked towards the fire. Daisy knew he meant to sit down on one of the creaky fireside chairs, but Paddy Kildare obviously misunderstood. 'Stop right there!' he shouted. 'Them's only what they calls facsimiles; the real documents is lodged with Mitch's firm in Noo York, so if you throw 'em in the fire all you'll do is delay things, and annoy me, and I'm tellin' you, brother, I ain't the man as it's wise to annoy.'

Colm turned round, astonished eyes upon the older man. 'Burn 'em? Why in God's name should I burn 'em before I've read a single one of 'em?' he said blankly. 'Remember, though Mr Prescott tried to explain when you arrived, he did so in legal language, so me family and meself don't rightly know why you're here at all, at all.'

The coffee-coloured one opened a mouth as ugly as a rat trap and began to bluster, but Daisy, who had been staring at the two men, her eyes going from face to face, said suddenly: 'Mammy, are these two fellers brothers? They's ever so alike.'

Maggie and Colm both started to speak, doubtless to tell her to be quiet, but Paddy Kildare turned and stared at her, then gave a reluctant grin. 'Well I never did! This 'un's a bright kid. Mitch 'n' me is half-brothers, as it happens; not that it makes no odds, but most folk don't see no likeness.'

'Half-brothers?' Daisy said. She had never heard of such a thing. Indeed, when she looked hard at

22

the two men, she was amazed by her own perspicacity, for they were not superficially alike. But it seemed as though her remark had broken the ice, for Paddy Kildare actually unbent enough to explain.

'We've the same mammy but two different daddies,' he said. 'That's what being a half-brother means, get it?'

Taking advantage of the moment of calm, Mr Prescott cleared his throat once more. 'I think we may take it that Mr Colm Kildare has no intention of destroying these documents, gentlemen, so I think it would be best if you made yourselves scarce for half an hour whilst he reads them, both to himself and possibly to his family, since the contents will affect them all. I would prefer to be on hand to explain any legal jargon which may confuse the issue. What do you say?'

The two brothers moved away from the centre of the room and stood by the back door, talking in low voices, and once again Daisy saw the resemblance between them. It was not in their colouring, but they both had big, square faces and both had an air of bull-like determination and something which, for want of a better word, she found herself thinking of as ill-will. She was sure that neither of them had lied when they intimated that they were dangerous men to cross.

The short colloquy by the door ended and Paddy Kildare turned towards the lawyer. 'Very well; we'll stroll around and have a look at the place. Anywhere we can't go?' He did not wait for a reply but left the room, shutting the door behind him with a violence which Daisy guessed was his usual way of doing things, rather than a show of annoyance.

Once the room was quiet the family looked at one another and then at the solicitor, before Colm spoke. 'I t'ink it would be best if you explained in simple language just what me cousin – if he truly is me cousin – means,' he said quietly. 'When they first come in there was a lot of talk about documentary evidence and the rights of the elder son, and mebbe I'm t'ick, but somewhere along the line I missed the point. So if you wouldn't mind, Mr Prescott, sir . . .'

'Of course I wouldn't mind,' Mr Prescott said with a sort of false heartiness. It struck Daisy that he was a nice man who had been bullocked into doing an unpleasant job. 'I'll make it simple, then you can read the documents with more under-standing. As you know, your family, the Kildares of Benmacraig, have owned the land and this cottage for many generations. It seems that your grandfather had an older brother who decided that he did not want to work on the croft whilst his father – the father of them both – still lived, though he had every intention of coming back and claiming his inheritance when the old man died. Apparently there had been bad blood between them, and bad blood also between the son and the younger brother, who had courted and won the girl that the elder brother, Padraig, had wanted.

'So Padraig and his father and the younger son, Tomas, went into Clifden and drew up a document – a will, in fact – saying that the old man left all he possessed to his eldest son. I am sorry to say it of a connection of my own firm, but the will was badly drawn up by an ignorant person, because it ignored Tomas's rights, being solely concerned with seeing that Padraig did not lose out.

'Only Padraig sailed for the United States taking the will with him and the family heard no more of him, not so much as a letter. His mother, your great-grandmother, mourned him for dead but your great-grandfather said he was the sort to survive anything the world might throw at him and simply put him out of his mind. After all, many an Irishman has gone to America and done well, coming home, sometimes after many years, to shower money on his family. So probably, if he thought about Padraig at all, your great-granddad would have looked upon him as a sort of prodigal son who might one day surprise them all.'

'And so he has, bad cess to him,' Maggie muttered. Speaking aloud, she added: 'So what he's saying is that he has a legal right to our croft? The cottage, the land ... even the boat?'

'That's what the documents say,' Mr Prescott said unhappily. 'You see, old Mr Kildare's will is all absolutely legal and binding. I believe his sole

25

intent was to ensure that Padraig would leave the croft and go to the States, confident that he would not lose out by so doing. Yet for some reason which is now, alas, lost in the mists of time, the will didn't even mention the second son, your grandfather. I suspect that, because old Mr Kildare knew nothing of the law, he imagined that if Tomas lived and worked on the croft all his life it would naturally go to him, and when he said, in his Will, all my property, he meant whatever sum of money he had managed to salt away. He surely could not have dreamed that Padraig's grandson would return, after all these years, and take the croft as of right.'

For a moment the room was absolutely still; so quiet that the sound of the burning peat settling made Daisy turn her head. Then her father, who had been standing whilst Mr Prescott spoke, sank into one of the home-made wooden chairs and began to study the papers, which he spread out upon the table once more. 'Yes, I see,' he said heavily, after a moment. 'But this will was made in favour of a man who's been dead and gone for many years. I understand that if Padraig had come back he would have been en-titled to take the croft, but I don't see why this feller should have it. It weren't willed to him but to his grandfer.'

Mr Prescott sighed. 'That's why there's so much documentation. Because each generation, Padraig and his son, though they have never returned to claim the croft, have willed it on to *their* sons. Can you understand that, Mr Kildare?'

'Yes, I can understand. But, Mr Prescott, suppose my father had willed the croft to meself in honest ignorance of that other, older will? What would happen then? After all, 'tis me own grandfather and father who have kept the place in decent order, bought more land, increased the value of our stock . . .'

'Ah, that might put a different complexion on things. If such a will existed . . .' Mr Prescott began, his tone brightening, but his face fell as Colm shook his head.

'No, we've never been a family to go to law, seein' as it's an expensive business and not one we considered necessary,' he admitted. 'There's never been any need, it being taken for granted by all parties that the croft would be passed from father to son. And as you know, I've no brothers or sisters, which is why I gave up me job on the railways in Liverpool as soon as my father died and my mammy admitted she couldn't manage the croft alone.'

'So you can see, Mr Prescott, that the Kildares never had no need for wills and such,' Maggie put in. 'But don't they say possession is nine-tenths of the law? If so . . .'

But Mr Prescott was shaking his head. 'I'm afraid that doesn't apply in this case, Mrs Kildare, since although you have been living on and working the croft for many years it has belonged,

27

in law, to the American side of the family since your husband's great-grandfather died. You can contest their right to it through the courts, but I fear you would end up the loser, which would mean you would have to pay heavy legal costs and would lose your home anyway. However, there is no doubt that you have considerably improved both the cottage and the demesne during your occupancy, and some part at least of the value this has added to the property should be paid back to you.'

Colm said nothing; Daisy could see that he was still trying to find a way out of the impossible dilemma in which he found himself, but her mother spoke up at once, her chin jutting with a belligerence that Daisy had never seen her show before. 'Why, the *Mary Ellen* lost her mast and her sail in the storm yesterday, but she's a grand sturdy boat and new since Colm's great-grandfather's time, I'm sure. They can't take her from us, surely? Nor the donkey and cart because they really are new; Colm and meself bought them. And the house cow, and her calf . . .'

'They may argue that you bought such things with the proceeds from the croft,' Mr Prescott said sadly. 'However, we must be able to apply for more time in order that you may find some-where to live. Have you relatives who would take you in?'

Colm began to shake his head, to explain again that he was an only child and that Maggie, coming from England, was only in touch with her elder sister who had a live-in job and so could not offer them shelter. But Amanda, who had been listening intently, with her head slightly on one side, broke in. 'But Mr Prescott, if my daddy had known the croft was not his, he would have expected – and got – wages for the work he did. Mammy too, because she would not sell fish and slave in the house for nothing. Surely that must be taken into account?'

Daisy saw some of the worry leave Colm's face as he took Amanda's hand and gave it a comforting squeeze. 'Thank God I've a daughter wit' a head on her shoulders,' he said, and turned to Mr Prescott. 'She's right, isn't she, sir? We'd not have laboured for another man's gain if we'd known how things stood. And, you know, me cousin – if he is me cousin – hasn't done well by us, leaving us in ignorance all these years, for I'd put him at fifty if he's a day.'

'Yes, you're right. Mr Paddy Kildare is fifty-five,' Mr Prescott said. 'I wondered myself why he'd chosen this moment to claim his inheritance, but got no satisfactory answer save that he'd a fancy to visit the old country. He says he doesn't mean this cottage to be his first place of residence, but wants it as a sort of holiday home which, if it is true, must mean he has sufficient money to set you up somewhere else.'

'I don't see why we can't stay here. If he's really rich he can buy a place for himself,' Maggie said eagerly. 'We'd do anything we could to help him get somewhere to live in the area if only he'd leave us our croft.'

Mr Prescott shook his head once more. 'Mr Paddy Kildare is not a straightforward man,' he said quietly. 'I don't know why he wants this place so badly, but want it he does, and he dislikes being questioned. But we will proceed on the lines suggested by Miss Kildare . . .'

He stopped speaking abruptly as the door opened and the two men re-entered the room. Daisy saw that the resemblance between them was more marked than ever, for their faces bore the same expression of threatening aggression. Mr Prescott began to speak but was rudely interrupted. 'Well? D'you understand?' Paddy Kildare barked, addressing Colm. 'This place is mine, everything's legal and above board, and I want you out by the end of the week.'

Colm glanced uneasily around the table, but it was Maggie who spoke. 'We need time – a good deal more than a few days,' she said quietly. 'We've small children and goods an' chattels, and we need a roof over our heads. Besides, I dare say the lawyers will still have questions which must be answered.'

Paddy Kildare, fat though he already was, seemed to swell to twice his size. 'This is my place,' he shouted, 'and I want you out! We ain't interested in your problems, an' so far as I can see every stick an' stone, every horse an' hen, is rightfully ours. Ain't that so, Mitch?'

The other man began to answer, but Colm suddenly got to his feet, his eyes blazing with indignation, and Daisy realised that her father was a good six inches taller than either of the brothers, and, now that he was angry, looked quite capable of the sort of aggression the Americans had threatened. 'I know you say this is your property and right now I can't deny it, but folk have rights in Ireland even if they don't have none where you come from,' he said. 'We shall need at least a month's notice in writing, and when we go we'll take what's ours.' He strode to the door and flung it open. 'Good day, gentlemen.'

There was a moment's hesitation whilst the brothers stared up into Colm's angry face. Then Mr Prescott crossed the room, took his hat and raincoat from the hooks upon which he must have hung them when he arrived, and ushered the two men firmly out of the cottage and down the path. 'I'll be in touch, Mr Kildare, and I'll explain to these gentlemen that there must be a cash settlement before you move so much as a foot from this place,' he called over his shoulder. 'I shall visit you again before returning to Dublin.'

Colm closed the door gently and went straight across to his wife, taking her in his arms and murmuring love-words against her neck. She had borne up bravely whilst the uninvited guests were with them, but now Daisy saw that tears were running down her cheeks and obeyed instantly when Amanda took her hand, beckoned to Brendan to follow, and left the cottage. They walked slowly down to the shore, where Annabel and the little boys were shrimping with a flour bag on a split cane in the little pools left by the ebbing tide. As the three older ones settled themselves on a sun-warmed slab of rock it struck Daisy that only an hour or so before she had been humping her bucket of mussels back to the cottage, full of delighted anticipation because she had picked so many and would be praised by her parents for her hard work. But in that hour everything had changed; the mussels had been forgotten. All she could think of now was that they were about to lose their home. Even if Mr Prescott managed to force the brothers into letting them keep the *Mary Ellen* and some at least of the livestock, they could scarcely camp on the beach. She supposed, doubtfully, that they would have to sell everything – the boat, the donkey cart, the livestock – and then try to rent a room somewhere. She knew people did rent rooms in big cities because the only thing about school she enjoyed was reading. The school had a small library and Daisy had read every book in it, and was now on her second time round. She particularly loved stories of poor children in big cities who made their way up in the world, but now she found she had no desire to emulate such heroines.

'. . . I'll do what I said and try to get work on a fishing boat leaving from Roundstone,' Brendan was saying. 'I think Daddy should fight the case, or else we should just sit tight and refuse to move out. After all, what can they do to us?'

'Kill us,' Daisy and Amanda said in chorus, Amanda adding: 'Or hurt the little ones. You heard what they said, Bren; they meant it.'

'Ye-es, but t'ings is said in the heat of the moment what a person would never do when his blood cools.'

Amanda snorted. 'They're really bad men and when I say bad I mean wicked, like in the Bible,' she said with conviction. 'Daddy's too fond of his family to put us in danger. He'll move us all out when he has to, so he will. It's not so bad for me because I can go into service – one less mouth to feed – but it'll be hard on the youngsters.'

Annabel had joined them and now looked imploringly from one to the other. 'What's it all about?' she said plaintively. 'What did those horrible men want? They scared me; I was glad when Daddy told me to take the babies down to the shore and not to come back until he sent for us. Was it about the boat? Is it going to cost a mint o' money to mend the *Mary Ellen*? And what did you mean when you said that you'd go into service, Amanda? You've always said you never would.'

'Oh, I just thought it might help Daddy to get the boat mended if I took paid work for a while,' Amanda said vaguely. She shot a warning glance at Brendan and Daisy. 'As for those two men, it turns out they are Daddy's cousins. They – they

33

wanted to meet us and – and see round the cottage, but they've gone now, so we might as well go home.' She turned to Daisy. 'I never noticed; did you get some mussels?'

Daisy jumped off the rock and took Annabel's sandy hand in her own, giving it a comforting squeeze. 'Yes, the men have gone,' she said with false cheerfulness. 'And I picked a grosh of mussels so we'll have a real feast. Did Mammy bake? The table was cleared when I brought the mussels in.'

Annabel nodded vigorously, then held out her own hand to Finn, for Dermot was already settled on Amanda's hip. 'Yes, she made sody bread and brack, and some dumplings to put in a stew,' she said happily. 'I'll help you scrub the mussels and take off the beards, Daisy, then we'll get our dinners all the sooner.'

When they returned to the kitchen, however, no attempt had been made to start the meal, though it was well overdue. To be sure, Colm had emptied the mussels into the sink and was scrubbing half-heartedly at the shells whilst addressing his wife over his shoulder, though he stopped speaking immediately when the children came in. Their mother had pen, ink and writing paper spread out before her and was scribbling away, her attention so fixed on her task that she scarcely seemed aware of the opening and closing of the door. Daisy went quietly over and stood at her mother's shoulder, half expecting a rebuke for nosiness, but Maggie

34

merely looked up and smiled, then returned to her work once more. 'I'm writing to your Aunt Jane,' she said quietly. 'If anyone can help us it's my elder sister and oh, Daisy love, I'm thinking we need help desperate bad!'

Chapter Two

Jane Dalton stood at the rail of the ferry and watched as the shore of Ireland appeared out of the mist. It was a welcome sight, for she had never been a good sailor, and though other passengers had not thought the crossing a rough one Jane's stomach did not agree. It had felt queasy as soon as the ferry left the shelter of the Mersey harbour and would only settle down, she knew, once her feet were on firm ground again.

She had never liked the sea despite the fact that she had been born and bred in the port of Liverpool. Since Maggie's marriage, however, she had crossed the Irish Sea a good many times though she hated doing so, especially when the ferry ran into bad weather, which it always seemed to do when she was aboard. When Maggie and Colm had first married, Jane had imagined that they would stay in Liverpool because he had a good job with the railways, but this had not proved to be the case. Within a month of their wedding, Colm had carried his Maggie back to Ireland to meet his mother, who had been recently widowed, and was struggling with the work of the croft and quite unable to make use of the fishing boat. Colm had speedily realised that he would have to return to Benmacraig, and fortunately Maggie had taken to the life like a duck to water.

When she had written to say she was expecting her first child, Jane had thrown up her job in a milliner's shop on Church Street and gone to her sister, so that she should not be alone in a strange land when her baby was born. She had found Maggie happily employed in helping her husband to build an extra bedroom on the end of their cottage, whilst old Mrs Kildare was teaching her how to rear a pig, keep chickens, plant potatoes and cook over the open kitchen fire.

Jane had been horrified by what she saw as primitive conditions and wondered at her sister's happy acceptance of such a hard life. It had soon become apparent to her that Maggie was in love not only with Colm but with his country as well. She frequently pointed out the beauty of the shore and the moors, taking Jane on expeditions in the old donkey cart, but though Jane pretended to appreciate the landscape her own idea of beauty was a well-swept city street, a milliner's window display where the colours and shapes complemented one another in a way that matched her personal taste, or the closely shaven lawns and bright flower beds of Prince's Park.

When she returned to Liverpool after that first visit, she had changed her job, taking a live-in post as parlourmaid to a doctor and his wife on Rodney Street, and had quickly risen to the position of housekeeper, though she knew that her employer, Mrs Venables, now considered her a friend as well as an employee.

When she had first been confirmed in her present post she had explained to Mrs Venables that she had a sister living in Ireland, on the west coast. 'Our mam died when our Maggie was only ten, so I more or less brought her up,' she had said. 'Our dad died a few years ago, so now there are just the two of us and if it can be arranged, madam, I'd like to take myself off whenever she needs me, though of course I wouldn't expect you to pay me a wage while I was away.'

Mrs Venables had patted her shoulder very kindly. 'You work hard, Miss Dalton, and I know how well you manage the other servants,' she had said. 'You shall have a fortnight's holiday a year, and if you work over public holidays such as Christmas and Easter I will allow you extra time off when your sister needs you. The only stipulation I shall make is that you train someone else to do your job in your absence.'

Jane had thought this was more than generous and had done her best to comply with her mistress's wishes. In fact some years she had not taken her holiday, but had saved it up so that she could spend longer with her sister when Maggie needed her. Naturally, she had journeyed to Ireland immediately after the birth of each of her younger nephews and nieces, knowing herself to be particularly useful then and therefore more than usually welcome, especially after old Mrs Kildare had died. By then, Amanda had been old enough to be a big help, but even so, Maggie and Colm were grateful for Jane's presence.

Gradually, however, Jane had begun to feel that the children, at any rate, did not appreciate her as they should. All of them, apart from the two little boys, had their own tasks to perform and in Jane's view at least they did not do their jobs properly. In spring and summer, the back door was usually left open and Shep, Colm's old dog, the small flock of hens and even the large grey goose, the gander and sometimes half a dozen goslings would wander in and out of the kitchen at will. When she had remonstrated with Maggie, her sister had laughed and said that the birds pecked up remnants of food from the earth floor and the old dog was one of the family, so he was, and welcome to come in at any time. Jane had tried to persuade Colm to cover the earth floor with bricks or tiles, or even wooden planks, but Colm had smiled and said an earth floor had been good enough for his parents, so it was good enough for him. She had suggested selling the donkey cart and buying a pony and trap but Colm had assured her, in his easy-going way, that a pony and trap for a man in his position would be absurd; crofters could graze a donkey on the moor, secure in the knowledge that the canny little beasts would thrive on the most meagre pasturage, whereas a pony would need hay and oats. A trap, furthermore, though it might be better sprung than a donkey cart, was meant to take fine ladies driving, not to carry large quantities of fish. He had laughed at Jane and told her that Maggie was no idle lady taking the air in a fancy vehicle; she was a fisherman's wife, selling his catch around the town and spending the money she made on the necessities of life and not on its luxuries.

As the years had gone by, Jane had had to admit that her sister's marriage had been not a mistake but rather the best thing that could have happened to Maggie. Oh, to be sure, she had thought Maggie's fine blonde hair and blue eyes were wasted on Colm, for her sister had had many beaux, all eager to wed her, but none of them could have made her sister as happy as Colm had done.

Then there were the children. Jane loved them all, of course she did: tall, golden-haired Amanda, who was the image of Maggie at a similar age; the two babies, both as fair as their mother – in fact as fair as Jane herself for she, too, was a blonde. Brendan, Annabel and Daisy took after their father, being dark-haired and dark-eyed with skin which tanned easily. But there the resemblance ended, for Colm was sweet-tempered, easy-going and placid, as indeed was Annabel; it was Daisy, even more than Brendan, who was difficult, quick to flare into anger, disobedient, wilful . . .

But I'm being unfair, Jane told herself now. There's nothing wrong with Daisy that a little discipline wouldn't cure. I'm sure she means well and, when she's older, will take life more seriously.

But right now, of course, the Kildares had worries far greater than any Jane could have imagined, for though the letter from her sister had been long and fairly detailed, Jane still found it difficult to believe that the strange American cousins could actually take over the property upon which Colm had worked so hard.

Thinking back, Jane realised with great surprise how the croft, the cottage and indeed the Kildares' lives had improved since her first visits. Colm had added two further rooms, and built a stable for the donkey and the house cow, and a neat shed for the new cart in which he also housed the implements he had bought as the size of his holding increased. At first, he and Maggie had been hard put to it to grow sufficient food for the family but now, in summer, they were able to sell vegetables at Clifden market whilst still having plenty for themselves. And Colm's latest venture had been to buy a ewe and a ram, going all the way to Galway to get good breeding stock. 'They are the start of me entry into the wool trade,' he had joked, and when the ewe gave birth to twins he had been triumphant, calling Annabel his little shepherdess because it was she and old Shep who were most often sent to round up his sheep when he wanted them down from the moor. Colm had doubled the worth of the property; surely it was not possible that these Americans could simply walk in and take over? Jane regretted now that she had not stayed in Liverpool for long enough to put the problem to a lawyer, but upon receiving Maggie's letter she had gone straight to Mrs Venables, explained the situation, packed a bag and left on the next available ferry.

Jane's meditations came to an abrupt halt as she realised that the deck was no longer moving beneath her feet. They had docked and already folk were streaming down the gangway. Hastily she joined the jostling crowd and was soon heading for the railway station. She had sent a telegram so that the family would know her time of arrival at Clifden, but she had no idea whether or not it would have reached the Kildares in time for Colm to meet her. If not, she would have to get a taxi since she had no intention of setting out on the long walk carrying not only her case, but also a canvas bag full of bits and pieces. She always tried to bring a little present for each of the children, some tobacco for Colm, who liked a quiet pipe occasionally, and something practical for Maggie to wear: a woolly jumper, for instance, or a brightly coloured headscarf, and once a pair of stout leather boots. Maggie adored those boots and wore them whenever she went into Clifden, for they were too good for work on the croft; clogs in summer and gumboots in winter sufficed for that.

The train journey was uneventful. Jane obtained a corner seat and tried not to worry over her sister's predicament, but it was impossible. She adored Maggie, was truly fond of Colm and loved the children, though she acknowledged now that she found

42

Amanda, Annabel and Brendan easier to deal with than young Daisy. Which was just as well, because even before hearing of the Kildares' problem she had intended to come to Ireland with a proposal which involved Annabel. She and Daisy were very alike to look at but, Jane thought thankfully, very different in temperament. And in a way, she told herself now, gazing out at the countryside as it passed, the suggestion she intended to make might be easier to put forward in the Kildares' changed circumstances. But it would not do to start worrying until she had heard the full story of the American cousins from Colm's own lips. Maggie's letter had been written immediately upon hearing the dreadful news; since then, surely, things might have altered? The lawyer, Mr Prescott, sounded a sensible, kindly man, who would guide the Kildares in the right direction. Jane settled back in her seat. Yes, by now the problem might be solved and they would all be able to laugh at their fears.

The train arrived at Clifden on time, and the very first person Jane saw as she stepped down on to the platform was Colm. He must have seen her immediately too, for she saw the flash of his white teeth as he grinned, and then he was taking her luggage and steering her towards the station entrance. 'We got your telegram so I drove the donkey cart down and picked up a sack of seed potatoes for Mr Vaughan on my way, but there'll still be plenty of room for you and your luggage. And how is me beautiful sister-in-law?'

'Worried sick,' Jane said frankly. She looked hard at Colm and saw the tiny signs of stress in an extra line or two about his eyes. Even so, she reflected, he was easily the best-looking man she knew. He was broad of shoulder and slim of waist, with an abundance of thickly curling black hair and a strongly cleft chin. His dark eyes were warm and when he grinned at her his teeth were white and even. But now he was speaking as he helped her into the donkey cart and untied the rope halter which had fastened Tina to the tethering post. 'Yes, I'm afraid we're in trouble and 'tis natural for you to worry. Maggie explained? Now, amn't I the foolish one to ask such a question when Maggie read the letter to me herself before I drove into Clifden to post it!'

'Are they still insisting that the place is theirs?' Jane asked. 'I felt sure that nice Mr Prescott would find a way out for you.'

'He's still tryin',' Colm said quietly. 'Though I doubt he can do much, but no use talkin' to me 'cos it's Maggie that has the clear head when it comes to legal matters. She wondered whether we might buy them off but the trouble is, it would cost a mint, which we don't have . . .'

'I've got a bit put by,' Jane said at once. 'Norralot, but a bit. You'd be welcome to it, though I doubt it 'ud buy back more'n the donkey and its cart.'

She had meant it as a joke but it fell very flat. However, Colm shrugged his big shoulders and said quietly: 'You're a grand girl, so you are, Jane

44

Dalton; we knew you'd help if you could. And now, how's Mrs Venables?'

Jane felt a rush of warmth for this man who treated her with affectionate respect and never, by word or look, let her believe he resented her visits or his wife's fondness for her. Colm might not take her advice, might go his own way, but he always did so with unfailing courtesy. She reflected that her brother-in-law had never raised his hand to anyone and even now, when he was facing the loss of his livelihood and terrible hardship, he could still smile and ask after her employer, her friends and acquaintances, with real interest and without allowing his own troubles to surface. Jane had been wondering when she should tell him that things had changed at the Venables house but Colm, all unthinking, made it easy for her. 'And how is Mrs Venables's poor young sister, the one you told us about last time you visited?' he asked. 'I disremember her name, but I do recall you said she was very frail and sickly and has a daughter a bit older than our Daisy.' He chuckled. 'And if the child is like Daisy in other ways, no wonder her poor mam is never well, for that girl of mine is enough to drive a man to drink, I'm tellin' you.'

'Oh Colm, I'm afraid Mrs Darlington-Crewe passed away a couple of weeks ago. Before she died, she asked Mrs Venables to take care of the child – to become her guardian, in fact – and of course Mrs Venables agreed at once, though then she was still hoping that her sister would recover.'

'Well, and isn't that tragical news,' Colm said, and Jane knew that he meant every word. Perhaps it even made his own lot seem less hard. 'Has the child moved in with Mrs Venables, then? And how about you, Jane; will it change things for you?'

'I suppose it's bound to do so,' Jane said. 'Particularly as Mrs Venables has never had children of her own. I understand that Cynthia is sickly, very different from your Daisy. She has never attended school but has a governess who comes in each day to give her simple lessons. She'll arrive tomorrow, poor little scrap, but she couldn't have a kinder or better guardian than Mrs Venables.'

'That's true,' Colm said thoughtfully, nodding his dark head. 'In the circumstances, it were real good of Mrs Venables to let you come to us.'

Jane shot him a quick, sideways glance, then spoke up boldly. 'Colm, I don't want to upset you, but Mrs Venables made a suggestion when I told her of your troubles. She thought it might ease matters if, when I leave at the end of my week, I take one of your girls back with me. She'd have a grand big bedroom, be clothed and fed, and she would be company for little Cynthia. And . . . and it would be one less mouth for you to feed.'

Colm was so startled that he pulled the donkey up short, then turned to stare at his sister-in-law. 'Is it – is it a sort of holiday you're proposin'?' he asked at length. 'Or would you be wantin' her for longer, like? Because if so, there's no doubt it would make things easier. Amanda's goin' into service with a family in Galway, that's all arranged, and Brendan has signed on with Mícheál Connor, to work his fishing boat out of Roundstone harbour. Annabel's a good little girl so she and Daisy will be in charge of the wee lads while Maggie and meself do any paid work we can get.'

Jane gazed admiringly at her brother-in-law. Faced with a disaster so enormous, Colm and Maggie were already putting plans into action, even though those plans would mean the breaking up of the Kildare family, something which Jane knew both her sister and her brother-in-law would hate. She said as much and Colm, clicking his tongue to give Tina the office to start, nodded slowly. 'Aye, and it's not only Maggie and meself what'll hate it,' he observed. 'Amanda never wanted to move away from Benmacraig, and the thought of leaving Daisy and Annabel in charge of Finn and Dermot is hard on all four of them, but one thing helps us to bear it. Mícheál's near on seventy. His wife died ten years back and his children moved away before that. His cottage is small but he's offered us a room in it, in return for Maggie managing the food, shopping, cleaning and so on. So you see, we'll be able to keep most of the family together while I repair the *Mary Ellen*. Once she's fit for the fishing, old Mícheál will join Brendan and meself aboard her, for his boat is little better than a currach and can only be took out when there's no sort of a sea runnin'.'

'Is – is there a garden to your friend's property?'

47

Jane asked cautiously, and was not surprised when Colm shook his head.

'No, it's a fisherman's cottage down by the quay. But I plan to try to drain a few yards of peat bog and grow taties on it,' Colm told her. 'Old Mícheál will pay Brendan in fish for workin' on the boat, and Amanda will send most of her wages home.' He chuckled suddenly, shooting a quick glance at Jane. 'Daisy was all set to dress up as a boy and try to get work on one of the big farms near Galway. She's a little monkey, but always full of good intentions. Brendan told her she'd eat up any wages she got, buying sweeties from the Galway shops, but she swears she's a changed person and if she can't get a paid job she'll work in Mícheál's cottage and help Annabel to mind the boys so that their mammy can look for a job. Only, if she goes back to Liverpool with you, what about her schooling? She's a rare one for mitchin' off school is our Daisy. Once she'd learned to read, she couldn't see no point in lessons, so mostly she left the cottage of a mornin' and come back in time for her tea, and heaven alone knew where she was in between, except that it were rarely school.'

Jane sighed to herself but decided not to explain that it was Annabel and not Daisy whom she intended to take back to Liverpool. Neat, obedient Annabel would be a far more suitable companion for Cynthia than wild, unbiddable Daisy. But she would not say anything now; Maggie would understand why she wanted the younger, quieter girl. 'I dare say she could share Cynthia's governess; indeed, since Mrs Venables thinks a good deal of the child's troubles can be put down to loneliness and a fear of other children, that would be an obvious solution,' she said carefully. 'Then, when Cynthia becomes less ill and more self-reliant, both girls could go to a local school. And she'll be paid a small sum weekly, which she will be able to send home.' Jane had not suggested paying the child when she and Mrs Venables had discussed the plan, but she knew her employer well enough to guess that the older woman would at least give Annabel pocket money which Jane herself could augment from her own good salary.

There was a long pause during which the donkey cart reached the cottage. Colm carried Jane's cases across to the back door, and the children must have seen him through the low little window, for the back door burst open and Maggie and the girls ran out, Maggie clasping her sister so tightly that Jane could scarcely breathe.

'Oh, I knew you'd come, dearest Jane,' she cried. 'I knew we could rely on you. Now you're here everything will be all right.'

Poor Jane mumbled that of course she would do her best, though she did not delude herself that she could solve a problem which neither Colm, Maggie herself, nor the lawyer had managed to sort out. Then she turned to greet her nieces and small nephews, for Brendan was not one of the group standing rather shyly in the doorway.

She went towards them, but even as she did so Colm tapped her shoulder and leaned towards her. 'Say nothin' about Cynthia, nor any o' that,' he whispered. 'I'll have to sound Maggie out and it'll be best if she has a quiet word wit' our Daisy before it's spoke of, like.' Aloud, he said jovially: 'Let your aunt get into the house, girls, so's she can wash off the dust o' the journey. And then you can make us all a nice pot o' tea, for I'm that dry I'm near dyin' o' thirst, and I'm sure your Aunt Jane feels the same.'

When her mother had suggested that she and Daisy might take a walk along the shore and see whether the new land lines which Colm had put out had caught any fish, Daisy had been surprised but very pleased. It was rare for her mother to go down to the shore for there was plenty of work on the croft which needed doing, and if Maggie wanted to discuss something she would go with Colm, or with Amanda. Daisy knew, sadly, that even Brendan was preferred to herself as a confidant, though she was sure she was every bit as helpful and practical as her brother.

Aunt Jane had been with them for almost three days and Daisy had strained every nerve to help the family in any way she could . . . well, she had done so for the first two days, anyway. Thinking back, perhaps her efforts had really only been noticeable on the first day but that was because, with Aunt Jane helping in the house and Amanda doing everything she possibly could to assist her parents whilst she was still under their roof, there really had not been a tremendous amount left for Daisy to do.

Guiltily now, she thought back to the previous day when she had been sent up to the farm with a message. Her mother had decided that they would keep Tina and the donkey cart as long as possible, but she had hoped that Mr Vaughan would allow Trudy, their house cow, to live with his beasts in return, obviously, for the milk she produced. Then, when they had sorted out some grazing rights near Roundstone harbour, they would be able to reclaim the cow. Mindful of the fact that her mother had said she meant to make butter that day and would need all the help she could get, Daisy had hurried to the farm and delivered her message. Mrs Vaughan, a fat, good-natured woman always ready to help a neighbour, had said she would be glad to graze Trudy and added that if their mother had butter or cheese to spare she would happily take it, with her own produce, into Clifden next market day, and sell it on her stall.

Feeling herself the bearer of good tidings, Daisy had meant to go straight home but had been diverted as she trotted across open country by the recollection that she was near the cliffs upon which many seabirds nested. How lovely it would be to bring her mother not only good news from Mrs Vaughan, but a quantity of eggs as well! The hens

51

would not be in full lay until summer, and heaven knew where the Kildares would be by then, let alone Maggie's treasured flock of sleek and bright-eyed poultry.

Having decided on her course of action, she had been delighted to meet Sean O'Grady, one of Brendan's oldest friends, also making his way towards the cliff edge. The O'Gradys lived on a similar croft to the Kildares', a mile further along the coast, and the two families had been exchanging visits for as long as Daisy could remember.

'Sean! Where's you goin'?' Daisy had asked eagerly. 'I'm away to get some seagulls' eggs for Mammy, but if it's Brendan you're wantin' he's not at home. He's gone fishin' wit' Mícheál.'

Sean had grinned down at her. He was a handsome lad, curly-haired and blue-eyed, and never patronised Daisy, even though she was five years younger than he. Indeed, he had several times insisted that she be allowed to join himself and Brendan when they went fishing for trout in a small freshwater lake up on the moors, and had told her that she was as good as a boy; high praise indeed from one who had no sisters of his own, but only two older brothers. 'As if I'd be wantin' Brendan, alanna! I'm headin' for the cliffs, same as you.' He flourished a reed basket under her nose. ''Tis gulls' eggs I'm after too. Me mammy will be bakin' just as soon as I get home.'

'Then we can go together,' Daisy said. 'Mammy

might be cross if I climbed down alone, but if you're wit' me, she won't mind at all, at all.'

'Right, but I'm only after a couple, then I've got to get back,' Sean warned her. 'I'll be seein' Brendan this evenin' though, to get the latest news.'

By this time they had reached the edge of the cliff and started scrambling down, ignoring the furious attacks of the nearest birds. 'Never take all the eggs from a nest, alanna, just one from each,' Sean roared above the seagulls' shrieks and flapping wings. 'Here we are, I've got three . . . no four . . . which is all I need. You must have about the same. Are you coming back wit' me?'

But this Daisy had declined to do, for though she thought Sean quite the nicest boy she knew she was afire to prove to her mother that she was every bit as useful a member of the family as either Brendan or Amanda. So she bade Sean a regretful goodbye and continued down the cliff, placing one egg from every nest carefully in the pocket of her skirt.

After she had collected half a dozen eggs, she scrambled down on to the shore, deciding to pick some mussels, for her previous offering had been much enjoyed by the whole family. Colm had given her a hug and told her she was a good little girl so she was and Daisy, so often in hot water over tasks half done or not done at all, found that she enjoyed such praise and longed for more. Picking mussels off the rocks, she suddenly realised that there was only room in her pocket for a handful of the shellfish, so she made her skirt into a sort of basket and began to cram them into its folds. Naturally enough, the mussels were wet so she did not at first realise that the weight of them had broken two of the eggs in her pocket, making a horrible slimy mess of her skirt. Cursing herself for her foolishness, Daisy tried to mend matters by dipping her skirt in the sea, realising that by now her mother would be making butter and wondering where on earth Daisy had got to. She headed for the cottage at a run and somehow managed to break two more eggs, so that by the time she entered the kitchen she was in a sorry state, her skirt still slimy with the broken eggs and soaked with sea water, and the mussels which she had collected slimy as well.

Aunt Jane had scolded, but Mammy just looked resigned. 'I know you meant to be helpful, alanna, but do try to remember in future to do one thing at a time,' she said gently, taking the eggy mussels out of her daughter's skirt and dropping them into the low stone sink. Sighing, Daisy produced the only two unbroken eggs, expecting that at least her mother would be grateful for these, but this proved not to be the case. Maggie had stared at them for an unbelieving moment and had then said sharply: 'Daisy Kildare, how many times have I told you that on no condition were any of my children to go egg-huntin' on the cliffs alone? And don't try to tell me that you were with Brendan because he's gone off to Roundstone, as you very well know.'

Daisy, very untypically, had burst into tears. She had meant to be so helpful, had not given a thought to the prohibition. 'It – it weren't a very high cliff, Mammy,' she sobbed. 'And I had a whole pocketful of eggs, honest I did. Sean O'Grady helped me at first only . . . only I wanted to get you even more eggs, and then the mussels mashed 'em.'

Her mother had sighed. 'You always mean well, but you simply never think,' she said. 'I don't know how many times I've told you to think before you act, but it must run into hundreds. Now go and change out of that filthy skirt so I can rinse it through and put it on the line before the weather changes.'

'I'll wash it meself, save you the trouble,' Daisy had said. She was so mortified that when her mother told her she would prefer to do the job herself, she had had to hurry from the room to hide the tears which threatened to spill from her eyes. Why was she such a thoughtless, stupid girl? Amanda and Annabel would never have been so foolish, but then Amanda and Annabel would never, in a thousand years, have even thought of collecting seabirds' eggs. That was a job for lads, not lasses.

But at this point Daisy jerked her mind back to the present, suddenly aware that her mother was addressing her. 'Well, Daisy, do you know we've been walking for five minutes and you've not said a word? Your Aunt Jane would ask if the cat had got your tongue!'

Daisy jumped. She had been so busy remembering her own stupidity that she had quite forgotten the treat she was enjoying – that of her mother's undivided attention. They had reached the path which led down to the shore, and she smiled up at Maggie, saying as she did so: 'Oh, Mammy, I were thinkin' about the eggs and the mussels and how I wanted to please you. I'm real sorry, so I am.'

'It's all right, chuck,' her mother said almost absently. 'You meant well and that's what counts. But I've not brought you out here to talk about eggs or mussels, or jobs half done. I've something far more important to discuss with you. Let's go and sit on that rock, because this may take a while.'

She sounded so serious that Daisy's heart gave a frightened hop. 'But I thought we were going to check the shore lines, Mammy,' she quavered. 'And even though you didn't punish me for muckin' up me skirt an' climbin' the cliffs, I got a right tellin' off from Aunt Jane. She went over all the bad things I've done since I were born, just about, and said I were the only Kildare she were ashamed to own as her niece. Mammy, I know she's your sister, an' I know she were ever so good to you when you were a kid, but she's horrible, so she is.'

'Don't say things like that, or even think them, because Aunt Jane is going to help us over this wretched business with the American cousins,' Maggie said. 'Now just sit quiet, and listen to what I'm telling you.'

'But what about the shore lines?' Daisy said wildly. She suddenly realised she did not wish to hear what her mother had to say. 'Hadn't we better walk along to the check them?'

Her mother sighed. 'Looking at the shore lines was just an excuse to get you to myself,' she said. 'So forget fish, mussels, eggs and everything else and listen to what I have to say to you. And don't interrupt,' she added firmly, for Daisy had already begun to protest. 'For once in your life, do as I tell you!'

Cowed by the sharpness of her mother's voice, Daisy subsided, listening with growing horror as her mother outlined the plan which she and Aunt Jane had made for Daisy. When she finished at last, Daisy found herself for once bereft of words and could only stare, whilst tears formed in her eyes and trickled down her cheeks. She was to be sent away from the family she adored and the only place she knew. She was to go across the sea with Aunt Jane, whom she hated, to live in a big city with only a nasty, sickly child for company. Of course, she had known that things would have to change when they were all crammed into Mícheál's cottage, but wasn't Aunt Jane here to help them out of their difficulties? Why should she, Daisy, be sent away? Why could not Annabel go? It was true that Annabel, despite being only eight years old, was far better at minding Finn and Dermot than she was herself. But she could change; she *would* change! She must persuade Mammy to send

57

Annabel with Aunt Jane, instead of herself. And wouldn't that be better all round, now? Aunt Jane liked Annabel and she certainly did not like Daisy.

But Mammy was talking again and Daisy dragged her mind back to the present. 'I know what you're going to say, queen; you're going to say why can't Annabel go?' her mother said, uncannily voicing Daisy's own thoughts. 'But as you must know very well, she's far better wi' the babies than you are yourself. What's more, she likes being indoors and amusing them. Oh, I know she takes them down to the shore sometimes and plays with them there, but she'd never go off and leave them. And she can put a meal together without burning the bottom out of the pan, or near on slicing her thumb off with the bread knife.'

Daisy sniffed sulkily. 'That were months ago . . . well, weeks ago,' she said, then brightened. 'Suppose I do that when I'm at Aunt Jane's? Will they send me home? If so, I'll burn the bottom out of every bleedin' pan in the place.'

'You will not, young lady,' her mother said angrily, flushing. 'For one thing, you won't get the chance because Mrs Venables has a staff of servants so you'll be livin' in the lap of luxury, as they say. And something I've not told you. Mrs Venables will give you pocket money – if you're good, that is, and behave properly to young Cynthia, and don't go causin' unhappiness or distress – which you can send home. So you see, you'll be earnin' money for us just like Amanda will.'

'Oh,' Daisy said doubtfully. Her mother's remark had taken the wind out of her sails, as no doubt Maggie had intended. If, by going back to Liverpool with Aunt Jane, she would ease the Kildare family's lot, then how could she possibly refuse to go? Amanda was going, and to a far less agreeable situation, for Daisy had twice been woken in the night by her sister's muffled sobbing, and when she had rolled over to give Amanda a cuddle her sister had confessed that she had not liked the woman who was to employ her and was afraid of the other servants, all of whom had seemed to consider her beneath them.

'Well? Have you any further objections? I'm sorry I can't tell you more but I'm sure Aunt Jane will be happy to answer any questions you may have. I know you're cross with her at the moment because she scolded you, but you brought it on yourself, queen; isn't that right?'

Daisy scowled down at her feet. Life was so unfair! If she had known that this was in the wind, how careful she would have been to do exactly as she was told! And though she felt truly sorry for Amanda, her sister was fifteen, grown up, and should be able to take care of herself. Then, Amanda was not being sent far across the sea to another country. Her big sister had already told her parents that she would come home on her day off whereas she, Daisy, might only be able to return to Ireland when Aunt Jane visited. She said as much and her mother looked evasive. 'Whilst we're livin'

59

with Mícheál, we shan't be able to have anyone to stay overnight,' she said. 'But I'm sure we'll manage something. And remember, queen, this plan isn't for ever. It's just until your daddy and myself have sorted things out.'

'But how long will that take?' Daisy wailed. 'Aunt Jane says Liverpool's bigger'n Clifden. I t'ink I'd go mad livin' away from Benmacraig for more'n a few weeks.'

'Liverpool is a huge city, but size isn't important,' her mother said. 'And after all, you aren't the only one who won't be living at Benmacraig. This is hard on all of us, not just you, but everyone has to accept what life throws at 'em. There's no exceptions. As for how long we'll be homeless, I wish I knew. All I can tell you for sure is that we shall strain every nerve to reclaim the croft or to rent ourselves a cottage with some land so we can start all over again.'

'And then will I come back home to you?' Daisy asked hopefully. 'Tell you what, Mammy, suppose I promise to be good and do my best to help Aunt Jane for a while, then couldn't Annabel and I swap places? Couldn't Annabel go to Liverpool so's I can come back to you?'

'Oh, Daisy, just *think*,' her mother said. 'No one, not even good Mrs Venables, would pay a child of eight to be a companion to one of nearly ten.'

Daisy was forced to admit that this was so, but when her mother got to her feet and said that they must return to the cottage, she clutched Maggie's arm, drawing her to a halt. 'Mammy, you do love me, don't you?' she asked urgently. 'Only you and Aunt Jane must have talked over which of us she could take and I know she don't like me nearly as much as she likes the others, so it must have been you – and Daddy of course – what picked on me.'

For the first time since they had left the cottage, Daisy saw her mother laugh. 'Oh, Daisy, you answered your own question, not two minutes ago,' she said. 'It has to be you because you're about the same age as Cynthia, and Daddy and myself love every one of our children equally, yet each has a special place in our hearts. We love you specially because you are lively and sweet and because you try so hard to be good.'

She slipped her hand into Daisy's as she spoke and Daisy suddenly felt full of happiness and the certainty that she was loved and would be brought home as soon as such a thing were possible. 'I *do* try hard, don't I, Mammy?' she said contentedly. 'And I'll go on trying even though it'll be rare hard, so it will. I'll pretend Aunt Jane is you and give her a bedtime kiss without being told, and I'll tell Cynthia all about Benmacraig and help her with her lessons, and never put a button in the collection at church, nor take the biggest piece of cake when it's handed round.'

This made Maggie laugh again. Stopping abruptly, she lifted Daisy up, gave her a hard hug and kissed the tip of her small nose. 'If you live up to all them promises, we shall have to call you Saint

Daisy,' she said. 'Tell you what, queen, I'll make you a promise – just a little one – and you can make me one in return. I'll keep a sort of diary, each day – a letter diary – and post it off to you every Saturday, so likely you'll get it on the Monday or Tuesday. And you can do the same for me.'

The idea was a novel one and Daisy was not at all sure that she liked it, for though she loved reading she seldom put pencil to paper and guessed that such a task might well be beyond her. Then she remembered a book she had read in which one of the characters had written a diary. It had started well enough with short descriptions of an argument, an extra nice meal or a game. But after a while the entries largely consisted of the words *Forget what did*, or *Ate twenty apples; was sick*, and she thought she could manage that all right. 'I promise, Mammy,' she said gaily therefore. 'And I'll write to Amanda because she'll be lonely in that big old house, same as I shall. And – and it won't be for long, will it?'

It had taken Maggie time and patience to persuade Jane to accept Daisy in Annabel's place, but in the end her sister had had to admit that the younger girl would be of much more use at home with her brothers than Daisy would ever be, however good her intentions. Maggie had spoken the truth when she had told Daisy that she loved all her children equally; letting go of either girl would be a wrench, but there was no denying that in the confines of old

Mícheál's cottage the meek and biddable Annabel would be an easier companion than her boisterous older sister. Sighing, Jane had conceded that there was never any telling what Daisy would get up to next, and inwardly shuddered at the thought of the havoc she might wreak in the well-ordered Venables household. However, she was a good sister, and sincerely wishful of helping Maggie in any way she could, so she concealed the worst of her qualms and prepared to make the best of things.

Despite herself, Daisy quite enjoyed the next couple of days. Aunt Jane had talked to her very kindly, explaining that she would be helping a poor, sick child whilst earning money for which her family stood sorely in need. She had described the house and the old nursery on the third floor, which was being turned into a beautiful suite of rooms for the two small girls and the governess. None of these descriptions meant anything to Daisy, who had never entered a house with stairs and rooms above. Nevertheless, she appreciated that Aunt Jane was doing her best to prepare her for what was to come, and responded by not complaining when she was taken into Clifden to be trailed round the shops and forced to try on any number of dresses, blouses and frocks, as well as a neat pair of button shoes and a coat, so soft and warm that even Amanda was impressed.

'But we won't buy much; this is mainly to give us ideas,' her aunt told her. 'For there's places in

Liverpool – TJ's for example – what'll sell us a whole outfit for a quarter of the price you'd pay in Clifden.'

This seemed unlikely to Daisy, for surely a big city would charge big prices, but her mother assured her that Aunt Jane was right; clothing in Liverpool was cheap compared with Clifden. 'I reckon it's competition what keeps the prices down,' she said wisely, when Amanda questioned her on the subject. 'Then there's lots of women with a crowd of kids, what likes to work from home. They learn their trade in factories and shops, then they buy materials cheap and make 'em up for you, and what they make is as good as what's in the shops, only nowhere near as pricey.'

Daisy, sublimely uninterested in clothes, was quite content with the things they had bought in Clifden, but Amanda said eagerly that she meant to spend some of her first wages on suitable garments for a girl working in a big city. 'They give us uniform of course, but I'll need something a bit smarter for me days off,' she told Jane. 'You've got excellent taste, Aunt; if I send you me measurements and some money, could you – would you – buy me somethin' suitable?'

Aunt Jane agreed but said that she would take Amanda's measurements herself before she left. Then she and Maggie began the formidable task of deciding just which of Daisy's possessions should accompany her to the big city. After much wrangling with Daisy, who wanted to take all her own things and several objects which were not hers at all but she had always coveted, Aunt Jane put her foot down. 'You can have the rag doll your mammy made for you, the book of poems she gave you and the big shell your daddy brought home after it got caught in his fishing net, but I refuse to take that horrible dried octopus – if it is an octopus – or the shark's teeth . . . yuck . . . or that awful old blanket which is more moth holes than wool.'

Daisy longed to say she would not go to Liverpool if she could not take her most precious things, but when she began to object Amanda gave her such a quelling look that the sentence mumbled off into silence. Later in their room preparing for bed, Amanda reminded her rather sharply that she was not going to Liverpool on a pleasure trip but to help the family to regain their lost fortunes. 'And anyway, that horrible old dried octopus isn't the sort of thing you can put on a mantelpiece, and the shark's teeth smell really nasty,' she told her small sister. 'Besides, from what Aunt Jane says, you're going to be given money each week and I dare say you'll spend a little of it on yourself, though I know you mean to send most of it home. So you will doubtless see things in the shops which you'll like much better than the stuff you're leaving behind.'

Daisy muttered that she was sorry, but she could not imagine that anything bought in a shop could ever be as precious to her as the results of the

65

diligent beachcombing which all the Kildares so much enjoyed. However, the little book of poems, the big pearly shell and Topsy, her rag doll, were all reminders of the love – and the life – which she would be leaving behind.

On her last day in Benmacraig everyone was especially nice to her, though Brendan was out fishing with Mícheál, and Amanda had left for Galway the previous day. Mammy made her favourite dinner, then Daddy took her for a walk on the shore, ostensibly to gather mussels but really, Daisy thought, to tell her how much he would miss her and to make her promise that she would not try to run away from kind Aunt Jane. 'If you're very unhappy, alanna, and can't abide the big city, then you must write and tell us and if we're able we'll come over and spend an hour or two wit' you,' he said. 'But from what your aunt has said you'll not be unhappy; quite the opposite in fact. And remember, we truly need the money you'll be earning for us.'

'I know it, Daddy, and I'll do me best to be good,' Daisy promised fervently. 'And it won't be for ever, will it?'

Her father chuckled and gave her a squeeze, but Daisy saw that his eyes were sad and her heart gave a great uncomfortable lurch. She had never, in all her life, been further from Benmacraig than Clifden, and she had never spent a single night away from her own home. How would she bear it? Aunt Jane had been kind to her recently, but it was impossible not to remember other occasions when Aunt Jane had aired her frank opinion about Daisy, by no means her favourite niece. But by this time they were approaching a huge mass of rocks upon which the blue-black mussels clustered in great family groups, and Colm was rolling up his trouser legs in order to wade into the water, the big bucket swinging from his hand. He began to pull the mussels from the rock and drop them into the bucket, and Daisy was following suit when suddenly, just for a second or two, the moment crystallised into one she knew she would never forget, not if she lived to be a hundred. The feeling of the wet sand between her toes and the salt water sloshing halfway up her calves, the sun warm on the back of her neck and the wonderful salty smell of rocks and seaweed, the freedom of the wind on her cheek, and the sound of seabirds mewing as they headed for their nesting places on the cliffs, were all indelibly impressed on her mind. Her fingers gripped a mussel and pulled and the moment was broken, but she knew that whenever she thought of Benmacraig, the cottage or the shore, this moment would return to her, crystal clear, to remind her of what she had lost.

Presently, her father stood the bucket down on a ledge of rock and put his arms about her. 'Don't cry, alanna,' he said gently. 'You'll come back to us and we'll get our home again; I feel it in me bones. Now, I've a suggestion to make. Your aunt were saying how fond Mrs Venables is of fresh mussels. Why not take her a bucket of them? I swear there's no mussels as good as ours. If you fill the bucket half full of sea water . . .'

It had been said to make her laugh and it succeeded, and perhaps it lightened the atmosphere, for Daisy let the wind dry the tears on her cheeks and wept no more that day, though next morning, when she was woken in darkness, bundled into her clothes and presented with a bowl of creamy porridge, the tears simply would not be suppressed, and trickled down her cheeks until Colm said it was no wonder she did not fancy her porridge, for it must be awash with salt by now.

Aunt Jane, sitting opposite her niece in the lamplit kitchen, reminded Daisy that they had a long day's journey in front of them and advised her, kindly, to eat up. But though Daisy tried to swallow, the lump in her throat got in the way and by the time Colm had fetched Tina round to the door, she had scarcely reduced the porridge by more than a couple of spoonfuls.

'Never mind, chuck; it 'ud be a miracle if you could eat when so much is going to happen,' her mother said consolingly, helping Daisy into her new coat. 'Now don't forget, write me a letter just as soon as you arrive in Rodney Street, and I'll write back and tell you what's happening here. I wish I could come to see you off, but you know I can't leave the little ones.' She bent over her daughter, giving her a hug and a kiss on the cheek. 'Be a good girl for your Aunt Jane,' she said, her voice breaking. 'Ah God, you're terrible young to be sent away from your own folk! How I wish . . . but if wishes were horses, then beggars would ride.'

Daisy forced back the tears and gave her mother her cheekiest grin. 'I'll be all right, Mammy,' she said, and heard the confidence in her own voice with some surprise. 'Aunt Jane and me's goin' to get along just fine, so we are, and I'll write as soon as I've unpacked me t'ings.' And then, because she could feel the treacherous tears welling up once more, she patted her mother's hand rather blindly, and rushed out to climb aboard the donkey cart, leaving her mother and Aunt Jane to say their goodbyes in private.

Chapter Three

It was a long journey, and for Aunt Jane probably a tedious one, but for Daisy it was a totally new experience. The parting with her father at Clifden had been painful because Colm could not hide his distress. He had meant to wait until the train left so that Daisy would have someone to wave her off, but as soon as he had carried their luggage on to the platform he had whisked Daisy off her feet, given her a kiss and a cuddle and had then stood her down, wiping his eyes with the backs of his hands as though he were still a small boy. 'I can't watch you get into that train and leave us,' he had said. 'Better I go now. Besides, your mammy will be wantin' me back at Benmacraig just as soon as possible.' He had headed for the station exit, then turned back. 'Never forget we love you, Daisy,' he had called in a choked voice. 'And we love you too, me dear Jane; so be good to one another.' And with that he had disappeared. Daisy had promptly abandoned her aunt and the pile of luggage and had run to the exit, so in the end it was she who had waved her father off rather than vice versa, and she had kept waving until the donkey cart had disappeared before returning, reluctantly, to the platform.

It was by sheer luck, as the train drew away, that she looked out of the window once more and saw a figure waving frantically in her direction. She promptly rattled the window down and leaned out as Sean O'Grady began to trot alongside the carriage. 'Brendan told me you were off so I thought you'd mebbe like something to remind you of Benmacraig,' he said, thrusting a small parcel into her hands. 'I'd promise to write only I'm no hand wit' a pen so I made you this.' The train began to pick up speed and Sean dropped behind. 'Come home soon, alanna,' he roared. 'We'll miss you, so we shall.'

Daisy stared back towards the platform until the tiny figure disappeared, then she pulled up the window and returned to her seat. Her aunt smiled at her encouragingly. 'That were kind of Sean,' she said approvingly. 'What's he given you, queen?'

Daisy had unwrapped the newspaper and looked down at a small piece of driftwood, carved into the shape of a gull. She showed her aunt, torn between tears and laughter as she thought of her last meeting with Sean, when they had searched the cliffs together and been briskly attacked by angry birds.

'That's very pretty; a nice keepsake,' Aunt Jane said. 'Now how about sharing one of the chocolate bars I bought from the machine on the station? I know your mammy made us a grand breakfast, but I wouldn't say no to some chocolate.'

71

Daisy turned towards the window, surreptitiously flicking away tears and saying, in a muffled voice, that chocolate was a grand idea, so it was, whilst hoping that Aunt Jane had not noticed her childish behaviour.

Despite her sadness, however, Daisy rather enjoyed her first train journey, though she was overawed by the size and splendour of Dublin, and clung very close to her aunt as they made their way along the quays to where the ferry for England awaited its passengers. It was a fine day but there was a stiff breeze blowing, and as soon as they got aboard Aunt Jane gave a moan and settled herself on one of the long wooden benches beside the ship's rail. 'I never know whether it's better to be sick on a full stomach, or to feel like death out walking on an empty one,' she said pathetically. 'But you're used to the water, queen, so no doubt you won't mind the motion.'

'There isn't any motion,' Daisy said, rather surprised, for they were still tied up and she did not consider that the small movements as folk came aboard could upset anyone. 'But I'm awful hungry, Aunt Jane. The bun and the glass of milk you bought me when we changed trains was ages ago, and I couldn't eat me porridge at breakfast ... it were too early, I dare say.'

Aunt Jane moaned and closed her eyes, then opened them again and dug around in one of the large bags she carried, producing her purse from its depths. 'I can't go below for I always feel worse there,' she said. 'But I'll give you some money. As soon as we sail they'll open up the bar down them stairs and you can buy yourself a drink and a snack. Only don't bring it too near me 'cos even the smell of food is enough to make me throw up.'

Daisy took the money eagerly, then leaned on the rail and watched the seamen as they cast off the mooring ropes. She waited until they were out of the harbour and chugging through the surf, then went below and examined the money she had been given with considerable satisfaction. Two beautiful shiny half-crowns, enough to buy a whole dinner if she wanted it. In the end, after much thought – and to the steward's amusement – she bought sausage rolls, doughnuts, apple turnovers and a wedge of pork pie, as well as a large bottle of ginger beer. She carried her provender back to the deck and, forgetting the prohibition, sat down beside Aunt Jane, suggesting that they might share the food and drink. Aunt Jane gave another moan and flapped one hand weakly at her niece. 'Take it away,' she whispered. 'Even the smell . . . oh, God, that doughnut . . . *please*, Daisy . . . I can't – I can't . . .'

With an abruptness which almost caused Daisy to drop her half-eaten doughnut, Aunt Jane lurched to her feet and hung over the rail, her shoulders heaving. Daisy, feeling guilty, put her food down a short distance away and timidly patted her aunt's back, but this did not seem to help in the least so she abandoned the older woman, picked up her plate of food and the bottle of ginger beer, and trotted up to the bows. For the rest of the voyage she stayed where she was, returning to her aunt a couple of times, but soon realising that there was nothing she could do to help except, in fact, to leave that afflicted woman severely alone.

Presently, she fell into conversation with a large Irishman, who told her that he was a navvy, working on the roads in England, and had been home to see his old parents. When she told him about her aunt, he assured her that seasick persons recovered as soon as they reached land once more, which was a great relief to Daisy, who had been worrying that her aunt might be incapable of leading her to Rodney Street, for she herself had no idea in which part of the city it lay.

The two of them had been watching as they approached land and as the ferry entered the Mersey Daisy stared, round-eyed, at her very first sight of the city of Liverpool. 'It's absolutely *huge*,' she said to her new friend. 'I thought Dublin was big, so I did, but Liverpool is – is taller, as well as bigger. Why, some of them buildings must reach up to the clouds, pretty near. Is they houses? Or palaces?'

Her companion laughed. 'Mostly they're offices, warehouses and such,' he informed her. 'They tell me Liverpool ain't nowhere near as big as London, but I doubt that can be true meself. All the big

74

ships come here, bringing cargo in – or taking it out, o' course. In the bad old days, they brung black slaves here.' He chuckled. 'Imagine, missy, how them black fellers must ha' felt, comin' from straw huts in the jungle, wit' only little skirt t'ings round their waistses to keep them decent, and seein' this. No wonder so many of them died.'

Daisy shuddered. 'Do they – do they still bring them here?' she enquired tentatively.

The navvy shook his head. 'Nah, 'course not. We's civilised now. You'll see folk of all colours in Liverpool, though: black, yaller, coffee-coloured – sky blue pink for all I know – but they's seamen, not slaves.' He turned reluctantly away from the bows as the ship began to slow. 'Best get back to your auntie, alanna, because I knows how it is wit' folk what's been seasick. They're that keen to gerroff and on to firm ground that they're usually hoverin' by the gangway, and the two of you don't want to lose each other, 'cos, as you've already observed, this here's one helluva big city.'

To Daisy's secret surprise, Aunt Jane was indeed already on her feet and collecting their luggage. She smiled rather wanly at her niece but bade her pick up her baggage and make for the gangway. 'As soon as we're ashore we'll get ourselves a taxi straight to Rodney Street,' she said. 'I don't mean to struggle aboard a tram with all this stuff to carry.'

A taxi! Daisy knew such things existed – there were a couple at Clifden station – but she had

75

never expected to have a ride in one, and was very impressed. Her aunt must be quite rich, as well as at home in the city, even to consider such a thing.

They began to make their way to the side of the ship, but they did not have to carry all their bags since the navvy, spotting them, came over and seized their two large cases, assuring Aunt Jane that he could manage them with ease. He chatted amiably to them as they descended the gangway and saw them into a waiting taxi, asking for their address so that he might tell the driver where to take them. Aunt Jane thanked him for his help and Daisy saw a dark flush invade his weather-beaten countenance before he said that it was a pleasure.

Aunt Jane replied graciously that it was very kind of him but added, as the taxi moved off, that no doubt he was lonely and anxious to fall into conversation with anyone who seemed friendly. Daisy looked speculatively at her aunt, realising for the first time that she was a handsome woman even though she must be in her mid forties. Her thick fair hair was almost untouched by grey, and Daisy thought it a pity that she had not taken to a modern bob or shingle, or even allowed her hair to flow loose, but dragged it back from her face into a hard knob at the nape of her neck, which gave her a severe appearance. Aunt Jane had a trim figure, but again the clothes that she chose were neither pretty nor colourful. She favoured black or navy, shapeless dresses or dark jackets and skirts over plain white blouses which looked more like shirts. Her stockings were thick and her shoes flat and practical. Daisy, who had never been the least interested in clothes, suddenly realised that she must have inherited this trait from Aunt Jane, for her own mother loved pretty things, her one extravagance being a subscription to the *Ladies' Journal*, which was sent to her monthly and she perused from cover to cover, often refurbishing an old dress as it advised with a pretty collar and cuffs, or making up a pattern obtained free from the magazine.

Because Daisy had been so engrossed in her own thoughts she had taken no notice of the streets along which the taxi passed but now, as the vehicle slowed at a crossing, she looked rather apprehensively out of the window. The pavement was crowded with people of all ages, shapes and sizes, but it was not a colourful crowd. Both men and women wore mainly black, though some of the younger ones, she saw with relief, were brightly dressed. She nudged her aunt. 'Where's this?' she hissed. 'Ain't it busy, though? I've never seen so many folk in one place before.'

'You should have looked out at Bold Street where the fashionables shop. This here's St Luke's Place and we're turning into Leece Street, so we'll be home before you know it,' her aunt said authoritatively. 'As for the people, you'll get used to them. Why, when there's a football match on, I'm

77

told you can cross the streets leading to the ground by treading on the heads of the folk hurrying along and you'd not need to descend to the earth once.'

'Golly!' Daisy said reverently. 'I wish I may see it, that's all. D'you mean it, Aunt Jane? Do folk really cross the road by treadin' on other people's heads?'

Aunt Jane laughed, and to her humiliation Daisy saw that the taxi driver was grinning broadly as he drew his cab to a halt and turned to shoot back the little window which divided him from his fares. ''Ere you are, ladies, number thirty-nine Rodney Street. I'll get your traps out and carry 'em to the front door.' He winked at Daisy. 'No doubt the butler will carry them in the rest of the way,' he added in a plummy squeezed-up voice, which Daisy imagined he thought posh people must use.

Since she had no idea what a butler was, the remark might have passed her by, but her aunt said haughtily: 'That's quite enough of that silly talk, my man. How much do I owe you?'

Money changed hands and Daisy was gratified by the altered expression on the driver's face when Aunt Jane pressed an extra coin into his palm. 'Thank you, madam,' he said humbly. 'I didn't mean to give offence, but hearin' the little gal so impressed wi' the crowds and knowin' you come off the Irish ferry . . .'

'You shouldn't leap to conclusions. My niece is here for a visit, but I was born and bred in

78

Liverpool so it's as well you didn't try to over-charge me,' Aunt Jane said reprovingly. 'I've heard as how some folk try to cheat the Irish when the ferries come into port and I'm glad you aren't one of them.'

'I'm Irish meself, way back, same as most Scousers. Me gran'parents came over last century 'cos o' the famine, so I wouldn't cheat anyone.' The man looked at No. 39 and at the brass plate beside the front door, and his expression changed. 'Ain't the little girl well? She looks so bonny that I never thought . . . but if she's comin' to see the doctor . . .'

'She's not; not coming to visit the doctor, I mean – or not as a patient, at any rate,' Aunt Jane said, unbending at the man's obvious concern. 'I'm Dr Venables's housekeeper, so we're neither of us patients. But thank you for your concern. Good day to you.'

'Ta-ra, ladies,' the taxi driver said, climbing back into his cab, just as Aunt Jane rang the bell.

Daisy stared after the cab but turned to face the door once more when she heard footsteps approaching. It swung open to reveal a neat, dark-haired woman in a nurse's uniform, with a white cap perched on her head. Her face wore a bright and falsely welcoming smile, which became real as she recognised Aunt Jane, who smiled back with equal warmth, saying apologetically: 'Good evening. I'm so sorry to have brought you to the door' – she indicated the pile of baggage at her

79

feet – 'but I really couldn't face carrying these round to the back, having given the taxi driver the Rodney Street address. Is Pilcher about? If so, do you think you could ask him to come and carry our bags up to the housekeeper's room? But what are you doing here at this hour? I'm sure it's well past six.'

Nurse Evans smiled. 'It's Thursday, remember – evening surgery,' she said, now including Daisy in her smile. 'And this will be the young lady who is to be companion to Mrs Venables's niece, I suppose.' She held out a slender hand. 'How do you do? I'm Nurse Evans. I work for Dr Venables and come to the house whenever he is holding a surgery, so I dare say you and I will get to know each other quite well. But what am I doing, keeping you standing on the doorstep?' She turned back to Aunt Jane. 'If you carry one big suitcase and I take the other, we can get them through to the kitchen. Pilcher is in there having a cup of tea, so he'll carry them up the back stairs in no time, whilst Cook puts together a supper for the pair of you, because I'm sure you'll both be hungry as hunters after your long journey.'

'I don't know about both of us,' Aunt Jane said rather grumpily, as they stepped into the hall. 'I was sick as a dog, as always, and now I'm as empty as any drum, but the youngster here started eating and drinking the moment the ship left Dublin and didn't stop until we moored at the Pier Head. Still, I dare say she might manage a bite.'

'Yes I could manage – a bite, I mean,' Daisy said at once. 'I've never been in a train or on a big ship or in a taxi before in my whole life, and I think such things must make me hungry. Anyway, I only ate four doughnuts, two apple turnovers, a couple of sausage rolls and a piece of pork pie . . .'

'All right, all right, Nurse Evans doesn't want to know what a horrible mixture of grub is churning round in your stomach . . . indeed, it makes me feel quite ill only to think of it,' Aunt Jane said repressively. 'Follow me, Daisy.'

Nurse Evans had taken the larger suitcase and now Aunt Jane picked up the other one, leaving Daisy only two small bags to carry. Obeying an injunction to shut the front door behind her, Daisy trotted along an imposing hallway. It was floored with black and white tiles, lit by a magnificent chandelier, and seemed to Daisy's dazzled eyes as wonderful as a royal palace. She saw that the walls were panelled and hung with portraits, mainly pictures of elderly men with side whiskers and collars so stiff and high that Daisy thought their wearers must have been in danger of strangulation. Then the nurse pushed open a green baize door at the end of the hall and held it so that Aunt Jane and Daisy could pass through into the corridor beyond and down the stairs to the basement kitchen. Daisy had noticed several doors in the main hall, one of which was labelled *Waiting Room*, another *Reception* and a third *Surgery*. She supposed she must have known that her aunt worked for a doctor but so far as she could recall he was seldom mentioned. Aunt Jane spoke of her employer as Mrs Venables and Daisy had not realised that the doctor carried on his business actually in the house on Rodney Street. No wonder it had to be so large! It also made sense of her aunt's remark about going round the back, because with nurses and patients using the front door life would be simpler for everyone if family and friends used the rear entrance. But now they were entering the kitchen and Daisy promptly forgot her awe as she glanced around the warm and comfortable room. It was very like the kitchen up at the Vaughans' farm, only even bigger, and Daisy recognised from her reading – both of the *Ladies' Journal* and of the pile of magazines which Aunt Jane brought with her on every visit – a large white gas cooker and, wonder of wonders, a great box-like object which she was pretty sure was a refrigerator.

'Daisy!'

Daisy, suddenly aware of her rounding eyes and dropped jaw, jerked herself back to the present and to the realisation that her aunt had been addressing her. 'Sorry, Aunt Jane,' she whispered. 'Only I've never seen . . .' She pointed to the wonderful kitchen appliances at which she had been gazing. 'I've never seen them things in real life, only in me mammy's magazines, and I were took aback, you might say.'

'Well, now you're with us again I'd better introduce you,' Aunt Jane said, and for the first time

82

Daisy looked at the people in the room instead of at the room itself. They were seated round a large table covered in checked American cloth, at the head of which sat an enormous woman, grey-haired and fiftyish, wearing a brown dress which was almost hidden by a voluminous white apron. Next to her was a row of young girls, all clad in gingham, with their hair cut in a variety of modern shapes, and opposite them sat a tall, good-looking man, with crisp dark hair. He was wearing a blue shirt and navy trousers, and he was polishing the brass buttons on a navy jacket. He was using a button stick, which Daisy knew all about because one of Mr Vaughan's sons was a naval officer, and always used a button stick when cleaning his uniform. Immediately, she leapt to the conclusion that this young man must also be in the Navy and wondered what he was doing in the doctor's kitchen.

Next to the button polisher sat an elderly man in worn corduroy trousers and waistcoat. He was supping noisily at a tin mug of tea and had a hunk of bread and cheese in his free hand. Beside him sat a boy of sixteen or seventeen, roughly clad and also eating, whilst at the foot of the table and turning round to stare at her was a lad of no more than ten or eleven. Relieved to find herself not the only child in the room, Daisy smiled at him, where-upon he stuck his middle finger against the end of his nose and used his other fingers to pull down his lower lids until his eyes were rimmed with scarlet. Daisy promptly put out her tongue as far as it would go, then held her nose and blew a raspberry. She had done it on the spur of the moment and expected a reprimand, even though the boy had started it, but everyone laughed, except Aunt Jane, who had not seen what Daisy had done but was wagging a reproving finger at the boy.

'That's no way to greet a young lady, Jake,' she said, then indicated the large woman at the head of the table. 'The lady in the apron is our cook, Mrs Bellamy, but we mostly call her Cook. The girls are the maids, Ruth, Molly, Annie and Biddy. Ruth helps Mrs Bellamy in the kitchen and will wait on you and Miss Cynthia. Molly is the upstairs maid; she makes the beds, dusts and cleans, lays fires and so on. Annie runs errands and helps Mrs Bellamy with her marketing and ordering, and young Biddy here works mostly for the doctor, or at any rate she keeps the surgery, reception room and waiting room clean, and answers the door when Nurse is busy.'

The four girls grinned at Daisy and said hello, to which Daisy responded with a polite 'How do you do?' which made Mrs Bellamy give an approving nod.

'That's right, chuck,' she said in a warm, fat sort of voice, 'and this here, on me left, is the doctor's chauffeur, Mr Elgin. Next to him is Pilcher, the gardener, then Roddy, what helps with the car and the garden – Doctor calls him Odd-job – and last of all Mr Elgin's son, Jake, what's the wickedest boy I ever met, and the most troublesome.'

The chauffeur smiled at her, as did Roddy, but Jake hunched an offended shoulder and muttered that he were a poor motherless boy what did his best to please, a remark which set the four girls giggling, though the cook and the male members of the household took no notice.

'Well, now you know everyone,' Aunt Jane said. She turned to indicate her niece. 'This here's Daisy Kildare, ladies and gentleman, what's come to be a companion to Miss Cynthia. And now, if you wouldn't mind, Pilcher, I'd be glad if you and Odd-job could take me traps up to the house-keeper's room.' She turned to the cook. 'I see you've finished your evenin' meal, Mrs Bellamy, but is there any chance of us having our suppers straight away?'

Mrs Bellamy surged to her feet and waddled over to the Aga. She opened the oven door and a wonderful smell wafted to Daisy's nostrils, making her mouth water. Mrs Bellamy produced an earthenware pot with the aid of a thick cloth, and put it down on a large cork mat in the middle of the table with a triumphant air. 'Me Lancashire hotpot,' she said proudly, as the maids left their seats, each hurrying to perform some prearranged task. One of them fetched plates from the big Welsh dresser against one wall, another began to

85

make a pot of fresh tea, the third cleared the table, brushing the crumbs into a flat little pan with a small silver brush, whilst the fourth – Daisy had already forgotten which was which – collected cutlery from a baize-lined drawer, and made up two places at the now cleared board.

The chauffeur stood up leisurely and slipped on the jacket with its now gleaming buttons, then jerked his head at his son. 'Gerra move on, young Jake. You've not done your homework yet an' I'm damned if I'll take another tellin' off from your teacher because of work not done,' he said.

Jake sniffed and wiped his nose on his sleeve. 'All right, all right, don't nag,' he said sulkily. 'I'm comin', ain't I? But why can't I stay an' do it here, like I usually does? It's perishin' cold above them stables an' it's nice 'n' warm in here.'

'Because these ladies don't want to eat their meal with you jabberin' away nineteen to the dozen,' his father said. 'Why d'you have to argue over everythin', Jake? Just do as you're told or I'll give you a clack you won't forget in a hurry.'

Jake sniffed again, and as his father herded him towards the back door he turned and pulled another awful face at Daisy. This time she ignored him, partly because she was taking her place at the table before a plate already piled with a generous helping of Lancashire hotpot, but also because she did not wish to make an enemy of a boy probably a year older than she, and consequently stronger.

*

86

Jake slouched out of the kitchen and set off towards the flat above the garage, still known as the coachman's quarters, where he and his father lived. As they climbed the stairs, Mr Elgin said reprovingly: 'Why'd you go pullin' faces at the little gal, young feller-me-lad? This is a good job and one I don't mean to lose. I thought you liked it an' all, so don't you go makin' yourself difficult.'

'I weren't,' Jake mumbled as his father opened the door which led straight into their kitchen. 'But I don't like girls an' I bet she'll be just like t'other one, once she settles in.'

Mr Elgin laughed. 'Miss Darlington-Crewe won't have nothin' to do with either of us, if she can help it,' he observed. 'This 'un's different. She's just Miss Dalton's niece, what her family can't afford to feed no more. I pity her, honest to God I do, so don't you go makin' things hard for her. Just you remember what life was like before I got this job. And now gerron with your home-work. I've got to check me tyre pressures.'

As his father left the room, Jake opened his satchel and spread out his books, but his father's words had brought vividly back to his mind what life had been like before Robert Elgin had obtained the post of chauffeur to the doctor, rather less than a year ago. They had lodged in one of the tall ramshackle houses on Mere Lane. Their room had been in the attic and until he had started school Jake had been 'looked after' by their landlady, a fat and slatternly woman whom

87

he had called Aunt Ruby, though she was in fact no relation. His father had had a number of badly paid jobs and Jake had never had quite enough to eat, for Aunt Ruby had six kids of her own, all older than him, and naturally, he supposed now, she had been more interested in their welfare than in his.

Things had improved a bit when he started school, but boots were a perpetual problem, for no child was allowed in school barefoot. Robert Elgin bought Jake boots for winter and plimsolls for summer, but as soon as his back was turned this footwear was either taken to the pawnbroker's or simply handed to one of Aunt Ruby's children and Jake, who was bright and enjoyed school, had to use considerable ingenuity to keep himself shod. His father had understood the problem and had confronted Ruby on the subject, but she had told him that his son hated school and was using his lack of footwear as an excuse not to attend. Jake had known that his father did not believe her but had been, so to speak, in a cleft stick. The room the Elgins had occupied was cheap, and though Aunt Ruby was lazy and scarcely ever cooked, she had always fed them with watery porridge for breakfast and some sort of evening meal, even though Jake had often been expected to make do with bread and jam and a slice of bought cake.

But all that was in the past. Since the move to Rodney Street, Jake's whole life had changed. Mrs

Bellamy was a marvellous cook and the Venables were generous employers. The coachman's flat was a little paradise compared with Aunt Ruby's filthy and neglected house and because it was all their own to do as they liked with – they paid no rent since the flat went with the job – Robert and Jake kept the place spotless and were proud of their little abode.

Now, Jake pulled his arithmetic homework towards him and began on the first problem. Sometimes, he thought, I puzzle meself. Why did I pull a face at that girl? True, he was not fond of girls as a general rule but this one, though a good deal younger than himself – at least a year – seemed a decent enough kid. He had seen Miss Darlington-Crewe a couple of times and had not been impressed, thinking her stuck up and snobbish. Why, she didn't even go to school but had a governess, something unheard of so far as Jake was concerned. He supposed he had pulled a face simply because the girl had been staring at him, and he decided that in future he would be polite, though he meant to keep her at arm's length. Besides, he had heard Miss Dalton saying that her niece would be living on the nursery floor and probably not joining the rest of the staff for meals, except on special occasions, so the girl was no threat to his pleasant existence. As the only child in an otherwise adult household, he realised he was privileged. No one ever asked him to wash up or clear away, to do messages or to fetch the washing in off the line. Indeed, it was quite otherwise. Mrs Bellamy saved him little extras, the maids bought sweets and shared them with him, and when his father was not driving his employer he was at liberty to use the car to take Jake on outings to the beach, or into the countryside.

Jake knew his father had been brought up in the country and loved it there. When he and Jake's mother had first married, they had run a small market garden and had been both happy and successful. But then Jake's mother had fallen ill and by the time she died the place had been neglected for too long and Robert, with a two-year-old son to look after, had sold up and moved into the city, believing that he would do better as an employee, and would find it easier to get help in bringing up his son.

Jake could not remember the market garden, or his mother, and his father scarcely ever mentioned them, but Robert still loved the country and had taught his son to love it too. 'When I retire, we'll mebbe move back, take a cottage with a big garden, and grow our own grub,' Robert sometimes said. 'Mr Venables told me the other day a feller could rent an allotment – grow vegetables, fruit, the lot – but there ain't much point in doin' that now. No, I'd rather save me money in the Post Office so that one day, when I'm too old for driving, I'll have another string to me bow.'

Now, Jake finished the last problem he had been

set, closed the exercise book and shoved it back in his satchel, then pulled out the next. English – not as much fun as arithmetic, but it had to be done. Resolutely, he began to write, heading his essay *The day we went aboard the good ship Tantalus*.

As soon as the door had shut behind the Elgins, Daisy and her aunt began to eat and the maids, apart from the youngest and smallest of them, left the kitchen. The one remaining went straight to the sink and began to run hot water from a big tap on to a pile of dirty plates. Daisy guessed this must be the kitchen maid, though she still could not remember her name. Presently, however, Mrs Bellamy addressed the girl as Ruth, and Daisy, more relaxed now, thought thankfully that she would remember this one name at least. She had seen the hot water gush out of the tap with tremendous awe and as soon as she had cleared her plate – for her mother had always told the children not to talk whilst they were eating – she turned to her aunt. 'Did you see that, Aunt Jane? The hot water didn't come from no kettle, but straight out of the tap. How can that be? I've seen water come from a tap in the Vaughans' kitchen, but it come out cold; they needed the kettle and a fire to get it hot.'

Aunt Jane finished her own helping of hotpot and turned to her niece. 'This here is a very modern house, or at least it's a very old house what's been modernised,' she explained. 'Doctor wants everything up to date, and not only in his surgery but in the rest of the house as well. Presently, when we go upstairs, I'll show you the bathroom what the staff use.' She chuckled, smiling across at Mrs Bellamy, who had reseated herself and was sipping a cup of tea whilst perusing a copy of the *Liverpool Echo*. 'That's so, ain't it, Mrs B? Doctor spares no expense when it comes to keepin' up to date.'

'Very true,' Mrs Bellamy said absently, her eyes still on her paper. 'My goodness, they've caught the feller what's been misbehavin' on the underground trains late at night! I hopes as they cuts his –' She glanced across at Daisy. 'I mean I hope he gets a harsh punishment; aye, that's what I mean,' she concluded.

'A bathroom!' Daisy breathed, ignoring the cook's remark. She knew such things as bathrooms existed, had seen pictures of them in the *Good Housekeeping* magazine, but had never dreamt that she might use one in real life. 'Wait till I write and tell me mammy. I bet even she has never used a bathroom. No wonder you didn't like our earth floors, nor the hens runnin' in an' out, when you'd lived in a house wit' a real bathroom. Is there a privy in the yard? Don't say that's indoors 'n' all?'

Mrs Bellamy, engrossed in her newspaper, took no notice, but Aunt Jane shook her head warningly and put her finger to her lips. 'It won't do to talk too much about Benmacraig,' she whispered. 'I've not told folk how – how countrified your home is, so just you keep such remarks to yourself, young lady.' She picked up her cup and drained it, then addressed the cook. 'Thank you very much, Mrs Bellamy. That was delicious. Now I wonder if I should take Daisy up to see Miss Cynthia? What do you think?'

Mrs Bellamy put her newspaper down and shook her head. 'No indeed. Madam knew you would be arrivin' late and gave strict orders that you were to have the child in your own room tonight – she's provided a truckle bed – so that she might make the introductions herself tomorrow mornin'.' She lowered her voice. 'I reckon she knew you'd be tired, hungry and travel-stained, and didn't mean you to make a bad impression. Oh, not on the child, but on this here governess of hers. My lor', but she's a right tartar. Everything's gorra be just so, and she talks that far back, crackin' her jaw to sound like a princess. What's more, she's livin' in, which Madam didn't allow for and isn't best pleased about.' She surged across the kitchen, bent down and gave Daisy a pat on the cheek. 'So you go off with your auntie, chuck, and don't worry about a thing. You'll be welcome as the flowers in May to that poor sick kid. Sleep well.'

She ushered the two of them out of her kitchen. Daisy expected her aunt to make straight for the stairs and asked, rather plaintively, where they were going when her aunt bypassed the flight and made for a narrow corridor leading towards the rear of the house. 'We use the back stairs except when we're servin' the family,' Aunt Jane explained. She looked kindly down at her niece. 'What a day, chuck! You'll sleep like a log, I'll warrant.'

'Aunt Jane, why do you speak different when you're in the kitchen from when you're talkin' to Nurse Evans and me?' Daisy asked diffidently, as they toiled up the back stairs. 'If I'd had me eyes shut I'd ha' thought you were two different people.'

Her aunt laughed. 'We all have to be different people sometimes, Daisy, and I advise you to copy my example,' she said. 'When I am with the other servants I let my Scouse accent show because . . . well, you heard what Mrs Bellamy said about the governess. She clearly thinks she's "putting on the style", pretending to be one of the gentry. But when I'm with Madam, or Nurse Evans, or anyone else who talks what you might call posh, then I speak as they do. Do you see what I mean?'

'Yes, I think so,' Daisy said as her aunt opened a door and ushered her into a pleasant bedroom. The windows were curtained in gold brocade; there was a brightly patterned carpet on the floor, and a comfortable-looking bed covered in a gold silk counterpane with, next to it, a smaller and much narrower bed, already made up with sheets, blankets and a beautiful blue eiderdown. 'I say, is that little bed for me? And what a beautiful room, Aunt Jane. I'm sure it's nicer than any of the bedrooms they show in the magazines.'

'Yes, it's a lovely room,' Aunt Jane said, sounding gratified. 'You'll find every room in this house is much superior to those at Benmacraig.' Daisy scowled, but before she could reply her aunt spoke again. 'I'll say nothing against Benmacraig, dear Daisy, because your parents have done their best and – and the cottage is delightful.' She gave a little laugh. 'Why, how absurd it would be to have carpets on your floors when the animals run in and out, and though you children take off your boots by the kitchen door the little ones drop food all over the place. So you see, what is suitable – indeed very nice – for a city house would be ridiculous in a country one. Can you understand?'

'Yes, and of course you are right: carpets would simply get filthy in Benmacraig and how could Mammy possibly sweep them, as she does her nice earth floor? Though I do see, Aunt Jane, that bricks or – or tiles in the kitchen at home would be nice, because when I was in the kitchen here I saw the floor was clean as a new pin and those little squares are tiles, aren't they?'

'That's right,' her aunt said. 'And now no more talking, my dear, but get yourself undressed and into your nightgown, and I'll take you along to the bathroom so you can have a good wash. As you can see, there's a washstand here which I use when the bathroom is occupied, but most of the staff are still downstairs so we shall have it to ourselves.'

Greatly intrigued, Daisy undressed, struggled

95

into her nightgown and the brand new slippers which her aunt had bought, and followed Aunt Jane back on to the landing and along to the bathroom. She thought it magnificent, with its huge bath and the great white object above it that Aunt Jane explained was the geyser that heated the water. There was also a very large lavatory with a cistern up by the ceiling, from which dangled a silver chain ending in a porcelain pear. Daisy had used the lavatory on Dublin station and had thought it very smart and modern, but by now she needed to use it again and hesitated to do so in front of Aunt Jane. Her aunt must have realised how she felt, for she said tactfully that she would leave her niece whilst she herself got undressed in the bedroom. When they had first entered the bathroom, she had flung open the doors of an enormous cupboard and extracted a large white towel which she had handed to Daisy. 'You must use this towel whenever you have a bath or a wash, for a week,' she explained. 'Then you may put it in the laundry basket and take a clean one from the cupboard.' Now she went towards the door and opened it, but turned to smile reassuringly. 'You remember which room is mine? When you come out of the bathroom you must turn to your right, and it's the third door along. Oh, and when you are bathing or using the convenience, you should lock the door. The bolt is just below the handle.'

She left the room, closing the door softly behind

her, and Daisy immediately shot across, seized the
bolt and rammed it home. Then she used the lavatory and pulled the porcelain pear, though she
had to stand on tiptoe to do so. After that, she decided to explore. She peeped inside the cupboard
from which her aunt had taken the towel and saw
a huge metal drum which seemed to be radiating
heat, and slatted wooden shelves upon which were
stacked piles of linen. Then she went over to the
hand basin, in which one could quite easily have
bathed a small child. She ran the tap but the water
all gurgled away down a round hole framed in
some silvery metal. She washed her hands under
the flow, using a fat white bar of soap, then discovered the plug and fitted that into place. Her aunt
had told her to take her flannel, soap and tooth-
brush into the bathroom with her, but she saw no
need to waste her own soap when there was such
a fine piece sitting on the side of the basin, so she
rubbed some of it on to her flannel, soaped her
face, neck, hands and arms, and then had a noisy
and enjoyable splash to rinse herself off. After that
she decided to wash her feet, not an easy task
because the hand basin was above her waist level.
She looked around for some means of gaining the
extra height she needed and saw a cork-topped
stool, which she dragged over. She realised afterwards that she should never have stepped from
the stool into the hand basin, for she had not been
paddling long when the basin gave an ominous
creak. Quickly, she stepped out again and was

97

sitting on the stool and beginning to dry her feet when her aunt's voice spoke to her from outside the locked door. 'Daisy? What on earth are you doing, child? Unlock the door and we'll get ourselves to bed, for I'm sure you must be clean as a whistle by now. And remember, I've not had a wash myself yet.'

Dismayed, Daisy jumped down from the stool, sending it crashing to the floor, noticing as she did so how very wet the linoleum was. Hastily she righted the stool and dropped her lovely white towel into the puddles. It absorbed them all right, but such treatment did little for the towel itself.

'Daisy! Will you please open this door! And what was that noise?'

Daisy rushed over to the door and began to tug at the bolt. 'I was washin' me feet and I knocked the stool over, Aunt,' she said breathlessly. 'Oh, oh, oh!'

'What is it *now*?' her aunt said impatiently. 'Will you do as I say, child? Open this door before I get really angry.'

Daisy gulped, and when she spoke her voice quivered with suppressed emotion. 'Oh, Aunt, I dunno what's the matter . . . well I do . . . but I can't open the door. That little knob thing, what you pull the bolt back with, has come off in me hand.'

There was a moment of stunned silence from the other side of the door. Then Aunt Jane spoke, her voice rising. 'You can't open the door? But the bolt can't have broken – it's made of metal, it's really strong. Are you sure you haven't just twisted it in the wrong direction?'

'It's broke all right,' Daisy said, her voice trembling. 'Here, I'll shove it under the door – the broken bit I mean – so you can see for yourself.' Bending down, she poked the small metal knob under the door and saw her aunt's fingers close over it, heard her deep, dramatic sigh.

'Oh my God, Daisy, you haven't been in the house above an hour and already you're wrecking the place! How on earth are we going to get you out of there? I dare say Pilcher and Odd-Job could break the door down, but that bolt's real strong and likely forcing it will wreck the door an' all.' Aunt Jane sighed gustily. 'And here's me hoppin' from one foot to the other . . . Look, I'll have to go and use the downstairs cloakroom, and I suppose I'll have to explain to the Venables and get help. Tell you what, see if you can wiggle the bolt out with your fingers. That'll keep you out of mischief while I'm gone, and just you stay right where you are and don't do anything else.'

'All right, Aunt,' Daisy said, repressing the desire to say she was unlikely to leave the bathroom since she was far too fat to squiggle under the door. She heard her aunt's footsteps receding down the stairs and glanced round the bathroom. The window was not wide and the glass was frosted, so she had no idea what it overlooked, but right now that seemed less important than clearing up the mess. She picked up her soaking towel, wrung it over the basin and trotted across to the linen cupboard. Folding it carefully, she pushed it right to the back and abstracted a clean one which she laid on the cork-topped stool. Then she rinsed the bar of soap, unwrapped her own cheap little tablet and wet it under the tap before wrapping it in her flannel. She had not had time to clean her teeth but ran the brush under the tap anyway, swilled the basin round carefully, then turned to examine her handiwork. So far as she could judge, the bathroom now looked perfectly respectable so she went back to the bolt and tried, unavailingly, to grip it between her water-softened fingers. Giving up on that, she went over to the window and pushed it wide. Immediately below was a paved courtyard. There was a drainpipe down which someone might have climbed, but even as she considered it she realised that escape by such a route would be pointless, since even supposing she got down safely someone would still have to break open the bathroom door.

Sighing, she closed the window and went and squatted on the bathroom stool, feeling both homesick and miserable. It was not her fault that the bolt had sheared; it must have been faulty, weakened by constant use, but she had an uncanny feeling that she would get the blame nevertheless. Aunt Jane would say she had rammed it home too hard, or tried to tug it back too impetuously. When the staff found themselves locked out, their friendliness would vanish and they would think her a real troublemaker. Daisy drew up her knees and linked her arms round them. She would *not* cry, she simply would *not*! Whatever anyone said, she was, in this instance at least, innocent of any wrongdoing. To be sure, she never should have paddled in the hand basin – she saw that it had come a little way away from the wall – nor should she have splashed water about with such abandon. And some people might say that swapping the dirty towel for a clean one had been somewhat deceitful. But I'm a long way from home, and I've never been in a bathroom before, Daisy excused herself dolefully. I'm only nine years old and I've never even seen a little bolt like the one on this door, though of course there were big bolts on the outside of the stables at Deinniacraig, as well as a couple, seldom used, on the back door. Oh, if only I were home with Mammy and Daddy, if only they hadn't sent me away!

Despite her resolve to be brave, Daisy felt the tears begin to gather behind her eyes and was just about to give way to a hearty bout when she heard footsteps ascending the stairs – several footsteps – and Aunt Jane's voice came to her ears. 'Daisy? Are you still there?'

Stupid woman, where else could I be, Daisy thought, and all fear of tears disappeared. She spoke humbly, however, not wanting to antagonise the only person she truly knew in the whole house. 'Yes,

I'm here, Aunt Jane,' she said, infusing a shake into her voice. 'I've tried and tried to pull the bolt back, but there's nothing left to grip. It's all smooth and shiny, so I've had no luck.'

Aunt Jane began to speak, but a man's voice cut across her. 'Hold on, missy. Your aunt says you passed the broken bit of the bolt under the door. If I push through a screwdriver, do you reckon you could unscrew the bracket? That's the bit of metal the bolt slides into. If you could unfasten that then the door would open immediately.'

'I'm sure I could,' Daisy said eagerly, and presently found herself picking up a small screwdriver as it was pushed beneath the door, and beginning the task. After five minutes, however, she was forced to admit that the screws were so old, and had been painted so many times, that she was having no luck at all.

The man on the other side of the door said a bad word beneath his breath; Daisy just hoped her aunt had not heard. 'Right,' he said at last, having clearly given the matter some thought. 'I've had another idea. Have you tried opening the window?'

'Yes, but it's a long way down and the drainpipe don't look too stout,' Daisy said, and was rewarded with a chuckle.

'Now what good would it do, queen, if you climbed out of the window, lerralone if you broke your neck – and the drainpipe – by crashin' on to the pavin' below? No, all I want you to do is to open the window wide and sit tight. It won't be long before we have you out of there.'

Daisy did as she was told, then sat on the window ledge, gazing out into the dusk, and presently she saw the chauffeur, his young son and the youth named Odd-job, below her, carrying between them a long ladder. They propped it up against the house wall – it reached the sill of the bathroom window easily – and the chauffeur began to climb, adjuring Odd-job to hold the ladder still, for Gawd's sake, since it were old as the hills and several of the rungs were rotten. He proved this last statement when he was, fortunately, no more than four or five feet up. One of the rungs broke in two as he put his weight on it, and he fell back into the yard, using words so strange and colourful that Daisy memorised them for future use.

Below her, the chauffeur scrambled to his feet, ordering Odd-job to ascend the ladder in his place. 'You're younger'n me and a good deal lighter,' he pointed out, but Odd-job shook his head.

'I ain't got no head for heights,' he said obstinately. 'And what's more, that bleedin' ladder's a perishin' death trap. You didn't oughta h'expect it o' me, Mr Elgin, sir.'

The chauffeur began to explain that Odd-job should test each rung before putting his full weight on it, and Odd-job was still insisting that it were not his place to go climbing rotten ladders, when the matter was settled for them. The boy Jake said impatiently: 'Oh my Gawd, wharra fuss about nothin'! Hold the ladder steady, Pa, an' I'll be up there and have the bleedin' door open before you can say Jack Robinson. I'm lighter'n anyone, apart from that stupid girl, an' I'm as likely to be able to undo the screws as ever Odd-job could. I've helped wi' all sorts of jobs on the car . . .'

He began to climb the ladder as he spoke and reached the window so swiftly and with so little fuss that Daisy had to jump off the windowsill in some disorder to get out of his way as he entered the room. He glanced around him as he did so and it occurred to Daisy that she was not the only one who had had no experience of such a room before, because his eyes widened and he spent quite ten seconds staring at the geyser before turning to Daisy and snapping his fingers impatiently. 'C'mon, girl, hand over that bleedin' screwdriver!' he said imperatively. 'Hmm, perhaps I'd ha' done better to bring a bigger one up from the garage, but I dare say this'll do.'

He approached the door and began hacking away at the paint-embedded screws, then gave a grunt of satisfaction and wedged the implement into a screw head. He twisted it sharply three or four times and there was a tinkle as the screw fell to the ground. Daisy pounced on it, but before she had given it more than the most cursory glance a second screw hit the linoleum and Jake, with a crow of triumph, snatched the bracket from the door frame and swung the door wide. 'There you are,' he said proudly, as Aunt Jane, the cook and one of the maids surged into the room. 'It weren't as easy as I thought it would be 'cos the screws was all covered in paint; that's why the kid couldn't get no purchase. But it's all right now, though someone will have to buy a new bolt . . .' He sniggered, shooting a sly look at Daisy. ''Cos you won't want to be caught on the lavvy with your knickers round your ankles,' he added rudely.

Daisy opened her mouth to tell him what she thought of him but her aunt was before her. 'You're a cheeky little varmint, Jacob Elgin,' she said angrily. 'I'd tell your pa and see he gave you a wallopin' only I reckon you've done me niece a good turn, comin' up that ladder and gettin' the door open without no mess or fuss. Now off wi' you 'cos it's high time we were all thinkin' of bed, and there's others what'll want to use the bathroom.' She grabbed at the boy's arm as he set off towards the window. 'No you don't, young man. You'll come down the stairs like a Christian, for I've no doubt your father and Odd-job have taken the ladder back to the stable block and your pa will be waiting for you in the kitchen.'

'Well, I don't mind usin' the stairs, seein' as how that perishin' ladder is half rotten,' Jake conceded, following them out of the room.

Mrs Bellamy, who had gone first, turned on the landing and addressed him. 'You ain't a bad boy, Jake, if only you'd learn to treat your elders wi' more respect. I've a fruitcake on the kitchen table and a fresh-brewed pot of tea, so I reckon as you're the hero of the hour you might enjoy a piece.'

Jake nodded eagerly. 'Aye, Mrs B, I wouldn't say no,' he said.

Daisy was about to agree with him, to say that she was starving, so she was, but her aunt fore-stalled her. 'I must say I wouldn't mind a cuppa meself,' she said. 'But me niece ain't used to late hours and she's a long day ahead of her tomorrow, so I think you'd best say goodnight, Daisy.' She turned a rather cool glance on her niece. 'I know it weren't your fault and perhaps you'll say it could have happened to anyone, but I don't see as you should be rewarded wi' cake for gettin' the whole house in an uproar.'

Ruth, the maid who had done the washing up, turned a pair of round, astonished eyes upon Aunt Jane and started to speak. But when Mrs Bellamy began to descend the flight the girl stopped short, and the little cavalcade disappeared into the corridor below. Aunt Jane ushered her niece into the bedroom they were to share, for this night at least, saying severely as she did so: 'Don't look at me as if I were a monster, Daisy Kildare, because rich food late in the evening is bad for children and anyway, you've been stuffin' yourself with pork pie and doughnuts and God knows what beside, so it won't harm you to go straight to bed now. Say your prayers before you get into bed . . . I'll wait while you do that . . . and then you aren't to get out again until morning, understand?'

'S'pose I want to pee?' Daisy said sulkily. 'You wouldn't like it if I peed the bed.'

She had said it to annoy, knowing her aunt would dislike the expression, and knew at once that she had succeeded, for her aunt's brows drew together and she heaved an impatient sigh. 'There's a chamber pot in the bedside cabinet; you may use that,' she said austerely. 'And don't you dare leave this room, or go anywhere near the bathroom, unless I'm with you. Now go on, say your prayers.'

Daisy gave her aunt a sullen glare before dropping to her knees and covering her face with both hands. She began to mutter very fast. 'God bless Mammy and Daddy, Amanda and Brendan, Annabel and me, Finn and Dermot. Oh, and Aunt Jane, I suppose. Give Daddy good catches in the *Mary Ellen* – oh, no, sorry God, I forgot the *Mary Ellen*'s laid up. Give Daddy good catches on the shore lines instead, and let there be lots of mussels, and let the potato crop be a good 'un and let there be a real bolt on the bathroom door, not one so weak that a poor little girl who ain't even ten yet finds it comes off in her hand. And please God, take away my anger 'cos I've had no cake, and make me a good little girl, amen.'

She scrambled to her feet on the last words and climbed into her little bed, keeping her back ostentatiously towards her aunt. Aunt Jane had turned away, but when she reached the door she looked back. 'I dare say God will manage to provide a new bolt for the bathroom door, but I think He'll have his work cut out to make you a good little girl,' she said. Daisy thought her voice trembled a little and was half sorry if she had upset the older woman, but she still resented the lack of cake. However, the bed was soft and warm and she might have fallen asleep, had not the saying of her prayers reminded her so strongly of Benmacraig that a wave of homesickness overcame her, and she buried her head in her pillow for a quiet little weep.

She was just wondering how Amanda felt and what her older sister was doing now when the bedroom door creaked open very, very softly and a voice whispered: 'Are you awake, chuck?' It was not Aunt Jane's voice. Daisy's eyes shot open and even in the half-light from the landing she recognised the little maid. 'I've brung you some cake, chuck,' Ruth whispered. 'I thought your aunt were awful mean to say you couldn't have none, even though it weren't your fault that the bolt sheared through.' She came over to the bed, delved in the pocket of her apron, and produced a large slice of fruitcake. 'It's a mite crumbly from bein' jammed into me pocket, so you'd best gobble it up right away. Your aunt won't be up for a while. There's a right party goin' on in the kitchen, only they sent me off 'cos I'm the youngest,' she ended.

'Thanks ever so much, Ruth,' Daisy said, taking the cake and beginning to eat. 'You're real kind, so you are. But I don't see why you were sent off just because you're the youngest. How old are you? What about that Jake? He's only a kid, but they were goin' to give him cake.'

Ruth sat down on the side of the bed. 'Oh, I had cake all right, but when I'd finished Mrs Bellamy told me to go to bed and Jake had already gone. His pa's awright, quite nice really, but I reckon the older ones wanted to talk wi'out no kids flappin' their ears.' She smiled at Daisy as the younger girl finished her piece of cake and dusted the crumbs off her hands on to the carpet. 'Jake's only ten – well, nearly eleven really – but I'm fourteen, a fair bit older'n you both.'

'That's true; I'm only nine,' Daisy admitted. 'Why do you live in, though, Ruth? Why don't you go home each evening to your mammy and daddy?'

'Because I don't have none. I'm an orphing,' Ruth explained. She pulled back the covers and tutted over the crumbs on the bottom sheet. 'Hop out for a second, chuck, and we'll brush them crumbs on to the floor so's I can pick 'em all up at once an' pop 'em into me apron pocket. Then I can put them on me windowsill.'

'On your *windowsill*?' Daisy said. 'What's the use of that? At Benmacraig we always shook the cloth into the yard so's the poultry could pick up the bits, but the hen ain't born what can flap up to a high window and I don't believe you keep hens here anyhow.'

Ruth had brushed the bed clean and was diligently collecting crumbs, but she gave a gurgle of

109

laughter at Daisy's words. 'Course we don't keep hens, norrin the city we don't. No, it's the pigeons, and maybe even a blackbird, what comes to my windowsill. They knows I feed 'em, see? I've always wanted a pet of me own but that weren't allowed at the orphanage so feedin' the birds is the next best thing.'

Daisy gazed curiously at the other girl. She was familiar with the word pets, but so far as her own life at Benmacraig was concerned it meant nothing, for all the animals, from Tina the donkey down to the tiniest day-old chick, had their own place in the life of the farm. Poultry laid eggs and when they could no longer do so were slaughtered for the table. Cows gave milk and bullocks were sold for meat. Tina carried heavy loads and pulled the donkey cart, as well as providing the yearly foal which was sold at the market. Sheep were kept for their wool and for the lambs, which again were sold at market, and Shep, Colm's crafty old sheepdog, rounded up the stock when ordered to do so, barked when strangers approached and generally made himself useful. Fortunately, however, Daisy's omnivorous reading had intro-duced her to the idea of pets – animals which were kept by rich folk, apparently for the enjoyment of seeing them about the place, but were of no prac-tical use.

She explained this to Ruth, who nodded wisely but proved how little she understood by saying: 'How you'll miss all them animals and birds and things! Course, I'd like a dog best of all 'cos a dog can be a real pal, but the Venables won't have nothin' like that in the place 'cos it's the doctor's surgery and such places have to be specially clean. Mrs Bellamy once telled me that before she come here her old mistress had two canaries in a cage in her front parlour, and she let Mrs Bellamy keep a budgie what lived in a cage in the scullery.'

'What happened to the budgie if she weren't allowed to bring it here?' Daisy asked curiously.

'Cat gorrit,' Ruth said briefly. 'Mrs B were cleanin' the cage and Joey – that were the budgie's name – nipped out and the old tabby cat had him before you could say knife.'

'Poor thing,' Daisy said absently. 'Mammy talked about getting a cat at one time when we were pestered wi' mice, but Daddy bought some traps and we got rid o' them that way.'

'Oh aye? Well, I'd better be gerrin' up them stairs to the attic or I'll have Mrs Bellamy fetchin' me a clout,' Ruth said, beginning to move towards the door. ''Spec I'll see you at breakfast, chuck.'

'Hey, wait a moment, Ruth, there's summat I want to ask you,' Daisy said urgently. 'What's this Cynthia like? Is she nice? D'you reckon she'll like me? Mrs Bellamy says the governess is a tartar but she didn't say nothin' about Cynthia.'

Ruth paused in the doorway. 'I dunno, 'cos I've not seen much of her. I spends most of me time acting as kitchen maid to Mrs Bellamy,' she said.

'But when I go up there with meals an' that, I've took a look at her, and tried a smile. She's pretty, wi' fair hair, but . . . oh, a bit sulky, like, I reckon, an' quick to find fault.'

She made to leave the room but Daisy jumped out of bed and ran across to the doorway to clutch her new friend's arm. 'Oh, but that were the governess, weren't it?' she said urgently. 'Cynthia's only nine, same as me. Kids like us don't find fault as a rule. Or do you reckon she just likes her own way?'

Ruth shrugged. 'I dunno, but you'll find out for yourself tomorrer, after breakfast,' she said cheerfully. 'Tell you what, when you get a chance, come down to the kitchen and we'll have a bit of a crack and you can tell *me* what you think of her. Now leggo me arm 'cos I've gorra go, else I'll be in big trouble.'

'Sorry, Ruth. See you tomorrow then,' Daisy said. She closed the bedroom door softly and climbed back into her small bed, pulling the blankets up round her ears and realising, as she did so, that she was very tired indeed, but she felt far happier than she had done when she had climbed into this same bed earlier. She was no longer completely alone, apart from her aunt, for she was very sure that Ruth would stand her friend. And even if Cynthia was a girl who liked things done right, that did not mean they would not get on. By the end of a week I reckon the two of us will have joined forces against that governess, Daisy told herself. No one likes being forced to do lessons so I reckon we'll plot how to give her the slip and have some fun.

She snuggled down, meaning to live again, in memory, the fullest and most exciting day she had ever spent, but sleep overcame her almost as soon as her head touched the pillow, and though she was aware of her aunt re-entering the room, she did not wake.

Jake had enjoyed both the cake and the party atmosphere which prevailed, but to his own surprise he found himself feeling sorry for Daisy. He had been impressed, upon entering through the bathroom window, to find her neither in tears nor in any great distress and thought, reluctantly, that she was not such a bad kid after all. Indeed, she was almost as good as a boy, for his father had told him about her examining the drainpipe and he guessed that, had it been possible, she would have clambered down the thing. Clearly, she had plenty of guts; it was simply her misfortune to have been born a girl. What was more, he thought Miss Dalton had been downright mean to send the kid off to bed, thus denying her both cake and party, and was glad when he saw Ruth secreting a slice of cake in her apron pocket before muttering that she'd best get off to bed or she'd never wake in the morning. He liked Ruth, who was only four years older than himself, and guessed that the cake was for Daisy. So she would not lose out on everything.

One thing puzzled him, though. There had been much discussion in the kitchen before Miss Dalton had left for Ireland as to whether she was doing the right thing in bringing her niece to be a companion for Miss Darlington-Crewe. He had listened with some interest and it occurred to him now that when Miss Dalton had talked about her niece then, she had never once called her Daisy. She had referred to her as Anna . . . Annie . . . well, at any rate, he was pretty sure the name had not been Daisy. Perhaps Daisy was a nickname. Telling himself that he would find out one day, Jake put the matter from his mind and, after receiving yet more congratulations, said his goodnights and made his way to bed.

Chapter Four

'Wake up, Daisy! I let you lie in because Madam agreed that you must be worn out, but it's nine o'clock and Cook can't keep your breakfast waiting for ever. Come along now, up with you!'

Daisy groaned and clutched the blankets, trying to curl yet lower in the bed, but her aunt, for it was she who had spoken, seized the covers and pulled them back. 'Up with you,' she said again, and now she sounded really cross. 'I had a long day yesterday, just like you, but as soon as the alarm went off I was out of bed and splashing cold water into my face, so if you don't get up at once, young woman, I'll pick you up and dunk your head in my washing water, an' I'll warrant you won't like that much.'

Hastily Daisy opened her eyes, then swung her legs out of bed and stood up. 'Sorry, Aunt Jane. I didn't know where I was for a minute,' she said. 'You should ha' woke me before.'

'Well, I'm waking you now,' Aunt Jane said. 'Have a quick wash, queen – there's clean water in the basin – then we'll make our way downstairs and you can have some porridge and a nice mug of milk, only you'll have to hurry because

Mrs Venables wants to see you as soon as possible.'

Wanting to make a good impression, Daisy positively flew. She raced down the stairs, ignoring her aunt's warning cries, and shot into the kitchen. Mrs Bellamy was chopping meat into small cubes on the long table under the window, but as soon as Daisy appeared Ruth hurried over to the Aga and carried a pan of porridge to the table, which was already set with a bowl, spoon and mug. She grinned conspiratorially at Daisy as she tipped porridge into the round blue dish, splashed milk into the mug, then took the pan over to the sink to soak. A few minutes later, Daisy scraped her spoon round the now empty dish, drained the milk and turned expectantly to her aunt. 'I've done,' she said breezily, though at home she would have asked for a piece of soda bread to fill up the chinks. 'Good thing me hair's short 'cos it only needs a dab with a brush and it's as tidy as it'll ever be. Am I all right to go and meet Cynthia now, Aunt Jane?'

Her aunt looked her over critically, then nodded. 'You'll do,' she said. 'It's a pity I've not had time to buy you some decent clothes – apart from the ones you travelled in – but we'll do that on my next day off. Follow me.'

Daisy trotted obediently up the basement stairs, through the green baize door and into the main hall. Aunt Jane ignored the doors which were part of the doctor's establishment, but opened one whose plate simply said *Private* and ushered her niece inside. Daisy glanced around her. It was a pretty room, yet it was also a business-like one, for though there were flowers and ornaments on the shelves, and a great many books, there was also a large desk, behind which sat a tall and stately lady. She had dark red hair, cut short in the modern style and greying at the temples, a thin hooked nose, which made Daisy think apprehensively of witches, and a pair of large, grey-green eyes which fixed themselves upon her small visitor. She stared for a moment, then smiled rather thinly. 'So this is your little niece, Miss Dalton,' she said in a cultured voice. 'How do you do, Daisy?'

'How do you do, Mrs Venables?' Daisy said when her aunt dug her in the back. 'It's glad I am to meet you, I'm sure. Me aunt's told us so much . . .'

Another dig in the back caused her to stop talking which was as well, since Mrs Venables had ignored her reply but was speaking to her once again. 'You are very late, but I'm sure that is because you had a long journey yesterday. However, it will not do for you to lie in bed every morning, so I must ask your good aunt here to purchase an alarm clock for your use. Miss Redditch – she is Cynthia's governess – wants the pair of you to keep school hours. She says that, because of her frequent bouts of ill-health, Cynthia's education is sadly lacking and she will need to work extremely hard to catch up with other

117

children of her age. Your aunt tells me that you, too, have missed a good deal of schooling, so you will both have to attend to your books.'

Once again Daisy opened her mouth to reply but was not given the opportunity. 'I'm sure Daisy will be grateful for any extra learning,' Aunt Jane said encouragingly, although secretly she was nothing of the sort. 'I'll go out this very morning and buy an alarm clock. And now do you wish me to accompany you to the school-room? I know you said you wanted to introduce the girls yourself.'

'No, I will take Daisy and you may go about your business,' Mrs Venables said, heading for the door. 'Come, Daisy.'

Daisy, following Mrs Venables up two very long flights of stairs, thought that it would be a good thing when she knew her way around this big old house. All I see is their back views and all I hear is *follow me, do this, do that,* she thought rebelliously. And now I'm going to meet the tartar, which won't be any fun at all, though I'm real anxious to meet Cynthia.

They reached the head of the second flight of stairs and Daisy found herself on a small square landing. There were two doors to her left and two doors to her right, but halfway across Mrs Venables stopped so abruptly that Daisy cannoned into her. She began to apologise but Mrs Venables flapped a hand. 'My fault,' she said. 'I was going to take you straight into the schoolroom to meet Cynthia but I've decided it would be best if I show you the other rooms first.'

She flung open a door on her right, revealing a pleasant bedroom with two small beds, two easy chairs and a washstand. Daisy was not surprised to see that the pink curtains at the window matched the silky pink counterpanes on the beds, for plainly this was commonplace in a rich man's house. She looked curiously at the tall cupboards to her left and at the enormous chest of drawers which stood beside the window, but before she could ask what they contained Mrs Venables had flung open the cupboard doors to reveal a long rail, completely filled with clothing. She looked slightly taken aback. 'Oh!' she said. 'I was about to tell you that you two girls must share this built-in wardrobe, but it's pretty full simply with Cynthia's garments. Never mind, you may have the two bottom drawers in the chest beside the window, and I dare say we can make room in the wardrobe by taking out Cynthia's winter clothing and storing it elsewhere.' She turned and indicated the two beds. 'I don't know which one Cynthia has chosen, for the maid has already done this room, but we'll ask her which is to be yours.'

The two left the room, Daisy closing the door carefully behind her. She expected Mrs Venables to open the next door but she did not do so, explaining that it led to the governess's bedroom. Instead, she indicated the door on the opposite side of the landing. 'That is a small parlour where you and Cynthia may go to amuse yourselves after lessons. I've managed to acquire a great many children's books from patients whose own families have outgrown them, as well as a quantity of jigsaw puzzles and board games. Do you play chess? There is a very fine chess set which you and Cynthia can use, as well as Ludo, Snakes and Ladders and Monopoly. Doubtless you will enjoy playing such games.'

She opened the door as she spoke, giving Daisy a glimpse of another pleasant room furnished with a sofa, two easy chairs, a low round table, and two glass-fronted cupboards, as well as a couple of bookcases stuffed with children's books. Daisy's heart gave a happy leap, for many of the titles were well known and loved and felt, to Daisy, like old friends, met by chance in an alien land. She started forward, saying as she did so: 'Oh, there's *Alice's Adventures in Wonderland* as well as *Anne of Green Gables* and *Simple Susan*! Can I . . .'

But Mrs Venables closed the door firmly, causing Daisy to wonder if the older woman were somewhat deaf, for she had twice appeared to ignore what Daisy said. Now she led the way to what Daisy realised must be the schoolroom and opened the door, ushering her charge inside. It was a large airy room, but Daisy had no eyes for anything except the woman seated behind the big desk which faced the door, and the girl standing beside her. Daisy did not know precisely what she had expected Cynthia to look like, but she had thought the other girl would be about her own size and shape. Instead, she was several inches taller than Daisy and a great deal thinner. She had a long plait of fair hair, skin as white as milk, and eyes of such a pale blue that they looked almost colourless. She had glanced up as the door opened and Daisy, anxious to make a good impression on the girl with whom she would be sharing so much, started forward, a big smile breaking out. 'Hello, Cynthia! Sure and haven't I been longin' to meet yourself? This is a grand room, so it is ... I'm Daisy Kildare, what's come to keep you company and share your lessons.' She turned towards the woman seated behind the desk. 'And you'll be Miss Redditch, what's going to teach us. Glad I am to meet you ...'

Her voice faded into silence. Daisy was a friendly and forthcoming child, and was wondering why Cynthia was staring at her so coldly when she suddenly remembered why the other girl had come to live in this house. Her hand flew to her mouth. 'Oh, Cynthia, me wretched tongue! I clean forgot that your mammy died only a few months ago. I'm so sorry ... no wonder you look so pale and sad.' She did not add, as she might well have done, that Cynthia was not exactly dressed in mourning, for she wore a grey pleated skirt and a frilly pink blouse, over which she had donned a deeper pink cardigan.

There was an uncomfortable silence and for an awful moment Daisy thought that Cynthia was so angry – or, indeed, so shocked – that she did not mean to reply. Behind her, she heard Mrs Venables draw in a breath, and saw the woman seated at the desk turn an admonitory glance on Cynthia. At last the other girl spoke. 'I was not well acquainted with my mama, if that's what you mean,' she said flatly. 'She was always ill for as long as I can remember, and, in any case, found my company tiring.' She shot another cold glance at Daisy. 'Not that it's any business of yours. And I can see you are wondering why I'm not wearing black. It's because I refuse to do so. It doesn't suit me and it made me miserable.'

'I see,' Daisy mumbled, feeling thoroughly uncomfortable. She looked hopefully towards the governess. Miss Redditch was a large, angular woman, probably in her forties, with dark hair strained so harshly back from her face that her eyes were tilted at the corners, giving her an oriental look. Daisy, still anxious to make a good impression, smiled at the older woman. 'How do you do, Miss Redditch?' she said formally. 'Me mammy tells me to do as you bid me and try to learn me lessons, so when I go home I'll mebbe get a better job than I would have before.'

The governess's thin, black brows rose. 'I beg your pardon?' she said. 'I'm afraid you will have to speak more clearly if you wish me to understand what you're saying. I made the acquaintance of your aunt last evening, and she informed me that your mother has tried to prevent you from speaking with a strong brogue, so I shall not hesitate to correct you when you slip into idle ways.'

Daisy could not imagine why a touch of brogue should apparently annoy the governess so much, but she did remember that Mammy had bidden her to watch her tongue, and this must have been what Aunt Jane had meant. More than ever, she felt herself to be a stranger in a strange land, and wished with all her heart that it had been Aunt Jane standing behind her instead of Mrs Venables. So she smiled at the governess again and spoke with great care. 'I'm sorry, Miss Redditch; I'll do me best to speak proper, but it will be strange to me at first. In fact, everything here is strange . . .'

Her voice broke on the words, for suddenly a picture of the kitchen at home had come into her mind, with her own dear mammy making soda bread, Daddy gutting fish at the sink, and the little ones playing on the hearth. Daisy tried to push the picture from her mind and fought for self-control. She would not cry under Cynthia's chilly but curious gaze, nor with the governess's accusing eyes upon her; she would *not*. She half turned away, longing to rush from the room, but Mrs Venables's hand closed on her shoulder, giving her an admonitory little shake. 'It's all right, Daisy. Your aunt told us that in times of stress your brogue might thicken, and this must be a difficult moment for you.' She had lowered her voice, but raised it again to address her niece. 'Cynthia, that was no way to speak to a child you have met for the first time today and one, furthermore, who has never done you any harm and is a guest in my house. Remember, Daisy is a long way from home and has never received a formal education such as you have enjoyed. She has been brought here to share your lessons, games and pastimes, so it behoves you to be friends. And now I think Miss Redditch and myself have things to discuss, so you two children may go along to your parlour. As I told Daisy, there's plenty to amuse you in there.' She gave Daisy a little push towards the door, still open behind her. 'Off with you; I declare today a holiday from lessons.'

Daisy however, lingered, looking up at Mrs Venables and seeing that despite the severity of her expression she had, as her aunt had said, a kind heart. 'Please, Mrs Venables, I promised my mammy and daddy that I'd write them a letter as soon as I arrived, to let them know I was safely here. I don't have no pencil or paper . . . is there a scrap and an envelope I could have?'

Mrs Venables was beginning to reply when the governess stood up, fumbled in the desk for a moment, and then crossed the room towards them, holding out a postcard, already stamped, and a pencil. 'I told your aunt I would see to it that this was written and despatched,' she said. Her voice was calm but her eyes would not meet Daisy's. 'In the afternoons, when the weather is clement, I mean to take you to walk in the park, so today, when you have had your luncheon, the three of us will go at least as far as the postbox and see your card on the first stage of its journey.' She turned and beckoned to Cynthia, who was still standing by the desk, an expression of obstinacy on her small white face. 'Come, Cynthia, do as your aunt bids you.'

Cynthia crossed the room as slowly as she dared, Daisy thought, trailed into the parlour in Daisy's wake, then slammed the door and walked over to the window, staring out at the sunshine. 'I shall *not* go for a walk; I'm not strong enough,' she said, without turning her head. 'People of a consumptive habit should never be expected to take walks. Indeed, fresh air is poison to me. I hate it.'

Daisy crossed the room and stood beside the other girl. For a moment she was silent, pondering what she should say, for it was pretty plain that Cynthia did not mean to like her. Or perhaps this was just how sickly persons behaved? But Daisy felt she could not let the silence lengthen any further without being as rude as she felt Cynthia had been, so she cleared her throat and spoke. 'I've not heard of a consumptive habit,' she said, enunciating every word with great care. 'Is it a bad habit, like biting your fingernails, or picking your nose?'

She had thought the remark an innocent one, but realised her mistake when Cynthia spun round, her eyes hot with fury. 'How *dare* you?' Cynthia hissed. 'Everyone knows what a consumptive habit means, even a nasty little guttersnipe like you! My

125

poor mama died of consumption, and I shall, too, if I'm forced to go out into the fresh air . . . and to share my life with a common brat who can't even speak English properly.'

Count to ten, Daisy Kildare, Daisy told herself fiercely. Remember all the things your mammy and daddy taught you. Sticks and stones may break your bones, but names will never hurt you. A soft answer turneth away wrath. She's only a kid herself, after all . . . and she's lost her mammy, even though she pretends not to care. She folded her lips tightly on the words which were longing to burst forth and let the silence between them lengthen whilst she searched for the right thing to say. Finally, it came. 'I'm sorry if I misunderstood you, but, you know, illness is something I don't know much about, so you must forgive me ignorance. It's an odd thing, though – me and all me fambly spend more time in the open air than ever we do within doors, and we're all fit as fleas. So maybe it ain't – I mean, it's not – fresh air what gives you bad habits, but bein' too much alone and shut up in the schoolroom, studyin' your books.'

She half expected Cynthia to say something cutting, but the other girl merely turned and gave her a contemptuous glance, then stalked over to the nearest bookcase, pulled out a volume, and began leafing through the pages. After a moment's hesitation, Daisy went and stood beside her again, peering at the book. It was the most marvellous thing she had ever seen, for it was illustrated, every other page being a beautiful picture, in full and glorious colour. It was a copy of *The Water Babies* by Charles Kingsley and Daisy, who had read the book and loved it despite the many long and difficult words it contained, yearned to touch the beautiful pictures and turn the pages for herself, for Cynthia had opened the book quite near the beginning, when Tom was still a chimney sweep, and had not yet become transformed into a water baby. However, Cynthia saw her looking and closed the book. 'Am I to do nothing without you following me around like a wretched shadow?' she enquired. 'Aunt Venables told you this room was full of games and books and such. Find your own amusements, can't you?'

Her voice was so full of malice that Daisy's good resolutions wavered for a moment, especially when Cynthia slung the book down so hard on a nearby table that it slid right across the surface and landed with a thump on the floor. Daisy might not have been a regular attender at the village school, but she had been taught to respect and value books, both by her parents and by her teachers, and would never have dreamed of mistreating a common primer, let alone a beautiful and expensive volume like this one. She glanced reproachfully at Cynthia, then went and picked up the book. It had landed open, and she smoothed the crumpled pages and closed it carefully before replacing it on the table and glancing doubtfully at her companion. She realised that the situation in which she found herself was completely outside her experience. There had been bullies at school, but one steered clear of them, and she did not think that Cynthia was a bully precisely. It seemed to her that the other girl must be most dreadfully spoiled and used to having her own way in everything, and she supposed, rather dubiously, that Cynthia had not wished for a companion, but would be far happier with Miss Redditch's whole attention focused upon herself. As for hating fresh air, Daisy was sure that it would do the other girl a great deal of good to spend more time out of doors. Indeed, Miss Redditch had made it plain that she intended to divide their time between morning lessons in the schoolroom and afternoons spent in the fresh air. She still felt sorry for Cynthia who had no mammy or daddy, but realised that if her own life in this house was to be tolerable the two of them would simply have to come to an understanding. Resolutely, she approached the couch where Cynthia was now sitting, idly turning the pages of another beautiful book, and sat down beside her, though she was careful to leave a good six inches of cushion between them. 'I've said I'm sorry once, Cynthia, and I don't mind saying it again, if it'll make you happier,' she said. 'But you're going to have to put up with me, you know, so I think we'd best start with some explaining. What did you mean when you said you had a consumptive habit?'

Silence. Cynthia raised her eyes to heaven and rolled them expressively, but said nothing. Daisy waited for a moment, wondering what the devil to do, then decided that perhaps shock tactics might work where meekness had failed.

'Hasn't nobody ever telled you it's bloody rude not to answer when someone asks you a question?' she said, letting her anger show. 'You think I'm common and – and a gutter thing, but it's you who ought to know better, 'cos you've had education, and all I've had is a bit of schooling when I couldn't get out of it. So are you going to tell me what you mean by a consumptive habit, or am I going to give you a clack round the ear that will make your head sing?'

Cynthia's mouth dropped open and her eyes rounded with astonishment, and Daisy realised with satisfaction that the other girl had expected Daisy to accept her spiteful remarks without so much as a word. It was equally clear that no one had ever threatened to clack her ear, or, indeed, to cross her will in any way. When she saw Cynthia's eyes begin to brim with tears, she was tempted to retract, to give the other girl a hug and say she had never hit anyone yet and did not mean to start now, but some instinct told her that this would be a fatal mistake. Instead, she said brusquely: 'Well? Are you going to tell me, or . . . ?'

Cynthia fished around in the sleeve of her pink cardigan, and produced a dainty lace handkerchief. She dabbed at her eyes, then blew her nose.

Then she heaved a deep sigh, and spoke. 'I think it means your lungs aren't very good, because my mama said it hurt her to cough, and sometimes, if I get upset, I can hear a little wheeze, deep down in my chest,' she said. 'Once, when the doctor had been to see Mama, he came to see me, because I'd had a really bad cold, even worse than usual. He said something about a consumptive habit then, so I knew I'd got whatever my mama had. I expect I'll die of it when I'm her age.'

Daisy thought she sounded rather smug, and this effectively stopped her from sympathising, though she would have liked to do so. Instead, she said bracingly: 'That's rubbish, so it is. If you ask me, you're talking yourself into this consumptive thing because you're bored and alone too much. Why, me daddy told me Aunt Jane said that most of what ails you was being by yourself. She said, once you were better, you could go to a proper school, and then you'd be quite well and wouldn't need Miss Redditch, or anyone else for that matter.'

'But I'm ill, you can *see* I'm ill,' Cynthia wailed. 'Look how thin I am, and so pale! Why, I'm only a few months older than you, but I couldn't clack your ear, because you'd give me one good shove and I'd be flat on the floor.'

'I don't know about that; you're a good bit taller than me, but at any rate you'd best not try – clackin' me, I mean – because I dare say you've never fought anyone in your life, an' I've got brothers,' Daisy said. 'Come to think of it, if you'd had a brother or two, or even a sister, you'd not be so pale 'n' skinny. They'd drag you off to play hurley wit' a bundle of rags as a ball, or they'd take you fishin' for tiddlers wit' a flour bag on a split cane, or they'd lift you up on the donkey to play circuses, when your mammy wasn't usin' it to sell fish of course. I never thought of it before, but things like that mean you've got to be tough, whether you're a girl or a boy. I'm tellin' you, Cynthia, if you'd had brothers, it 'ud be you threatenin' me with a clack on the ear.'

Cynthia looked wistful, but said slowly: 'I don't know. As for going to school, that's the last thing I'd want. When Aunt Venables told me you were coming to keep me company, I cried for a whole night and a whole day. And when she told me my old nurse was going to retire, and not look after me any more, I cried for two whole nights and days. Miss Redditch is just a teaching person, though the maid they've given us – she's called Ruth – is always willing to fetch and carry for me and to do as I tell her. But Goody – she was my nurse – was just like my mama would have been, if she'd not been so ill. Goody often said so. She called me her little lamb, and her bestest girl, and gave me cuddles, and nice things to eat when I felt poorly, and – and – let me win when we played I Spy and Snakes and Ladders.'

Daisy thought that Goody was probably responsible for most of Cynthia's bad manners and the belief that she was sickly, but fortunately did not say so. Instead, she picked up *The Water Babies* and asked Cynthia whether she had enjoyed the book.

She thought this was an innocent enough remark, but it had a strange effect upon Cynthia, who blushed to the roots of her hair and then looked slyly at Daisy through her lashes. 'I don't like reading, so I don't do it much,' she said. 'I like the pictures, though.' She closed the book she was holding. 'But I don't know why we're talking about books when you are supposed to be writing to your mammy and daddy.' She sniffed, and again the glance she shot at her companion seemed to hold a meaning which Daisy could not interpret. 'Go on, write your postcard; that's what you want to do, isn't it?'

'Yes, I'll do that,' Daisy said with alacrity. She had been clutching the postcard and the pencil, and now she laid it on her knee and began to write.

Dear all,
  I am safe in Liverpool. I liked the ferry, but Aunt Jane felt sick. This is a very big house. Me and Cynthia has a grand playroom and there are heaps of books. I miss you all and send you love and kisses,
    Daisy.

She read it through; then, seeing Cynthia's eyes upon it, pushed it towards the other girl. There was nothing private about a postcard, she reasoned. 'Is that how you spell your name?' she asked, though she was pretty sure she had got it right. Cynthia made no attempt to take the card, so Daisy pushed it into the other girl's hand, saying impatiently: 'Oh, Janey Mack, there's nothin' private writ here, so you might as well read it and have done. *Is* that how you spell your name?'

'Mumble, mumble, mumble; your writing's so bad ... anyway, it's rude to read other people's letters,' Cynthia muttered. 'And I'm sure you're so clever that you never make a spelling mistake.'

Daisy stared at her, round-eyed. 'I'm not clever, but me writin' isn't that bad,' she said, rather reproachfully. 'For goodness' sake, read the perishin' thing so's you can see I've not telled me parents anything you wouldn't like. Then I'll address it and mebbe we can play one of the games in the cupboards until Miss Redditch finishes talkin' to Mrs Venables.'

Cynthia bent her head over the card, then suddenly jumped up and threw the card on to Daisy's lap. 'I – I can't read, you stupid girl! Miss Redditch only came a few days ago, and though Goody did her best to teach me, she – she was awfully old, and when I got tired and cried, and said reading was too hard, she'd cuddle me up in the big armchair by the nursery fire, and tell me stories about when my mama was a little girl. Or she'd read to me; stories out of *Peg's Paper* or the *Red Letter*.'

'Holy Mother of God!' Daisy said reverently.

'And you goin' on for ten years old! Does Miss Redditch know you can't read?'

Cynthia shrugged. 'I don't think so. She said we should not start lessons until you arrived. Several times she's given me books and told me to read them, but she's never asked me to do so aloud. Oh, I know she's going to find out, but I don't care about that. It's her job to teach me, so she'll just have to get on with it.'

'Does Mrs Venables know? I shouldn't have thought it was the sort of thing you could hide from an aunt . . .' Daisy was beginning, but Cynthia turned on her, two bright spots of colour appearing on her pale cheeks.

'I don't know and I don't care! You sound as if not being able to read was my fault, as though I'd done it on purpose. I've been too ill to learn and – and Goody said it would come to me one day, so I never really bothered. And I think you're horrible, Daisy Kildare, to mock me for something I can't help.'

'I am not mocking you . . .' Daisy was beginning when she found herself grabbed by the shoulders and shaken.

'Yes you are! You hate me and I hate you, and I won't, I won't have you sharing my lessons! I'll tell Aunt Venables to send you away, back to your horrible mammy and daddy, and then Miss Redditch won't have to bother with you, and will teach me to read and write in no time at all.'

But Daisy had had enough. She got to her feet

and slapped Cynthia resoundingly and in seconds the two girls were fighting like wildcats, rolling around on the parlour carpet, completely oblivious of everything but the hatred which was smouldering between them.

In the schoolroom, Miss Redditch and Mrs Venables stood, one on either side of the desk, whilst the governess told her employer that teaching the two girls together was not going to be the simple matter she had at first supposed. Mrs Venables eyed the governess with some exasperation. She had worked extremely hard to get this floor of the big old house fitted out suitably for the governess and her pupils. She had bought a teaching desk for Miss Redditch herself, and two smaller ones for Cynthia and Daisy. At Miss Redditch's instigation, she had purchased quantities of educational material, exercise books, sketch pads and watercolours. She had bought an instrument described as a cottage piano in case either girl should prove musical, and had planned menus which Cook thought suitable for nine-year-old girls. And now Miss Redditch seemed about to tell her that the preparations she had made were not going to work. Mrs Venables sighed. 'I'm sorry, Miss Redditch, I'm afraid you will have to be a little more explicit,' she said. 'Why should you not be able to teach the two girls together?'

'I think I had better be blunt with you, Mrs Venables,' the governess said. 'Your niece can neither read nor write, despite the fact that she's almost ten years old. You warned me that her education had been neglected, but not that it was non-existent. She has tried to hide her ignorance from me, which is very understandable, and at first I thought I must be mistaken, but this morning my suspicions proved correct.'

Mrs Venables stared; she had known that Cynthia had never attended school, but when she had questioned her sister on the subject, she had been assured that Nurse Goody was teaching the child the basics. It had never occurred to her for one moment that Goody had failed so lamentably to instil any knowledge at all into her charge's head. But surely Miss Redditch must be wrong! Cynthia might be a poor reader but she could not be completely illiterate. Could she?

She said as much, but Miss Redditch shook her head. 'This morning I laid three simple reading books out on my desk, and asked her to bring me one of them. I asked for it by title, and after a moment she asked if I meant the red book or the blue one. I pretended not to understand and repeated that it was *Fairy Tales for Little Ones*.' Miss Redditch smiled thinly. 'One thing I must say for her, Cynthia is not unintelligent. She counted the words, hesitated, I think, over whether fairy tales was one word or two, and picked up *Fairy Stories for the Children*. She hesitated for a moment and then put it neatly on the corner of my desk. I said nothing, of course, and no doubt she assumed that her guess had been right, but it confirmed my worst fears. Cynthia most definitely cannot read, which means of course that she cannot write either.'

Mrs Venables sighed again. 'You've shocked me, Miss Redditch, and I don't mind admitting it. What the doctor will say when I tell him I hate to think, for he will blame my poor sister for her neglect. However, I don't understand why Cynthia's woeful ignorance should make it difficult for you to teach her. Surely it is simply a case of . . .'

Her voice faded away as Miss Redditch shook her head firmly. 'Mrs Venables, it will not be easy for me to teach Cynthia such basic skills without Daisy Kildare realising what is happening, and your niece will not wish the younger child to know how woefully behind she has fallen.'

Mrs Venables gazed at her thoughtfully. 'But I understand from her aunt that Daisy has also missed a great deal of schooling. Is it not possible that Daisy, too, is still struggling with the basic skills?'

Once more Miss Redditch shook her head. 'No indeed. If you remember, Daisy said she meant to write a letter to her parents, telling of her safe arrival. She did not ask for aid, but simply for materials with which to write such a letter – or postcard rather, since that seemed simpler. But I talked to Miss Dalton last evening and she told me the child was an avid reader, devouring books, magazines or newspapers. So you see, she may look down on your niece, not understanding why

137

a child from a well-to-do family should be so ignorant. And if she shows contempt, then I fear their relationship is doomed and teaching them together will be impossible.'

'Then what do you suggest?' Mrs Venables asked rather hopelessly. 'It never occurred to me that the girls might not be evenly matched. That is, of course, it did occur to me but I thought Daisy would be a long way behind Cynthia, and not the other way about.'

'Yes; if that had been the case, it would have been far simpler. Indeed, it might have helped their relationship if Cynthia had been able to assist Daisy with her lessons, instead of vice versa.' She smiled encouragingly at her employer. 'But I do have a solution of sorts. I suggest that you send Daisy to a local school, possibly just for one term, whilst I undertake to concentrate on bringing Cynthia's reading and writing up to standard.'

Mrs Venables let out her breath in a long sigh of relief. So there was a solution, and one which did not involve having to send poor little Daisy back to Ireland which, for one moment, she had feared Miss Redditch was about to suggest. It was a shame, of course, because she knew her husband was of the opinion that her niece was living an unnatural life, cut off from the companionship which he believed every child needed. But facts had to be faced. There was a school probably no more than ten or fifteen minutes' walk away, which Daisy could attend. Mrs Venables had often seen the children coming out of the playground in the afternoon, so the girls could be together when lessons were over. And if this meant that Daisy need not learn her companion's shameful secret, then it was definitely worthwhile. But Miss Redditch was still waiting for her employer to agree or disagree with the scheme, so Mrs Venables nodded and inclined her head. 'I think you have the answer, Miss Redditch. But what shall we tell Daisy? She knew she was to learn with Cynthia and may feel she is being punished for some sin unknowingly committed.'

'I'll think of a convincing reason. Possibly I might explain that Cynthia's health means she will have to take her lessons very slowly, until she is stronger. Then Daisy will accept that it would be best for them to work separately for a few weeks,' Miss Redditch said. She headed for the door, holding it open for her employer. 'And now I'll go and see whether Daisy has written her postcard. If she has done so, we might as well walk down to the box on the corner and post it before luncheon, since it is such a lovely day.'

As she finished speaking, she opened the door into the parlour and for a moment both adults were frozen to the spot. Before them, rolling about on the floor, the two small girls fought in silence, save for the odd squeak when hair was pulled, or a sharp elbow landed in someone's ribs. Mrs Venables was horrified and astounded. She and her sister had never fallen out, would not have dreamed of exchanging blows, yet here was her pampered and protected niece fighting like an alley cat with the tough little Irish girl from across the water.

She opened her mouth to reprimand, but Miss Redditch was before her. The governess strode across the room, bent down and seized dark curls in her left hand and a flaxen plait in her right, and her voice, cold and harsh, broke the stunned silence even as she jerked the combatants apart and dragged them to their feet by their hair. 'How dare you behave like street urchins! You are young ladies, or have you forgotten? Now sit down, the pair of you, and calm yourselves. Then I must have an explanation of this disgraceful behaviour. Cynthia?'

Cynthia stared sullenly at the governess, then glanced at Daisy. Mrs Venables saw how her thin chest was heaving, but had sufficient sense to realise that Cynthia was clearly a good deal stronger than she appeared, for Daisy's chest was heaving as well. When Cynthia said nothing, the governess compressed her lips and turned to the other girl. 'Daisy?'

'We – we disagreed,' Daisy muttered. 'We – we wasn't really fighting, was we, Cynthia? It were – it were a game what got a bit hectic like. Ain't that so, Cynthia?'

Cynthia nodded and then, to her aunt's astonishment, began to giggle. She nudged Daisy, who looked at her, gasped, and then began to giggle as well. In less time than it takes to tell, both children were laughing so hard that their mirth infected their elders, who began to smile and then to laugh in sympathy. 'Well, if it was a game, it was an extremely rough one,' Mrs Venables said at last. How odd children were; she thought she would never understand them. 'But if you've quite recovered, you'd best put on your coats so that you can accompany Miss Redditch to the letter box to post Daisy's card. I take it you wrote it before you began your – er – game?'

Daisy nodded and picked up the card. 'I finished it and done the address 'n' all,' she said, handing the card to Mrs Venables.

The older woman glanced at the card, which was neatly written, then turned it over to examine the address. She was beginning to hand it back to the child when she realised something. 'Yes, this is fine, but don't forget – your parents will soon be moving away from Benmacraig. I have another address to which you may send your next letter . . . let me see, it is care of Connor, The Quay, Roundstone Harbour.'

Daisy took the card without a word but, to Mrs Venables's horror, the smile was wiped off her face, tears forming in her eyes and beginning to run down her cheeks. 'I'd forgotten,' she muttered, 'but I'll remember next time.'

Mrs Venables thought sadly that the child was not only a long way from home but had clearly just realised she no longer had a home, not in

Ireland at any rate. She had been told all about the Kildares' situation and had been happy to be able to offer some help, but the sight of Daisy's tears had brought home to her how truly unhappy the child must be. She had hidden it well, had put on a cheery face, but underneath it she must have felt not only lost and bewildered but most terribly alone. And now, Mrs Venables thought remorsefully, we are going to make it even worse because we have to tell her that she will be going to school, whilst Cynthia will be educated at home. Oh dear, I feel I'm reneging on a promise, but I'll make it up to her and after a term or two she will be able to join Cynthia and Miss Redditch as I had planned.

The girls donned their coats and hats and made for the outside world, though Cynthia pulled a sour face and said she would much prefer to remain in their little parlour. Miss Redditch, however, was firm. 'We are all going to post Daisy's card,' she said. 'When we return, Mrs Venables wants to talk to Daisy and I must have a word with you, Cynthia. After that, we will discuss how we should occupy ourselves until teatime.'

Daisy had managed to control the miserable rush of homesickness which had overcome her when she had thought of Benmacraig in the hands of horrible Paddy Kildare, and as they stepped out into Rodney Street she took a deep breath of the fresh air and turned to smile encouragingly at

Cynthia. 'Isn't it grand now to feel the breeze in your face?' she said. 'Oh, I know you think it's bad for you, but you'll soon learn different.'

'I shall not,' Cynthia said obstinately, turning to glare at her companion. 'Why, when Goody took me shopping we always took a taxi cab and made the driver stop right outside the department store so we could hurry in and not catch cold from the fresh air which you think is so wonderful.'

'But you did catch cold; you caught colds all the time, you said so,' Daisy pointed out. 'You used to spend all your time indoors and you were always ill, so now I truly think you ought to give fresh air a chance.'

The two girls were walking along the pavement beside Miss Redditch and Daisy, glancing up at the governess, saw her nod approvingly. 'Daisy is right, Cynthia. You really must get over your absurd conviction that fresh air is injurious to your health,' she said. 'Your Uncle Venables is a highly esteemed doctor of medicine and he has told me that you should do your lessons in the mornings and spend at least an hour outside in the afternoons, and I mean to obey him, naturally, for one cannot ignore a doctor's advice.'

Cynthia's scowl deepened and her mouth tightened, but she said nothing until they had posted the card and were on their way back, with Miss Redditch now walking ahead of them. Only then did she turn to Daisy. 'This is all your fault, you hateful little prig,' she hissed. 'Just because you lived in a tiny, stuffy hovel, with no room to swing a cat so your parents had to chuck you out of doors whatever the weather, you think everyone else has to do the same. But you're wrong, so you can just stop smarming round Miss Redditch and taking her side against me because it won't work. I shall be ill – I can feel my chest tightening already – and I'll make sure you get the blame.'

Daisy turned to her, eyes blazing with indignation. 'You're a horrible girl, so you are!' she said passionately. 'Our home was beautiful and Mammy and Daddy never had to throw us out because unless it was raining cats and dogs there was always lots to do outside. Our home was by the sea; we played on the beach and the cliffs, or up on the moor. And we never ailed, none of us.' She glanced consideringly at the governess's figure, striding ahead, then lowered her voice once more. 'So don't you dare say one word against my family or Benmacraig, because who the devil do you think you are to be hateful about us? Why, you can't even read!' She saw Cynthia's hand curl into a claw and dodged, but the other girl's nails caught her across the cheek. She grabbed Cynthia's hand, feeling blood begin to seep from a long scratch, and, forgetting discretion, slapped wildly at the furious face so near her own, shouting as she did so: 'All right, so you hate me, but nowhere near as much as I hate you!'

It was at this point that Miss Redditch turned and grabbed a shoulder of each, giving them a good shake. 'Whatever is it *now*?' the governess demanded acidly. 'Daisy Kildare, I'd not have taken you for a troublemaker, but –' She stopped short, clearly seeing for the first time the long scratch on Daisy's face, yet it was Cynthia who was now in tears and pointing a trembling finger at the younger girl.

'She started it, Miss Redditch,' Cynthia whined. 'She called me names and said I was a fool and couldn't even read. She – she slapped my face. It really hurt, and she should be punished.'

Miss Redditch ignored the remark, merely giving Cynthia a speaking glance. They had left the house by the front door, but Miss Redditch now turned down Mount Street, saying grimly that she had no intention of using the Rodney Street entrance since that would mean ringing the bell and bringing the doctor's receptionist to the door. 'And I don't intend to let anyone see one of my charges with finger marks on her cheek and the other with a scratch from the corner of her eye to her mouth, so we will go in the back way,' she said. 'And you, Cynthia, must stay on my right hand side whilst Daisy must stay on my left. That way, you can only glare and mutter at one another, if argue you must.'

'I don't want to argue,' Cynthia said primly. 'I'm not used to arguing. Well, I've never had anyone to argue with. I shall tell Aunt Venables that Daisy slapped my face and I expect she'll send her back to Ireland, where she belongs.'

'I wish she would,' Daisy said rather wistfully. 'Me brothers and sisters may have a bit of a barney from time to time – well, they do – but we ain't into scratchin' faces, nor we don't tell lies.' She peered round Miss Redditch's angular figure. 'And *you* tell lies, Cynthia Crewe . . .'

'My name is Darlington-Crewe,' Cynthia said coldly. 'If you must address me, at least use my proper name.'

Daisy began to say that she would as lief not speak to Cynthia at all, but Miss Redditch interrupted. 'Be quiet, Daisy. I don't want to hear another word from either of you until we are back in the schoolroom and then I expect a proper apology, first to each other and then to myself, for your disgraceful behaviour. I was not aware when I agreed to work for Mrs Venables that she expected me to teach two wild, ill-mannered little savages, but now I feel I may have to reconsider my position.'

By now they had reached the back garden gate. Miss Redditch pushed the two children in ahead of her, choosing to ignore Cynthia's muttered remark that she must have expected to educate one little savage since she had known from the start that Daisy Kildare came from Ireland. Daisy would have liked to refute this spiteful remark but one glance at Miss Redditch's face convinced her that this would be a mistake, so she compressed her lips, stuck her nose in the air and followed the governess and Cynthia through the side door, along the corridor and up the two steep flights of stairs to the schoolroom.

Once inside, they removed their outer clothing in complete silence. Daisy hung her coat on one of the hooks, took a deep breath, and turned to Cynthia. 'I'm sorry I slapped you, Cynthia,' she said stiffly. 'But we both know why I did it, doesn't we?'

There was a long pause before Cynthia spoke. 'I'm sorry if my nail caught your face,' she said grudgingly.

Miss Redditch turned away for a moment and Daisy wondered if it was to hide a smile. She did not think Cynthia's reply had been amusing and thought her companion foolish to try to wriggle out of a simple thing like a straightforward apology. But then Miss Redditch turned to face them again and she looked perfectly serious. 'That was not very generous, Cynthia,' she said quietly. 'However, if it's the best you can do . . . Daisy?'

For a moment, Daisy could not think what she meant, then she remembered. 'I'm sorry I behaved so badly, Miss Redditch,' she said humbly. 'It were very bad; me mammy and daddy would be ashamed of me, so they would.'

This was perhaps unfortunate since it gave Cynthia the opportunity to look wistful for she had neither father nor mother to approve or dis-approve her actions. She glanced up at Miss Redditch, putting on what Daisy now thought of as her 'orphan face', before saying meekly: 'I'm sorry, Miss Redditch. I won't do anything like that again, not even if I'm provoked.'

Miss Redditch nodded curtly and was opening her mouth to speak when a knock sounded on the schoolroom door, which was pushed open to reveal Ruth. She looked up at Miss Redditch, twisting her hands together. 'Oh, please, miss, I know it were agreed that you and the young ladies was to have your dinners an' that in your parlour, but when I 'splained to Cook about how hard it was carryin' all that heavy stuff up three flights of stairs even when it were only for two, she said as how now Miss Daisy's arrived you could have your meals – all of 'em – in the small breakfast parlour. I've laid up the table and put out the food, so if you'd all like to come downstairs wi' me . . .'

She turned on the words and began to clatter down the stairs, opening a door when they reached the ground floor to reveal a small sunny room furnished with a table, a number of upright chairs and a long sideboard. The table was laid for three and Miss Redditch took her place at the head of it, gesturing for Daisy to sit on her right and Cynthia on her left. Ruth seized a covered dish from the sideboard and served cold meat on to each plate, then pointed to the tureen in the middle of the table. 'Them's mashed taters,' she said. 'I loves mashed taters, I does. We're havin' 'em an' all today.' She swung round and picked up an enormous bowl containing a salad of lettuce, tomatoes and cucumber, eyeing Miss Redditch anxiously as

148

she did so. 'Do you want me to serve you, miss, or would you rather help yourselves? And there's some salad dressing in that funny-shaped jug . . . Cook makes lovely salad dressing wi' all sorts . . . egg yolks, cream, oil, vinegar . . . ooh, it's prime is Cook's dressing.'

Miss Redditch blinked. 'Thank you, er . . . you may put the salad dressing on the table and we'll help ourselves,' she said, rather repressively. 'I'll ring for you when it's time to clear and bring up the pudding.'

'It's semolina with raspberry jam, and me name's Ruth,' the maid said, beaming at the three of them. 'Cook makes lovely –'

'That will do, Ruth,' Miss Redditch interrupted, and Daisy felt sorry for the little maid, who clearly enjoyed a bit of a chat.

But Ruth did not appear to feel that she had been snubbed, for she said cheerfully: 'Right you are, miss, an' just you give that old bell a good bang if I don't come quick enough.'

She left the room, slamming the door behind her, and Miss Redditch stood up and began to serve mashed potato and salad on to each plate. Cynthia said rather pettishly that she did not like salad and would not eat it, but the governess ignored her. When they had all been served, Miss Redditch closed her eyes, bowed her head, and said a short grace. 'For what we are about to receive, may the Lord make us truly thankful, amen.' Raising her head, Daisy looked towards

Miss Redditch, for she had been taught never to begin to eat until her father and mother picked up their knives and forks, and assumed that Miss Redditch would give the signal when they might start. Cynthia, however, had no such inhibitions. She picked up her cutlery straight away and began to push her salad around the plate. As soon as Miss Redditch began to eat, Daisy followed suit. She was hungry and the creamy mashed potatoes, crisp salad and delicious slices of thick pink ham were irresistible. She was rather pleased to notice that by the time she had almost finished, Cynthia too was making inroads into the food on her plate. Daisy wondered if this was an especially grand meal because it was their first under the Venables' roof, then decided this could not be so since Miss Redditch and Cynthia had arrived at Rodney Street a week earlier. It looked as though the food would always be delicious.

When the meal was over, Daisy began to gather plates and dishes together and asked the governess if she should go down to the kitchen to help with the washing-up. Cynthia snorted rudely and said something which Daisy did not catch, though she did see the governess give the other girl a quelling look. However, Miss Redditch explained that the Venables had servants whose job it was to carry out such tasks, and swept her charges up the two flights of stairs and back into the parlour. Then she put a hand to her mouth. 'Gracious, I quite forgot. Daisy, you are to go down to Mrs Venables's study.

She would like a word with you whilst I talk to Cynthia. I'll ring for Ruth, and she can show you where to go. When you come back, we will brave the elements' – she glanced towards the sunny window with a wry smile – 'and take a walk down to the Pier Head where you may see the shipping coming and going.'

By bedtime, Daisy and Cynthia both knew what was in store for them, and knew also that they must keep a tight rein on the antipathy which had flared up between them. Daisy had been told that she was to go to school until Cynthia was more accustomed to regular lessons, and she had been delighted. It would mean mixing with other children, getting to know people, and spending at least some time away from 39 Rodney Street, and from Cynthia. The governess had insisted, too, that they should talk openly over what had caused so much unpleasantness that morning, and now each knew what subject would inflame the other and had promised – grudgingly on Cynthia's part – not to mention Daisy's family or Cynthia's inability to read and write.

Because Miss Redditch now realised that Cynthia's illiteracy was no secret, she had suggested to her employer, and to the two girls, that they might put aside the school plan for the moment and have lessons together, but both girls had shrunk from the idea and even Mrs Venables thought it best that they should be separated for at least some of the day.

151

So on the following morning Miss Redditch took Daisy to the Queen Mary School for Girls on Rathbone Street where she was accepted as a pupil by the headmistress, a middle-aged woman who wore tiny gold-rimmed pince-nez. Daisy sat a short examination and was placed in the juniors, in Standard IV, though Miss Beaver said that if she found the work too difficult – or for that matter too easy – she could remain in Standard IV for two years, or could skip to Standard VI after twelve months.

A young teacher with frizzy brown hair and a droopy dress then accompanied Daisy on a tour of the school, explaining breathlessly that though Queen Mary's had no playing fields adjacent to it, the pupils would be taken at least once a week out to the recreation grounds at Sefton Park, for games such as hockey and lacrosse in winter, and cricket and rounders in summer. Daisy, who had never played in an organised game in her life, nodded wisely and said she was sure she would like to have a game, so she would, and thought of the cramped little playground at the school she had scarcely ever attended back in Ireland and wondered what the devil a 'recreation ground' was when it was at home. She liked the look of the school, though, with its big airy classrooms, gymnasium, large assembly hall and cloakrooms, where the pegs for the little ones started at no more than three feet from the ground, going up to full adult height for senior girls.

152

When they had left the school behind and were crossing Upper Duke Street, Miss Redditch asked Daisy what she had thought of her new school, and showed her pleasure when Daisy said it was grand, so it was. 'Even Cynthia would like it, I'm sure,' she said, but was not surprised when the governess merely smiled and began to walk towards Rodney Street without further comment.

They were almost back at the house when there was the sound of running footsteps behind them and someone snatched at Daisy's elbow. 'Hey, is you too bleedin' 'portant to reckernise your pals?' a voice said breathlessly in her ear. 'Where's you been? And where's that other girl? The one wot's like two yards of tap water?'

Daisy turned and recognised the boy Jake, who had rescued her from the bathroom. Miss Redditch gave him a chilly glance and said severely: 'Young ladies do not speak to strange boys in the street, Daisy, particularly rude ones. Come along now.'

Daisy sighed. She had been taught that if anyone asked you a question you should answer it, but here was Miss Redditch, a very superior lady, telling her otherwise. It seemed that there was nothing simple in this new life, but she had sufficient common sense to know that silence would merely antagonise Jake, meaning there was another person who disliked her. So looking up at Miss Redditch she said firmly: 'Jake isn't a strange boy. He's Mr Elgin's son, and Mr Elgin is the doctor's chauffeur.' She wondered why Miss Redditch did not know this, and then remembered that the governess spent most of her time on the school-room floor and apart from Ruth had little to do with other members of the household.

'Oh, I see,' Miss Redditch said, and Daisy thought she spoke reluctantly. 'Very well, you may tell Jacob where you've been.'

'I've been to me school, me new school,' Daisy informed her companion. 'They gave me some papers with questions on, so's they'd know what class I were to go in to, and I'm startin' there next Monday. As for Cynthia, she don't want to go to school, and she wouldn't have been able to answer the questions 'cos she can't re—' She broke off, horrified by what she had so nearly said, and adroitly changed it. '. . . she can't really go to school until she's fit and well, which she ain't at present,' she ended in a rush.

Jake sniffed. 'I seen that other girl when she arrived, but I ain't seen her since,' he said. 'I wanted to go wi' me dad to fetch her in the car, but old Ma Venables – sorry, sorry, I mean Mrs Venables – wouldn't let me, and when I seen that girl – wozzername – I were glad.' He snorted and wiped his nose on the sleeve of his jersey, which Daisy thought unfortunate since he was quite neatly dressed, having obviously just come from his own school, wherever that might be. 'I never seen no one look so glum.'

'Ye-es, but remember, she ain't well,' Daisy said

154

excusingly. 'And her name is Cynthia Darlington-Crewe.'

'Wharra mouthful!' Jake scoffed. 'D'you like her?'

Daisy hesitated. It would be politic to tell an untruth, particularly with Miss Redditch listening, yet on the other hand if she did so Miss Redditch would know she was fibbing and might write Daisy down as a liar, so she said cautiously: 'We don't know each other very well yet. And now tell me about you. Me aunt says you've got the coachman's flat over the stable. Is it just you and your dad and mum?'

Jake heaved an exaggerated sigh and rolled his eyes heavenwards. 'You don't know nothin', do you?' he said rudely. 'Me mam died eight years back, an' I live with me dad and nobody else.'

'What about Roddy?' Daisy said. 'I thought he were your brother. You know the fellow I mean, the one with big ears what grow straight out, like.'

Jake snorted. 'I wouldn't want him for a brother, even if he didn't have big ears and sticky-out teeth,' he said dismissively. 'He's daft as a brush is Roddy – can't add two and two without makin' five. He's Pilcher's son, you eejit; Pilcher the gardener.'

Daisy sighed. It had taken her some time to sort out the maids, though of course she knew Ruth quite well by now, but it would not do to let Jake think she had not recognised his father's superior

155

position to that of a mere gardener. 'Sorry, but it's all a bit confusing. Back home in Ireland, there's just me family; even neighbours are folk I've known all me life. This here is strange to me.'

Jake nodded. 'I reckon it is a bit confusing,' he admitted. 'Is you goin' to go to the gals' school on Rathbone Street? If so, I don't mind walking you there tomorrer, 'cos it's on me way to Gilbert Street.'

'What's Gilbert Street got to do with it?' Daisy asked.

Jake rolled his eyes heavenward once more. 'It's where me own school is,' he said patiently. He began to walk faster, then turned to give her a cheeky grin. 'Ever heard that song? It reminds me of you.' He began to sing in a husky, not untuneful voice. '*Oh dear, what can the matter be, Two old ladies locked in the lavatory, They'll be there from Monday to Saturday, Nobody knew they were there.*'

Daisy started forward, intending to give him a good clout, but Miss Redditch grabbed her arm. By this time they had turned down Mount Street and were heading for Pilgrim Street, which ran along the back of all the Rodney Street houses. 'Just ignore him,' the governess said grimly. 'You must learn, Daisy, to ignore ignorant remarks made by ignorant little boys.'

'He's not a little boy, he's nearly eleven; Ruth told me so,' Daisy objected. 'And – and I didn't mean to hit him, I just wanted to . . . to . . .' Her voice died away since of course had she caught Jake up she would undoubtedly have tried to thump him. '. . . but I know you're right really. He was only teasing, after all.'

Miss Redditch nodded approvingly. 'That's right. You must learn to take teasing without resorting to violence,' she said. 'Ah, this is our back gate.'

They reached the gate and Miss Redditch took hold of the latch, but Jake did not wait for her to open up. He scaled the wall as though it were a stairway, straddled the top of it, made an extremely rude sign to Daisy, uttered a hoarse laugh and plunged out of sight. Faintly, Daisy heard his voice. 'Bleedin' girls! Can't even gerrover a little old wall.'

Daisy grinned to herself, feeling that she already knew a good deal more about Jake than he had realised. Boys always wanted the last word – usually a rude one – and clearly Jake was no exception. She was glad she had not revealed Cynthia's secret and was quite prepared when Miss Redditch began to say that Jacob, despite his parentage, was a rough sort of boy, best avoided. 'And his language!' she said. 'I do trust, Daisy my dear, that you will not try to emulate him.'

Daisy, who had no idea what emulate meant but imagined it was another way of saying 'become friendly with', crossed her fingers behind her back and said she was sure that the last thing Jake wanted was to have anything to do with a girl. 'I don't suppose you know, Miss Redditch, but most boys think girls is sissies and no good for games and such,' she said, as they walked up the garden and entered the house by the side door. 'And he ain't bad, as boys go. I mean, he did run to catch us up.'

'Well, I hope he will not bother to do so again,' Miss Redditch said tartly. 'Obviously, you're going to have to walk to and from school by yourself, but I dare say you won't mind that. If, however, Jacob becomes a nuisance, you must tell me and I shall speak to his father. I've no doubt he's a sensible man and will deal with his son if it becomes necessary.'

Daisy murmured that she was sure a complaint would not be necessary and Miss Redditch said, with the first sign of real approval she had so far shown, that Daisy herself had behaved just as she ought. 'It would have been very unfortunate had you revealed the fact that Cynthia cannot read to that boy,' she said. 'As for his offer to walk you to school tomorrow, perhaps it was kindly meant and will save me a task which would have been awkward, because Cynthia is going to need me to help her to arrange her lessons early in the morning. But once you've familiarised yourself with the route, I'm sure you won't need anyone to accompany you. It would be better in fact if you walked to school with some other girl and avoided doing so in Jake's company.'

At this point they entered the schoolroom and Daisy was able to murmur agreement, though as she began to shed her outdoor things she realised that she had no intention of avoiding Jake. She would enjoy walking to school with him, and despite the bad language and the strange, rather uncouth expressions he had used she liked him a good deal more than she liked Cynthia. Him and me's both common, ordinary folk, she told herself as the three of them went through to the parlour where they would read, do jigsaw puzzles or play games until Ruth came panting up the stairs to tell them their high tea was laid out in the breakfast parlour. There ain't no airs and graces about me and Jake.

Miss Redditch ushered Daisy into the small parlour where Cynthia was already ensconced, announced that she was going back to the school-room to prepare the next day's lessons for Cynthia, and disappeared, closing the door gently behind her. Cynthia immediately went over to the window seat and sat down, then took a small leather case from her pocket. She began to rub her nails with a soft leathery implement, and then she produced a mirror and began a minute examination of her own face.

She's weird, Daisy thought. Here we are, surrounded by beautiful books, games, puzzles . . . all sorts . . . and all she wants to do is look at her face and shine her fingernails. Oh well, we're all different, as Daddy used to say. The memory of his words brought her daddy's face before her inner eye and Daisy felt a lump rise in her throat and knew that for two pins tears would start.

Oh, how she missed Benmacraig and all the family! But thinking about them did no good, so she crossed to the bookcase, pulled out a volume at random, settled herself comfortably in one of the fireside chairs, and began to read.

Chapter Five

July 1933

Daisy woke betimes because the curtains had not been pulled properly the night before, and a ray of sunshine fell across her face. She sighed and turned over, glancing at the little alarm clock standing on the cabinet which separated her bed from Cynthia's. It was very early; she could go back to sleep secure in the knowledge that the alarm would go off and wake her again in good time for school. She closed her eyes but sleep would not come and she realised that this was thanks, partly at least, to excitement, for she and Aunt Jane meant to go over to Ireland to spend a week near her family as soon as the school holidays started.

They had been once before, in August 1931, which had been unfortunate to say the least. It had been the wettest, windiest August on record, with gales and thunderstorms almost every day, meaning that outdoor activities had been impossible and everyone had grown fractious, even Daisy, who had longed for this reunion for more than two years. Naturally, this had affected the entire week, for the Kildares were still living in one room of Mícheál Connor's cottage and though Aunt Jane and Daisy had taken a room in a boarding house nearby, the

161

addition of two extra people, no matter how welcome, in the fisherman's tiny cottage had put a tremendous strain on them all.

'But it will be different this time,' Aunt Jane had assured her niece only the previous day. 'We've had a lovely summer so far, so if we go as soon as your school breaks up we're bound to have better weather, which will mean we'll all be able to spend time out of doors. Besides, ever since you won the scholarship to Queen Mary's, Maggie and Colm have benefited, since Mrs Venables insisted on sending the fees she would have paid straight to your parents.'

The scholarship had come as a complete surprise to Daisy when her English teacher had told her about it and suggested she might try for it, explaining that it would mean her education would be free for the next few years.

Now Daisy smiled at Aunt Jane, who was repeating her remark. 'I know,' Daisy said. 'But I think the extra money goes into the Benmacraig fund.'

'That's true, but just think, queen. If the weather's nice and sunny, we'll all be able to get away from the Connor place and have picnics on the beach and walks on the moors. Why, we can even take a crafty look around Benmacraig, which wasn't possible last time with the rain lashing down and the wind blowing a gale, to say nothing of that thunderstorm. I tell you, I thought me last hour had come.'

Daisy, remembering, gave an involuntary giggle. Their stay in Ireland had been so restricted and uncomfortable, though the lodging house had been a pleasant enough place, that they had been downright glad to board the ferry bound for Liverpool. But when the thunderstorm had broken halfway across the Irish Sea, poor Aunt Jane, green-faced and trembling, had been so sick that Daisy had honestly wondered how she would get her back to Rodney Street when they reached the Pier Head. However, solid ground beneath her aunt's feet had acted like magic and she had completed the journey almost jauntily.

The following year they had not attempted another such trip, but apparently Aunt Jane's courage had returned since she had suggested another visit this year and had immediately written to her sister, asking Maggie to book the lodging house for the third week in July. Daisy had been glad, of course she had, though the memory of her parents' strained faces and of Annabel, Finn and Dermot dressed in ragged clothing, and desperate at mealtimes to devour the food which Aunt Jane had provided, was something she would never forget. Daddy and Brendan went fishing whenever the weather allowed and Maggie sold their catch from the donkey cart whilst Annabel looked after her little brothers, but the Kildares were not the only family suffering. Unemployment was high, wages were low and getting lower, so naturally the price of fish had slumped. Amanda had taken a cut in wages and Maggie, cleaning at the big houses in Clifden, had had to do the same. Daisy knew that times were hard in Liverpool as well as in Ireland, for she had become very friendly with Ruth and had several times visited Ruth's aunt's house, which was in a court off Scotland Road. Ruth had seven cousins and she gave her aunt most of her wages to support the family, so she and Daisy were in a similar position for Daisy, too, handed over every penny of her allowance that she could spare.

Despite everything, Daisy was looking forward eagerly to the third week in July. She just knew things must be better; she had read in the papers that unemployment had fallen for the first time for ages, and in her last letter her mother had written that Colm and Brendan were supplying a big hotel with crabs and lobsters and were doing quite well out of it.

Daisy was just telling herself that this visit would be much nicer than the previous one when the sunlight fell across Cynthia's eyes, causing her to give a long moan and sit up on one elbow. 'Why are you shining that light in my eyes?' she asked in an aggrieved tone. 'Is it time to get up? Oh, I hope not, because it's double maths this morning . . . or is it Thursday? If it's Thursday, it's French, and I quite like that.'

Daisy chuckled. When she and Aunt Jane had returned from their first trip to Ireland, they had entered the Rodney Street house to be given stunning news. Miss Redditch had given in her notice because she and a gentleman friend meant to get married and move to London, where Mr Claude Spencer had been appointed chief clerk to a firm of solicitors. The girls had been incredulous, for they thought Miss Redditch old and plain, and could not imagine any man wanting to marry her, but Mrs Venables had assured them that it was so. At the time, Cynthia had simply stated that her aunt would have to employ another governess, but to the great surprise of both girls Dr Venables had put his foot down, interfering for the first time with his wife's upbringing of her niece. He had come up to the schoolroom, a thing he seldom did, and told Cynthia bluntly that it was time she mixed with girls of her own age and stopped hiding away from the outside world. Cynthia had protested that she would be ill, that fresh air was poison to her, and that she had no desire to mix with girls of her own age, but the doctor had been firm, simply stating that attending school and playing games such as hockey and netball would do her a great deal of good. Then he had patted her head and left, so had not had to see Cynthia's tantrums, or hear the names she called him once he was safely out of earshot.

Daisy had been not at all pleased at the prospect of having Cynthia at Queen Mary's, since she and Jake always walked to and from school together. They had become good friends, though Jake continued to tease and torment Daisy whenever the fancy took him. Daisy, remembering how

Brendan used to treat her, rather liked Jake's teasing, though she would never have admitted it to him. But it had soon appeared that Cynthia did not intend to become a pupil at Queen Mary's, if she could possibly avoid it. Daisy might not have known this had not she and Jake spent a good deal of their spare time in one another's company and had recently been caught red-handed purloining pears, ripe and juicy, from a neighbour's garden. As a punishment, the gardener had told them to weed the herbaceous borders, one of which was directly under the doctor's study window. The window was open and the two wrong-doers had been able to hear every word of the conversation between Dr and Mrs Venables which was taking place within.

'As I've already told you, I forbid you to bring another governess into this house to spoil that young madam even more than old Goody did,' Dr Venables had said. 'My dear, you are doing her no favours by allowing her to remain solitary. Oh, I know she has Daisy's companionship when lessons are over and during school holidays, but that is not the same as mixing with a group of children her own age. I have explained to her and she seemed to accept what I said.'

'But Albert, what am I to do?' Mrs Venables had wailed. 'If I tell her that I agree with you she will work herself into a state, particularly since Daisy will be at least a year ahead of her; so humiliating for the poor child since she is the elder. Why, even the mention of joining Daisy at Queen Mary's upsets her so much that she makes herself ill.'

'Rubbish,' the doctor had said firmly. 'If she doesn't want to go to Queen Mary's then choose some other school. Heaven knows there are enough such establishments in the neighbourhood . . . indeed, since her school fees are paid from the fund her mother left for that purpose, she could go to the most exclusive and expensive boarding school in England if she wished.'

Mrs Venables had immediately vetoed the idea, but at this point the doctor's voice had seemed to be approaching the window, so Daisy and Jake had scuttled on all fours round the corner, and heard no more. But it had been enough. Daisy had not been surprised when Cynthia had announced that she had been enrolled as a day pupil at the Calderstones School for Young Ladies in Allerton, a very superior academy which was extremely expensive and offered no scholarships or bursaries, so the pupils were all fee-paying. Since it was a considerable distance from Rodney Street, Mr Elgin drove her to school each day and picked her up each afternoon – for Cynthia had refused even to consider going by bus or tram – which left Daisy free to continue to walk to and from school with Jake.

'Well? Is it Wednesday or Thursday? And have I missed the alarm? Or was it just the sunshine that woke me?'

Cynthia's rather peevish voice brought Daisy back to the present with a jerk. She blinked across at the girl in the other bed. They had not become close friends despite living cheek by jowl for the past four years, but at least they were on reasonably good terms now. Daisy considered the questions, then answered them, ticking them off on her fingers as she did so. 'One, it's Wednesday and two, it was the sunshine that woke you. But I wouldn't go back to sleep again, Cyn, because the alarm will go off in ten minutes.'

'Don't call me that,' Cynthia said automatically; she hated the abbreviation and Daisy knew it, but sometimes Cynthia seemed such a mouthful. People at school often shortened Daisy to Day, but of course that had a much pleasanter meaning than sin. 'Right, I'll get up now then.' She swung her legs out of bed, then smiled across at her companion. 'Only a few more days and the holidays will be upon us. You'll be off to Connywhatsit and I'll be heading for a glorious two weeks in Southport with my mama's oldest friend. We'll do the lovely shops, have lunch at all the smart places, and go for drives in her Rolls-Royce. I can't wait!'

'Nor me,' Daisy said joyfully. It was true that she was longing to return to Ireland and to see her beloved family, though she couldn't help hoping desperately that Aunt Jane was right and she would find them happier and better off than they had been on her previous visit.

As soon as she and Cynthia were washed and

168

dressed they went to the schoolroom and picked up their coats, hats and satchels, then thundered down the stairs and were making for the break-fast parlour when Aunt Jane appeared from the direction of the basement kitchen. 'There's a letter for you, queen,' she said breathlessly, holding out a familiar blue envelope towards her niece. 'It's from your mammy, of course. I expect it's to confirm that she's managed to book lodgings for us. Mebbe this time Amanda will be able to get a day or two off so we can all meet up; wouldn't that be just grand?'

'It would, it really would,' Daisy said, taking the envelope. For her mother's last birthday she had sent her paper, envelopes and an inexpensive fountain pen, knowing that writing materials were a luxury which her parents could ill afford. She hadn't had to break into her allowance either since Jake, who was always short of money, had begged orange boxes from the greengrocer who occasion-ally employed him to deliver goods. She and Jake had then sneaked into the garden shed when Mr Pilcher was not around and borrowed a small axe with which they had chopped the orange boxes into kindling. Daisy had then 'borrowed' a ball of string from the schoolroom to tie the kindling into ha'penny bunches which they had sold around the neighbourhood.

Had the Venables known, Daisy was sure there would have been a row, but Mr Elgin, when he found his son and Daisy traipsing from door to door, had merely grinned and reminisced about his own youth. 'Me and me pals were always short of cash and always thinkin' of ways to earn the odd penny, which were often a real help when me dad was out of work,' he had told them. 'This 'ere Depression means we're all glad of any cash we can bring in, so if you can make a bob or two, why not?'

Jake had been generous too, Daisy considered, for his father was seldom able to hand out pocket money. Yet Jake had insisted that since she had done her fair share of the work, she should also have a fair share of the money, and it was with this that Daisy had bought her mother's gift.

Now, Aunt Jane gave Daisy's shoulder a little pat. 'If there's nowt private in the letter, mebbe you could come and read it to me after school,' she suggested. 'If Maggie has booked us into the same lodging house, I'd like to know. I dare say the price may have risen a bit but Mrs Flanagan was so good to us last time that I'd like to take her a little present. Nothing much, but mebbe a box of really good chocolates or some of them crystallised fruit. She's got a sweet tooth has Mrs Flanagan.'

'That would be nice. If we are staying with her again I'll buy her a little gift, too,' Daisy said. 'And I'll come down to the kitchen when I've finished school so you can read my letter. Oh, I do hope you're right and we can see Amanda as well this time.'

Aunt Jane smiled and turned back towards the kitchen, and Daisy followed Cynthia into the breakfast parlour. There was always porridge in a big silver dish on the sideboard, and such things as sausages, bacon or eggs in a covered chafing dish. Both girls helped themselves to porridge and sat down to eat. Daisy was scraping her bowl clean as Cynthia got up and lifted the lid off the chafing dish. 'It's lovely crispy bacon and scrambled egg,' she announced. 'Shall I help you to some of each while you read your letter?'

'Yes please,' Daisy said, slitting open the envelope and pulling out the sheets which it contained. 'My goodness, it's a lovely long letter. I wonder . . .' Her voice trailed away as she began to read.

My own dear Daisy,

I'm afraid this letter is going to be a shock to you because things here have changed completely. When I received Aunt Jane's letter asking me to book you into Mrs Flanagan's lodging house, I was delighted and meant to go round to her place the very next day. But, as I have said, everything here has changed. But I see I had better begin at the beginning so that you understand why your visit is no longer possible.

Daisy's heart descended into her boots. Whatever could have happened? She was sure it could be nothing good but braced herself and read on.

Let me assure you, dear Daisy, that shocked as you must be by our news, you could not be more shocked than we were ourselves. As I believe I've already told you in previous letters, Paddy Kildare has been doing up the cottage and changing it from what it was. Everyone said he was going to sell it, but we could not think who would want it since the land has been totally neglected for four years now. It appears, however, that we had not reckoned with Paddy's connections, for he is selling it to an Irishman who went to America years ago and made a pile of money. Now he wants to retire to the old country as he calls it, and means to buy our place, intending to modernise it even further. Mr Prescott, who has been a good friend to us, is doing his best to prevent the sale, saying that there was still some doubt as to the legality of Paddy Kildare's claim, but it seems to be going ahead.

We discovered the asking price and realised we could not afford a tenth of such a sum, yet your father and myself – and, I believe, Mr Prescott – are still convinced that somehow Daddy has been cheated out of his birthright. Truth will always out in the end, your daddy says, but it's been four years and still we've no absolute proof that Paddy had no right to claim our home as his own.

However, we took the train to Dublin a week ago and had a long talk with Mr Prescott. He reminded us that the document proving Paddy's ownership was a copy of the original though it had all sorts of stamps and seals to prove it was legal. Mr Prescott says that he does not think it would be possible to fake these things, yet he is convinced that, somehow, Paddy has cheated us. He says that since the property is being offered for sale things have reached a desperate pass and therefore call for desperate measures. He wants us to go to America and find the lawyer there who holds the original document and see whether there is some proof that Paddy Kildare does not own, and has never owned, the Benmacraig cottage. The really big snag is the sale of the property because the man who is buying it believes every word Paddy Kildare has said, and so is acting in good faith, which means that if the sale goes through it will be harder to get it back. Your daddy wishes Mr Prescott had suggested a visit to America earlier, if that would settle the matter, but if the truth be known we would not have been able to afford such an expedition even twelve months ago. We shall go at the cheapest possible rate, taking only Annabel, Finn and Dermot with us, for you older ones, my darling, are well able to fend for yourselves until we return.

Daddy has had to sell Tina, the donkey cart and even the Mary Ellen to help finance our voyage. Brendan would really like to accompany us but has agreed that he cannot possibly do such a thing, for he is to work for the man who bought Daddy's boat and cannot let him down.

My dearest, I know what a shock this must be,

but it seems to us that we will never get our home back by any other means and, of course, if Paddy's claim is proved to be false he will have to compensate us for the past four years. Mr Prescott is sure we will at least be able to buy the **Mary Ellen** *back and it was this which decided your daddy to make a push.*

I will of course continue to write to you weekly, and I know Amanda drops you a line whenever she has time. Even Brendan, who hates letter writing, will keep in touch. I am writing to Aunt Jane, and as soon as we are settled we shall send you an address so that you may write. I wish Mr Prescott could come as well for we shall be lost, at first, in such a big country, but of course that is impossible. However, he has recommended a firm of lawyers in New York to whom we may turn if we find ourselves unable to manage alone. But that will cost money. Daddy means to get work almost as soon as we land and I shall try to do the same, for Annabel is a sensible child and Finn and Dermot obey her as they obey Daddy and myself.

When your aunt's letter arrived we regretted bitterly that we could not remain for a few more weeks so that we could have talked the matter over face to face, but our passage is booked; we leave in ten days.

Take care of yourself, dear little Daisy, and you know you are always in our hearts,

    From your ever loving mother.

Daisy sat very still, staring down at the letter in her hand whilst the words before her blurred with the tears which formed in her eyes and trickled down her cheeks. It was bad enough to be separated from her parents by the Irish Sea, but the thought of them on the further side of the great Atlantic Ocean was almost unbearable. Hundreds, maybe thousands, of Irish people crossed that sea but very few of them ever came back. If only she could go with them – but even a moment's thought was enough to assure her that to make such a suggestion would only add to their troubles. A thirteen-year-old girl, no matter how eager to help, would be an added expense and responsibility. Worse, if she were not in Liverpool, there could be no reason for Mrs Venables to send her school fees on to her parents, nor to pay her an allowance, so in fact if she did try to join them the Kildares would be very much worse off.

'Daisy, whatever is the matter? Is someone ill?'

Daisy pulled herself together. 'No, not ill,' she said stiffly. 'The fact is, my parents have decided to take ship for America. Our – our home is being sold and Mr Prescott – he's a lawyer – thinks Mammy and Daddy should go to America in the hope of discovering that Paddy Kildare lied about my great-great-grandfather's will. So – so Aunt Jane and me won't be going to Connemara after all.'

She half expected Cynthia to make some slighting remark, or at best to suggest that Daisy should accompany her parents, but Cynthia did no such thing. She got up from her place and came round the table to give Daisy's shoulders a comforting squeeze. 'Oh, I'm *so* sorry, Daisy. What a dreadful thing to happen,' she said. 'I know how much you were looking forward to seeing them again, and I know how important it must be for your family to get their home back. When you told me about Mr Paddy Kildare and how he had behaved I thought he sounded like a cheat and a liar, but now I'm sure of it. I expect you wish you could go with them, but if they're leaving so soon that won't be possible, and . . .'

'And a passage to America must cost a lot of money,' Daisy finished for her when Cynthia hesitated. 'Amanda and Brenda aren't going either so I'm not the only Kildare left behind. But oh, how I wish they didn't have to go!'

'I dare say they won't be gone for long though,' Cynthia said hopefully. 'Before you know it you'll have another letter saying they've returned and telling you to come over to Ireland to help them settle back into your old home.'

Daisy scrubbed the tears from her cheeks and stood up, giving Cynthia her most resolute smile. 'You're absolutely right. Do you remember how Miss Redditch always used to tell us to look on the bright side? Well, that's just what I'm going to do. And in a way, it's worse for Aunt Jane, because she was so looking forward to her little holiday and there would be no point in going all the way to Connemara just to see Brendan, nice though he is . . .'

'Yes, and I remember you saying several months back that Amanda and her young man are saving up to get married, so there wouldn't be much point in you travelling to Galway to see her, because she'll want to spend her time off with him,' Cynthia said. 'I say, do eat your brekker. Nice food always makes me feel more cheerful and I expect you are the same.'

'I don't really feel hungry . . .' Daisy was beginning when she thought of Aunt Jane and what she would say if her niece's plate returned to the kitchen still laden with the delicious eggs and bacon. She gave the scrambled egg a desultory poke with her fork and then realised that in fact she was hungry. After all, in her heart she was sure that her parents were doing the right thing, and why should she assume that they might not return just as soon as they possibly could? She knew, of course, that the Depression was as bad in America as it was in England, but her father and mother were hard-working, resourceful people. She was sure they would soon get jobs and begin to amass money, and if they were unsuccessful in their claim then such money would be saved up to pay for the passage home. Yes, she must look on the bright side. Naturally, she would miss Mammy and Daddy, Annabel, Finn and Dermot like anything, but she had been away from them now for four and a half years, had only seen them once in all that time, and she had survived. Indeed, in one sense, she would be no more separated from them now than she had been before.

She said as much to Cynthia whilst hastily eating her breakfast, adding, however, that she was dreading having to break the news to Aunt Jane. 'There's no need for you to say a word; just rush down to the kitchen, hand over the letter and say you'll see her when school's over,' Cynthia advised.

Daisy finished the food on her plate and stood up. 'Thank you for being so nice, Cynthia,' she said humbly. 'And I'll do as you say and give Aunt Jane the letter to read for herself. And now you'd better leave or Mr Elgin will hoot his horn and you know he hates doing that.'

'Right,' Cynthia said, struggling into her blazer and cramming her panama down over her long fair hair. She snatched her satchel, which was a good deal lighter than Daisy's, and hurried out of the breakfast room, heading for the front door and calling over her shoulder, 'See you at teatime!' as she went.

Daisy struggled into her own blazer and hat and heaved her satchel on to her shoulder, then set off for the kitchen. There was nothing unusual in this since Jake always ate his meals in the kitchen with the other members of staff, so Daisy joined him there and they left by the back door. She must have been a little earlier than usual, however, for her friend was only just finishing his porridge, his spiky black head bent over the bowl. He looked up as she came in, his sharp narrow face breaking into a grin which changed into a questioning look as he saw her face. 'What's up?' he asked curiously. 'Lost sixpence and found a farthing? Don't say you're upset 'cos of what happened to the old Philharmonic last night?'

'I dunno what you mean,' Daisy said, avoiding his eye. Trust Jake to spot that all was not well with her – and trust him to bring it to everyone's attention, too. Her aunt, polishing the best silver cutlery, glanced inquisitively across at her, but Daisy cut in quickly before the older woman could speak. 'What's happened to the Phil, anyroad? Not that I care one way or t'other. Do get a move on, Jake. I didn't finish my maths homework last night so I want to get to school in time to do it before my next class.'

'Oh, ain't we a clever little scholarship girl?' Jake mocked. 'As for the Phil, you'd best come with me an' see for yourself, and you can tell me what's botherin' you at the same time,' he added.

'Ever heard what the initials MYOB stand for?' Daisy said caustically. She turned to her aunt, holding out the envelope. 'There you are, Aunt Jane; I'm afraid we shan't be going to Connemara yet awhile, but when you've read the letter you'll understand why.'

As she and Jake left the kitchen and turned to walk down the long garden path, Jake said triumphantly: 'So that's why you've been snivelling! Bloomin' cheek I calls it, since if you ain't goin' to Ireland you 'n' me will have an extra week to earn ourselves a bit of gelt. This'll be my last

179

summer holiday before I start work, I reckon, though me dad says I did ought to stay on in school, like what you're goin' to do. But now I'm fourteen I reckon it'll be more fun to gerra job, then I can go to the flicks three or four times a week if I want.'

'I think you ought to stay on at school,' Daisy said decidedly. 'You're better at maths even than my teacher is. Well, you explain better, at any rate. I heard your dad telling my aunt that they'd offered to coach you so you could try for your School Certificate. He said he was all for it, but you weren't too keen. I'm telling you, Jake Elgin, the folk who chuck away chances like that live to regret it.' Jake began to protest that he'd had enough of school, but Daisy cut across his words. 'Anyway, you know I said I'd not finished my maths homework . . .' she began persuasively, but Jake forestalled her.

'All right, all right, I know what you're goin' to say. Sure I'll finish off your maths for you, and I'll check the answers you have done, make sure you've gorr'em right. But first I want to know why else you're upset. Has that snooty Cynthia been havin' a dig at you? I know you said once she'd been horrible about your mam and dad; is it that?'

Daisy sighed. 'No, Cynthia has been really nice,' she said resignedly. 'The truth is, Jake, that the feller who took our cottage off us is selling it, and once the sale goes through – if it does – then there's not much chance of us getting it back unless we can prove that Paddy never owned it to begin with.

So Mam, Dad and the little ones have bought a passage to New York in the hope of finding evidence that Paddy lied.'

Jake whistled softly under his breath. 'Course he lied,' he said stoutly. 'You've told me how he behaved and how horrible him and the feller with him were, and if you ask me they've lied and cheated right from the start. But if this lawyer of yours really believes the truth lies in America, why didn't he say so years ago?'

Daisy shrugged helplessly. 'I don't know. It might have been because he believed, as my daddy did, that Paddy would soon get sick of the hard work of the croft and let us buy it back for whatever money Daddy could raise. Or it may have been because there wasn't enough money for a passage to America; Daddy had to sell Tina and the cart, and the *Mary Ellen*, to pay for the voyage across the Atlantic for all of them. But whatever the reason, they're going and Brendan, Amanda and myself will be left behind.'

Jake whistled again, looking thoughtful. By this time they were on Pilgrim Street and for a moment he hurried on in silence, a crease between his brows. Then they reached a low wall upon which they often sat to exchange news and views, and Jake settled himself on it, pulled Daisy down beside him, and reaching over began to rummage in her satchel for her maths book. 'Best get this cleared up before we go any further,' he said. 'Then we'll go along to the Phil 'n' take a look. If it makes you late for school you can tell your teacher you have bad news from home. And since you're such a little goody-goody, she'll let you off wi' a caution. I'll check your answers first . . . yup, yup, yup, they're all right; now I'll do the ones you've left.'

Daisy watched in awe as Jake finished her work. He had done it faintly in pencil and now he handed her the exercise book, telling her as he did so how he had come to each conclusion, since it would be of little use to simply write down the answers. Teachers, both children knew, always demanded workings-out as well.

As soon as she had completed the task to Jake's satisfaction, they both got to their feet and started down Pilgrim Street again, but as they turned into Hope Place Daisy caught at Jake's sleeve, raised her chin and sniffed. 'There's a really horrible smell around here . . .' she was beginning, when she realised what it was. Burning! 'Oh, Jake, I don't think I want to go any further. Suppose people died in the fire; it would be very wrong of us to stare at something like that.'

Jake, however, grabbed her arm and towed her along. 'Don't be such a little ninny,' he said scornfully as they reached the junction with Hope Street, upon which the Philharmonic Hall was situated. 'If folk got burned up, it's too late to be squeamish about it. And besides, me dad said it happened after everyone had gone home, so that's all right.'

By now the smell of burning was stronger and the street was beginning to be peopled by curious onlookers. Daisy looked to her left and at first saw only the Unitarian church, standing calm and unruffled in its grounds. Yet something about it looked strange and Daisy realised, with a little stab of surprise, that in normal circumstances one saw the church against the enormous bulk of the Philharmonic Hall. Now that bulk looked . . . different. It was still there, but it looked as though it were leaning up on one elbow. They began to walk towards it, or rather Jake did so, towing Daisy behind him. 'C'mon, you perishin' goose, else you won't be able to tell your pals what you seen,' he said. 'Good thing we was early or there'd be a crowd o' kids here by now, but it's mainly police and firemen and grown-ups. Coo, it's still smoulderin', and the roof looks kinda odd; I reckon all the innards is burnt out, though it don't look as bad as I expected.'

He sounded disappointed, but Daisy was too interested in the scene before her to reproach him. Two fire engines partly blocked the road and there was a large police presence. Firemen wandered about, erecting barriers and occasionally stopping to gossip with passers-by, though no one spoke to the children. Jake, however, spotted a policeman who was a regular on the Rodney Street beat. 'Hey, Mr O'Toole, when did this happen?' he asked eagerly. 'Me Dad said dead o' night, but he weren't around then. Were there many folk killed?'

The constable grinned and cuffed Jake lightly across the ear. 'You 'orrible little ghoul,' he said.

'As your dad said, it happened last night after the final performance. No one don't know for sure how it come to go on fire but the brigade reckon it were an accident, not arson. No one was hurt, you'll be disappointed to learn, but someone will be if you hang around here when you ought to be in school.'

'Right you are, Mr O'Toole; now we knows what's what, we'll be off,' Jake said cheerfully. 'You can't blame us for wantin' to have a look, though. It ain't often as something this excitin' happens so near Rodney Street. When I got up this mornin', early, there were a sort of haze and an odd smell. Me dad told me there'd bin a fire at the old Phil, so me and me pal here thought we'd take a look.'

The constable shook his head reprovingly. 'It ain't excitin' so much as sad, 'cos the building was a grand one and nearly a hundred years old,' he said. 'They were plannin' a celebration but the fire's killed that off good an' proper. It'll need a deal of money to rebuild a hall of that size, I'm tellin' you. And now be off, the pair of you.'

Daisy would willingly have left the scene but Jake insisted upon a prowl round just in case the Presbyterian church at the back of the hall had also caught fire. It had not, but stood there in the warm July sunshine, solid as a rock, so Jake allowed Daisy to pull him away along Hope Street. She broke into a run, her satchel bumping on her back, her panama slipping from her head

184

to hang round her neck by its elastic. Jake swore colourfully, but kept pace with her, though he grumbled that she was daft. 'We've got a cast iron excuse for bein' a bit late; I'm goin' to say me dad's employer was at the Phil last night, so we went round there to make sure the old feller weren't a burnt-up corpse,' he said, with much relish. 'You could say the same and don't go protestin' you don't tell lies, 'cos it ain't a lie, not really.'

'Oh, shut up and run,' Daisy said breathlessly. They swerved into Upper Duke Street, slowing slightly, for the pavement was already crowded, then belted along until they reached the junction of Berry and Great George streets, where they dropped to a walk, Daisy at least mindful that teachers did not approve of their pupils running in the street. At Great George Square their ways parted, Jake turning right to make for Gilbert Street and Daisy going back on herself, entering Rathbone Street just as the school bell sounded and the pupils began to make their way into the building. Smiling to herself, Daisy thought what an idiot she had been. Because she and Jake always walked to and from school together, parting and meeting on the corner of the square, she had come that way today even though it would have been far quicker, from the Philharmonic Hall, to take the more direct route. But there you were, habit was stronger some- times than common sense.

She let her breath out in a long whistling sigh

and was glad she had done so when someone tapped her on the shoulder. 'Daisy, was it you I saw running like a maniac as I passed the end of Hope Street? Was that young man chasing you? You know the school rules . . .'

'Yes, Miss Davies; we aren't supposed to talk to boys when we are wearing school uniform unless they are brothers or cousins,' Daisy said glibly, smiling up at the teacher who had addressed her. 'I was afraid I might be late because I went round by the Philharmonic Hall – did you know it was destroyed by fire last night? – to take a look. I ran all the way back because I didn't want to be late for school.'

'The Phil? I mean, the Philharmonic Hall? You say it was destroyed by fire? But that's terrible news; how did you hear about it? I do trust no one was hurt.'

Daisy realised with some relief that she would not have to explain her relationship with Jake, for the teacher's mind was now firmly fixed on the fire at the Phil. As they entered the building she began to tell Miss Davies all that the constable had told Jake, and very soon she was heading for the assembly hall, realising with some surprise that she had completely forgotten her own troubles and the deep disappointment she had felt upon reading her mother's letter that morning. Cynthia was right to remind me that Mammy and Daddy will come home just as soon as they can, she told herself resolutely. And I'm sure Aunt

Jane will suggest that we have a little holiday of our own, here in England, even if we can't go to Connemara. I must be positive. Come to think of it, I must write back to Mammy immediately, as soon as I get indoors, or she won't get the letter before they leave the country. And I'll make it a really happy cheerful letter and tell her I know that she and Daddy are doing the right thing. Then I'll write to Amanda and Brendan because they must be feeling just as miserable as I am. After all, though America is a long way off, it's not the end of the earth. I wonder whether they will be back in time for Christmas? Yes, they're bound to be, probably a lot sooner. I shall make a big calendar and cross off a square each day and before I know it a letter will come saying that Paddy Kildare's papers were fakes and that Mammy, Daddy and the kids have booked their passage home.

Aunt Jane came towards Daisy that afternoon as soon as her niece entered the kitchen, holding out her arms, and Daisy flew into them. 'Oh, Daisy, I know how disappointed you must be,' she said. 'As disappointed as I am myself. Come along to the housekeeper's room and I'll make you a nice cup of tea whilst we talk.'

Daisy was about to point out that the kettle was steaming on the kitchen hob and cups were set out ready, but then she realised they could scarcely talk confidentially here with other members of staff coming and going, and followed her aunt out of the kitchen and into the housekeeper's room, closing the door softly behind her.

The kettle perched on the small fire was already boiling. Aunt Jane made and poured the tea, handing a cup to Daisy, and then they both sat down on the small sofa. 'It's been a hard day for you and meself,' Aunt Jane said. 'But I believe Maggie and Colm are doing the right thing, indeed the only thing. Doubtless they will feel lost and unhappy when they first reach America, but they have a goal in mind and because reaching that goal may mean Benmacraig will be theirs once more they'll put aside their fears and tackle whatever comes bravely.'

'I know they will. And if they can't prove Paddy Kildare a liar, if he really does own Benmacraig, then they'll come home at once, don't you think?' Daisy said rather shakily. She took a sip of her tea. 'Only . . . so often folk go to America, find good jobs, and – and never come back.'

Aunt Jane laughed. 'I know what you mean, chuck, but folk who do that take their families with them. Your mammy and daddy would no more desert you and your brother and sister than fly to the moon, so don't give that another thought. Now, I think you and meself should still take our week's holiday, even if we only go to a seaside place nearby for a few days. What do you think?'

'That would be lovely; but I wouldn't want to spend our Connemara money, because if they do come back quite quickly, we could still go over and have time with them,' Daisy pointed out. 'How soon could they come back, Aunt Jane? I've been telling myself Christmas at the latest . . .'

'By Christmas we will have saved up our holiday money all over again,' Aunt Jane said reassuringly. 'So don't worry about it any more. Promise me to look at the business in a positive way.'

Daisy laughed. 'I've been telling myself all day to look on the bright side, which is what you mean, isn't it?' she said. 'And I'll really try to do so.'

'Good girl. And if you get very down, just you come along and tell me how you feel and we'll talk it all through,' Aunt Jane said. 'Now drink up that cuppa and we'll go along to the kitchen and join the others for high tea.'

Daisy was immensely heartened by her aunt's cheerful optimism, especially since having high tea in the kitchen was a rare treat. On this particular occasion everyone sympathised over their lost holiday but said, reassuringly, that her parents were taking the only sensible course. 'And they won't linger in a foreign country any longer than they need,' Cook said comfortably. 'They'll be back before you know it, just you see.'

Later, when she and Cynthia were settling down in the schoolroom to do their homework, Cynthia too was kinder and far more understanding than usual. 'It's a good thing the school holidays are about to start because you always enjoy mucking about with that Jake and exploring the streets and

189

museums and that,' she said. 'I know you say your Aunt Jane means to take you to New Brighton whilst I'm in Southport, but honestly, Daisy, if you'd like to come with me I'm sure you'd enjoy yourself as much as I do. After all, Southport *is* a seaside town, though the sea goes out about a million miles, I should think. But it leaves plenty of sand, I can tell you.'

Daisy laughed. 'I bet you've never been on that sand in your life,' she remarked. 'I bet you've never made a sand pie, or dug a moat round a castle, or paddled in a pool, let alone gone shrimping with a flour bag on a split cane. Were you *ever* a child, Cynthia Darlington-Crewe?'

After a tiny pause, Cynthia joined in her laughter. 'I see what you mean, though I've never thought of it like that before. The truth is, Goody didn't like the beach at all and my mama was so afraid I'd catch a chill that she never even suggested I might go to the shore. And if I'm honest, I wouldn't have liked it anyway. We did walk along the prom sometimes, and if it was windy I'd end up with sand in my shoes.' She shuddered expressively. 'Horrible stuff! And sea water's sticky, or so Goody used to say.'

'It is rather; and of course when you're on the beach you take your shoes and socks off, so the sea water and sand gets between your toes,' Daisy said, and laughed again when Cynthia pulled a face. 'But most kids like it. Why, Jake and me sometimes skip a lecky out to Seaforth Sands and have a grand time, though of course Aunt Jane and the Venables would have heart attacks if they knew half of what we got up to.'

'I dare say your aunt guesses, though,' Cynthia said. She sighed. 'You and I are so different, Daisy. You were very free in Connemara, weren't you? Free to do what you wanted, I mean, whereas I have always been fussed over. But how on earth did we get on to this subject? All I meant to say was I'm sure Mrs Winterton would welcome you if you wanted to come to Southport with me.'

'It's very kind of you but I'd rather be here with Jake, thanks,' Daisy said. 'I know you, Cynthia, you'll spend all your time in the shops and I'd hate that.' She grinned suddenly as a thought struck her. 'But you're only going for a couple of weeks, aren't you? When you come home, why don't you come out with Jake and me? We'd teach you to swim in the Scaldy – that's what they call the bit of the canal where the water's always warm because Tate's sugar factory pumps its used water back into it there. And then we could go on the Overhead Railway to have a good look at the docks. Or we could . . .'

'Or we could get on with our homework, which is what we're supposed to be doing,' Cynthia said reproachfully. 'As for what I shall do when I come back to Liverpool, I've plans of my own. Aunt Venables likes taking me shopping with her, or visiting relatives and friends. You know she would take you as well, only you always say no thank you when she suggests that you accompany us.'

'I do hope she doesn't think I'm ungrateful, but the thing is I have to behave the way she expects me to do in term time, so I feel it's only fair that I spend the hols with Jake, or some of my school friends,' Daisy said rather remorsefully. 'Mrs Venables is ever so kind – generous, too – and I do believe she understands how I feel. At any rate, she never tries to persuade me.' The two girls had been sitting at the neat tables which had taken the place of their old desks and now Daisy reached out, picked up her satchel, and began to ferret for the books she needed. 'C'mon, let's get our home-work done, then we can take our skipping ropes and a ball down into the garden and mess around until bedtime.'

Because it was mid-week neither girl had very much homework, and what they had was soon finished. They were in the garden, Daisy skipping energetically and Cynthia more languidly, when Mrs Venables found them. She called them, and the two girls stopped skipping immediately and went over to where she stood.

Daisy opened her mouth to speak, but Mrs Venables was before her. 'Daisy, my dear, I've only just heard from your aunt that your parents are off to America to try to sort out the ownership of your cottage. I know you must be distressed to think of them going so far away, but one must be practical. I'm very sure they're doing the right thing and it's better by far that they pursue the matter, even though you must feel sad not to be going home.' She smiled kindly. 'America must seem a very long way away to you, but these days the voyage takes only a couple of weeks. The time will soon pass, so you must look forward to their return and hope that their visit will end the un-happiness of not knowing who owns Benmacraig.'

'I know. And I know they're doing the right thing as well,' Daisy said rapidly. She smiled brightly at Mrs Venables. 'It's not as though they're going to the moon, after all!'

Chapter Six

Daisy found it difficult to get to sleep that night, and when she did so she had a most peculiar dream. She dreamed that she was in beautiful countryside which did not look real, but more like an illustration from a book. She was surrounded by brilliant balloons and realised, suddenly, that she was a balloon too, one of a bunch held by an old woman in a scarlet dress with the sort of crinolined and panniered skirt which she had seen many times in illustrations of Little Bo-Peep or the Old Woman who Lived in a Shoe, over which was a billowing white pinafore.

Daisy glanced round at the other balloons and realised that they had faces. Her daddy smiled at her from a large red balloon, her mammy from a blue one, and bobbing just below them were Annabel, pink, and Finn and Dermot, yellow. Daisy waved and smiled excitedly, seeing Amanda looking prettier than ever in a violet balloon, and Brendan in a green one. She could see that the people themselves, frail and misty, were not truly in the balloons. But then she reasoned that when she went to the cinema the people she saw on the screen were not there either. She called out: 'Daddy,

Mammy, it's grand to see you, so it is,' and her parents and brothers and sisters answered at once that it was good to see her, too. 'And it won't be long before we're home again,' her father said reassuringly. 'It's not as if we were going to the moon . . . the moon . . . the moon . . .'

His voice seemed to grow fainter, and even as she wondered why Daisy realised what had happened. The old woman was rearranging her balloons, holding one out to a child, and somehow she had let go of Daisy's string and Daisy was floating gradually up into the sky. 'Daddy, Mammy, fetch me down!' she shrieked. 'I don't want to go off by meself, I want to be with you.' And on the words she began to struggle, trying to return to the brilliantly coloured bunch beneath her. She was succeeding, too, when, with a suddenness which made her cry out, she awoke to find Cynthia bending over her.

'Daisy? You were having a nightmare. Do wake up! My goodness, what on earth were you dreaming about? I bet a crocodile had you by the toe judging by the way you squawked when I shook your shoulder.'

Daisy sat up and rubbed her eyes. She glanced at the alarm clock and saw that it was only five o'clock. 'How odd; it wasn't really a nightmare, or not until the end at any rate,' she said slowly. 'I dreamed I was a balloon, one of a big bunch of the things, and when I looked around, my family were all balloons, too. We were quite high in the air, on long strings which the balloon woman held, and it was fairy-tale country, if you know what I mean, not a bit real. I called out to Mammy and Daddy and the others, and they all answered me. It was really jolly and I liked it, only then a kid came up to the woman to buy a balloon and somehow she must have let go of my string, because I started floating up, away from the others. I began to struggle and fight to get down again, because I was frightened I'd get separated. I shouted out . . . and then you woke me up.'

Cynthia, who had been bending over the bed, squatted back on her heels, shaking her head sadly. 'Mad, quite mad!' she said. 'When you say you were a balloon, and your family were balloons too, how did you recognise them?'

'Oh, it was just their faces inside the balloons, misty and faint, but of course I knew them at once,' Daisy explained. 'And they knew me, too. Aren't dreams odd, though? I wonder what would have happened if you'd not woken me up? I think I would have got back to the bunch, but I don't know how I would have stayed with them, because I didn't have hands, or anything like that.'

Cynthia chuckled. 'You don't need hands in dreams, nor feet, nor bodies,' she said. 'And now let's try to get back to sleep because tomorrow is my last exam – it's history – and I really do think I might pass this one.'

'I've got two more to go,' Daisy said ruefully. 'And I'm wide awake. I could do some revision,

I suppose . . . oh, but I can't be bothered. I've been revising for weeks, so if I don't know my stuff by now I never will. I'll see if I can get back to sleep for a couple of hours.'

Examinations finished and the results were pinned to the board. Daisy had done well, and when she carried her report home her aunt was pleased both with her position in class and by the teachers' comments. 'You must write to your parents today, letting them know how well you've done,' Mrs Venables said when Daisy handed her the long cream-coloured report sheet. 'Cynthia has done rather well, too; better than I expected. I have suggested that she should spend some time in France next year, since French is her best subject; perhaps you might like to accompany her?'

Daisy returned a noncommittal answer for she was hopeful that by the following year she would be back in Benmacraig with her family, but when she said as much to Aunt Jane, that sensible woman shook her head. 'What, and waste the schooling which you've worked so hard to acquire? My dear, even if your parents are successful and return to the croft, you must not throw everything up. The Depression has hit Ireland even harder than it has hit Liverpool, and well-paid jobs there will be scarce indeed. Of course you'll go back for holidays, but I fear you will have to look elsewhere when it comes to earning a living.'

Daisy pretended to agree, but in her heart the

memory of halcyon days spent at Benmacraig refused to be dismissed. She told herself that her parents would need all the help they could get to bring the croft back to what it had been four years ago, and refused to admit, even to herself, that Colm and Maggie would need the money she could earn far more than they would need the sort of help a girl of her age could provide.

But all this was for the future. Right now, she intended to enjoy the long summer holidays. She and her aunt went to New Brighton and had a lazy and enjoyable week, for the weather continued hot and sunny and they spent long hours on the beach, Aunt Jane snoozing in a deckchair whilst Daisy splashed in and out of the little waves and made friends with other holidaying children.

Then one day they had a wonderful surprise. It was a sunny evening and Daisy and her aunt were strolling along the wide promenade when someone hailed them. 'Daisy! Miss Dalton! Hang on a moment while we catches you up!'

It was Jake and his father hurrying along behind them, both smiling broadly. Aunt Jane and Daisy waited for them to catch up and Daisy burst into speech at once. 'Jake! Oh, it's grand to see you, so it is; and Mr Elgin, of course. But whatever are you doing here? Don't say you brought Dr Venables over to see a patient!'

Mr Elgin grinned but shook his head. 'No, no, you're out there. I've got a weekend off and young Jake here suggested we spend it in New Brighton.

We've booked into a boarding house on Virginia Road – Mrs Venables told us where you were staying – so I reckon us two old 'uns might take ourselves off for a ride in the country, or to the theatre, whilst you kids amuse yourselves.'

'Oh, I'm not sure, Bob,' Aunt Jane began, but Mr Elgin cut in.

'Jake's a sensible lad, Jane, and will take good care of young Daisy here.'

Daisy glanced at her aunt and saw pink colour steal into her cheeks; Aunt Jane was blushing! Turning her gaze on to Mr Elgin, Daisy saw that he was looking eager, his eyes brighter than usual in his tanned face. He's really awfully good-looking, she told herself, and Aunt Jane looks quite pretty when she blushes; how strange that I've never noticed it before! But then Mr Elgin asked them if they had yet eaten, and when Aunt Jane said they had had nothing since a sandwich lunch taken at noon he gallantly offered to buy them a meal at the Royal Victoria Hotel, an invitation which Aunt Jane seemed to have no hesitation in accepting.

Over the meal, Aunt Jane and Mr Elgin talked a great deal. Listening to their conversation, Daisy realised that the two knew each other a good deal better than she had supposed. During the school holidays, when I was off with Jake, I do believe Aunt Jane was off with Mr Elgin, she thought, and was astonished at her own blindness. How could she not have realised why Aunt Jane had never really queried what her niece was doing? She had probably been afraid that such interest in her niece's activities might be reciprocated. Not that it would have been, for Daisy realised with some shame that she had always considered her aunt too old to have a life of her own.

As they were served with a delicious iced pudding, Daisy saw that Jake was staring at his parent, eyes round with astonishment, and realised that her friend had had no more idea than she that his father knew Aunt Jane so well. She was bursting to discuss the whole matter with her pal, and as soon as the meal was over she thanked Mr Elgin then suggested that she and Jake might go to the funfair whilst their elders looked at the shops – which were closed – or simply walked along the prom to admire the sunset.

As soon as Aunt Jane and Mr Elgin were out of earshot, the two children stared at one another, wide-eyed. 'Well, who'd have thought it?' Jake said. 'My dad and your Aunt Jane! I reckon they're sweet on each other. I never seen me dad blush afore but he coloured up like – like a perishin' tomato when Miss Dalton started talkin' about that theatre show they'd both seen.' He grinned at Daisy, pulling what he no doubt thought was an appealing face. 'How would you like to be me little sister?' he squeaked in falsetto. 'I wonder if old Venables knows his chauffeur is makin' eyes at his housekeeper?'

'I should think they must have some idea

because Mrs Venables told your dad where we were staying,' Daisy said after a moment's thought, 'and she wouldn't have done that if she didn't know they were friendly.'

Jake thought this over and then nodded. 'Aye; and the doc lent us the car, you know, so I reckon he's in on the secret an' all. In fact, you and me is probably the only people livin' in Rodney Street what don't know.'

'I feel ashamed because she is my aunt and she's been good to me, so I really should have noticed what was going on,' Daisy admitted. 'I would have told my parents, too, because my mammy has always wanted her sister to get married and blamed herself for Aunt Jane's still being single. You see, Aunt Jane's a lot older'n me mammy and after their own mam – my gran – died, Aunt Jane was like a mother to her little sister. She took jobs which would allow her to go on taking care of Mammy and of course it must have spoiled her chances. Well, that's what Mammy says, at any rate. So if your dad pops the question, my mam will be thrilled, so she will.'

By this time the two children had reached the funfair and were able to forget everything but rides, shooting galleries, hoop-la stalls and ice cream stands. And indeed, for the whole of that weekend they had a really marvellous time. Both were determined to find out how Mr Elgin and Aunt Jane felt about each other when they got back to Rodney Street, but for now the holiday took their minds off everything else. Even Daisy's preoccupation with her parents' quest was pushed into the background, though she was delighted, when they re-entered Rodney Street late on Sunday night, to find three letters awaiting her.

A glance told her who they were from: Amanda, Brendan and her mother. Her fingers itched to open her mother's first but she decided to save the best until last and instead turned to Brendan's epistle. It was short, as she had guessed it would be, but very much to the point.

> . . . *I don't get paid all that much because times are pretty hard, but every penny extra is going into an old wooden box labelled* 'Mary Ellen' [he had written]. *Of course, I hope Daddy and Mammy will find that they really do own Benmacraig, but if they don't it will be even more important to get our boat back, because without it, we're sunk. I know Mammy and Daddy say you must stay at school, maybe for years, but I dare say you might get a holiday job. If you do, put the money aside so's we can get the* Mary Ellen *back one day . . .*

Daisy was reading her letters in the parlour, rather enjoying having it to herself, as Cynthia would not be back for another week. She nodded her head, promising Brendan in her mind that she, too, would put money aside for the *Mary Ellen*; if the worst happened, that was.

202

Next she opened Amanda's letter, which was longer and chattier, and very cheerful. She could not help wondering whether the cheerfulness was for her benefit but decided that it did not matter. She had already sent extremely cheerful letters to her family, though at the time she had still been suffering from bouts of misery over her lost holiday and her parents' departure. So she must accept Amanda's letter at its face value and not try to read into it any of the misery which her sister may have felt upon learning the news. The letter began in the usual way.

Dear Daisy,

Many thanks for yours, recently received. I'm sure Mammy and Daddy are doing the right thing and will come home again just as soon as every-thing is sorted out. I hated Paddy Kildare and his horrible brother, so it will serve them right to be kicked out of our home and to have to pay Daddy for what they've done. My friend, Gerald, is actu-ally putting aside some of the money he earns especially for Brendan's boat fund, though neither of us think it will come to that. I wish you could meet Gerald – you would like him, I'm sure. He reminds me of Daddy, being tall and dark, and he is very kind. We mean to get married some time next year, so you will meet him then. Mammy and Daddy have met him and like him very much.

As you know, I had to take a cut in wages last year but Mrs Tomais says the business is beginning to pull round and has put my pay back to what it was before. I offered to send money to America but Mammy said not to do so. They will get work of some sort. However, should they need it, I would be happy to help out.

The rest of the letter was mainly concerned with the charms of Gerald and her friendship with other servants at Mrs Tomais's grand house. Daisy skimmed through it and then turned, with a sigh of pleasure, to the familiar blue envelope. She slit it open and began to read.

Dear Daisy,

I am going to start by explaining to you that postage is rather expensive and writing letters time consuming. So I hope you will forgive me for what I am about to suggest. I mean to write to you at least once a week, perhaps more often if anything happens, and I want you to faithfully copy my letters, once for Amanda and once for Brendan, and then I want you to post them off with a covering letter explaining what we are doing and why. You might think I should write to Amanda, or even to Brendan, since they are older, asking them to do this for me, but I have chosen you because you have more time than Amanda in which to copy letters, and poor Brendan is no scholar and would find such a task extremely difficult. Also, your school has taught you to write beautifully – and to spell correctly – so Daddy and I decided that you were the obvious choice. I know I don't have to ask if you will do it; you would not dream of refusing, alanna. But you need not copy this explanation so now I shall begin all over again.

Daisy chuckled. For years now, her mother had penned weekly letters to her absent children; it was about time she had a break. And I mean to write to Amanda and Brendan each week, so it won't cost me any more to send on the copies, she thought. Then she turned back to her mother's letter.

Dear Amanda, Brendan and Daisy,

Well, we arrived here five days ago and found a cheap lodging house. I won't pretend it's a pleasant place because it is not, but we do not intend to stay here once our week is up. The proprietor insisted that we pay a week in advance which fortunately we were able to do, thanks to all the help we have received from our children. Your father has found work in a warehouse down by the docks and I will be cleaning in a huge hotel, starting in a week's time.

New York is very strange after Ireland, but the nice thing about it is the number of Irish already well established here. They are truly friendly and helpful and refer constantly to 'the old country', but though they talk of returning, I am sure they realise they will never do so. Most of the garda – they call them cops – seem to be Irish and one of them, his name is Mick, has befriended us. It was he who got Colm the warehouse job and he's found us a room with a rent we can afford. He didn't know the lawyers but advised us not to visit them until he has had a word with a friend of his who does know them. And we are happy enough to wait for we are still finding it difficult to understand the many different accents we hear every day. But your father says in a week or two things will grow clearer; I do hope he's right.

One of the reasons we do not like our present lodging is because everyone is turned out at nine o'clock each morning and no one may return until after seven in the evening. This means that while Daddy goes off to his place of work, I cannot start at the hotel because of Annabel and the boys. It is very hot here and there is an enormous park where Annabel said she would be happy to remain all day with her brothers, for it is like real country, and one can ramble for miles. However, Mick told us that Central Park – that is its name – is not a safe place for children unless accompanied by an adult, so though the four of us are spending long hours roaming the park, it will be out of the question for Annabel to take the boys there once I am in work. She is a very good girl and will doubt-less manage to keep the boys amused when we have moved into the new room.

Well, my dears, I don't think I have any more news for you now. It takes rather a long time for *the post to reach us here, so if you write to the new address below we shall be living there by the time your letters arrive.*

Take care of yourselves, my darlings; we think about you every day and miss you most dreadfully. The boys and Annabel send kisses and hugs, as do your loving mammy and daddy.

Daisy read the letter through three times with increasing pleasure, and then got out her diary and carefully wrote the strange address into it. Then she crossed the room and switched on the electric light, for dusk was deepening and she meant to copy her mother's letter straight away so that she might send it off to Amanda and Brendan the following morning.

Dipping her pen into the ink bottle, she began to write.

Despite Daisy's fears, the days and weeks passed incredibly quickly. Letters arrived regularly from her mother, and each one cheered Daisy more, for all attempts to find the original of the will which Colm's great-grandfather was supposed to have made had proved unsuccessful . . . *and that must mean that it never existed at all, but we shall continue to search, just in case,* her father had scrawled on the end of one of her mother's nice, newsy epistles.

Daisy carried this screed to Aunt Jane, as she did all her mother's letters, and her aunt took it to Mrs

Venables. 'If the will leaving Benmacraig to Paddy Kildare's grandpa never existed, then what's the point in searching for it?' Aunt Jane enquired, a worried frown creasing her forehead. 'How can not finding a will help my poor sister?'

'I imagine what your sister is hoping to find is a proper will which is different from the copy Mr Paddy Kildare showed them,' Mrs Venables explained. 'If the two are not identical, then it will probably be easy for an expert to prove that Mr Kildare lied.'

School started again in mid-September, and halfway through October Daisy thought sadly that her original estimate of a Christmas homecoming might not be possible after all. Then a letter arrived which changed everything and caused Daisy, after reading only the first few sentences, to fly down the stairs and into the basement kitchen, accompanied by Cynthia, anxious to know why Daisy was so excited. Daisy flung herself at Aunt Jane, waving the letter before her aunt's startled eyes. 'It's all right! They've found the original will in a dusty little law office in a part of New York called Brooklyn,' she gabbled. 'Daddy had to get another lawyer to go with him and the other lawyer took the will away with him because he said it was really nothing to do with Paddy Kildare but belonged to our own daddy. I'd better read you the letter . . .'

Dear Daisy, Amanda and Brendan [she read aloud],

Everything has now been sorted out. Your great-great-grandfather's will leaves all his property and any money he may have possessed at the time of his death to his son Tomas, your great-grandfather. When the lawyer confirmed it, he told your father and myself to leave our jobs, and is loaning us the money for the train journey to Boston, where he believes Paddy Kildare to be living at present.

We now know, also, just why and how Paddy Kildare came to forge the document which he brought to Ireland. It was through his friend and partner in crime, Mitch Mitchell, who was working for the firm which held the will amongst its archives. He could see that it had all the relevant details needed to create a false document, and that is exactly what he did, falsifying everything, seals, signatures, the lot. He was never a lawyer, but just a filing clerk, and shortly after making a copy of the will he was dismissed for some other misdemeanour, we don't know what.

Upon talking it over with all the lawyers concerned, we came to the conclusion that Mr Mitchell, already hand-in-glove with Paddy Kildare over other crooked matters, had seized upon us as victims because his friend's name happened to be Kildare. The lawyer traced him as far back as his great-grandfather, and though his family had come from Ireland once, it was from Dublin and not Connemara.

There remains the question of why Padraig Kildare took his father's will with him to America in the first place, since it did not benefit him in any way. We fear he cannot have been an honest man, and must have intended to cheat his younger brother out of his inheritance very much as Paddy Kildare has tried to cheat us. By hanging on to the only authentic copy of the will he ensured that Tomas would not be able to prove his own claim, but for one reason or another he never returned to Ireland and it has taken all this time for the truth to come to light.

My dears, I felt bitter at first, because if we had acted sooner we might have been together at Benmacraig years ago, but at least we now know that we shall be together in the future. The lawyer has already assured us that Paddy Kildare has no choice but to sell his hotel in Boston and repay us whatever the courts decide, unless he agrees to settle out of court, which Mr O'Leary – that is the name of our lawyer – is sure he will do, rather than risk imprisonment for fraud.

So you see, my darlings, the shadows are lifting and the sun is going to shine on us at last. Take good care of yourselves. I must write no more, as our train departs in an hour. The children send their love, as do your daddy and I.

Aunt Jane beamed and hugged her niece, and then the two of them danced a jig of triumph round and round the kitchen, whilst Cynthia and the staff applauded and laughed, Cook had a little weep and Mr Elgin gave Aunt Jane a kiss on the cheek, saying that they would celebrate by taking the kids back to New Brighton at the weekend for a day out and a slap-up dinner at the Royal Victoria.

'I'm so happy, it's almost unbelievable,' Daisy said presently, handing the letter to her aunt. 'Oh, Aunt Jane, does this mean they really could be back by Christmas?'

'If those two scoundrels agree to settle out of court, your parents will only have to wait until the money which has been agreed is actually in their hands. Then I just know they'll make for home as fast as they can,' Aunt Jane assured her. 'They could be home by Christmas, I suppose, but having waited so long I'm sure we can wait a further few weeks. If the crooks decide to be awkward and force your father to go to court, then of course it could take longer.' She smiled very fondly at Daisy. 'Can you be patient, queen? It's much easier to wait for something good than to fear something bad.'

'I could wait a whole year if it meant that Mammy and Daddy could come back to Benmacraig knowing that it was their own home,' Daisy said joyfully. 'Besides, don't they say time flies when you're having fun? I'm sure it's true because our

211

week in New Brighton simply whizzed past. And I shall have a grand time spending the money I've saved up on really nice Christmas presents for everyone.' She looked anxiously at her aunt. 'Will it be all right to do that, Aunt Jane? I know our land has been allowed to go to rack and ruin, but if Paddy Kildare has to pay Daddy for the past four years, then he won't need my savings, will he? If he does, of course I wouldn't dream of squandering my money.'

'Oh, Daisy, what a nice, generous child you are,' Aunt Jane said. 'But you're quite right: if Maggie and Colm get their just deserts, they won't need any help from anyone.' She tucked the letter into her skirt pocket.

Since it had arrived on a school day, Daisy had to wait until four o'clock to copy it, but all day she thought of nothing else and when she and Cynthia had finished their homework, she repeated her pleasure in the news again.

'I'm jolly thrilled for you, of course, Daisy, and for your parents. They must be so excited and happy,' Cynthia said. 'But I do hope it doesn't mean that you'll go home once your parents get back. I know we sometimes disagree, but I'd miss you most horribly if you left Rodney Street.'

'Oh, I shan't. I wouldn't dream of it, because my parents need me to get a good job so I can support myself when I leave school,' Daisy said blithely. 'You know I've said several times that I'd quite like to be a teacher; well, you can't do that from Benmacraig because the school I used to go to doesn't teach French or science, or anything like that, just the three Rs as they say. But I'll spend holidays back home, helping Mammy and Daddy to get the croft into decent order.' She beamed at the other girl. 'The man who has it now has put in a proper bathroom, and there's running water from a tap in the kitchen, which not even Farmer Vaughan has.'

'I'm amazed; what did you have before?' Cynthia said sarcastically. 'Oh, Daisy, you've lived here for ages but you still think a bathroom and water from a tap are modern wonders. I'm really glad that you won't be leaving Rodney Street, though, and I expect you are, too, when you think about it. You've got heaps of friends at school, I know, and you're quite fond of that horrible Jake, as well as liking Ruth so much. Do you know, I was quite jealous of Ruth at one time, because the two of you got on so well and she took you back to her aunt's house on her days off . . . but then you and I got to know one another better and I got school friends of my own and it didn't seem to matter any more.'

Daisy stared at her companion. They were in their comfortable little parlour, their exercise books stowed in their satchels once more, and Cynthia was embroidering a tablecloth which was to be a Christmas gift for her Aunt Venables. Daisy had been darning a huge hole in the heel of a black woollen stocking, but she lowered her work as Cynthia spoke. 'Jealous of Ruth?' she squeaked. 'Cynthia, you must have been mad! Her family live in one of the courts off the Scotland Road, in a tumbledown house with almost no furniture, a lodger in the only decent bedroom, and all the kids crammed into the other one. When I go round I take a big chunk of slab cake and at teatime they fall on it as if they'd never seen cake in their lives before. And don't say nasty things about Jake, please. He's really nice and so is his pa.'

Cynthia smoothed a hand across her tablecloth, then held it up for Daisy to see. 'These flowers are primroses, most awfully pretty, but there's a butterfly perched on one of them and I don't believe I've ever seen a butterfly that early in the year,' she said. 'Still, I suppose it's like poetic licence, and if I make it a blue butterfly it will look quite good. And you are daft, Daisy; when I said I used to be jealous of Ruth I didn't mean I envied her things like her home, or her family. I envied her your friendship, only now you and me are friendly anyway. As for Jake, I don't really know him very well. Understand? Savvy?'

'Yes, of course I do, but as I said before Jake is not horrible. He's really nice when you get to know him,' Daisy said defensively. 'I used to think he was rough and rude – well, he was – but he's improved no end. Remember, his mammy died when he was only two and I don't believe fathers manage too well when they're left to bring up a

214

child alone. Anyway, you like Mr Elgin, don't you? You must know him pretty well because he takes you to school each day.'

'Oh yes, Elgin's nice enough,' Cynthia said carelessly. 'Yes, he's a good sort. Sometimes he lets me give one of my friends a lift home, which he doesn't have to do. Yes, Elgin's quite nice.'

'He isn't quite nice, he's very nice,' Daisy said firmly. For some reason, she had never told Cynthia that the chauffeur and her aunt were good friends. She and Jake had done their best to discover just how close Mr Elgin and Aunt Jane had grown, with very little success. For one thing, Daisy guessed that her aunt and the chauffeur went out together in the evenings after she, and probably Jake, had been sent to bed. If they were together during the day, it was when she and Jake had gone off on some ploy of their own, so were unable to check up on their relatives. Daisy did not think any other members of staff knew what was going on, but when she and Jake discussed the matter they agreed that probably the Venables knew and very likely approved. After all, if Aunt Jane and Mr Elgin were to marry, nothing very much would change at No. 39. Dr Venables would not have to look for a new chauffeur, and Mrs Venables could retain the services of her housekeeper, because neither Aunt Jane nor Mr Elgin would dream of leaving such good jobs when the Depression was biting more deeply with every day that passed.

'And they're far too old, both of them, to start having kids,' Jake had said when she had put the point to him. 'So it 'ud suit the Venables down to the ground if Miss Dalton and me dad got wed. They'd keep both of 'em, see, because who else is likely to need a new chauffeur and a new house-keeper at the same time?'

Daisy had agreed with this eminently practical viewpoint and now, as she watched Cynthia thread a needle with a length of blue silk, it crossed her mind to wonder why her friend had never noticed what was going on – if indeed it was going on. But in the end she concluded that Cynthia noticed very little, her thoughts being mainly concerned with herself. Daisy doubted if it ever occurred to the other girl that servants were people with interesting lives of their own, whereas she, Daisy, knew all sorts of things about everyone living or working in the Venables household. Cook was one of an enormous family, most of whom lived within a mile or so of Rodney Street. One or other of them was always popping in for a gossip and a cup of tea, or for advice. She knew that Roddy, who helped his father in the garden, was simple, being able to neither read nor write, but had a great affinity with all growing things. Pilcher's wife had run off with a sailor a couple of years before Daisy had come to the city. He and Roddy lived in the basement flat of a neighbouring house, acting as night watchmen, since the house in question had been divided into consulting and waiting rooms for four or five doctors, and was unoccupied during the hours of darkness. The maids were all friendly and went around together, dancing at the Grafton ballroom, going for trips on the Mersey, and falling in and out of love, sometimes with the young men they met, sometimes with the stars on the silver screen or the actors at the Empire.

At this point the door of the parlour opened and Aunt Jane came in.

'You and Jake can go along to Carter's and buy fancy cakes, enough for everyone, because they will all want to celebrate your good fortune.'

'Ooh, I'll get something really creamy and delicious! Thank you, Aunt Jane,' Daisy said. She ran into the schoolroom to fetch her hat and coat and to change her slippers for boots, and to her great astonishment Cynthia accompanied her and seized her own outdoor clothing. 'I'll come with you,' she said positively. 'I don't want to be left upstairs all by myself whilst you have all the excitement. Jake won't mind, will he?'

'Of course he won't,' Daisy said. 'But wouldn't you rather go with my aunt to tell Dr and Mrs Venables?' She turned to her aunt, waiting on the landing. 'You'll want to tell them now the doctor is free, won't you, Aunt Jane?'

Her aunt agreed to this and Cynthia, who had been struggling into her coat, struggled out of it again, saying as she did so: 'All right, I'll go

with you, Miss Dalton; I hate playing gooseberry. My goodness, Aunt Venables will be so
pleased.'

The three of them hurried down the stairs, Daisy
at least so excited that she ran too fast and skidded
down the last six steps on her bottom, though she
jumped up immediately, assuring Aunt Jane,
following with her purse, that she was not hurt in
the least. Then her aunt and Cynthia hurried away
to the main part of the house, whilst Daisy thundered into the basement and entered the kitchen
at a run. Cook was at the stove; Daisy could see
Ruth preparing vegetables in the scullery and
Biddy and Molly were seated at the table, chattering away whilst they polished the silver cutlery
with Goddard's pink powder, Molly applying the
mixture and Biddy rubbing if off. Everyone looked
up expectantly.

'Anyone seen Jake?' Daisy asked. 'Me aunt
wants us to do some messages.'

Cook turned round and frowned in a considering sort of way. 'Last time I see 'im, he were
in the yard helping his pa to clean the motor,'
she said. 'But I reckon it's too dark for them to
work out of doors now, so likely they're in the
coachman's quarters.' She smiled kindly at Daisy.
'No need to climb them rickety stairs, just give
a good loud holler, an' he'll come running.'

'Thanks, Mrs Bellamy,' Daisy said, heading for
the back door, and very soon she and Jake were
gloating over her news.

'But what'll happen if that feller – the wrong 'un, I mean – simply takes off the minute he realises he's gorra part with his gelt?' Jake said as the two of them strolled companionably along Rodney Street, then turned right into Upper Duke Street, heading for Carter's the confectioners, where Daisy meant to spend the money she had been given on the delicious chocolate éclairs for which Mr Carter was famous.

Now she considered Jake's remark but immediately saw a flaw in it. 'No fear of that, you stupid boy,' she said happily. 'Someone who's bought a hotel and is making money doesn't just up sticks and disappear. Why, if he did, the court would take possession of the hotel, so Daddy might get all his money instead of just what's owed.'

Jake thought deeply, then a wide grin split his face. 'One way and another, youse gonna be rich,' he said exultantly. 'Eh, Daisy, don't forget your old pals when you're up there, livin' in Buck'nam Palace with the old king and queen.'

Daisy giggled. 'Just as soon as the family's settled into our cottage, I'm going to ask me mam if you can come and stay with us,' she said. 'I'm not going to pretend it's Buckingham Palace, but it's a grand little place, so it is. Did I tell you there's a real bathroom in it now . . .'

'. . . and runnin' water in the kitchen,' Jake finished for her. 'If there's one person in Liverpool what don't know your cottage has got

219

runnin' water, I'd be that surprised you could knock me down with a feather. No, don't go hittin' me just for speakin' the truth. And I've got news for you an' all, news what nobody else don't know yet. I might even tell you if you promise I can have first pick of the éclairs.'

'Course you can. What have you done?' Daisy said rather apprehensively. She knew Jake had been hoping for work during the break, but she also knew she would miss him if he did get a job, since Cynthia liked to go off to Southport shopping, and this year would be no exception. Jake however shook his head. 'No, it ain't that. Have another guess,' he said provocatively, causing Daisy to give a yelp of annoyance and to punch him as hard on the shoulder as she could.

'Less of that. Just you tell me or I'll make sure you get the tiniest éclair with the least chocolate on the top,' Daisy threatened, seeing Jake's face and knowing that he was bursting to tell her anyway.

'All right, all right,' he said, fending her off. 'Last spring someone told me dad that the Charles Mortimer School for Boys, out by Prince's Park, were offering two free places to boys from council schools, so's they could study for their School Certificate. There was a pretty stiff exam, but Dad said there were no harm in me havin' a go. And the letter came this morning; I've got one of the two places. I'll be going there after

Christmas. Now you ain't the only one with a scholarship.' He was beaming with triumph and Daisy, remembering how he had kept insisting that he had had enough of school and meant to start work just as soon as he could persuade his father to let him leave, gave him an impulsive hug and a slapping kiss on the cheek. 'Gerroff!' Jake said indignantly. 'That's typical of a girl, that is, kissin' a feller in the street where anyone might see.'

Daisy giggled. 'Sorry, but I'm just so thrilled for you that I forgot myself,' she said apologetically. 'But why on earth didn't you tell me you were taking the exam? I wouldn't have let on to anyone else 'cos you're me best pal, so you are, and naturally you wouldn't want anyone else to know in case . . . in case . . .'

Jake grinned. 'I know what you mean; in case I didn't gerrit,' he said. 'D'you know how many fellers entered? The letter said that out of a hundred and ninety-eight, me and Freddie Boscombe were top. Not bad, eh?'

'I think you're brilliant, but I always knew you were clever, especially at maths,' Daisy said. 'I'll tell you something though, Jacob Elgin, you're gonna have to talk proper, an' I know very well you can 'cos I've heard you when Dr or Mrs Venables asks you a question.'

'Oh aye, I can crack me jaw with the best,' Jake admitted. 'Ain't all kids the same? Why, I've noticed over and over that you talk real

221

posh to Cynthia and the Venables – and the girls at your school – and real common when you're with me.'

'Do I?' Daisy asked, truly astonished. 'I thought I talked the same all the time, but now you mention it, when Ruth takes me to her aunt's house I'd feel silly talking posh; it would make me . . . oh, seem different, I suppose.'

'There you are then,' Jake said triumphantly as they turned into the confectionery shop. 'Gosh, look at them éclairs! I can't wait to get me gob round one of them!'

True to her promise Daisy had begun to buy Christmas presents, though the habit of economy was so ingrained in her that she never even considered buying from the expensive department stores, such as Lewis's or Blackler's. Instead, she went to them first to see what was in fashion, then tried to buy something similar from the stalls on Byrom Street or the Scotland Road. She had decided to save the money she would have spent on her parents, Annabel, Finn and Dermot, since the postage to America would be a waste of money if they meant to return as soon as they could. For Amanda and Brendan, however, she had bought presents and would send them off so that they arrived well before Christmas Day.

Daisy had meant to buy holly and mistletoe too, and possibly wreaths of ivy from the stalls in Byrom Street, but Jake had regarded her with such horrified astonishment that she had felt obliged to listen to his plans. 'Buy holly and that?' he had squeaked. 'There ain't a kid in Liverpool – 'cept for you – what'd dream of buyin' holly when half the hedges round the big posh houses by Prince's Park are crammed wi' the stuff. Holly's a wild tree, ain't it? If it's wild, then it should be free to everyone and I don't mean to spend me hard-earned cash on something which you can get for nowt if you don't mind a few scratches. Them buggers on Byrom Street charge tuppence or threepence for a tiny bunch, whereas you and me can cut enough to decorate all of Rodney Street in ten or fifteen minutes without payin' a penny.'

'But what if a scuffer sees us chopping holly off someone's hedge?' Daisy had said doubt-fully. 'And what about mistletoe? I know it grows on apple trees – or at least it does in Connemara – but there's none in the Rodney Street garden.'

Jake had agreed that mistletoe would have to be bought but had decreed that the purchase should be left till the last possible minute. ''Cos we don't want the berries to fall off when they get hot inside the house,' he had said wisely. 'As for scuffers seein' us, they won't get the chance 'cos we'll leave cuttin' the holly until late afternoon, when it's dark.'

So they had caught a tram to Prince's Park and

now, as dusk thickened, each child produced a sack which had once contained potatoes, selected a fine thick holly hedge, and began to cut. Jake used his pocket knife, the one his father had given him for getting the scholarship to the Charles Mortimer school, and Daisy used Cynthia's embroidery scissors, or rather she tried to do so. They were fine for twigs, but not much use when it came to a decent-sized branch and Daisy sighed to herself, knowing that if she ruined the wretched things she would have to replace them, which would make the holly as expensive as though it had been purchased from the sellers on Byrom Street after all. However, Jake saw her difficulty and hacked off a couple of branches for her, saying that when they got home she could find something sturdier with which to reduce them to manageable pieces, and presently he announced that they had plenty of holly and some fine garlands of ivy, and could make their way home.

As they hurried away, Daisy cast a glance over her shoulder and was horrified at the raggedness of what had once been a formal hedge, but when she hissed at Jake he said simply that by the time every other kid had followed their example, the hedge would probably look tidy once more. Daisy sighed, but it was too late to argue and anyway hedges would grow again. She meant to present the maids with a bunch each and to decorate the parlour as well as the hall and dining room. With

224

so much holly in their possession they could afford to be generous and she knew Jake meant to beautify the coachman's quarters, even though the Elgins would probably spend most of Christmas in the kitchen of No. 39.

Daisy had been somewhat wary of lugging their sacks aboard the tram, but Jake had no such inhibitions. He stowed the holly away beneath the stair, and when they got off at St Luke's Place they had to move a number of packages belonging to other shoppers before they could reclaim their booty.

'What the devil have you got in there?' the conductor said, unwisely seizing one of the sacks and swearing as the holly pierced his fingers. 'Ouch! I just hope you paid for this little lot.'

Daisy muttered something, then saw that he was grinning, and grinned back before jumping off the platform and hurrying along in Jake's wake. 'You'll get me hanged, you will,' she grumbled as they turned into Rodney Street. 'I thought he'd guessed there were holly in the sacks, but he couldn't have. Poor chap, my scratches sting, but not nearly as much as his do, I bet.'

'Serve him right for being nosy,' Jake said, as they swerved down Mount Street and then into Pilgrim. 'Here, I'll go first, and when I'm on top of the wall you can hand the sacks up. I take it the gate's locked as it's after dark?'

It was, but Jake climbed the wall with his customary ease and straddled the coping, taking the sacks from Daisy's outstretched arms and throwing them into the garden. He remained on top of the wall to give Daisy a hand as she scrambled up beside him, then the pair of them dropped down into the garden, picked up their sacks and made for the house.

They erupted into the kitchen and found everyone assembled there. 'We've got some holly . . .' Jake began, then his voice trailed into silence. He looked wildly around the circle of faces. 'What's up?'

Daisy dropped her sack on the floor and stared across at her aunt. 'What is it, Aunt Jane?' she said, and even to herself her voice sounded strange. 'Is it – is it bad news?'

Aunt Jane came across the kitchen very slowly and took Daisy in her arms. 'Daisy, you must be very brave,' she said, her voice shaking. 'There's been a terrible train crash on the New York to Boston line. Your mammy and daddy, and the children, were in the very last carriage. Oh, my dear, I'm afraid – I'm afraid . . .'

'Are they hurt bad?' Daisy said huskily. But even as she said the words, she knew what the answer would be. She saw the tears trickling down her aunt's cheeks, and the way her mouth worked, though no words came out. She pulled herself free from her aunt's embrace and felt the tears begin to spill from her own eyes. 'They're dead, ain't they?' she said in a thin, reedy voice. 'Is it – is it all of them? The kids as well?'

Aunt Jane's mouth opened again, then closed. She held out a telegram form with printed letters upon it. 'Yes, all of them,' she whispered.

Chapter Seven

Cynthia did not know what had woken her and for a moment she simply lay in her bed, wondering why she felt so unhappy. She remembered how she had felt when her mama had died and Goody had decided to retire rather than move to the Venables' home in Liverpool. But that had been a long time ago; surely she could not still feel . . . abruptly, the happenings of the previous day came flooding back. She had been sitting with her aunt in the room they called her office when there had been a ring at the doorbell. Cynthia had been awaiting the delivery of a new dress and had jumped to her feet and run to the door, easily beating Biddy bound on the same errand. But instead of a man bearing the the longed-for box, a small boy in a navy uniform, with a round pillbox hat on his head, had stood before her. 'Telegram for Miss Dalton,' he had said. He handed the envelope over. 'Will there be a reply?'

'I don't know . . .' Cynthia had been beginning, when a step sounded in the hall behind her. She had turned, and there was the housekeeper, a tray of tea in her hands.

'Oh, Miss Dalton, there's a telegram for you and

the boy wants to know if there's a reply,' Cynthia had said. She had looked at the tray. 'Shall I take that whilst you open it?'

Thinking back now, Cynthia felt a stab of real pain as she remembered how eagerly the older woman had slit open the envelope, speaking as she did so. 'Oh, it must be from my sister . . . I do hope this means that they're about to set out on the voyage home . . .'

Her voice had trailed off, and even as Cynthia had glanced at her face she had seen the colour drain out of it, had seen Miss Dalton sway, and then crash to the floor. Cynthia herself, forgetting the tray in her hands, had started forward, and the entire contents of the tray had slid on to the hall tiles, soaking the telegram, still in Miss Dalton's hand, with a mixture of tea, milk and sugar. At the sound of the breaking china, Mrs Venables had emerged from her office. 'What on earth . . . ?' she had begun, then had bent and twitched the telegram from her housekeeper's nerveless fingers. She read it, gave a strangled gasp, and then turned to her niece. 'Fetch your uncle,' she had commanded, kneeling down, regardless of broken china and pools of milk and tea. 'She's had the most terrible shock . . . the telegram says the Kildares have been killed in a train crash in America. Oh, my God, where's Daisy?'

From that moment on, the day had become a nightmare. The news had had to be broken to Daisy

when she and Jake had got back from their expedition, and to Cynthia's surprise, though her friend
had wept a little, she had not given way to grief
in the way that Miss Dalton had when she recovered from her faint. In fact, Daisy had said, very
quietly, that she needed to be alone and had left
the kitchen and gone straight to their bedroom.
Cynthia had followed her, hoping to be of some
use, but Daisy had repulsed her, though not
unkindly, and Cynthia had respected her wishes
and had spent the evening with her aunt and uncle,
discussing how best they could help aunt and niece
to come to terms with the terrible tragedy.

When Cynthia had at last returned to their
bedroom, Daisy had appeared to be fast asleep, so
Cynthia had crept into bed and pulled the covers
up to her ears. She had not expected to be able to
sleep herself, but had eventually done so, and now
she wondered why she had woken so early, since
the room was still in darkness. Had Daisy stirred?
Or perhaps got out of bed and gone down to the
lavatory? She glanced across at the other bed and
saw that it was empty, and suddenly she knew,
with absolute certainty, that Daisy had not just left
the room, but had done so some time before.

Cynthia got out of her own bed and went across
to Daisy's. She put a hand on the pillow and felt
how cold it was, and even in the dim light of a
winter's dawn she saw that the clothes which Daisy
had taken off and piled upon her chair were
missing. The only garment remaining was Daisy's

nightdress, neatly folded, and her scuffed scarlet slippers.

Poor Cynthia felt that she ought to rouse the household, but first she searched to make sure that her friend had not curled up in a chair somewhere. Then it occurred to her that if Daisy had left the house, she had probably done so through the side door rather than the front. She investigated and found the side door not only unlocked and unbolted, but still a trifle ajar. She had not dressed, but had pulled on her thick woollen dressing gown and thrust her feet into her slippers, so now she pushed the door open and stepped out into the early grey light. She glanced across the cobbled yard to the coachman's quarters and wondered, fleetingly, why they still used the old name since there were no sleek horses or handsome coaches kept there, but only the gleaming motor car and Jake's old bicycle. Should she climb the stairs up to the flat and tap on the door to wake Elgin and Jake? She realised that someone must be told, and as soon as possible, of Daisy's flight. It would be sensible to go first to the coachman's quarters, since if anyone knew Daisy's mind, it was Jake. He might be able to guess where she would go, and at that moment horrid thoughts of Daisy sleep-walking down to the docks, or trying to stow away aboard a ship bound for America, were chasing themselves through Cynthia's frightened mind.

She crossed the cobbles, feeling the cold of the frost strike up through the thin soles of her slippers, and found that she longed to turn tail and return to her bed. She could cuddle down beneath the covers and pretend to wake for the first time when the alarm went off. But even as the thought entered her head, she was mounting the stairs and banging on the Elgins' door, knowing she could not possibly let Daisy down.

It was Jake who came to the door, rubbing the sleep from his eyes. He stared at Cynthia uncomprehendingly for a moment, then appeared to take in the words which she kept repeating. 'Daisy's gone. Daisy's gone. Her clothes have gone, and her boots. I've looked everywhere. She's gone.'

Jake gave a quick, decisive nod, then turned away. 'I'll get dressed and wake me dad,' he called over his shoulder. You go back and rouse the household . . . everyone, mind. Don't worry, we'll find her.'

Daisy had not expected to go to sleep, for her misery was so deep and intense that sleep seemed impossible. Yet at some stage in the night she must have dropped off from sheer exhaustion for she immediately found herself back in fairy-tale land, a balloon once more, one of a brightly coloured bunch. Feeling a strange anxiety which she could not explain, she glanced around her and saw with immense relief that her parents and brothers and sisters surrounded her. Her mother said cheerily: 'Here we are again, alanna, the whole family. A shame it is that we can only meet up here, but sure and isn't it better than not meeting at all?'

'And the balloon lady's awful good, awful kind,' her father contributed. 'We only float away when our time comes; she makes sure of that.'

Daisy glanced down at the fat old balloon woman sitting on the green hill and holding the strings of all the balloons in a capable hand. And for the first time, the balloon woman looked up at her. Daisy saw round rosy cheeks and a pair of dark twinkling eyes, but instead of the smile she expected she saw such wild sorrow in the old woman's face that she turned at once to her father for an explanation. Before she could open her mouth, however, she realised that the old woman must have released her parents' strings, for their balloons, and those of Annabel, Finn and Dermot, were already well above her head. As she watched, the beautiful sunny day disappeared, the sky darkened and the balloons began to ascend, making for the stars at an incredible rate and ignoring her cries for them to return.

Then she awoke, heart pattering and tears running down her cheeks, for the dream was still with her and the painful knowledge that she would never again see her parents or her younger sister and brothers was like a knife in her heart. The room was in darkness and she knew from the heavy breathing emanating from the next bed that Cynthia was asleep beside her. Waking thus, for a few seconds, she merely wondered what had disturbed her, for Daisy was one of those lucky people who fall asleep as soon as their head touches the pillow, and wake only when either increasing daylight, or the shrilling of an alarm, announces that the night is over. She was still wondering when the recollection of the dream and the knowledge of the previous day's happenings opened up before her like a great black pit, and all the misery, the inconsolable sense of loss, came flooding back. The pain of the sudden revelation was so potent, so strong, that she sat up in bed, unable to remain physically cosy and comfortable when her mind was icy cold and full of her tragedy.

Without really considering what she was doing, she slipped out of bed, wincing as warm feet met icy linoleum and the chill air of the bedroom brought goose flesh pimpling up all over her body. Somehow it seemed fitting to feel cold so that her body suffered a little as her mind was suffering. For a moment she simply stood beside her bed, beginning to shiver; then Cynthia gave a little mumbling moan and shifted uneasily, and the movement galvanised Daisy into action. She pulled her nightdress over her head, folded it neatly and laid it on the chair, then grabbed her clothes and crept softly out of the room, closing the door gently behind her. Outside, the landing was in complete darkness and for a moment she hesitated there. What could she do? She had no idea of the time but guessed it was very late, or more probably very early, since when Dr Venables was on call he seldom went to bed before midnight. She told herself she had no wish for company yet knew,

234

perversely, that had Aunt Jane or Mrs Venables appeared she would have gone to them for whatever comfort they could offer.

Daisy tiptoed to the head of the stairs and looked down them into the landing below. No light glimmered; everyone slept. Slowly, she crossed the landing and went into the schoolroom. The curtains had not been drawn and she could read the time on the mantel clock by the faint starlight. Ten past two. It would be four hours at least before the servants were stirring, even longer before Cynthia and the Venables awoke. Plenty of time, she thought; but time for what? She had no idea, but realised, suddenly, that she must get away. In this house, as soon as it grew light, there would be sympathetic faces, voices mouthing meaningless phrases about heaven . . . suffer the little children . . . she knew, abruptly, that for the moment at any rate such comfort was not for her. She could see Dermot's round rosy face in her mind's eye as clearly as she had seen him two years previously. Innocence had shone from him, his little face smiled at the thought of the simplest treat. He and Finn had had no toys, but had played games with stones or shells from the shore, had learned little poems and songs which Annabel had taught them, had been content with whatever came their way. America must have been a huge adventure . . . and to end like that!

Without really being aware of what she was doing, Daisy had dressed herself. It seemed to her that movement helped, because though your mind continued to work as you pulled on woollen stockings, a pleated skirt and a thick jersey, it was better than lying in bed and letting the horror of it all overcome you. On the ground floor, in the little cloakroom by the side door, were her coat and her stout boots. She stole down the stairs and pulled on the boots, lacing them with fingers which trembled with cold. Then she reached her coat down from its hook and put it on. The outer door was locked and bolted, but the bolts had been recently oiled and she slid them back soundlessly, and the key turned in the lock without so much as a click. As Daisy pushed the door open the cold air rushed in. She felt faintly surprised since she was ice cold herself, but turned to twitch a scarf off one of the pegs and wrapped it round her head and neck, then stepped out into the yard. It really was bitterly cold. The cobbles were rimed with ice and she crossed them carefully, for despite her preoccupation she did not wish to fall, perhaps breaking a leg.

She gained the garden path without mishap and reached the back gate. It was locked and Mr Pilcher had the key but Daisy scaled the wall without a second thought, sitting for a moment on the coping and glancing rather doubtfully up at the heavens. She knew that frost was always accompanied by a clear sky, but now the stars and the moon, which had shone when she first woke, were hidden by thick and heavy clouds. Daisy, a country child, slid

236

down into Pilgrim Street and stood for a moment, sniffing the air. She could smell a change coming in the weather, but such a change would not alter her resolve. She had to get right away from the house in Rodney Street before she could come to terms with the terrible thing that had happened, and she knew instinctively that to face the deep and frightening loneliness which awaited her she must spend some time alone.

She thrust her hands into the pockets of her overcoat and felt the soft navy-blue gloves which Aunt Jane had knitted for her the previous Christmas. For a moment, guilt stabbed at her; Aunt Jane would be desperately worried to find her missing when she woke. I should have left her a note, Daisy thought, yet how could I possibly have done so? If I cannot explain even to myself why I had to leave Rodney Street, then how could I possibly explain to someone else?

By the time this thought had entered her head, she was making her way along Upper Duke Street. There was not a soul about, no trams rattling along their rails, no carter whipping up his horse, no motor van carrying vegetables or bread disturbing the silence. Suddenly, Daisy longed for the country, for a lane where the trees overhead would stand stark against the sky, for the sight of a flock of sheep, their fleeces sparkling with frost as they huddled together, their breath forming a mist, their small sharp hooves stamping the frozen grasses. In the country there would be ponds with ducks skittering on the ice, streams whose chuckling movements would be temporarily silenced. She would make for the country, simply walking until she reached it, and by the time she did so she might have managed to make sense of what had happened. If, as Mrs Venables had tried to say the previous evening, God had loved the Kildare family so much that He had taken them to live with Him in heaven, then why had He not taken Daisy also? Why had He left her here to suffer the unbearable loneliness and misery which was now her lot?

Daisy had no idea in which direction the country lay, nor in fact what she would do when she reached it, so she just kept on walking. As the night eased towards morning, lights began to appear in windows. People emerged from houses and hurried off to begin their day's work. Milk carts rattled past, the horses' breath steaming in the cold air, their hooves clattering on the frosty cobbles. Daisy walked briskly now, not only in order to keep warm, but also because instinct told her that if she wished to remain unnoticed, she must not wander aimlessly.

Daylight came, though it was a cold, grey light, and Daisy, looking around her, saw more gardens and trees, and guessed that she was traversing the suburbs, and the country could not be far off. Presently, it began to snow.

They had searched the neighbourhood as thoroughly as possible, and Aunt Jane had alerted the police, but by the time the snow started there had not been one sighting of a small dark-haired girl in a navy-blue coat, with a thick navy-blue scarf wrapped round her neck and possibly over her head. When she had first been told, Aunt Jane had succumbed to hysterics, but Dr Venables had given her a draught which had soothed her, and now the staff, including Jake and his father, were sitting round the kitchen table, devouring an enormous cooked breakfast and discussing what best to do next.

Aunt Jane glanced at the faces surrounding her and saw, with a little clutch of the heart, the sympathy and concern writ large on every countenance. Even Cynthia's. She caught the girl's eye and gave her a grateful smile, thinking guiltily that she had never really liked the child, until now. To be sure, at first Cynthia and Daisy had not got along, but she knew they had been good friends for the past couple of years and thought, remorsefully, that she had been so taken up with Daisy she had scarcely noticed Cynthia. She would know better in future. The girl had had the courage to wake the whole household at four in the morning, and Jane knew that she herself, at Cynthia's age, would have been extremely reluctant to awaken one person, let alone almost a dozen.

'She'll make her way to Ireland, I'm sure of it,' Aunt Jane said now, not for the first time that morning. She had both hands wrapped round a mug of tea and had eaten almost nothing from the plate of eggs, bacon, fried bread and black pudding which Cook had set before her. 'Poor little soul, I guess she'll have stowed away aboard the Irish ferry, as they do in books. But what'll she do when she lands? She'll have to cross the whole country to get to Connemara . . . I must go after her, I must!'

Ruth looked up from her own breakfast to shake her head at the older woman. 'She won't have done no such thing,' she said roundly. 'If she's a-going to stow away, she'll have got on a ship to America, and you can't folly her there 'cos there's no tellin' where she might have gone, not once she lands.'

'I don't think you can stow away to America, 'cos I've heared from pals about somewhere called Ellis Island, where they checks passports and papers and that,' Cook said. She turned to Aunt Jane. 'I reckon the scuffers will check on the Irish ferries, just in case. And now, Miss Dalton, you eat that good breakfast else you won't have the strength to go out lookin' again, like you said you was goin' to do.'

Aunt Jane obediently picked up her knife and fork and began to eat, then laid them down again. 'If it weren't for the snow I wouldn't be so worried,' she said. 'But if it continues to fall, and it don't show no sign of stopping, I keep getting this horrible picture . . .' Her voice trailed away.

Cynthia, seated beside the housekeeper and glancing from face to face as each person spoke, cleared her throat. 'If she goes to Ireland, then I suppose she'll go to Galway, to her sister Amanda,' she said nervously. 'You could send a telegram, Miss Dalton, asking Amanda to let you know if Daisy turns up, or at least explaining that she has gone missing. Then Amanda could get a search going in Ireland. I'm sure the police there know what route she's likeliest to take, and will find her pretty quickly.'

'You're a bright one, you are,' Cook said, smiling at Cynthia. 'We should have thought of that.'

Aunt Jane sighed. 'I telegraphed Amanda and Brendan with the dreadful news yesterday,' she said. 'I was afraid that the lawyer who contacted me might not have realised that the two older Kildare children were still in Connemara. Yes, I think Cynthia is right. I'll go to the telegraph office as soon as I've finished my breakfast.' She glanced towards the window as she spoke and gave a little moan at the sight of the flakes descending rapidly from the clouds overhead. 'And Daisy was so looking forward to today, it being the last day of the term. I wonder . . . you don't suppose she'll go into school later? She's mortal fond of her teachers; she might well turn to one of them . . .'

'Aye, she might,' Mr Elgin said. It was the first time he had spoken and now he reached across and squeezed Aunt Jane's hand. 'I've got to know Daisy pretty well and she's a sensible kid. I've listened to wild talk round this table about her walking into the docks and drowning, or stowing away on a ship to America, or doing something similar, and none of it sounds like Daisy to me.

241

So Jake and meself will take the car and go to any likely spots where Jake and Daisy have gone in the past. The rest of you can keep asking questions and searching nearer home.' He smiled at Aunt Jane. 'Wharrabout New Brighton? We had a grand time there, as I recall; she might want to go back, like going back to happier times. But before we do anything else, I think we owe it to Cook, and ourselves, to eat every scrap of this breakfast.'

When the food was finished, Cynthia said rather regretfully that she supposed she had better go back to her aunt and tell her what had been decided, and the party broke up. Aunt Jane, struggling into her coat, realised that despite her worry she felt better for the hot meal inside her, and for the advice and help which everyone had offered. Suddenly, hope blossomed and it was with a lighter heart that she prepared to make her way to Rathbone Street and the telegraph office.

Bob and Jake got into the car and the chauffeur drove with great care across the slippery cobbles, for the snow was laying, as far as the big double wooden doors which led on to Pilgrim Street. He handed Jake his key and the boy hopped out to unlock and open them, staying to swing the big doors shut again. They were never locked during the day when Pilcher was working somewhere in the grounds, but Bob and Pilcher both had a key, and always locked up at night. Jake climbed back into his seat, but when the car reached the intersection with Upper Duke Street he clutched at his father's arm. 'Hang on a minute, Pa,' he said urgently. 'There's something I've got to ask you, though I feels a bit awkward, like. But it's important now, so I hopes you won't get angry. You remember when my mam died?'

'Course I does,' Bob Elgin said gruffly. He did not add that it had taken him years to rid his mind of the dreadful moment when he had tiptoed into the bedroom with a cup of tea and found his sick wife cold and white as the snow which was even now falling, her bright hair spread out on the pillow, and with that in her face which told him at once that she had gone beyond recall. He could acknowledge now that the pain had lessened with every passing year, but the recollection still stabbed him like a knife. His son, however, had only been two years old, and his presence had helped Bob to face up to life without his beloved Chrissy. At first, of course, he had asked constantly for his mammy, but so far as Bob could recall he had not so much as mentioned her for many years, so it was with some surprise that he waited for his son's next remark.

'What did you do, Pa, after she died?'

There was a long silence whilst Bob Elgin thought back to that dreadful day. He could understand Jake's interest; the boy must be thinking that his father's experience might give him a clue to how Daisy would behave.

'Dad?' Jake's voice was tentative. 'If you'd rather not say . . . it's just that I were hopin' you might know better'n anyone how Daisy feels and what she'll do. But if you don't . . .'

Bob sighed. 'It'll sound pretty stupid,' he warned. 'But I simply walked out of the house, called to the landlady to give an eye to you, and set off. I didn't have any destination in mind or any plan, come to that. I reckon I were simply escaping, running away. It was October, and when I got into the country I left the road and walked through some woods. I remember the ground was thick with fallen leaves and someone had lit a bonfire. The smell of the smoke drifting through the air made me think of happier times, but I just kept walking. I must have covered miles and miles, because it got dark and I got pretty cold.'

He hesitated, remembering. He had turned back in the end because he had had an odd experience. He had been passing through a small village and it must have been early the following morning because lights were coming on as the cottagers prepared for the day ahead, and the smell of food cooking had come to his nostrils. For the first time he realised that he had eaten nothing for forty-eight hours and that he was far from home, yet still the urge to escape from the memory of that motionless figure in the bed haunted him. He had stopped, staring indecisively about him; what to do, what to do? And then he had heard a voice, though afterwards he thought that it must have come from inside his head. The voice had been light, gay, yet full of reproach. 'Robert Elgin, what the devil are you doing, miles from home, with your belly flapping against your backbone and no idea of where you are! Have you forgotten our little lad? There's not much I can do for him now, but you've got to be mother and father to Jake, so just you pull yourself together.'

Bob had looked wildly round him, his heart lifting, though he knew he would see nothing. 'Chrissy?' he had whispered. 'Chrissy, is that you? I – I've not forgot Jake, he's with Ruby downstairs. But I don't know as I can manage without you.'

The voice which had answered him was wistful, yet there had still been gaiety in it. 'Oh, Bob, I wish . . . but you'll manage just fine. You're strong and loving and I know you'll take good care of our little boy.'

Once more, Bob had looked wildly round him, and even as the voice had faded into the whisper of the wind in the trees he was turning to retrace his steps. He had not wasted time wondering about the voice; was it conscience, or a miracle, or simply his imagination, stirred into activity by hunger and grief? But whatever it was, he knew it had spoken the truth; his place at this sad time was with his little son.

'Dad?' Jake said again. 'Was you gone long? I

don't remember anything about that time, 'cept you bought me a lovely red tricycle.'

Bob chuckled reminiscently. 'That perishin' tricycle! If you took it to pieces once, you took it to pieces a dozen times.'

'Yes, and when I was old enough you taught me how to put it together,' Jake reminded his father. 'But you've not told me what made you turn back. It's important, Pa, or it may be.'

Bob hesitated. 'I suppose I could say that I suddenly remembered I'd got a little lad waiting for me,' he said slowly. 'I'd gone miles, trying to make sense of what had happened. I was right out in the country when I came to meself, and turned back.' He glanced at his son and saw Jake giving a decisive nod. 'D'you think that's what Daisy'll do? Just walk?'

'I reckon,' Jake said. 'You could say she's lost everything, just like you had when me mam died, so it's on the cards that she'll want to get away. I never did believe she'd go to Ireland, nor America. In fact the only question, Pa, is whether she turned right or left when she reached Upper Dukey.'

'We'll try both, but I believe we'll go right first because that's the way I went, all them years ago,' Bob said, as he steered the car across the square by the Sailors' Home and drove with extra care through the swirling flakes and into Paradise Street. The volume of traffic had kept the roads pretty clear, but the cobbles were still icy. 'Keep your eyes peeled, Jake, because for all we know she might see sense a lot quicker than I did and be on her way home by now.'

Daisy emerged into what she considered real country at what was probably around mid-morning, though she had no idea of the time. She had bought a couple of buns with some loose change she found in her pocket and had had some water from a drinking fountain, so she felt no hunger or thirst, just the sense of helpless misery which had haunted her from the start of her walk. She saw that the snow lay thicker here because there was not so much traffic, and she realised as well that she must be heading away from the sea since her father had always told her that it was the salt in the breeze which kept the coastal strip of Connemara free from the snow which piled up on the moors and the Twelve Bens. The thought of her father hurt so much that she stopped in her tracks. She wondered, dully, how Brendan and Amanda were coping, whether she should have turned to them rather than simply taking off, running away. But what would be the use? Even if she went to Ireland, neither her brother nor her sister could take on the responsibility of a girl her age. Amanda had a good job and a young man who hoped to marry her one day, and Brendan had a tiny room in a cheap lodging house, where he stayed when not aboard his distant-waters trawler, for he had recently gained a place as

247

decky-learner aboard the *Venturer*, a big modern vessel which sailed from Galway right up to the icy seas near the pole.

So I really am alone, Daisy thought without surprise. The Venables are very kind but they owe me nothing. There's Aunt Jane, who would do everything to help me, but she's just an aunt; it's not the same. I want my mammy and daddy, and my little sister and brothers. I want Benmacraig and a future to be spent with people I love. Aunt Jane and Mrs Venables talked about heaven, and a loving God, and at school they say that God is a father and we are His children, but I think that's just talk. Oh, Daisy Kildare, you can't think straight so stop trying and just keep walking! Perhaps you'll make sense of it all in time, if you walk far enough and fast enough.

Dusk came. The snow had ceased to fall, but Daisy was bitterly cold and aware that her boots were letting wet in through the lacings. Snow had long ago soaked through her scarf and her coat was sodden. The previous night, darkness had not worried her, perhaps because she had been in city streets, but now she felt considerable unease. She had somehow got on to a narrow lane, though she was unaware of having changed direction, and when snow came sliding from a tree overhead and plummeted to the ground, she was so frightened that she dived into the ditch and found herself up to her knees in melting snow water. Though the thaw had started earlier, as dusk fell it grew steadily colder, and an icy shell had formed over the soft melting stuff. Hauling herself out of the ditch, Daisy realised that she was sobbing with fright, and also realised that no matter how lonely, miserable and bereft she felt, she did not want to die. Earlier she had told herself that she longed for death, but this was not true. Yet if she gave in now, she could easily freeze to death.

So she turned in her tracks and began to retrace her steps, though she was so weary, wet and cold that she could hardly walk in a straight line. Presently, spotting a low, hunched dwelling to one side of the road, she staggered towards it, reached the low doorway, and banged feebly upon it. When the door abruptly opened inwards, she simply collapsed upon the rough earth floor, hearing the startled words: 'My word, wharrever have we here? Mabel, stoke up the fire and pull the kettle over the flame. There's a dead girl come a-calling, or nigh on dead at any rate.'

Daisy tried to sit up, to explain, but it was several moments before she was able to move, and then the bent old man, and the old woman he had addressed as Mabel, lifted her on to a sagging sofa and Mabel, without ceremony, stripped her of her soaking garments, wrapped her in a rough wool blanket, and held a mug of hot sweet tea to her lips. Daisy gulped the drink gratefully, then gave an enormous yawn. 'You'm wore out, queen, as well as clemmed and starved wi' cold,' Mabel said comfortingly. 'I don't suppose you know but it's past ten o'clock; lucky it is for you that my Will'm is a light sleeper 'cos I never heard a thing. But you settle down an' sleep now; you can tell us how you come here tomorrow.'

Daisy tried to explain, to thank them, but she was far too tired and was asleep before she had managed a word. She awoke next morning to find the fire blazing in the hearth and her hosts eating porridge at the kitchen table. To her delight and surprise, all her clothing, even the heavy coat and lace-up leather boots, had been dried whilst she slept, and when she sat up and began to thank her rescuers Mabel told her to hold her noise and get herself into their bedroom, so's to be dressed respectable before she joined them for breakfast. Daisy complied and presently came shyly back into the room and sat down at the rough wooden table. As she ate her porridge, she explained that she had gone for a long walk to try to come to terms with the loss of her parents, who had been killed in a railway accident, but she had gone astray somewhere and lost herself.

Mabel and William nodded understandingly. 'That's a terrible thing to happen to anyone,' William said. 'Good thing you're young and strong, missy, 'cos you were soaked to the skin and cold as ice when I brung you in. Now you'll have to tell us your name and where you'm come from so we can inform your folks, 'cos you can't simply set out to walk back the way you come. It's thawin' nicely, but there'll be a deal o' water on the roads, and I reckon you've come a fair way.'

Mabel shook her head and tutted disapprovingly. 'She ain't got no folks, you old fool, didn't you hear what she said?' She turned to Daisy. 'But you must have come from somewhere; stands to reason you must.'

Daisy sighed. 'I'm living with my Aunt Jane; she'll take care of me now my mammy and daddy have gone,' she said heavily. 'I don't have much money, but I think I've enough for a bus or tram ride back into the city. I'd rather do that than cause you any more trouble. You've been so good and you needn't worry that I won't go home, 'cos I promise you I will.'

The old man looked dubious but Mabel, after giving Daisy a long hard stare, nodded slowly. 'The trams don't come out this far, but there's a bus into Liverpool, goes by the end of our lane, in about an hour,' she said. 'How much money have you got?'

'Sixpence. Is that enough?' Daisy said baldly, and was relieved when both the old people nodded.

'Right you are; we'll walk down with 'ee to the bus and see you aboard,' Mabel said. 'Now get outside o' that porridge and the mug o' tea, then we'll set off, for we walks slow, Will'm and me.'

The bus was half full but Daisy had no difficulty in getting a window seat, and waved vigorously to the old couple as the vehicle drew away. Mabel had insisted upon lending her a shilling, though she was pretty sure that sixpence would cover the fare, because as she said, you never knew when you might need the odd copper or two. 'And besides,' she had added with a twinkle, 'if I lends you money, I knows you'll want to pay me back 'cos I can tell you're an honest gal, queen. And when you come to give me my shillin', we'll learn how you'm gettin' on, for it ain't every night a poor half-frozen little fledglin' lands on our doorstep.'

'I'd come and see you again with or without the shilling, because you saved my life last night and I'll be grateful to you both for the rest of my days,' Daisy had said sincerely. 'If my mammy and daddy were here . . . but Aunt Jane will want to thank you in their place, I'm sure.'

Both old people had smiled gap-toothed grins, assuring her that they had been thanked enough already. Then they had taken her to the end of the lane and now here she was, on the rattling old bus, facing the fact that she must have worried and upset a lot of people, and knowing that she would find it extremely difficult to explain what she had done and why she had done it.

She was bending her mind to the problem when the bus jerked to a stop and after a short pause someone slid into the seat beside her. Not wanting to talk, Daisy continued to stare out of the window, but a voice in her ear said: 'Well I'm blessed, if it's not little Miss Curly Top! Just what are you doing on my bus, pray?'

Startled, Daisy turned her head to gaze at her companion. He was a tall, red-haired lad of fifteen or so, with a great many freckles, greenish hazel eyes and a long, humorous chin. Daisy frowned. She did not know him from Adam, yet he must have thought he knew her, unless of course he travelled so often on this bus that he had spotted her as the only stranger aboard.

'Well? Cat got your tongue? Or has nobody taught you that a civil question demands a civil answer?'

Daisy was about to tell him, indignantly, that she had not fully understood his question when she saw his hazel eyes twinkling and realised that he was joking. 'I'm sorry, I didn't know this was *your* bus,' she said, returning his smile. 'But how did you know I'm not usually aboard? And why did you call me Miss Curly Top? I'm jolly sure I've never set eyes on you before!'

'No, you probably wouldn't have seen me, but I see you most days, or most schooldays at any rate,' the boy said tantalisingly. 'Sometimes you walk with a girl with yellow hair done up in two plaits, sometimes with a very tall girl who stoops a bit, but mostly I've seen you with a lad a bit older than you. He's got very black hair and eyes.'

The truth burst like sunlight into Daisy's mind. 'You must be on the bus that comes along Dukey,' she said triumphantly. 'Of course, what an idiot

253

I am; that's why you said *my* bus. But you haven't answered *my* question, either. Why did you call me Miss Curly Top?'

'Because in the summer you push your school hat off the back of your head so it's only held on by the elastic under your chin. Most girls keep their hats on so I never really notice their hair, but yours is in plain view. Even in winter, you often push your hat back. So my pal Simon and myself have always called you Miss Curly Top. What's your real name, by the way? I'm Tony Fordham.'

'I'm Daisy Kildare,' Daisy said. 'When term starts again, I'll keep an eye open and give you a wave as you go past. But where are you off to now, if not to school? And I can see you're not going there because you aren't wearing your cap.'

'How very observant of you to notice that I'm wearing civvies and not uniform, Miss Cur— Miss Kildare,' Tony said easily. 'Of course I'm not going to school, it's the holidays, halfwit. Actually, I'm going to Lewis's to buy my mother's Christmas present.' He cocked a sandy eyebrow. 'Want to come along?'

For a moment Daisy was truly tempted. She knew enough about boys to realise that his calling her a halfwit meant acceptance and she also realised, with a definite lifting of the heart, that because Tony knew nothing of the events which had been uppermost in her mind she could pretend that they had not happened, could respond to him as though she were the Daisy of three days ago, carefree, smiling and friendly with anyone who tossed her a kind remark. But it really would not do to accompany him to Lewis's. She owed it to Aunt Jane, the Venables and the rest of the household to go straight home and apologise to them for running off without a word.

So she shook her head regretfully. 'I'd love to come shopping with you but I've simply got to get home,' she said. 'But maybe we could meet up another day?'

Her companion pulled a face. 'I don't like "maybe",' he said gloomily. 'Tell you what, if you come to Lewis's with me, I'll treat you to the biggest ice cream in the store. I hate shopping alone, particularly for women's stuff.'

Daisy was beginning to tell him, all over again, that she had to get home when she saw that they were approaching her stop. Hastily, she stood up. 'Here's where I get off,' she said. 'Do you mind . . . ?'

She expected him to stand up and let her go past him, but instead he walked down the aisle ahead of her, jumped off the platform when the bus stopped, and held out his hand to help her down. 'I'll walk you home and we can discuss our next meeting . . .' he was beginning, when a car drew up with a screech of brakes, and a figure hurtled from the front passenger seat.

Daisy found herself grabbed and hugged tightly by Aunt Jane, who had tears of relief running down her cheeks. 'Where have you been, chuck?' she said, with a break in her voice. 'We've been that worried . . .' As she spoke, she was hustling Daisy towards the car where Jake and his father sat, beaming at her. Daisy began to say that she must tell her new friend that she was not being kidnapped or abducted, but before she could even begin to explain her aunt thrust her into the car and climbed back into the passenger seat. Mr Elgin slammed the car into gear, thrust his hand out of the window to indicate that he was pulling out, and joined the stream of traffic making its way down Upper Duke Street.

Daisy, screwing her head round at an uncomfortable angle, saw Tony, mouth open, eyes wide, staring after the car, and hastily gave him what she hoped was a reassuring wave through the rear window. Then she turned back and began to apologise to Aunt Jane for the worry she knew she must have caused, but Jake cut across her words, giving her a light punch on the shoulder as he did so. 'Well, you *are* a one!' he said reproachfully. 'Here's every scuffer in Liverpool searchin' for you, to say nothing of everyone at number thirty-nine, and you gerroff a perishin' bus, cool as a cucumber, with some smart feller in tow. You've got some explainin' to do, Daisy Kildare! Who is that feller? C'mon, explain.'

'I don't have to explain to *you*,' Daisy said frostily. 'But I'll tell Aunt Jane all about it when we get back home.' She leaned forward to address her aunt. 'I'm awful sorry, Aunt Jane, to have worried you so, but to tell you the truth, I don't think I was in my right mind, or at any rate I wasn't thinking straight. I just set out walking, and kept going until I was miles out in the country. I was pretty tired by then and darkness was coming on, so I went to a cottage and the old couple put me up for the night. They were ever so kind, gave me a hot drink and dried my clothes round their fire, and then this morning they lent me some money and walked me down to the bus stop. And here I am!'

Aunt Jane turned and squeezed her niece's hand. 'I think I can understand, but oh, love, why didn't you wake someone, tell us what you were going to do?' she said distractedly. 'Cynthia gave the alarm at four in the morning, when she woke to find your bed empty. We searched and searched . . . the snow was laying and it was bitterly cold . . . dreadful things happen to girls . . . we thought of the docks, wondered if you'd tried to get back to Ireland, go to America . . .'

'Don't!' Daisy said sharply. 'Please don't say any more, Aunt, you're bringing it all back. I – I have to forget those dreadful two days. I've told you what happened and I don't want to talk about it any more.'

Daisy saw her aunt glance quickly across at Mr Elgin, saw his hand leave the steering wheel for an instant to take Aunt Jane's in a comforting grasp. Then he slowed the car, turned into Pilgrim Street, and drew to a halt, turning in his seat so that he could look Daisy in the eyes. 'I know what you're feeling, queen, because it happened to me when my Chrissy died,' he said quietly. 'Like you, I walked myself into the ground, but I was a whole lot older and I had me laddo there' – he jerked a thumb at his son – 'to keep me from going round the bend. My wife had told me, you see, that I would have to be mother and father to Jake and her words made a deep impression. So as soon as I could think straight, I turned and came back home, and though you won't believe me, luv, the pain eases as time goes by, especially if you've the strength of will to remember the good times, not with grief but with pleasure. Can you do that, do you think?'

'I'll try,' Daisy said simply. 'There were so many good times . . . though the past four years were pretty grim for Mammy and Daddy. But I don't mean to think about that or – or the train crash, because it's happened and no one can turn back time.'

Mr Elgin nodded. 'You'll do,' he said. 'Open the gates, Jake, there's a good lad.'

'In a minute, but there's a question I want answered first,' Jake said. 'He turned to Daisy. 'Who was the feller who got off the bus with you? You said an old couple took you in, but I hopes as you ain't goin' to try to kid me that he were old, 'cos he weren't. And you waved to him; I seen you.'

'His name's Tony Fordham and he sat next to

me on the bus, and we got talking because he remembered seeing me with Clare and Lucy – and with you,' Daisy said. 'He was really nice, and wanted me to go shopping with him to buy a present for his mum, only I wouldn't, of course, because I knew I must get home so Aunt could stop worrying.'

'Ah, that explains it,' Jake said. 'He looked bleedin' rich – well worth knowing if you ask me.'

Aunt Jane tutted. 'Language, Jake,' she said reprovingly. 'You know what your father and meself have been telling you: if you want to make a good impression at that posh school, you'll have to mind your manners.'

Jake gave a contemptuous sniff. 'I'm a genius, I am,' he said, opening the car door and sliding out into the cold. 'The fellers are already queuing up to be pally with a genius, I'm tellin' you.' He hurried over and flung open the big double doors, gestured his father inside, then slammed them shut and ran after the car, easily overtaking it as his father inched it across the cobbles, still splattered with snow and puddles. He opened the door for Aunt Jane and helped her out, then tried to do the same for Daisy, though she ignored his proffered hand and hurried into the house behind her aunt. They entered the cosy kitchen and Daisy steeled herself as every face turned in her direction and voices demanded to know whether she was all right, where she had been, and how the Elgins and Aunt Jane had managed to find her.

Daisy took a deep breath but Mr Elgin, who had followed her in, forestalled her. 'No point in telling a story more than once,' he said quietly. 'I'll fetch Mrs Venables and young Cynthia down here so Daisy can get it all over with in one go. Dr Venables will still be in surgery, but I'm sure Mrs Ven will explain when he's free.' He smiled pleasantly across at Cook. 'How about some buttered scones and a hot cup of tea all round?' he suggested. 'It's mortal cold out and Jane and I missed breakfast to search for the young 'un, so we could both do with a bite.'

Chapter Eight
Summer 1936

When Jake heard a shout from the yard below him, he had just laid down his pen after completing a letter of application, for he was hoping to get a holiday job, preferably in one of the big insurance offices on Exchange Flags, where he knew they needed holiday cover, and often employed pupils from Charlie's. Carefully, not hurrying, he blotted the page, then went across to the window. He knew it could not be Daisy, because she and Aunt Jane had left for Ireland several days earlier and besides, he was almost sure he recognised the shout. Peering through the rather dusty panes, he saw curly ginger hair and knew that he'd been right: it was Tony Fordham. In the years that Jake had attended Charlie's, where Tony Fordham was a pupil, the two boys had become good friends, despite the fact that Tony was six months older. The two of them had taken their School Certificate and had matriculated with flying colours and Jake was grateful both to Tony and to Daisy, because the subjects in which he was a long way behind the others were French and Latin, and they had coached him in both, so that he had managed to scrape a pass in each.

Higher School Certificate, however, would be a different matter. Tony had taken it for granted that Jake, and eventually Daisy, would be sitting their Higher in order to gain a university place and, though it had not been his first intention, Jake was now every bit as keen as Tony, Simon and various other members of his class to get into university. 'If only to please my pa', Jake had told anyone who was interested, but this was not strictly true. A teacher had taken the class to visit Liverpool university, telling them that this was the first of what were known as the redbrick universities, the name deriving from the bright terracotta of the material used when it was built. Jake had been bowled over by the whole experience and was determined, if it was humanly possible, to go to college, but everything depended on getting his Higher. There were other boys in his class who hoped for a place at Oxford or Cambridge, but Jake was pretty sure that that would cost money; well, it stood to reason it must, since there would be lodgings and so on to be taken into consideration, whereas at Liverpool university he and Tony would both be able to live at home.

However, it was no use fretting over something so far in the future. If he failed, that would be that. He would simply have to forget university and enter the world of work, though Tony, lucky blighter, had said airily that if he failed he would sit the exam again the following year and hope for better luck next time.

So now Jake thrust the window open and poked his head out. 'What d'you want?' he shouted rudely. 'I've been writing a job application. Come up and I'll address the envelope and nick one of Dad's stamps, then we can post it on our way to – to wherever we're going.'

'Righty-ho,' Tony shouted and presently Jake heard his feet thundering up the stairs and the door burst open. 'I thought we might go up to the rec and bag a tennis court,' Tony said breathlessly as he entered. 'Or we could go up to the nets.'

Both boys were in Charlie's cricket team but lately, largely because of Daisy and Cynthia, they had played quite a lot of tennis in a foursome, swapping partners at the end of each set, though Jake thought they were pretty evenly matched. Daisy was still small for her age but she made up for her lack of inches with a great deal of bounce and energy whereas Cynthia, who was nearly as tall as Tony, seldom pursued a ball and relied on her height and her long reach to make up for her rather languid approach to the game.

Outside, the sun shone brightly and the leaves on the trees in the garden scarcely stirred in the breeze. Jake considered, addressing his envelope, licking the flap and then pulling open a drawer in the dresser behind him to take out the neat folder where his father kept stamps. 'I suppose you mean bag a court and play singles,' he said, licking the stamp and applying it carefully to the envelope. 'I don't know what Cynthia's doing, but I don't fancy

263

a threesome, and if you ask me, by the time we reach the rec the sun will be scorching down and every court will be taken. Why are you so late? If you wanted to play tennis, I should have thought you'd have been here hours ago.'

'Ho, ho, very funny,' Tony said sarcastically. 'You aren't the only one hoping for work, you know.' He delved in his jacket pocket and produced two somewhat crumpled envelopes. 'Only I'm not made of money, so I'm going to deliver 'em myself. I've got one for a firm in the Liver building, and another to Exchange Flags, same as you.'

'Bloody cheek,' Jake said absently. 'You've got fifty times more money than me, and you know it. But if we go round delivering these by hand, you can say goodbye to tennis or the nets. Tell you what, you can buy a couple of stamps off my pa, then we'll post all three applications in the box at the end of the road. And then I reckon we ought to go up to Prince's Park and take a boat out on the lake. It's too perishin' hot for cricket or tennis.'

'Yes, you're right,' Tony said, sounding surprised. 'Then when the sun goes down and everyone else is heading home for their tea, we'll grab a court and have a few games in the cool. My backhand could do with some practice, as I'm bloody sure you realise since you and Curly Top hit every ball towards me well to my left.'

'Good thing Daisy isn't around to hear you call her that; you know it makes her mad,' Jake said as they left the flat and headed down the stairs. 'Come to think of it, I don't much care for it when you call me Marbles, either. Daisy says she wants to check whether my arm's dropped off every time she hears it.' They emerged, blinking, into the hot sunshine. 'Have you got any money, though? I've got a bob, but that won't go far. I'm relying on you, as a rich farmer's son, to pay for the court, or the boat, or whatever.'

They were strolling towards the back gate into Pilgrim Street, but at Jake's words Tony stopped short. 'Don't you read the newspapers, you ignorant lout?' he asked incredulously. 'There's a Depression, remember, and it's hit farmers worst of all. The price per acre has sunk lower than ever before and farmers are leaving the land in droves because they simply can't make a living. It's all these cheap imports; there ought to be a law against 'em.'

'Yes, I know farmers have been selling up, or trying to do so,' Jake admitted. 'But your dad's all right, isn't he? I mean Wychbold Farm is huge.'

'We're all right now, but I know Dad's worried,' Tony said. 'He's forever reading the farming journals, trying to find out which crops will bring the best results. But farmers are so dependent on the weather; a wet summer or a severe winter can wipe out acres of what had been a good crop. Still, unless we have really bad weather for the next six weeks or so, we've got a good crop of apples and folk round here prefer a nice pippin to tasteless foreign rubbish. So we're managing to keep our heads above water.'

'My heart bleeds for you, as one whose head is perpetually plunging beneath the surface,' Jake said. They reached the post box and slipped their letters through the slit. 'Is that why you're applying for jobs? Because Daddy needs a bit of a hand?'

'Nasty, nasty,' Tony said reprovingly. 'Things aren't that desperate, not yet. But now we're on holiday I'd like some money of my own, and I don't want to keep asking my dad for hand-outs. He has had to lay off two of the farmhands until the grain harvest starts. He hated doing it but needs must.'

Jake opened his mouth, then shut it again. He had visited Wychbold Farm many times and thought that if Mr Fordham needed to save some money he could have sold off some of his antique furniture, or got rid of one of his three motor cars, but he knew better than to say so. Instead, as they turned into Upper Duke Street and headed for the nearest tram stop, he said wistfully: 'There's no getting away from it, times are hard for everyone. They say it's even worse in America than it is here. And I expect Ireland is suffering badly because they're a much smaller country than us, and still sorting themselves out after the civil war.' He sighed. 'Thank the Lord Daisy's only gone for a couple of weeks. You've no idea how horrible it is not having her cheery little face popping round the kitchen door each morning.'

'I can imagine,' Tony said. 'But you see more of her than you used to, don't you? I remember her saying that now Ruth and Biddy have left, and the cook too, she and Cynthia eat with the staff in the kitchen.'

'True,' Jake said, joining the queue at the tram stop. 'But of course with her Aunt Jane, who's been doing the cooking, away as well, meals aren't what they were. They aren't replacing any of the staff, either, because I suppose even doctors find patients harder to come by during a depression. So Daisy's really useful; she either washes or wipes up after each meal, and goes round with the maids who are left, dusting and hoovering, polishing furniture, making beds and so on. I think she likes it, though it takes up quite a bit of time.'

'Does Cynthia help as well?' Tony asked idly as the tram screeched to a halt and passengers began to get off. 'I can't imagine it, but I suppose she does her share.'

Jake snorted. 'Does she hell! She drifts in, eats her food and then drifts out again. Miss Dalton asked her to give a hand one day, when Molly was off with stomach cramps, but Cynthia said it wasn't her place to go interfering and her aunt wouldn't like it. And when my pa pointed out that Daisy did her share, Cynthia gave him a very sweet smile and said that Daisy was trying to pay the Venables back for their kindness to her because no one asks Daisy to pay a penny towards her keep.'

At this point they climbed aboard the tram and

headed for the stairs, finding a seat right up at the front, where they would get the benefit of what breeze there was. Tony, settling himself, turned to the other boy, eyes wide. 'What did your pa say? I never realised Cynthia could be so horrid.'

'She can be pretty critical,' Jake said cautiously. 'But in a way, she's right. I mean she's a relative and Daisy isn't. And though Miss Dalton buys most of Daisy's clothes and so on, I think Mrs Venables does help out. Still, it wouldn't hurt Cynthia to give a hand. Daughters help their mams without a second thought, so why shouldn't a niece help her aunt? You may be sure that Daisy would do anything for Miss Dalton.'

'Oh well, it's none of my business, I suppose,' Tony said. He chuckled suddenly. 'Is Cynthia going to hate it if Daisy really does go to university? Or will she pretend she never wanted to go anyway?'

'But she doesn't – want to go to university I mean,' Jake said positively. 'She isn't at all academic, you know, and when she's twenty-one she'll inherit so much money that she'll never need to work at anything. I didn't much care for Cynthia at first, I thought she was selfish and idle, but she's not that bad really. She gets a big allowance and though I'm sure Daisy has never realised, quite a lot of it goes on things Daisy needs, as well as on Cynthia herself.' He looked quizzically at his friend. 'It's bloody difficult to explain, but Cynthia is the way she is because of the way she's been brought up. First her mother and her nurse spoilt

268

her, let her get away with murder because they were afraid she had inherited her mother's frail constitution. Then her mother died so she was an orphan and the object of even more pity. After that, she came to live with her Aunt Venables and the doctor, and she used ill health for her own ends, but, do you see, the way her mother and her nurse treated her meant she was almost *taught* to be a bit devious. And of course Mrs Ven was anxious because Cynthia was in her care, so she let her have her own way in everything. Which didn't help Cynthia's character.'

'I think I see what you're getting at,' Tony said thoughtfully. 'I suppose you could say we are all the result of our upbringing. Daisy's a tough little nut because first her life in Connemara was pretty hard, and then she was sent away from home to live in a strange country where she knew no one but her Aunt Jane, and then of course there was that terrible accident when she lost her parents. It's made her self-reliant and, as I said, pretty tough.'

'Yes, you're right,' Jake admitted, and his mind went back to a terrible day in December, the year after Daisy's parents had been killed. For some reason – he could not now remember what it was – Daisy had decided to buy her aunt a bunch of chrysanthemums to cheer up her room, for though they would have liked to return to Ireland for the holiday, it was clearly not practicable. Despite the tragedy, Daisy had been her usual optimistic self, looking forward to Christmas and buying small presents for Brendan and Amanda, which she would pack in with Aunt Jane's gifts and send off in a couple of days. Ah, yes; Jake remembered now: the flowers were to have made up for the fact that Aunt Jane had been giving Daisy extra pocket money because Christmas was so close.

'We'll go to Clayton Square; there's flower sellers there who go early to the markets and sell a bit cheaper – well, a lot cheaper – than they do in the shops,' he had said. 'You must have been to Clayton Square?'

'Yes, but never in winter,' Daisy had said rather doubtfully. 'I've often been there in spring because I do so love primroses, and then in May there are great swags of lilac and narcissus, but it never occurred to me that they would be selling flowers at Christmas time too. Poor old things, they must be freezing on a day like this.'

Jake had nodded, for not only had it been extremely cold, but there had been flakes of snow drifting gently down in the cold air. 'Yes, it is cold, but you may rely upon it that the old shawlies will be selling away, or they'd be having a pretty lean Christmas,' he had assured her. 'And when we've bought the biggest bunch of chrysanthemums you can afford, I'll buy you a cuppa and a buttered scone at the Victoria tea rooms. Then, if you've any more shopping, we can nip along to Bunney's, or one of the other big stores.'

Daisy had assured him however that once she

had bought the flowers her Christmas shopping would be over, and the pair of them had hurried along Elliot Street and into Clayton Square. As Jake had predicted, the old flower sellers, surrounded by their wares, were in their usual positions, though most had pulled the shawls up over their heads to protect them from the lightly falling snow. Each was surrounded by a positive carpet of chrysanthemums, bronze, gold, white as the falling snow, and blood red.

Jake had been about to suggest that Daisy should choose a variety of colours when she gave a little sound, almost like a cat mewing. Jake had turned to glance at her and had been horrified and astonished to see gallant little Daisy, who never cried, weeping so hard that the tears actually seemed to spout from her eyes. Immediately, all Jake's protective instincts had been aroused. What on earth had happened? He had put an arm round her, asking urgently what was the matter. But it seemed that all she could do was continue to shake with sobs, hiccuping and gulping, trying to get words out and failing to do so, whilst pointing at one of the flower sellers.

Finding that kindness did not stem the flood, Jake had seized her by the shoulders and given her a fairly gentle shake. 'Pull yourself together, girl. What has that poor old woman done to get you into this state?' he had asked brusquely. 'Everyone's watching us; let's get these flowers and go. Which of the sellers upset you, anyhow?'

Once more Daisy had pointed, and this time Jake had realised she was indicating not a flower seller but a fat old woman sitting amongst them, with a big bunch of brilliantly coloured balloons bobbing above her head. Jake had never seen anyone selling balloons here before, but had imagined she was hoping folk would buy because it was Christmas. He had looked hopefully at Daisy. 'Do you want to buy a balloon for someone, queen? Only I think your aunt would prefer chrysanths . . . oh, Daisy love, what have I said now?'

And then, of course, it had all come out: the dreams of the old balloon seller, whose balloons were filled with the faces of Daisy's parents, brothers and sisters, and how she had seemed the only link with them that Daisy had left. But last time she had dreamed the dream, the balloon seller had released the strings and the Kildares' balloons had floated up to be extinguished amongst the stars.

'That's horrible,' Jake had said. He had slid his arm round Daisy's waist and begun to lead her out of the square. 'But I'm really glad you told me, because I don't believe it's good to keep things like that to yourself. A trouble shared is a trouble halved, you know.'

Daisy had tugged back against his arm, however. 'I'm all right now,' she had said huskily. 'It was just the shock of seeing a balloon seller, a real one, not a dream one. You're right about the flowers being cheaper here, Jake, so let's go back and buy as many as I can afford – and don't worry, I shan't go letting you down again.'

They had returned to the square and Jake had seen her casting covert glances at the balloon seller whilst she chose her chrysanthemums and bargained briskly with the flower lady. When she had a beautiful bouquet, she had paid and turned to Jake, and he had seen that her colour was a little lightened, the sparkle was back in her big eyes and her mouth was curved in her usual mischievous smile. 'The woman selling balloons isn't the one in me dream, she's quite different, and that means I'm not going round the bend after all,' she had said joyfully. 'Do you know, Jake, I'm real glad that this happened and real glad I told you as well. I feel . . . oh, lighter . . . as though it was true what you said, about a trouble shared. And now let's go along to the Victoria tea rooms; I didn't know crying and getting in a state could make you starving hungry, but that's just what I am!'

But that had all happened a long time ago and now Jake remembered how they had sat over their tea and scones and how he had told Daisy that this was the only occasion, in all the time he'd known her, that he had seen her cry. She had grinned up at him, through the wildly curling wet hair which hung over her brow. 'And it'll be the last time,' she had assured him. 'Kildares don't cry, except when they fall and skin their knees of course!'

He had laughed with her, but had never forgotten

the incident, and now he turned to grin at Tony. 'I wonder how Daisy's getting on?' he said. 'She wasn't that keen on revisiting her old home, but, knowing Daisy, she'll be making the best of it.'

'But Aunt Jane, I really don't want to go to Benmacraig, truly I don't. It's – it's full of ghosts for me. Oh, it's easy to say they're happy ghosts, but if I go there and see our cottage I shall remember everything, and I've trained myself to look forward and not back. It's – it's not so painful.'

She and Aunt Jane were walking along the shore, one moment crunching over sand and the next climbing on to the great slabs of rock against which the sea surged so hungrily. The Galway shore was very different from that which fringed Benmacraig, but it was better than being inland, for Daisy loved the ocean. Besides, it was difficult, if not impossible, to hold a private conversation in Amanda's busy kitchen. She had married her Gerald and they had a couple of rooms in an old, tumbledown house not far away from the great mansion where Amanda had worked. Now she was a married woman, however, she no longer went to the big house to scrub and polish, lay tables and clean silver and do the thousand and one other tasks which she had been given once the staff had been cut down from eight to four. Now she collected piles of linen which needed washing, ironing or mending, all of which she did in her own kitchen, so that the room was always crowded and often steamy, and though Amanda kept the windows open it sometimes grew uncomfortably hot, for the weather had remained sunny. This was good for getting the linen dry since Amanda could hang it out on the lines which stretched across the narrow alley, but Daisy dreaded to think what the kitchen must be like in winter, with wet laundry dripping from the drying rack overhead, and from every other available space.

When the work was completed and immaculate she took it round to the big house, but she was paid a very small sum indeed for doing such work, as little in fact as her employer could get away with. Gerald worked in an office, again for a small wage, but he had to be well dressed which was a worry sometimes, money being perpetually short. So even the small amount that Amanda earned from her laundering and mending helped, she explained to her aunt and her sister, and with a baby on the way . . .

It was the first time she had told them that she was expecting a child, and despite her resolve to be pleased with everything, and to greet her sister as lovingly as she knew how, Daisy felt her lips tighten with disapproval. She had decided long ago that she would never marry, never have children, because no one could foretell the future . . . look what had happened to the Kildares! They had been so happy at Benmacraig, but their happiness had been short-lived. First they had lost their home, then their lives . . . and Finn and Dermot had had such little lives! She had spent many nights in the Rodney Street house fighting the images that came, unbidden, into her mind when sleep would not be courted and the long hours of darkness stretched ahead, to be peopled with horrors she could clearly imagine. The moment before the train crash, when they were all full of delightful anticipation of what was to come. The little boys, noses pressed to the window, would have been marvelling at the changing scene. Annabel, as excited as they but, being older, hiding it better. Their parents and the lawyer, confident that their worries would soon be over . . . well, so they had been, but not in the way they had anticipated. And the crash . . . the moans, the desperate searchings, the dreadful suspicion that they had not died instantly, that they had suffered . . .

In her nightmares her mammy crawled around in the dark, dreadfully injured, looking everywhere for her children, for Colm. Or it was Colm, calling for his Daisy in a tiny, thin thread of a voice, forgetting that she was far away, unable to help, though in her dream she could see the blood running from his dear mouth . . . knew he was doomed. Oh no, she would never marry, never bring children into the world to suffer in such a terrible way.

But these nightmares had not haunted her for some time and Daisy had slept soundly for many months. Yet as soon as her feet touched Irish soil the dreams had begun again – not so terrible nor so violent as those which had haunted her in the weeks directly after the accident, but bad enough. They had been reading *Macbeth* at school, and the lines spoken by Macduff after the slaughter of his entire family haunted her. *All my pretty ones? Did you say all? All? What! All my pretty chickens and their dam, at one fell swoop?* and the agony in the words had been reflected in Daisy's dreams.

But now Aunt Jane was speaking, and Daisy wrenched her mind from the past to listen. 'Look, Daisy, closing your eyes to facts is the action of a child, and you are a young woman of sixteen, with your whole future before you. The wrangling over Benmacraig is still going on, but hopefully the lawyers will sort it out. Brendan says he no longer cares about the money Paddy owes the family, he just wants the croft back, but I think you should get the money, too, otherwise how is Brendan to get the land back into good heart? To say nothing of buying back the boat, or getting another . . . and then there's the donkey and cart . . . and you and Amanda to provide for, as well as Gerald and the children she intends to have. And you'll marry one day . . .'

'I shan't,' Daisy said, though so quietly that her aunt heard nothing and simply continued with the list of things for which they would need money.

'. . . and have a family to support, whether or not the croft is yours once more,' she concluded. 'So truly, Daisy, I think we should go over there and see what's what. If only all the papers had not been destroyed when the train crashed . . . but there's no use crying over spilt milk, and Mr Prescott seems to think that the whole awful muddle will be sorted out to your advantage, in the end. Will you come, my dear? Amanda means to do so and I believe Brendan visits regularly, whenever the *Venturer* is in port.'

Daisy would have liked to say that she would not, but she felt that to do so would be the action of a coward and she knew she was no such thing, so she nodded reluctantly. 'All right, Auntie, and I suppose you're right. I really should see the old place and judge for myself how badly the land has been neglected. But even if us Kildares got Benmacraig back tomorrow, I'll never live there again. I never thought I'd say it, but Liverpool's my home now, where I want to be. Oh, I love Ireland and Connemara with all my heart, but I couldn't live here again. I've changed, haven't I?'

Aunt Jane smiled and settled herself comfortably on a smooth slab of rock, with her legs dangling over the edge as though she were sitting on a chair or a sofa. She patted the rock beside her and Daisy sat down as well, then looked enquiringly at her aunt. 'Yes, you have changed,' Aunt Jane said quietly. 'Oh, I'm not talking about physically, because in seven years that would naturally change. When you came to Liverpool you were a child, and now you're a young woman. But you've changed in other ways. Do you know, when you first came to Rodney Street you used to make me

278

think of a puppy; you bounced around, so eager to help, to make friends, to become a part of the household. I could almost imagine you wagging your tail and getting excited at the thought of a walk. There must have been moments, my dear, when you were lonely and unhappy, longing for Benmacraig and the people you loved, but you never let it show. When Maggie suggested that you should be the one to return to Liverpool with me, I was . . . not best pleased, because – well, I thought you were a wild one. You hated housework, gardening, anything of that nature, and Maggie had said many times that whilst you went off to do her messages willingly enough, you usually came back with only half the things she wanted, or in some cases even forgot you'd been sent out for a purpose, and played on the shore or the moors until hunger drove you home. As you know, I've never had a child of my own, and the thought of trying to make you mind me was a frightening one. Furthermore, I knew you didn't like me very much, because, my love, you had never learned to hide your feelings. So you see, right from the start I was sure it wouldn't work. I thought that you'd seize the first opportunity to run back to Ireland, leaving me in a difficult position, for I'd promised Mrs Venables that I would return with a meek, sweet-natured child, who would be the ideal companion for her orphaned niece.'

'But you must have known I was the one nearest to Cynthia in age,' Daisy pointed out. She was smiling because nothing her aunt told her was news; she had known all along that she would not have been Aunt Jane's choice. 'So why did you tell Mrs Venables such an enormous fib?'

Aunt Jane put her arm round Daisy's shoulder and gave her a squeeze. 'Forgive me, my dear, but I hoped to persuade Maggie to let me take Annabel instead. There was only ten months between you, after all, and she was so serious and responsible that she actually seemed older than the wild tomboy who spent so much of her time out of doors that I hardly ever saw her anyway.'

'Oh, I *see*,' Daisy said, enlightenment dawning. 'Poor Aunt Jane – you must have been very disappointed!'

Aunt Jane laughed. 'Well, I was a bit worried at first, but I soon realised that you had unexpected qualities which came to the fore under duress. And you were academically bright, which I certainly had not expected, because Maggie told me how you were always sagging off school, only going in a couple of times a term to fetch books because you were an avid reader.'

Daisy smiled guiltily. 'Perhaps if I'd not come to Liverpool I'd have gone on sagging off school – only we call it mitching in Ireland – but it was different in Rodney Street. Going to school meant getting away from Cynthia, for a start, and being with kids my own age. Then it was fee-paying, so I couldn't let Mrs Venables down by mitching off. And I soon discovered that I enjoyed the lessons,

280

though I found maths difficult at first. Then there was Jake. Cynthia wasn't much of a companion, so if it hadn't been for Jake I'd have been awful lonely in the school holidays. The majority of girls in my class live outside the city, you know, and come in each day by bus or tram, or by car, so I had no one in the neighbourhood to go about with. And most of the other girls have parents who are well off, if not actually rich. They have what they call holiday homes on the Wirral, or the Welsh coast, so they aren't around. One or two of them have invited me to stay during the summer, but of course I couldn't possibly accept, could I?'

'I don't know why not,' Aunt Jane said. 'After all, Cynthia goes to stay in Southport at least three times a year; if you felt guilty at leaving her to her own devices, you could have gone then.'

Daisy however, shook her head. 'No, I couldn't do that, for three good reasons,' she said, ticking them off on her fingers. 'One, I never knew exactly when Cynthia was going to be away, or for how long. Two, I could never return the compliment by asking a friend to stay with my family. And three, because Jake has always been such a good friend to me that I couldn't let him down by going away during the holidays. I know he has school friends, but he's a funny one is Jake; or rather he was. Whilst he was at the Gilbert Street school he was always kind of solitary, I'm not sure why. Perhaps it was because he was cleverer than the others, or maybe it was because Mr Elgin's a chauffeur and always

281

dressed in a smart uniform. Perhaps the other kids thought it was his own car; I don't know, but anyway, I was pretty well Jake's only friend until he got a scholarship to Charlie's. So you see, I couldn't possibly have left him. And anyway, the two of us have had some grand times together. I've learned so much about the city that I dare say a stranger would think I'd lived there all my life. As you say, at first I was homesick, but here we are, back in Ireland, with my sister and brother near at hand, and I'm homesick for perishin' Rodney Street, and me pals back there. Isn't life strange, Auntie?'

Aunt Jane smiled. 'Yes, it is, and you have no idea how nice it is to hear you call me Auntie, instead of plain old Aunt.' She sighed. 'I shall miss you most dreadfully if you go to university, but I shan't be lonely. Can you guess why?'

'Is it anything to do with Mr Elgin?' Daisy asked, rather shyly. She knew that her aunt spent most of her spare time in the chauffeur's company, but had never questioned her on the subject, feeling that it was none of her business. As she spoke, she turned her head to look at her aunt and saw a flush deepen the colour in her cheeks.

'Yes, queen. Bob Elgin and myself have always been good friends, but we've grown closer over the past few years. He – he asked me to marry him quite soon after our little holiday in New Brighton, but I said I wanted to see you happily settled with your parents once more before I took such an important step. He agreed to wait, both of us thinking that it would not be long. After the tragedy he understood that I couldn't dream of making such a change, but I realised some time ago that you were becoming more independent with every day that passed, and scarcely needed me. So we're to wed a year next October, when Jake goes to university, and I shall no longer live in at Rodney Street.'

'You'll only be in the coachman's quarters, though, won't you?' Daisy said hopefully, for her heart had given a swoop towards her boots when her aunt talked of her marriage. Daisy realised, suddenly, that one of the main causes of her contentment, and indeed happiness, had been that she felt comfortably aware of her aunt's presence in the big old house. She knew she had a place there, that Cynthia and the Venables were fond of her, but she also knew that it was to Aunt Jane she ran when things went wrong, or when reassurance was needed. So now she waited for an answer to her question with some trepidation.

'Well, no. There is only one bedroom in the coachman's quarters and besides, Bob has always said he wants a full-time wife and not a working woman, always tired and always at someone else's beck and call,' Aunt Jane said apologetically. 'To tell you the truth, love, Bob is still a country boy at heart and – and he's had a bit of luck. An old bachelor uncle who lived on a tiny farm in a little Welsh village in the hills behind Abergele willed his property to Bob's father, only he's been dead for years, as you know. It's taken a while to get it all sorted, but Bob had a letter only last week to say that the farm is now his, and that he can take possession just as soon as he likes. It's not a big house – it's really more of a cottage – and the land is very neglected, very poor really, because the old man couldn't cope. He employed a fellow from the village to look after what stock he had – pigs, chickens and the like – but of late years money was short and he dispensed with paid help except for a woman who came in a couple of times a week to cook him a meal and keep the dirt down. In short, the place has gone to rack and ruin, rather like your family croft, my dear. I've not seen it myself yet, but Bob is sure that between us we can make a thriving place of it once more. He remembers how it was when he was a boy and is absolutely longing to get to work. So when we marry, we shall move out there.'

'Oh, I see,' Daisy said slowly. 'And I suppose Mr Elgin will drive into the city each day to take Dr Venables on his rounds.'

'Well no, dear, he won't be doing that because he'll be working the farm, and it's much, much too far to travel to and from Liverpool. Goodness, it must be fifty miles! Bob has offered to find the doctor another chauffeur, but he means to learn to drive – Bob is going to teach him – so the coachman's quarters will become empty.'

'But why shouldn't Jake stay there?' Daisy asked

eagerly. 'I dare say the Venables wouldn't charge him rent – they're most awfully kind – and he could go on having his meals in the kitchen with the rest of us.'

Aunt Jane looked doubtful. 'I believe it's customary for students to live on campus, as they say, during term time. And during his holidays, only I think they're called vacations, Bob will want Jake to work on the farm, helping him to bring it back to what it was.'

'But Jake's a city boy. He knows nothing about farming,' Daisy pointed out. 'He'll probably hate it – lots of people do.'

'Well, that remains to be seen,' Aunt Jane said cautiously. 'If he hates it, then we'll have to think again. But Bob believes farming is in Jake's blood and will come to the surface once we take possession of Ty Gwyn. However, there wouldn't be enough work on the farm for both of them, so Bob takes it for granted that it will just be a sort of holiday job for Jake until he gets his degree and begins a career of his own.'

'I see,' Daisy said rather numbly. She gazed around her at the sunny shore and the little waves breaking on the hard wet sand. She realised, suddenly, that she had been taking Jake's continued friendship for granted, assuming that even when he was at university things would not change. Life would go on, separately during school hours, but as soon as they were free they would spend their time together. Oh, sometimes they quarrelled, disagreed, marched away from one another in high dudgeon. Sometimes they laughed or scoffed at each other, even called names, but that was only natural; she thought of Jake as though he were a brother, like Brendan, and she could still remember the rows which had blown up suddenly between herself and Brendan, and how such disagreements had disappeared and been forgotten.

She realised now that, missing the brothers and sisters with whom she had shared her life, she had almost subconsciously relied upon Jake for the understanding which had existed between herself and her siblings. It had not occurred to her before that she had taken Jake for granted, but it was true; losing Cynthia's companionship would not be half as painful as losing Jake's.

But Aunt Jane's thoughts were still plainly focused on what was before her, and Daisy thought her aunt a perfect heroine to have sublimated her own wishes in order to take care of her niece for so long. Aunt Jane, however, was talking, still flushed and excited. '. . . I know Bob's going to ask Jake to be his best man, and I would like it very much, my love, if you would be my bridal attendant. I'd like to ask Amanda as well; I mean to pay for her, Gerald, and of course Brendan, to cross the water so that they can attend the ceremony.'

'Oh Auntie, I'd be honoured to be your bridesmaid,' Daisy said at once. 'But how dreadfully I shall miss you!'

'No you won't, because I shall come back to

Rodney Street to see all my old friends as often as I can,' Aunt Jane said. 'I wish you could come with us but that's plainly impossible whilst you'll still have a year at school, and it would leave poor Cynthia alone and break the agreement we made with Mrs Venables all those years ago.'

'I do understand that; it's much too far to travel to and from school each day,' Daisy said slowly. 'And Cynthia is a pain in some ways but if I did move out I guess I'd miss her too. Though if I really do go to university, she'll have to learn to manage without me, won't she?'

'Yes, of course she will,' Aunt Jane agreed. 'Mrs Venables said that Cynthia thinks of you as a sister, but everyone knows that as sisters grow up they go their separate ways.'

Daisy chuckled. 'A good few sisters I know can't wait to get away from one another,' she observed. 'I dare say Cynthia and I will feel like that in a year or two, but right now it's nice to have someone your own age sharing the same house. Perhaps Cynthia and I need each other more because neither of us completely belongs with the Venables. Oh, I know they have made us truly welcome, but it's not quite the same, is it, Auntie?'

'No, it's not,' Aunt Jane said. 'But I don't know how we got on to this subject! I meant to tell you that Ty Gwyn will always be your home once your education is finished and you no longer want to live in Rodney Street.'

'Thank you for saying that. When we get back

to Liverpool, Auntie, will you take me to see the farm? We could catch a bus or a train or something, because I don't suppose Dr Venables will want his chauffeur jauntering off such a distance.'

'No, no, you're quite wrong. The very first Sunday after we get back to Rodney Street, Dr Venables has said that Bob can borrow the car so that we can take you and Jake to show you the cottage. I must warn you that it's not only the land which has been neglected; the house too needs a great deal of work but we have over a year to get it made habitable before we move in. The old chap doesn't seem to have done a thing to it. And now, queen, we ought to be getting back because our landlady will have a meal on the table in twenty minutes and I've a feeling she likes her guests to arrive on time.'

Daisy got to her feet and jumped down on to the sand, then held out her hands to help Aunt Jane. 'Yes, you're right, we'd best be on our way,' she agreed, as Aunt Jane landed, somewhat heavily, on the sand beside her. 'How are we getting to the croft, incidentally? I trust you don't expect us to walk!'

Aunt Jane laughed. 'Scarcely! But Brendan said that if you are agreeable, we'll catch a bus to Clifden and he'll borrow a donkey cart. I think we'd better go tomorrow because if we leave it too long the fine weather may finish, and I don't fancy travelling all that way in the pouring rain.'

The next day was fine and Daisy went round to

288

Amanda's house soon after breakfast. She and Aunt Jane had arranged with Brendan that he would meet the bus at Clifden, so that they might travel to Benmacraig together. Brendan had grown to be a strong and handsome young man, very like his father so that at first, every time she saw him, Daisy suffered a pang of real pain. He had Colm's very dark eyes, curly hair and shy smile, but the determination which had been so dominant a part of her father's character was not so strong in Brendan. She mentioned the fact to Amanda as the two girls worked in the kitchen, getting ready for the day's outing, and Amanda said, somewhat tartly, that Colm had worked for himself and been his own boss until Benmacraig had been snatched from him, whereas poor Brendan had been taking orders from men who didn't have half his strength of mind, or intelligence, for a long time now.

'I didn't mean to criticise,' Daisy began to say quickly, seeing the indignation on her sister's fair face. 'It's just that he's so like Daddy to look at that I suppose I expected him to be like him in other ways. I'm sorry, Amanda. You're quite right, of course.'

'Yes, I am,' Amanda said. Her voice was still sharp. 'Brendan's had a terrible time, so he has, and my life hasn't been all roses since we lost Benmacraig. You've had it easy compared with us. You had Aunt Jane, and from the sound of it a beautiful home. You've wanted for nothing, and you didn't even have to work for it! Brendan and me never stopped working and I know Brendan was often hungry in the early days because he gave every penny, and quite often his share of the catch, to Mammy and Daddy so that they could feed the little ones. So if you come here and criticise Brendan to me you'll get a dusty answer, my girl.'

Daisy was shocked at Amanda's violent reaction, though she could understand it. Aunt Jane had gone off to buy food for their expedition and, looking round the crowded, unattractive kitchen, smoky from the peat which Amanda had just put on the fire, Daisy knew that her sister would find it difficult to forgive her for her thoughtless remark. Amanda had turned away from the sink in which she had been scrubbing potatoes the better to attack her sister, and she looked so fierce, with her blue eyes blazing and her mouth a tight line, that for a moment Daisy hesitated. Then she hurled herself across the room and grabbed Amanda round her thickening waist, realising that she must put things right immediately, or resentment on both sides would fester into something which would ruin their relationship.

'Amanda, I'm so, so sorry! It was a wicked and stupid thing to say and I'm ashamed the thought even crossed me mind,' she gabbled. 'And you're absolutely right that I've had it easy, living with the Venables and going to a good school, and that. It – it was just that Brendan looks so like Daddy that it hurts me. So maybe I was trying to look for differences; please try to understand! You and Brendan have borne the brunt of it; I've been spoilt rotten compared with you. I'm so sorry.'

There was an appalling moment when Daisy thought she was about to be rejected, but then Amanda's arms tightened round her. 'You're the only sister I've got and I know, really, that you didn't mean no harm,' Amanda said in a muffled voice. 'It weren't your fault that you had the best of it; why, when you first left, I cried myself to sleep night after night, knowing how lonely and homesick you must have been feeling. The truth is, I was jealous when you first came back here and I saw your nice clothes and heard you speakin' as though you'd been born and bred in England, without so much as a touch of the brogue. So we mustn't fall out now, alanna.'

'I'll never fall out with you, nor with Brendan,' Daisy assured her sister. 'Has Aunt Jane told you she's getting married? Well, when you come over to Liverpool for the wedding . . .'

'I'm not coming; nor's Brendan,' Amanda said firmly. 'I've got one decent dress to me name and it'll have to do me for many years yet. Besides, I don't fancy the crossing and by then the baby will be getting into everything. And Brendan needs every penny he can earn. He's putting it all away towards the day when Benmacraig is ours again.'

'Oh, but Aunt Jane will be heartbroken,' Daisy said, dismayed. 'Look, I've been saving up and sending money back to Brendan, but I've still got a lot more clothes than you have. I could send a dress and I know how clever you are with your needle, so I'm sure you could alter it to fit. If I did that, would you come? And I'd earn some extra money when I go home and send it straight to Brendan, honest to God I would. Aunt Jane would pay your fare and your lodgings and everything. Oh, Amanda, be a sport – think of Aunt Jane.'

Amanda however was adamant. 'Aunt Jane's been grand to you, so she has, but we've seen little enough of her these past years, me and Brendan,' she said. 'I can't speak for our brother – you may be able to change his mind – but for myself, I'm stayin' right here.'

At this point Aunt Jane entered the kitchen and the conversation had, perforce, to be cut short, but even as she climbed aboard the bus Daisy knew that the argument was lost. Neither her brother nor her sister would travel to England for Aunt Jane's wedding.

During the ride out to Benmacraig in the borrowed donkey cart, Aunt Jane mentioned her wedding plans to Brendan and Amanda, but did not seem unduly surprised when they both politely but firmly declined her invitation. She did not press them but changed the subject at once, asking Amanda whether she had visited Benmacraig since the new owner had taken over.

'I've not been at all,' Amanda admitted. 'I've been too busy, so I have. When I was working at the big house I spent all me spare time with Gerald, and once I had a home of me own that kept me occupied. Besides, we couldn't afford the fare.'

But Brendan turned in his seat to give his sister an indulgent smile. 'The truth is, Amanda didn't fancy seeing it when there was nothing we could do about getting it back,' he said. 'But it's different now, eh, Amanda?'

Amanda didn't answer, merely giving her brother a puzzled look, but Daisy said: 'What's different now?'

Brendan, however, only chuckled. 'You'll see,' he said. 'You'll see. And not a word will you get out of me until you *have* seen, so don't you go pesterin' me, Daisy Kildare.'

'All right, all right; I don't suppose it's anything very exciting anyway,' Daisy said. But as they neared the dear, familiar country which she had loved so well, she felt a lump rise up in her throat and tears dazzled her eyes, though she would not let them fall. They entered the deep little lane and she could see through the trees on her left the gleam of the sea and the mass of rocks where, on the very day that Paddy Kildare and his half-brother had entered their lives, she had been collecting mussels.

Daisy thought how happy she had been that day, paddling through the water with her skirt hitched up, clattering the mussels into her bucket, knowing that for once she was doing precisely as her mother had asked, anticipating the praise which would be hers when she returned to her home.

She remembered it all clearly, though it had happened so long ago. Yet she did not want to remember going into the kitchen and seeing the three strangers because that had been the start of the bad times. Instead, as the donkey cart approached the stream, she felt a jolt of surprise, for the stream was no longer bubbling across the rutted lane to tumble down the cliff on to the beach. There was no bucket standing ready to be filled and she turned to Amanda, a question on her lips. 'Where's the stream gone?' she enquired blankly. 'Oh, I *see*!' For, as they neared the spot, she did indeed see. Someone had re-routed the stream so that it no longer crossed the lane but dived beneath it. Then a fresh channel had been dug so that instead of falling over the cliff, the stream headed towards the cottage. 'Was that all they had to do to get running water into our kitchen?' Daisy said incredulously. 'Why, we could have done that ourselves; I'm surprised Mammy and Daddy never thought of it.'

Brendan turned and grinned at her. 'It's not as simple as that,' he said. 'But the stream forms a pool from which pipes lead into the cottage. It must have cost a grosh of money to do the work, which is why Daddy never considered it.'

Amanda, however, looked wistful. 'They don't need to come down to the stream now, then. They don't even have to carry water in a bucket. They just have to turn the tap,' she said. 'I wish Daddy could have afforded it. I hated carting water, so I did.'

'Me too,' Daisy said fervently and remembered with shame how often she had wriggled out of the task, leaving it to Amanda or Brendan, or even young Annabel, to fetch the water their mother needed. She hoped that Amanda would have forgotten, but if she remembered her sister made no sign, merely remarking that she was glad she did not have to cart water in Galway; her supply there came from a large brass tap over the stone sink.

At this point, the donkey cart swung round the last bend in the lane and Aunt Jane leaned across and took Daisy's hand in a comforting clasp. She began to speak, then stopped short as the cottage came into view. For a moment they all stared, horrified. Daisy had been told that their home had been modernised, though the land had been allowed to go back to nature. But the cottage, too, looked drab and deserted. The shingles were overgrown with moss and stonecrop in abundance. The whitewash, which Colm had renewed every other year, was cracked and peeling and the glass in two of the windows had gone, making the cottage look as though it were blinded.

Daisy's horrified gasp was echoed by Amanda and Aunt Jane, but Brendan was grinning. 'It's been empty for six months, so it has,' he said exultantly. 'I reckon we could move back in and no one the wiser. Why not? It's ours after all.' He had drawn the donkey cart to a halt and now he jumped down and looped the reins over a sagging gatepost. 'I dunno if we can get in, but at least we can see what's happened inside through that broken window . . .' he was beginning, when Aunt Jane caught his arm and gave it a little shake.

'There's someone in that wild patch just by the hedge to your left,' she said quietly. 'It's a feller, I think. Best have a word before you do anything else. Find out what he's up to.'

Brendan glanced to his left. 'It's probably some old tramp, sleepin' rough,' he said. 'No one's going to stop me havin' a look at my home. Besides, Daisy may not get another chance for months and months.'

Aunt Jane was beginning to say that it would not hurt to approach the man when he clearly spotted them. He had been crouching over something on the ground but now he waved a hand and came towards them. 'You're the early birds, so you are,' he shouted cheerfully as he approached. 'I take it you're interested in buying this property? I have to say this for 'em: the company's quick off the mark 'cos I've not even got the board up yet, let alone took a look inside.'

He was a tall, well-built young man, probably in his early thirties, and as he came closer Daisy saw that he was carrying a stout wooden pole in one hand and a mallet in the other. He grinned at them, then turned the pole so that they could see the sign at the top: *Michael O'Shea – House Agent*, it read. *This property, and land adjoining, for sale.*

Daisy could not speak. As soon as she had seen the dilapidated state of their home she had assumed, as Brendan had, that it would revert to them. After all, the man who had bought it must have left, no longer interested in his bit of 'the old country'. He must have got as tired as Paddy Kildare had been of the legal wrangling and decided to call it a day. In fact, when he had recovered from the shock, Brendan put their feelings into words.

'How do you do, Mr O'Shea? We are the Kildares what own this property, only we were cheated out of it, years back. But I don't under-stand. I went to the lawyer's office in town as soon as I heard Mr Morgan had moved out and was going back to America. We thought it would revert to us Kildares . . . I mean if Mr Morgan don't want it . . .'

The young man smiled. 'I'm not Mr O'Shea; he's my boss. I'm Mr Halloran,' he said. 'So you're the Kildares! Nice to meet you.' He shook hands with each of them, smiling in so friendly a fashion that Daisy could not help smiling back, though Brendan remained grave. 'As you can see, Mr Morgan doesn't want to live in Ireland any more. There's been too much fuss and bothera-tion. But he paid good money for the place so he means to sell it to get some of his investment back.' The young man glanced disparagingly at the croft behind him. 'Though he'd have done better to put it on the market two years ago when it was a decent little place, not a tumbledown wreck.'

Aunt Jane, who had been silently following the conversation, stepped forward. 'What's the asking price?' she said bluntly. 'I dare say, if it's reasonable, my nephew might be able to pay something for it which he would hope to get back when the legal battle is fought out. Surely it can't be much?'

The young man hissed his breath in between his teeth, glancing around at the wilderness which had once been a neat and productive vegetable garden. 'Maybe the asking price would be reasonable enough, but there's a snag,' he admitted. 'When Mr Morgan went, the place was in good heart and he rented it out to a lusty young feller with a wife and three or four children. The understanding was that they should till the land and keep the cottage itself repaired and decent. Unfortunately, as you can see, the tenant did neither. My boss thinks he was a tinker because he filled the place up with friends and relatives, none of whom lifted so much as a finger. We got them out six months ago and warned Mr Morgan how things were, but he didn't seem to believe us and his suggested price is absurd when you consider what has happened since he left.'

'But surely since you're his agent, you can insist

upon a realistic price?' Aunt Jane said incredulously. 'Otherwise nobody will buy it and his investment will be lost altogether.'

The young man shrugged. 'It's a similar story all over the country,' he told them. 'Good land, with decent cottages, are left empty and cannot be touched because the family who owned them originally found they could not make a living and emigrated. In some cases, this happened during the potato famine, almost a century ago, and quite possibly their descendants have no knowledge of the property their forefathers owned. They probably have no interest in reclaiming it anyway. So it is left like a scar on the landscape whilst families crowd together in tenement housing, unable to buy such holdings even if they could afford to do so.'

There was a long silence before Brendan spoke again. 'But we know the cottage and croft are ours,' he said dully. 'We can prove it's ours. The only thing we can't do is find the confidence trickster who sold it to Mr Morgan and ran off with his money. My parents were on his trail, accompanied by the New York lawyer who had discovered the cheat, when they were killed. I'd go to the States meself but the wicked feller will be long gone and anyway, I can't afford to go. But surely someone can persuade Mr Morgan to let us have our property back? Oh, I don't know, it just seems so unfair.'

'It does,' Mr Halloran agreed. 'I'll write to Mr

Morgan and put your suggestion to him. And now let's have a look inside the cottage and see what sort of a state it's in.'

Chapter Nine

When the small group got near the cottage, Mr Halloran produced a key and unlocked the padlock which fastened the small front door. Daisy hung back for a moment, letting the others enter first, then took a deep breath and followed them. She had dreaded this moment, but the cottage was so changed that it was not as bad as she had feared. There had been no need for Mr Halloran's key since the back door swung half open on broken hinges and the kitchen, which had once been a wonderfully warm and welcoming place, was unrecognisable. Dead leaves were piled up in every corner, sheep or some other animals had been stabled there at some time, leaving traces of their occupancy on the hard earth floor, and there were mounds of rags and filthy straw on every available surface. Of the furniture there was not a trace, and the stone sink with its unfamiliar tap was cracked across. To Daisy's secret relief, it did not resemble her mother's beautiful kitchen in the slightest, and when they went into the rest of the cottage they found broken windows, peeling whitewash and filth everywhere. The smell was pretty bad too, worse in the bedrooms than it had been in the kitchen, and worst of all in the bath-room which Mr Morgan had caused to be built, leading off the largest bedroom. It stank like a sewer and Daisy, with watering eyes, assumed that this was because whatever drains had led from it to the shore had become clogged, hence the stench.

They all left the cottage as soon as they could, including Mr Halloran. Dismay was writ large on every face except Brendan's, though he did not say a word until the family was a good half-mile from Benmacraig. Then he turned to speak to the others as the donkey trotted along. 'I know you t'ink it's turble and it won't never be decent again,' he told them. 'The shingles need a good clean and I reckon jackdaws have nested in the chimney. I'd clear all the filth out of every room and have a huge bonfire. Then I'd start scrubbin', repaintin' and makin' good windows and doors. I'd only need a few sticks of furniture at first and I'd buy seed so's I could grow me own vegetables. Tomorrer, or the day after, I'm goin' to get on the train and go to Dublin so's I can ask Mr Prescott for his advice. I don't fancy goin' all the way to America because I don't reckon I'd ever find Paddy Kildare, but I don't see . . .'

Aunt Jane had not spoken since they had left the cottage, but she must have been thinking deeply for she suddenly gave a squeak of excitement. 'But Brendan, Paddy Kildare's cheating of Mr Morgan is really not your concern. You must put it to Mr Prescott that the money which was paid over is a matter between Mr Morgan and the confidence trickster. It's up to Mr Morgan to pursue Paddy Kildare if he wants his money back. I believe it was different whilst Mr Morgan occupied Benmacraig, but he no longer does so. I honestly believe that if you put it to Mr Prescott in the right way, he'll see your point and contact Mr Morgan on your behalf. The only reason he might advise you not to move back into the cottage is because, if things went wrong and you were asked to pay, you might have improved the property, allowing Mr Morgan to charge a higher price.' She looked hard at Brendan's face, upon which hope was dawning. 'Do you understand what I'm getting at?'

There was a long pause whilst Brendan, brow furrowed, took on board what was clearly an absolutely new idea. Then he nodded and put a hand across to grasp Aunt Jane's. 'Sure and aren't you the clever one?' he said wonderingly. 'But would you come wi' me, Aunt Jane, to speak to Mr Prescott? Only left to meself I'd make a poor job of it, so I would.'

Aunt Jane agreed to accompany Brendan to the lawyer's office and the drive continued with much excited conversation between Daisy, her aunt and Brendan, though Amanda said nothing until the donkey cart drew to a halt at the bus stop. She climbed down, then put a detaining hand on the donkey's harness, when Brendan would have driven away. 'Sure and it's easy for you to talk about takin' on the old place again,' she said plaintively. 'But what about meself and Gerald? And then there's Daisy . . .'

'I'll make me own way and it'll be in England,' Daisy said quickly. 'I'd love to come and visit you, give you a hand, Brendan, once you begin work on Benmacraig, but I've got my own life now.'

'And when you marry, it won't be to an Irish crofter, but to some smart young feller wit' money in the bank and a grand big house,' Amanda said spitefully. 'Yes, Daisy's all right, Brendan; she's like an old tom cat what'll land on his feet whichever way you t'rows him.'

'I don't mean to marry anyone, Irish or English,' Daisy mumbled. 'But Amanda's right, you don't have to consider me.'

Brendan began to answer, but Aunt Jane cut in before he could do so. 'Your sister has been like a daughter to me,' she said quietly. 'She will have a home with Mr Elgin and myself for as long as she needs one. As for you, Amanda, I'm sure Brendan will be happy for you and Gerald to join him at Benmacraig, if that's what you would like.'

Amanda raised her brilliant eyes to Aunt Jane's face, looking a little guilty. 'I'd have to talk to Gerald; he's never gone more than a few miles from Galway in his life, so I don't know how he would feel about life on a croft, but oh, how I would love it! To live in Benmacraig, as it was once, is my idea of heaven.'

Aunt Jane kissed Amanda's softly flushing cheek. 'You are my darling niece; I knew I could not be mistaken in you,' she said softly. 'And now here comes the bus. Let's hope we get back to our lodgings in time or there'll be no supper for us tonight.'

1938

It was a fine summer evening in May. Cynthia and Daisy had decided to take advantage of the sunshine to go for a walk in the park. Aunt Jane and Uncle Bob had been living now at Ty Gwyn for six months and had been making great strides in improving both the land and the cottage itself. Since the Elgins' departure, Cynthia and Daisy had been thrown much more into one another's company. Daisy had always regarded Cynthia as someone who took the easy way out whenever possible, but her friend had changed greatly. She had met a young man, Clive Beamish, who was home from fighting for the Republicans in the Spanish Civil War. Cynthia knew that neither her aunt nor her uncle approved because Clive had been studying medicine when the war had started, and had promptly abandoned his studies to join the International Brigade and fight Franco's forces. Dr Venables had told Cynthia that the young man was a fool for throwing away his chance of a fine career but Cynthia, normally so self-absorbed, had begun to take an interest in what was happening in Europe, and was convinced that Clive was doing the right thing. She said the very fact that Hitler, the German Führer, was sending his air force to bomb Madrid and other towns held by the Republicans showed that Clive was fighting for justice and freedom and she, for one, would give him all the support she could. Dr Venables said that civil war was a matter for the country concerned and no other, but Cynthia disagreed and was not afraid to say so.

She had met Clive for the first time when he had come home after having been wounded at the battle for Santander. At the time Daisy had been helping her aunt at Ty Gwyn, so when she got back to find Cynthia engrossed in her new friendship, she had been both surprised and incredulous. Cynthia had not previously seemed particularly interested in what was happening in Europe, so her complete absorption in it now seemed strange, particularly when Clive had returned to the conflict. Daisy had thought that Cynthia's interest would wane as the weeks went by – letters were rare – but it had not.

And indeed, Cynthia was not the only one anxiously watching what was taking place in Europe, for the whole of Britain was, so to speak, waiting breathlessly for what was clearly about to happen. Hitler had annexed Austria and was strutting around, swearing eternal friendship with Mussolini, Italy's Duce. He had been holding enormous rallies in Berlin, at which his vast army of goose-stepping storm troopers put the fear of God into anyone who watched them on the cinema screen.

Everyone at No. 39, watching the newsreels and

reading the newspapers, was convinced that it was only a matter of time before Britain would be plunged into war, and Daisy knew Jake shared her fears. She and Jake corresponded pretty regularly for, contrary to all expectations, Jake had not gone to Liverpool university but had chosen instead to take up an offered place at Cambridge, where he was reading mathematics and science. Partly this had been sheer pleasure at the thought of attending the best college in the country, as he put it, and partly because his friend Tony had also gained a place at Cambridge, though in a different college since he would be reading the classics.

> *We meet up pretty often; either he comes to my stair or I go to his* [Jake had written]. *I expect you can guess what we talk about; the war which we both know is coming. Did I tell you I'd joined the Cambridge University Air Squadron? Judging from what has been happening in Spain, it will be air power which will affect the outcome for one side or the other, so I mean to be prepared. Besides, air force blue suits me better than khaki.*

But right now Daisy and Cynthia were in Prince's Park, neither thinking nor talking about war, but strolling beside the lake, enjoying the scent of a nearby lilac tree, wafted to them on the breeze, and discussing the letter which Daisy had just received. It was from Jake and it was, in fact, an invitation. There was to be a May ball at the university and Jake and Tony wanted Daisy and Cynthia to partner them.

You will be lodged in the rooms my college keeps for visitors for two nights, and I'll send you both your train fares [Jake had written]. *Judging by the state of the world there may not be many more May balls held, so I think you should grab the opportunity. You will see the town and the colleges at their best – Cambridge is very beautiful. The willows along the Backs are in delicate leaf and there are wild flowers everywhere.*

I know Cynthia has a young man, though I've not met him, but I also know he's gone back to Spain. However, it will be far more fun for us all if Cynthia will make up a foursome – Tony says no strings – so that we can take a punt out, or go for a meal, without Tony feeling he's playing gooseberry. Of course there are girls in Cambridge, but Tony has been studying far too hard to get to know any of them, so would be truly grateful if Cynthia could be persuaded to come with us.

Naturally Daisy had passed on the invitation and had been delighted when Cynthia had accepted without hesitation. 'I like Tony; he's good company, and as Jake says, Clive is a long way away,' she said, tucking her arm in Daisy's as they strolled beside the water. 'I try terribly hard not to worry about Clive but things are really bad for those of the International Brigade still in Spain. It's just a matter of saving as many lives as possible now the end has come. If only Clive would see reason and begin to make his way to the coast!'

'I'm sure he'll do so, because there's no point in staying in Spain now. Indeed, I read somewhere that the London non-intervention committee have discussed the withdrawal of the International Brigade,' Daisy said quickly. She had come to realise, over the past few weeks, how much Cynthia worried and how well her friend hid the fact. 'So you will come to the May ball, and you'll really try not to worry? I'm sure we'll both enjoy it immensely, and it's not something which is likely to come our way again.'

'No, you're right,' Cynthia agreed. 'There isn't time to write to Clive and ask him what he thinks I should do, but if I did I know darned well what his answer would be. Remember what he was like when he came out of hospital for his two weeks' convalescence before returning to Spain?'

Daisy nodded and grinned at the recollection. Cynthia had actually met Clive at the hospital. Daisy thought him pretty ordinary-looking, with soft brown hair which flopped across his forehead, toffee-brown eyes, a humorous mouth and a deter-mined chin. He was only an inch or two taller than Cynthia but built on much sturdier lines, and as soon as he had been released from the ward he had thrown himself into any amusement on offer. He had danced at the Grafton Ballroom, though his leg wound meant that he would probably always limp a little, taken Cynthia boating, boarded the ferry for New Brighton and paddled, built sandcastles and enjoyed the funfair as though he were ten instead of twenty-two. But beneath it all, Daisy had been aware of his sense of purpose and the underlying seriousness which he could not completely hide. A couple of evenings before he left to return to Spain he had told Cynthia something of the war which was being waged, and of the friends he had left behind. 'I can't desert the fellers who have looked to me for leadership,' he had said quietly. 'I know many people, including Dr Venables, will think I'm a fool to jump back into a fire which others are so eager to escape.' He had grinned deprecatingly. 'It's not my fault, it's the way I was brought up. My father's a doctor – you know that – and he goes in and out of cottages which are reeking of infection and would never dream of avoiding his responsibility to the sick. Naturally, he and my mother would be happier if I stayed in England, yet in their hearts they know I must go.'

Daisy had been deeply moved when Cynthia had repeated this conversation. Until that moment, she had thought Clive an unusual choice of boyfriend for Cynthia, but after that she had understood. For the first time, so far as she knew, Cynthia had looked beneath the surface of a young man, and liked – even admired – what she had seen.

'Well? You're very quiet all of a sudden!'

Daisy dragged her mind back from Clive and

the Republican army to the present. 'Sorry, I was daydreaming,' she said. 'Then, since we have decided to go to the ball, I think we ought to tell the Venables as soon as we get back to Rodney Street. I'm sure they'll be absolutely delighted, because Mrs Venables said only the other day that we're acting like two old married ladies instead of a couple of carefree young girls. She asked me why we didn't go along to the Grafton, or one of the other ballrooms – said we should be meeting young men and enjoying ourselves.'

'Yes, I know; the thing is, they still disapprove of poor Clive,' Cynthia said sadly. 'It's understandable in a way because by throwing up his course before he'd sat his finals Clive must seem to have dismissed medicine, which is the main interest in Dr Venables's life. Yet Clive's own father understands, so you'd think my uncle could at least try to see what a grand thing Clive is doing.'

'Oh, when Clive comes back and takes up his place at medical college once more, I expect your uncle will be all over him,' Daisy said encouragingly. 'He is going to do that, isn't he?'

Cynthia shrugged. 'I suppose so,' she said. 'But Dr Beamish isn't rich like my uncle; he's just a village doctor really, and Tony is a good catch because his father has heaps and heaps of money and is a very successful farmer. Once, before I met Clive, that would have mattered to me, but now it doesn't. I'd marry Clive if he didn't have a penny

311

to call his own . . . if he asked me, that is.'

Daisy stared at her friend, seeing her as if for the first time. The soft fair hair combed into a pageboy around her shoulders, the large light-blue eyes with their fringing of pale lashes, the fair skin and the little straight nose, dusted with freckles, were still as they had always been. But Cynthia's rosebud mouth seemed firmer and her chin jutted with a determination which had not been there before. Clive's done her an awful lot of good, Daisy found herself thinking. He's turned her from a nonentity into a personality . . . no, I don't mean that, precisely. He's turned her from a selfish young girl who thought of nothing but her own pleasure into . . . into someone who thinks of others, actually considers their point of view and admires grit and courage.

'Well? Why are you staring at me? I haven't grown an extra head, have I?'

Daisy giggled. 'You might just as well have done,' she said frankly. 'I've never heard the word marriage on your lips before, Cynthia Darlington-Crewe! Has Clive mentioned it, or are you jumping ahead of the gun so to speak?'

Cynthia gave a snort of amusement, then sobered abruptly. 'How can he ask anyone to marry him when he doesn't know when he goes to bed at night whether he'll still be alive by morning?' she asked rather bitterly. 'I don't think he could even ask me to go steady because he'd think it wasn't fair. But I told him I meant to wait for him;

I said no matter how many blokes might ask me out and no matter how many times I might agree to go with them, I'd still be here, waiting for him, even if he were away for half a lifetime.'

'Gosh!' Daisy said, awed. 'I've never felt like that about anyone and I hope I never shall.'

By this time they were making their way across the park towards Croxteth Road, and the tram. 'You must have,' Cynthia said, staring at her. 'What about Jake? You and he have been thick as thieves since you were kids. Or is it Tony Fordham you're interested in?'

'Neither; I'm sure I've told you I don't mean to marry anyone so what's the point of getting all het up?' Daisy asked. 'Didn't you believe me when I said I was never going to marry?'

'Of course I didn't; you were just a kid,' Cynthia said. 'But you're old enough now to fall in love. Why, if I hadn't met him first, you could easily have fallen in love with Clive . . . oh, even the thought makes me want to scratch your eyes out! But are you seriously telling me that you aren't really very fond of Jake?'

'Yes I am . . . telling you I mean. Jake and Tony are both pals, but so are you, Cynthia. I like all three of you and that's about it. As for Clive, I'm sure he's very nice but I'm beginning to think it isn't in me to fall in love with anyone. Girls at school are always oohing and aahing over the boys at Charlie's, or their brother's friends at university, or Gary Cooper or Clark Gable . . . you know, chaps like that. But I seem to be immune, and jolly glad I am. So you see, your Clive is safe from me and my eyes are safe from your claws. Hey, there's our tram . . . better run for it!'

Cambridge, and the colleges, bowled Daisy over. She had worked hard and hoped to get a place at Liverpool university, but the beauty of Cambridge made her long to pursue her studies there. After all, even if she never meant to marry anyone, Jake and Tony were her pals and it would be nice to have their company. When she said this to Jake, however, he looked rather guilty. 'The thing is, queen – I think I told you – I've joined the University Air Squadron to give myself a head start when I put my name down for the Royal Air Force,' he told her. 'So I'm not likely to be here if you come up.'

'You did tell me,' Daisy said. 'But if you do that, you won't get your degree. You'll be like Clive, chucking away your chances.'

Jake pulled a face. 'There'll be no hope of me taking a degree at all if we let Hitler overrun the whole of Europe, because we shall be next,' he said seriously. 'Some chance I'd have of doing a degree with storm troopers and Brown Shirts swarming across Britain. Besides, our best hope of keeping the Nazis at bay is to have properly trained and equipped forces. Can't you see that, Daisy?'

'Ye-es, only we are an island; surely the Channel will stop them, to say nothing of France. I mean, they've got to cross the whole of France and the Maginot Line in order to reach the Channel ports. That will mean it'll be a couple of years, maybe more . . .'

'For God's sake don't be such an idiot,' Jake said irritably. 'You're burying your head in the sand, just like any stupid ostrich. Distance didn't help Spain, did it? When war comes, aircraft could fly across France and drop paratroopers . . . oh, I don't know, I just know war is a certainty. Everyone in Cambridge knows it, so I'm going to join the air force and get ready to fight with everything I've got.'

'Perhaps I should do the same,' Daisy said slowly. 'Only I don't know what use I'd be.'

The two of them were sitting on the riverbank, watching punts and rowboats drift past. Presently, they hoped that Tony and Cynthia would join them for they had planned a trip down the river and a picnic and Tony had taken Cynthia off to hire a punt, promising to pick them up as soon as he had done so. The ball would start quite late so Jake had assured the girls that they would have plenty of time to change into what he termed their glad rags before it began.

'I don't know that women are joining up at this stage,' Jake said thoughtfully now. 'I think they'll need you to take over the jobs the men have left, but anyway that's all for the future. Ah, here they come; doesn't Cynthia look like the Queen of Sheba, lying amongst the cushions whilst Tony wields the pole? I just hope he doesn't splash her because that orange dress must have cost a pretty penny.'

'Don't you let Cynthia hear you call it an orange dress; it's flame chiffon,' Daisy said reproachfully as Tony steered his craft in to the bank. She hopped aboard then sat down hastily as the punt rocked. 'Can you manage the picnic basket? You can pass it to me and I'll stow it away under the seats.'

The ball was a great success. Daisy had graciously allowed Cynthia to lend her a frock which had a wonderful swirling skirt and a low bodice, held up by tiny narrow straps across her shoulders, and Jake had shyly presented her with a small heart-shaped locket on a chain. 'I wish it could have been gold and I wish I could have put a photograph of meself inside it,' he had said with a grin. 'But I've not gorra photo an' I don't mean to cut off a clump of me lovely hair, so you're at liberty to stick a picture of Rudolph Valentino or Gary Cooper inside it. I flatter meself there's norra lorra difference between them and me.'

She had laughed and punched his shoulder but had been touched by his thoughtfulness, for she had commented, wistfully, only the day before that she could have done with a necklace since the dress was cut so low. Now, when she looked in the mirror with the locket sparkling at her throat, she scarcely recognised herself, so glamorous did she appear. She had been doubtful about borrowing a gown which seemed to consist largely of white net and white satin, thinking that she would have preferred a brighter colour. But as soon as she put it on, she realised Cynthia had known best. It looked wonderful, and when she had daringly brushed Vaseline on to her curly dark lashes and added a touch of pink paint to her lips, she felt that she would not disgrace Jake.

And she was right. Jake's face glowed with pride as he introduced her to his friends and Daisy allowed her enjoyment to show, sparkling in a way she had never done at the Grafton. Jake had warned her that he was no dancer but she soon discovered that he got by very creditably; in fact she found it easier to dance with him than with his more expert friends.

'Half my pals are in love with you, Daisy Kildare, you little flirt,' Jake said as he took her down to supper. 'And I've always thought you were such a nice quiet girl!'

'So I am,' Daisy said demurely. 'I'm putting on an act; didn't you guess?'

Jake laughed and squeezed her hand. 'It's your true self coming out, after being repressed by school and the Venables, and your delightful Aunt Jane,' he said. 'And now let's follow everyone else's example and stroll along the Backs in the moonlight. It's most awfully romantic, or so I'm told.'

'I don't want to be romantic,' Daisy said frankly. 'But I'm ever so grateful to you, Jake, because I've had the most marvellous evening. Well, not just a marvellous evening, a magical time. Everything we've done has been such fun and it's all thanks to you, of course.'

'It has been grand,' Jake said absently. 'See that clump of willows ahead? There's a seat beneath the branches; there are things I want to say to you and we shan't have time for much talking tomorrow because your train leaves pretty early, doesn't it?'

Daisy agreed that this was so and presently they settled themselves on the bench, Daisy thinking how much she would love to study here but well aware that it was not likely to happen. There were only a couple of women's colleges, so competition must be twenty times harder than it was for men, who had a wide choice of places, and Daisy knew that she was nowhere near as clever as Tony, let alone Jake. But the silver moonlight and the scents of waterweed and the flowers which lined the bank, even the shadows cast by the willow beneath which they sat, were here for her to enjoy and remember, and she made herself comfortable, beginning to tell Jake how she envied him, how she wished she was cleverer so that she, too, might come here to take her degree.

And then Jake spoiled it all.

'If it's been magical for you, you've made it magical for me,' he said huskily. 'Oh, Daisy, I've loved you ever since you walked into the kitchen at Rodney Street, only now it's different . . . stronger . . . I can't explain . . . oh, Daisy.'

Thoroughly alarmed, Daisy found herself being

318

violently hugged and, when she opened her mouth to protest, equally violently kissed. She tried to wriggle free but all of a sudden Jake seemed to have at least four hands and all of them were in places which Daisy preferred to keep to herself. 'Gerroff, you bugger,' she shouted, feeling like a child again, and a child who was being attacked by someone she had trusted. 'Jake Elgin, if you don't gerroff, sure 'n' I'll kill you, so I will . . .'

Jake took no notice but continued to fondle and squeeze, until Daisy managed to get a hand free. She lashed out wildly in the direction of Jake's head, missing completely. If Jake had not laughed, she thought afterwards, she might have remembered that she was a lady, but the laugh, and the fact that he continued his amorous activities, spurred her into violence. She whacked out and felt her knuckles meet his nose. Jake's head jerked back and his eyes watered, but to Daisy's fury he continued to clasp her in one arm whilst fumbling for his handkerchief. Horrified at what she had done, for his nose was bleeding copiously, she began to apologise. 'I'm sorry, Jake, but you shouldn't have gone on when I told you to stop,' she said reproachfully. 'Oh, and you're bleeding like anything.'

'I'm sorry, too, but you didn't have to punch me,' Jake mumbled thickly. 'We's pals, ain't we? You know I wouldn't hurt you for all the world; dammit, Daisy, I love you!'

'Well I don't love you,' Daisy said crossly. 'You

should never start – start that sort of thing without so much as a by your leave! Oh, oh, and your beastly blood has speckled my frock – Cynthia's frock I mean. What on earth got into you to frighten me like that?'

'I told you, I love you,' Jake said miserably. 'I know we're both very young, but what does that matter? If you love someone, you love 'em, an' that's that; age don't matter.' He examined his handkerchief then glanced down at his shirt, formerly so crisp and white, but now dappled with dark stains. 'Gawd, girl, this bloomin' outfit is hired – even the shirt ain't mine! What'll Moss Bros say when I take it back lookin' as if I'd took part in the Valentine Day massacre? And I still don't gerrit. Why didn't you ask me to stop?'

'I did, honest I did,' Daisy said forlornly. 'You must have heard me and I wriggled like anything. What did you think that meant, eh?'

'I thought it were passion,' Jake said gruffly. 'How were I to know? You're the first girl I've kissed in a serious way, and . . .'

'Oh really?' Daisy said. 'And what happened when you kissed the others, pray? I didn't realise you made a habit of it.'

'I *don't*, I *told* you it were the first time I'd – I'd done anything like that,' Jake said sulkily. 'You're a bleedin' menace, Daisy Kildare; there's no way the blood will come out of this shirt so I reckon they'll make me pay for it. And don't go on about your frock because there's only little spots on the front whereas I'm soaked in the perishin' stuff.'

'Well I'm sorry . . .' Daisy was beginning when something struck her and she giggled. 'I say, where's your posh accent gone? And mine for that matter! As soon as we got upset and angry, you went back to talkin' Scouse, and I might have come over from Ireland yesterday! I tell you what though, Jake, Aunt Jane always says with blood stains that if you soak 'em in cold water before they've dried, they'll come out clean as a whistle. What say we try it?'

They had walked a long way before sitting down on the bench and now Jake, looking cautiously around, observed that they were alone; everyone else, presumably, having returned to the ballroom. 'All right, I'm game if you are,' he said, and began to struggle out of his jacket. 'Can you take that dress off? I reckon dabbing at it with water won't do much good.'

'Yes, I suppose I can; I'm wearing my own petticoat underneath,' Daisy said doubtfully. 'But – but suppose someone sees me? What'll they think? They'll think we're up to something!'

The willow beneath which they had been sitting was a vast old tree, its branches actually extending several feet over the water. Jake pointed this out and, having looked carefully around him, laid his jacket on the grass, then heaved the dress shirt over his head. 'There's no one about to think anything,' he observed. 'And if you imagine that the sight of you in your petticoat is going to inflame

321

me into trying to kiss you again, I can tell you you're worrying for nothing. God, my nose feels as if it's been hit with a sledgehammer! You're safe from me, Daisy Kildare.'

'Good,' Daisy said, kneeling on the bank beside him. 'How is your nose – is it still bleeding? Only I can't undo the little hooks at the back of my bodice, so you're going to have to help me, and it wouldn't do to get your beastly blood all over the back as well as the front.'

She turned her head to examine Jake and had to bite back a giggle when she saw him fingering his injured nose. 'Well? I can't see any more blood but you'd better wash your hands.'

'I think it has stopped,' Jake said grudgingly. 'But you'll have to wait until I've finished with my shirt.' He peered at the garment, swishing it back and forth in the water, then gave a crow of triumph. 'Your Aunt Jane was right! It's clean as a new pin. I'll go and hang it over the bench, then I'll give you a hand with your frock.'

'I wonder if I need to take it right off?' Daisy said doubtfully, as Jake began to undo the neat row of hooks and eyes. 'You were right, the splashes aren't too bad. But I suppose having gone this far . . .' She stood up, stepped carefully out of the dress and was actually lowering it into the water when she heard Jake hiss in his breath. She glanced at him, then followed the direction of his gaze. Someone was coming along the bank. It was a white-haired man smoking a pipe, strolling along with one hand in his pocket, his gown flapping, and gazing at the river.

'Oh, my God; I bet it's one of the teachers . . . dons I mean . . .' Daisy gabbled. She tried to pull her dress out of the water but the layers of net and the heavy satin defeated her, and before she could even beg Jake's aid the dress tore itself free from her grasp and sailed merrily off down the river.

'Daisy Kildare, if you think you can come creeping in here, wrapped up in a borrowed academic gown, with your petticoat damp to the waist and my second best dress streaked with mud and dripping water, then you are much mistaken. Don't say the admirable Jake tried to get fresh and started off by pushing you in the river! And where did the gown come in? Oh, I know every student has to have one, but Jake was in tails, or he was the last time I saw him.'

Daisy pulled off her petticoat and slung it on the floor, then hung the academic gown over the back of a chair, and sat down with a thump on the bed. She and Cynthia were sharing a pleasant twin-bedded room in Jake's college, but now she found herself wishing that she had had a single room, or alternatively that Cynthia had fallen asleep before her own return. However, explanations would have to be made eventually so perhaps it was better to get them over sooner rather than later. Nevertheless, she made an effort to stall her friend for a while at least. 'It's a long story and I'm dread-

fully tired . . .' she began, only to be firmly interrupted.

'I don't care how tired you are, I want an explanation,' Cynthia said. 'Spill the beans or I'll get out
of bed and shake the truth out of you.'

Daisy sighed, reached for her nightgown and
pulled it over her head. 'It was all perfectly innocent, the sort of thing which might happen to
anyone,' she said. 'Jake and I went for a walk along
the riverbank. It was so beautiful with the moonlight casting black shadows and the willows
leaning over the water, so we sat down for a
moment on a bench, to drink in the view. Jake got
out his handkerchief and blew his nose, and all of
a sudden I saw something running down his face.
He'd started a nosebleed, a really bad one. We did
our best to staunch the flow with his handkerchief
but it went on and on. It soaked his dress shirt –
it was a hired one – and even splashed the bodice
of your beautiful frock. Jake was really upset; he
thought they'd make him pay for the shirt because
it was absolutely covered. Then I remembered
Aunt Jane telling me once that if you soak a blood-
stain in cold water before it has had a chance to
set, it should come out completely. I told Jake and
he wriggled out of his shirt at once and began to
swish it about in the river, and Aunt Jane was right:
it came clean. So then I got him to unhook my –
your – frock, and I was just beginning to dunk the
bodice in the water when we saw someone coming.
In the moonlight I thought he was quite old

because his hair looked white and he was smoking a pipe . . .'

Cynthia giggled. 'Quite young men smoke pipes sometimes,' she observed. 'But I know what you mean . . . carry on with the story; I'm intrigued.'

'Yes, it's all very well for you, but I suddenly realised what the man would think when he saw Jake naked to the waist, and me in my brassiere and petticoat. I was so frightened that I let go of the dress and it sailed away down the river, just like Ophelia in *Hamlet*.' For the first time the humour of the situation struck her and she choked on a laugh. 'At least, that's what the don must have thought because he kicked off his shoes, chucked his gown and jacket on the bank, and dived into the water. Poor chap, he thought I was still inside the dress; that's why I said it was like Ophelia.

'Of course Jake and I burst out from under the willow and yelled to him, and we both jumped into the river and helped him ashore; not that he needed it. He had the dress in his arms, and when we explained he was really decent. He laughed like a drain – well we all did – and protested that it didn't matter, and then he wrapped me in his academic gown, I was beginning to shiver by then, and ran us all the way back to Jake's stair, which happened to be nearest. That was when I realised he was really quite young, only with hair so blond that it had looked white in the moonlight, and after Jake had made us all a hot cup of tea and we'd dried ourselves off as best we could, he told us to forget all about it and went off. After that, I thought it was time I came back to bed, and the rest you know.'

'Well, if anyone's going to get into hot water, it's you, Daisy Kildare,' Cynthia said, as both girls snuggled down. 'What was the fellow's name? The don, I mean. You'll have to return his gown before we leave, I suppose. Fortunately, it doesn't seem to have got dirty despite the adventurous life it's led.'

Daisy chuckled. 'His name is Guy Sanderson, but I shan't have to return it to him; Jake will do that. He's going to see us off though I told him that there was no need, so I shall hand over the gown first thing in the morning.' She sat up on one elbow and peered across at her companion. 'Look, Cyn, I'm most awfully sorry about your dress, but I'll have it dry cleaned and I'm sure it will look as good as new. The blood stains have come out and what's left is just plain old mud. Did you worry when we didn't come back to the dance? Only by the time we'd helped Mr Sanderson out of the river, the ball was long over and it never occurred to me that you might still be awake. How's Tony, by the way?'

'Fine, I suppose,' Cynthia said vaguely. 'He walked me back to our room but didn't try any funny business . . . well, he promised not to, if you remember. I take it Jake behaved himself? Or rather I take it he didn't behave himself and you loved every minute, because anyone can see Jake thinks you're pretty special and I guess you feel the same about him.'

'I told you, Jake is a friend, just like you and Tony,' Daisy said crossly. 'Because we've had a wonderful time and I was looking glamorous for once, that doesn't change anything. We're still only friends.'

'Oh come on, Daisy, a girl doesn't walk with a fellow in the moonlight unless she's at least a bit keen on him,' Cynthia said reproachfully. 'Why, even Tony gave me a goodnight kiss before we parted. Are you trying to tell me that Jake didn't get smoochy?'

Daisy sat up like a jack-in-the-box and hurled her pillow at Cynthia, causing her friend to fall, giggling, back on her own pillow. 'Shut up, Cynthia Darlington-Crewe,' she shouted. 'I've had enough . . .'

There was a sleepy mumble from the room next door and then someone rapped sharply on the dividing wall. Daisy jumped hastily out of bed and retrieved her pillow, saying in a whisper as she did so: 'I'm sorry, Cyn, but you asked for that. And now for goodness' sake, let's get to sleep or we'll look like a couple of hags in the morning.'

The girls arrived home in Rodney Street, Daisy at least longing to tell someone what a good time she had had. But of course there was no Aunt Jane in whom to confide, nor Jake in the coachman's quarters above the stable. Ruth was working in a factory out at Long Lane, making uniforms for the forces. She had a young man, a tram conductor, and though she was always pleased to see Daisy, their different circumstances made it impossible for Daisy to tell her much about Cambridge because it would have sounded like boasting. Dr and Mrs Venables were interested but again, Daisy never felt completely at her ease with them. So in the end, she decided to visit Aunt Jane just as soon as exams were over.

Of course by then Jake's term would have finished too, but she already knew that he would not be returning to the farm during the long vac. Despite his father's hopes, Jake had not taken to farming. He had applied for, and got, a job in a factory in the Midlands, where they made aeroplanes. 'I mean to learn as much as I can about aero engines and earn some money at the same time,' he had told Daisy as they sat out one of the dances at the May ball. 'Pa keeps telling me that money will be tight until the land is productive, so I wouldn't dream of asking him for pocket money, or money for books and so on. After all, Aunt Jane and Pa both earned decent salaries working for the Venables and Aunt Jane had a live-in job which meant food and rent and so on was all paid for. Now they're eking out their savings very carefully because Pa thinks it will be at least a year, and more likely two, before they can begin to sell their produce, so you see this is my opportunity to pay

Pa back for all he's laid out on my education. Of course I shall have to lodge with someone, but even so I shall be able to save money to send home.' Daisy had been very impressed and decided that when the school holidays came, she would follow Jake's example and try to get a paid job.

Back in Rodney Street once more, the two girls rapidly returned to their normal lives. Daisy went to school, studied and helped out round the house, and even Cynthia made her own bed, tidied their rooms and kept the stairs and the front hall brushed and dusted. She told Daisy frankly, however, that she did not mean to work outside the home; why should she? Her allowance was so generous that she seldom spent even half of it, and when Daisy landed a job as a holiday relief in Woolworth's Bazaar on Church Street Cynthia was quite dismayed and offered to pay her friend to stay at home.

'After all, you came here first to be with me, so what's different now?' she enquired rather tetchily. 'I can afford it, you know.'

'Yes, I do know. But quite honestly, Cyn, I want to get experience of work. And since I mean to send at least some of the money back home to Ireland, so that Brendan can add it to his boat fund, I'd feel bad not actually earning it when he and Amanda have to work so hard.'

'But how can Amanda work with an active toddler?' Cynthia objected. 'And I bet Woolworth's aren't going to pay you very much because everything there is so cheap.'

'No shop girls ever got rich so far as I know,' Daisy acknowledged. 'But it's experience, Cynthia. And anyway, if I get a place at college, you won't see much of me after October, so you might as well get used to the idea.'

Cynthia sniffed. 'You'll still be here when classes finish,' she pointed out. 'But the chances are, I may not be. Aunt Venables is going to send me to a finishing school in Switzerland and I'm most awfully keen to go, so that I can actually speak French and German all the time, and even possibly a bit of Italian. She knows I shall never need to work for my living but she says that to speak a language really well is always useful. I expect she wants to wean me away from Clive, give my thoughts another direction, but she won't do that.' The two girls were sitting in their small parlour, Daisy packing away her homework whilst Cynthia worked desultorily at the embroidered napkins she was making as a Christmas gift for her mother's friend in Southport. 'To tell you the truth, Daisy, when I told Clive about the money I shall inherit when I'm twenty-one, he said that I should give it to a worthy cause. I just laughed because I thought he was joking, but having had time to consider, I'm rather afraid he meant it. He doesn't believe in inherited wealth, it offends his socialist principles, so if I'm really serious about him, and I am, then I may have to get a job myself.'

She sounded so dismayed that Daisy had to choke back a laugh, but choke it back she did when

330

she saw that Cynthia was looking anxious. 'Are you really serious about Clive? Well, I know you are, but do you mean to marry him? If you do so, you won't just be embracing Clive, you know, but his socialist principles as well. Oh, Cynthia, I simply can't imagine you working at a factory bench or marching along the road carrying a banner saying "Fair deals for the working man; down with Capitalism".'

Cynthia giggled, though rather reluctantly. 'I never thought I'd feel like this about anyone, let alone someone whose whole way of life is the exact opposite of mine,' she admitted. 'But I'd do anything for Clive, anything at all. And that includes working in a proper job, though whether I could actually bring myself to hand over the money my mother left me to some good cause, I'm not sure.'

'I don't think you should,' Daisy said, having considered the matter. 'Nobody ever knows what's round the corner, Cynthia. Look at us Kildares! If we had had money behind us . . . Just remember that your Clive could be injured so that he could no longer work; or you could have a grosh of children and very little money coming in. All right, give some of the money away, but not all of it.'

'I expect you're right, but I shan't have to make a decision until I'm twenty-one,' Cynthia said airily. 'And right now I've got to kit myself out for this finishing school; term starts in September and

I mean to have a fabulous time because I'm sure you, Clive and Jake are right . . . oh, and Tony too . . . in believing that war will come, and I mean to enjoy life before that ends the fun and frolic. And I know you'll want to go and see Aunt Jane before you become a shop girl, so how about taking me with you? I'd like to see this farm I've heard so much about.'

They agreed that they would both visit the farm, and Daisy's examination results came through a couple of weeks later, assuring her of a place at Liverpool university. Her job at Woolworth's Bazaar would start the following Monday, so she and Cynthia seized what might be the only chance they would get to visit the farm. They got up incredibly early one morning and reached Abergele in good time, to be met by Aunt Jane and Uncle Bob in an ancient pony cart. Daisy had been worried that the couple might seem strained and anxious, but on the contrary they looked both fit and happy. 'I thought all the hard work and worry might have pulled you down, Auntie, but I've never seen you look so well,' Daisy said joyfully. 'Country living really suits you; and you, Mr . . . I mean Uncle Bob . . . look fit and happy as well.'

Her aunt laughed. 'You're right about the work being hard, but we've been pretty lucky so far. The weather hasn't let us down and we had an excellent crop of plums. What we didn't sell in Abergele market I either bottled or made into jam, and our hens have been laying well all summer. Do you remember the lemon curd I used to make for the Venables? Well, I must have made a hundred pots or more and I've sold every one. Then there are my fruitcakes; I'm using an old recipe which we found in one of Bob's mother's cookery books, and they are selling as well as the lemon curd . . .'

Bob turned and grinned at the girls. 'I tell her if she goes on as she has done, we'll need to start a shop and not just take a market stall,' he told them. 'At first we supplied other stalls, but one came vacant so we took the plunge and rented it, and haven't looked back.'

'That's wonderful,' Daisy said with real enthusiasm. 'And in a way you've got the Depression to thank, Auntie, because if Mrs Venables hadn't had to let the cook go you'd never have taken over her work as well as your own.'

'That's very true, though I think cooking is something you don't forget and I always was good at it,' her aunt said. 'I had a lot of practice when your mam was young, remember, and by the time she was off my hands I could bake my own bread, and make a sustaining meal out of a few bruised vegetables, a spoonful of flour, and anything else you could put in the pot. Still, you're right: cooking fancy stuff for the Venables taught me a lot.' She leaned over and patted Cynthia's hand. 'I know when I left I told Mrs Venables that I'd come back often, but we've been so busy that I've not visited as I had planned. And if there's a war – though of course we hope there won't be – it will put a stop to cheap imports from abroad and mean British farmers start getting a fair return when they sell their crops. So, dear Cynthia, please will you apologise to your aunt on my behalf and tell her that one of the reasons she's not seen more of me is because we're doing so well?'

Cynthia promised to do so and presently they arrived at the farm. Cynthia exclaimed at how pretty it was, with its whitewashed walls, blue paintwork and neatly tilled garden. She had not seen the farm before and Daisy, who had not visited it since the wedding, was even more impressed with the changes her aunt and Bob Elgin had wrought. Not only was there a tidy garden where waist-high weeds had flourished on her last visit, but great improvements had been made in the big living kitchen. The earth floor had been covered with quarry tiles and the rather shabby armchairs had been re-upholstered with a bright cotton material which matched the curtains at the windows. There was an old Welsh dresser against one wall covered in pretty, though not matching, china. 'We got it at a house sale for a song,' Bob Elgin informed them proudly. 'See the Aga? That's a blessing, I promise you . . . well, Janie wouldn't have been able to cook half the stuff we sell if we'd had to rely on the old stove my uncle used.'

'Where did you get that?' Daisy asked curiously.

'And the grandfather clock wasn't here last time I visited either. Nor that enormous table.'

'An old feller outside Conway died and his son didn't fancy taking on a rundown farm when he had a nice little business of his own down south,' Bob explained. 'Farming's been in such a poor way that there was almost no competition for the stuff, so we bought a good deal, including a tractor and trailer and two good carthorses. One of 'em brought you up from the station today,' he added with a grin.

After that, Aunt Jane took Cynthia on a tour of the farmhouse, whilst Bob and Daisy went round the farmyard and outbuildings, Daisy exclaiming with admiration at every improvement. Presently they returned to the house to find Aunt Jane dishing up whilst Cynthia laid the table. Once they were seated and eating an excellent beef stew, Daisy asked where Jake fitted into the scheme of things. Bob laughed. 'He doesn't,' he said. 'He's entirely taken up with aero engines at the moment, and talking about this war which he's so sure is coming. He isn't the only one either; they tell me the army's dug trenches across Hyde Park so's they can hide troops in 'em to shoot anyone parachuting into London. Heaven knows whose idea that was, but I reckon they'd do more good if they ripped up the grass and planted spuds or cabbages. Still, there you are: that's government for you. And the way I see it, the farm will be here if Jake

335

needs it when the war's over and forgotten.'

Daisy had been working at Woolworth's for several weeks when she received a rare letter from Brendan, which delighted her.

Dear Daisy,

Good news at last! I have moved into our old cottage with Mr Prescott's blessing, since Mr Morgan has give up all claim to the property. It seems his attorney pursued Paddy Kildare and got money from him, I don't know how much. There is no money for us, as yet – I doubt there ever will be – but we don't care. When I say we, you'll guess I mean Amanda, Gerald and myself, though Gerald must keep his job for a while at least, because we need every penny we can get. He's moved back in with his old mother but means to come over whenever he can to see us and give a hand. I've not got enough money yet to buy a boat. A boat would be a big help. I know you're off to college, so the money you've been sending will have to stop, but we'll manage. No use saying come home, because I know college is rare important, but some students work when they ain't in class, so if there's anything going spare, we'd be grateful.

Take care and remember this is your home as much as ours. We miss you. Your affec brother,
  Brendan.

Daisy read the letter through three times. She

and Cynthia had been sitting in their small parlour, going over the clothing Daisy would need for college and Cynthia would take with her to her finishing school. Daisy thrust the letter at Cynthia, beginning to tell her to read it, then snatched it back, flew out of the room, and ran down the stairs. She went straight to Mrs Venables's study, knocked and entered. Mrs Venables was seated at her desk, doing the paperwork for her husband. She looked up and smiled as Daisy entered the room.

'Now what can I do for you, my dear?' she said cheerfully.

'Mrs Venables, do you remember the doctor saying what a shame it was that I was working at Woolworth's Bazaar, because that was a job which someone with far fewer qualifications than myself might easily do? He had heard that one of the big shipping companies was looking for a clerical worker who would be paid double what I was getting on the shop floor, but then said it would probably be no use to me since he believed they wanted a full-time worker and not just a holiday relief.' She thrust the letter from Brendan into the older woman's hands. 'Will you read that?'

Mrs Venables read the short letter practically at a glance, then turned to Daisy, nodding slowly. 'You won't take up your place at college whilst your brother needs help so desperately,' she said matter-of-factly. 'I dare say the doctor will tell you that a university education will one day be worth very much more to you than a job as a shipping clerk, but I don't agree. Your family were tricked out of what was rightfully theirs and now that Brendan has got it back, you and Amanda are desperate that he should succeed. You could go your own way, telling yourself that the salary you would earn as a graduate could all go to Brendan in three or four years' time. But by then he may not need the money because he will have either succeeded or failed completely; he needs money now and it is your privilege as well, I think, as your duty, to do everything in your power to help him.'

Daisy was so relieved that tears came to her eyes and she had to blow her nose hard before replying. 'Oh, thank you, Mrs Venables. You've put into words exactly how I feel. And now is there any chance that the shipping clerk job is still open? If so, and you can give me their direction, I'll apply at once.'

Chapter Ten

The job at the shipping office had been filled, but Dr Venables advised her to try for a post as receptionist to four doctors, who shared a premises only a dozen doors from 39 Rodney Street. They had employed a nurse but found she could not keep up with the filing, letter-writing and general administrative duties which were the major part of her job, so they had asked Dr Venables for advice and he told them that though he always referred to his receptionist as 'Nurse' she was no such thing but merely wore a crisp white uniform, a white cap, sensible walking shoes – also white – and a fob watch dangling from her lapel, all provided by her employer.

Dr Venables had offered to help find a suitable person for the job, meaning to ask his own receptionist whether she knew anyone who might fit the bill. Now, when his wife told him that Daisy would not be going to university, he had agreed to recommend her for the job. He even arranged for the doctors to interview her first thing on Monday morning and advised her to wear a crisp white blouse and a dark skirt.

Daisy was afraid the doctors might reject her

application when they realised she was a connection of Dr Venables, but this did not prove to be the case. All four doctors had been impressed with her academic qualifications and thought she would soon prove to be in complete control of the job. They wanted her to start work the very next day but Daisy explained that she would need to tell Woolworth's she was leaving first, and then contact the college so that she might ask them if she could take up her place some time in the future, when her family no longer needed the money she could earn.

Rather to her surprise, once he was sure she did not intend to turn her back on a university education for ever, Dr Venables had applauded her decision. He also said that his wife would be glad of her company once Cynthia left. 'Over the years we've both got to enjoy having young people around,' he explained, 'and I miss Elgin. I like driving the car myself, but Elgin was an intelligent fellow and knew Liverpool like the back of his hand. Also, he had got to know my patients and could take me from one house to another without hesitation, even telling me who lived where. It takes me twice as long to do my rounds now, though I wouldn't admit it to anyone who wasn't part of the family.'

Daisy grinned at him. For some months now, she and Cynthia had been having dinner each night with the Venables and she was far less in awe of the doctor than she had been. She discovered that

he had a sense of humour and was deeply interested in the lives that she and Cynthia led. He
encouraged her to talk about her job at Woolworth's
Bazaar as well as such things as a trip to Seaforth
on the Overhead Railway, or life on the Elgins' farm.

The professor with whom Daisy had an interview about putting off her degree was very
understanding. He said it was a pity she could
not take up her English course immediately, but
added that in his opinion war was almost a
certainty, despite Mr Chamberlain's piece of paper,
so she would probably have had to quit some time
in the near future. He agreed there was nothing
to stop her re-applying when, as he tactfully put
it, there would be less need for her to earn. They
parted on the best of terms but Daisy could not
forbear a wistful glance around her as she left the
halls of learning, for she had dreamed of becoming
a part of the university ever since getting her
School Certificate.

'There's a letter for you, Brendan. Do you want
me to open it and read it to you while you eat
your porridge?'

Amanda's voice cut across Brendan's thoughts
and he looked up and grinned at her. The two of
them were in the kitchen of the Benmacraig cottage
whilst Amanda's little son, named Colm for his
dead grandfather but known as Colly, stood at his
uncle's elbow.

Brendan had been working out costings of some

description with a stub of pencil on a piece of wrapping paper, but now he nodded. 'You might as well, alanna, since I recognise the writing; it's from our Daisy, ain't it? It'll be meant for both of us even if it's only addressed to me.'

'True,' Amanda said, and Brendan thought how his sister's looks and attitude had improved since she had moved back to Benmacraig. She had arrived pale and exhausted, with lank hair and a greyish tinge to her skin, but this had soon changed. Now, her cheeks were flushed, her skin was like milk and her dark-gold hair had been cut and curled prettily round her small head. In the early days she had been inclined to find fault with the house, the garden and Brendan's own efforts, but now she worked as hard as he, putting all to rights, and it seemed to suit her. However, they had not, as yet, been able to buy a boat, a donkey, or the stock they so badly needed, which was why Brendan was working out the best way to spend his shrinking savings. Poultry must be purchased though they could only afford day-old chicks as yet, for the four hens which pecked and scraped a living around the croft were old and only produced eggs in the summer. A pig or a cow was, of course, out of the question whilst money was still so scarce, and as for a boat . . . Brendan desperately wanted a boat but knew it would be false economy to buy a poor, leaky old thing, which was all he could afford right now. He had considered a corrach but knew again that it would be a false economy, for the shore here was treacherous and could not be relied upon. A storm which the good old *Mary Ellen* could weather with ease would have swamped a corrach, made of tarred canvas stretched over a wooden frame, and broken it up before the wind had reached half-strength. And besides, there were his landlines. He put them out most days when the weather was clement and had had several decent catches of fish, which was one of the reasons, he thought, why his sister was beginning to gain condition. Why, once or twice they had even had hauls good enough to enable them to salt some of the fish down for winter use.

Then there were the crops. Back in the spring, before they even knew that Benmacraig might one day be theirs once more, Brendan had secretly dug and sieved and weeded a good large piece of land, closely surrounded by waist-high bracken and gorse which had hidden his efforts from prying eyes. Then he had haunted the narrow lanes and bigger byways with a small coal shovel in one hand and an ancient sack in the other. Every time he saw a pile of horse manure, pig dung or even cowpats, he had shovelled it into his sack and then dug the resultant stuff into his patch of good earth. He had buried the manure deep, so that it would not burn the potatoes, for it had not been rotted down the way he would have liked, but he knew it would be effective nevertheless. Then he had eaten nothing but bread and drunk nothing but water for a couple of weeks, putting the money he usually spent on food away until he had saved enough to buy seed potatoes. These he had planted in his 'stolen' and well-manured patch of earth, so that by the time the croft was officially Kildare property once more he had a good crop of potatoes, some to eat at once, some to put into a hay-filled clamp to see them through the winter. Then he had cleared more ground in order to plant winter cabbage which he would harvest as the cold months passed, ensuring them enough vegetables to keep them healthy, provided that the weather did not let him down.

But now it was July and he and Amanda, still wise in country ways despite their long absence from the land, knew that they must gather in everything possible to see them over the hard months to come. As soon as it was light, Amanda would put a rope round Colly's waist to tether him to her, and set off to collect wild strawberries and raspberries, the early plums which grew in the woods, and anything else which they could preserve for winter. She bought as much sugar as they could afford, which was not much, and bottled fruit or made it into jam. Rose hips, if you were not afraid of the hard work involved, could be turned into a delicious cordial which, bottled, corked and sealed, would keep all winter long.

And there was the peat. The best time of year to cut it was now, when the peat bogs were at their driest. Although lacking a donkey or any other beast of burden, Brendan cut the heavy peat and carted it back to Benmacraig himself, piling it up against the side of the cottage and covering it with a rough roofing of canvas to protect it when the bad weather came.

'Brendan? Shall I read you the letter, or do you want to do so yourself?'

'I said you could read it, but me mind's still wrestlin' wit' the money we've got left and how best to spend it,' Brendan explained. He reached across the table and patted Amanda's folded hands. 'Go on, open it. You know you're longin' to do so.'

Amanda smiled back, slit open the envelope and produced the sheets, saying as she did so: 'I expect it'll be all about college and how she's looking forward to it . . .' She ran her eyes swiftly down the page. 'No it ain't! Oh, Brendan, she's give up her college place and got a job so she has, and means to send us most of what she earns.' She turned over the page and gasped. 'Oh, my dear brother, I thought there were two sheets but the second one is a money order!' She drew in an ecstatic breath. 'It must be the money she was saving for college.'

Brendan leaned across the table and took the money order and the letter, eyes widening. 'Daisy's a grand girl, so she is,' he said reverently. He scanned the letter. 'And she says she'll send us money every month, because she means to take an evening job as well if she can get one. And not a grumble about giving up her place at that college;

she's a dote, so she is.' He frowned anxiously, glancing from the money order to his sister. 'Has she done right, alanna? I hope to God she's not ruined her chances just to help us.'

Amanda shook her head. 'She must have a real good job to be able to send money to us, so what's the odds?' she asked. 'What's that saying? Oh, I know – don't look a gift horse in the mouth. And remember, Bren, she's had it easy for years while we've been strugglin'. You mustn't send the money back or pretend we can manage without it; that would be a mad thing to do. Now that she is able to help, don't you dare try to stop her. After all, it's her future as well as ours.'

Brendan pretended to agree but in his heart he suspected that this was not so. Daisy had grown away from them, lived a life so different that he could scarcely imagine it, but he knew, suddenly, that his little sister needed to help in their struggle even more than she needed the college education which she had been so proud of earning. She had loved Benmacraig, her parents and the life they had all lived here. He was pretty certain she would never return to Ireland, save for brief visits, yet helping them to restore their home would give her enormous satisfaction and take away the guilt which he was sure she felt, because her life had been so much easier than theirs.

But across the table, Amanda was staring at him anxiously. So he smiled and tucked the money order into the pocket of his old corduroy trousers. 'I've not the slightest intention of handing the money back or telling her not to send more,' he said reassuringly. 'She'd be turble hurt, so she would, and anyway we can't afford such gestures. And now I'm off to the village to change this order for cash.'

Rather to her own surprise, Daisy loved her new job. Two of the doctors were young and all of them were honestly grateful for her efficiency and the speed with which she had learned to cope with both patients and paperwork. The surgery did not start its day's work until ten in the morning, though as secretary/receptionist she had to be there by nine in order to open up and arrange patients' visits. She finished each evening at five o'clock, for although the doctors took it in turns to have an evening surgery which lasted from six until eight, one of their wives did reception duty then, leaving Daisy free to look around her for an evening job. Mrs Venables thought she was working quite hard enough because before she left in the morning she helped Molly, who had been acting as cook since Aunt Jane left, to make the breakfast and to prepare vegetables, for the evening meal. Daisy, however, thought that she could cope perfectly well with another job. The truth was, she was missing Cynthia, who had gone to Southport to stay with her mother's friend and meant to remain there until she went to Switzerland, and Daisy found the long dark evenings spent alone in the little parlour the two girls had shared both boring and depressing. Furthermore, after she had been in the job with the doctors for a month, she had had a letter from Jake, who was still working in Derby, which decided her that she really should take on evening work if she could get it.

Well, old girl, I've been and gone and done it [he wrote exuberantly]. *I've put my name down for the Royal Air Force, signed a great many papers, had a medical and been accepted for aircrew training. Apparently this is subject to a great many other things; more medicals for a start, examinations, tests and so on, because only the cream of the crop, so to speak, actually end up flying planes. Even aircrew . . . I mean the fellows who man guns or plot one's course to and from the target . . . have to undergo the most rigorous training, so everyone has to be tremendously fit.*

I had to go to Adastral House, the London head-quarters of the air force, and they told me that a letter would be sent once the paperwork had been processed, telling me when and where I should report to start my initial training. They said it might be many weeks before I heard, but when the officer saw that I had already learned to fly at Cambridge he thought I might get priority over those who had had no experience and, in fact, my letter arrived this very morning.

I report to the centre on 18 September, so I hope to have a few days at home over Christmas; I trust you and I will see plenty of each other, even if you continue to insist that we are 'just good friends'. How is the new job going? You sounded pretty happy in your last letter but you also said you planned to join the WAAF when war broke out; I should say 'if' but I won't insult your intelligence because we both know it's going to happen, and probably quite soon. I don't have much faith in Mr Chamberlain's bit of paper, and would encourage you to join right away except that the pay is pretty pathetic and would mean you would not be able to help your brother and sister as much as you would like. But why not do a job in the evenings which would involve learning shorthand and typewriting? Or even driving? Then, when you apply for the WAAF they'll immediately see you have a trade which would be useful to them. Anyway, think about it. Every time I see a Waaf in the street, I am struck by how neat and pretty they look and have a mental picture of you, decked out in air force blue, which sends shivers up my spine.

Darling Daisy, I know you're very young still – I'm not exactly an old man myself – but despite everything you've said, I still hope that one day we'll be more than friends.

With lots of love from your almost-a-member of the Royal Air Force,

Jake.

Daisy read the letter with very mixed feelings. She had been telling herself for many weeks that war was a certainty, but she realised now that she had not truly believed it. In her heart she wanted Mr Chamberlain to be right because she had heard enough from Cynthia and Clive about the conflict in Spain to know that war was a terrible thing. In the course of the civil war thousands had died, thousands were imprisoned in dreadful conditions and whole cities had been razed to the ground, and though that war had now ended, Clive said it would take a lifetime to bring Spain back to what it had once been. He had returned home in such a poor state of health that his attempt to join one of the forces had been unsuccessful. Now he was following a regime designed to bring him back to fitness.

However, Jake's letter had made war with Germany seem not only inevitable, but real. People she loved would die, and if Jake's fears came true and Britain was invaded and crushed beneath the Nazi jackboot, then the future would be black indeed. The previous year the govern-ment had announced plans for a 'National Register' stating what everyone should do in time of war. Why had she not realised that this meant people in the know were no longer considering war a remote possibility? They knew it was coming, and coming fast.

Daisy had been reading her letter in the kitchen whilst Molly cooked eggs and bacon, kidneys and sausages, which Annie would presently carry up to the small breakfast parlour. Dr and Mrs

Venables might eat as much as half of the food provided; the rest would come back to the kitchen to be eaten by Mr Pilcher and his son, Roddy, as a part of their midday meal. Other members of staff ate earlier, when Daisy did, and for the first time it occurred to her that a good deal of food was wasted in the Venables household. Neither the doctor nor his wife was a big eater, and though Molly did her best it was not always possible to use up all the leftovers on staff meals. When war comes, Daisy thought, Auntie was saying that cheap imports will stop and I don't believe sufficient food has been grown here since the Depression to feed the whole country, so there will be rationing; bound to be. How strange that it will be Brendan and Amanda who will be better off than the Venables, despite their different circumstances, because though the Venables have a few fruit trees and currant bushes, and Pilcher grows vegetables on the little bit of garden that isn't laid down to flowers and lawn, that's nothing compared with the acres of ground available at Benmacraig, and I can't see the Venables building a pigsty or buying half a dozen hens, so rationing will hit them a good deal harder than it will hit the Kildares . . . or the Elgins for that matter.

Molly, sliding eggs and bacon into a beautiful silver dish and kidneys and sausage into another, whipped the pan to the side of the stove and turned to Daisy. 'I bet that's a letter from Cynthia;

and high time too,' she observed. 'Did you get that job, by the way?'

'If you mean the job at the hospital, no I didn't; they wanted an evening receptionist all right but the job started at five and ended at ten, so I had to say I couldn't manage,' Daisy admitted. 'But I've got another interview tonight. It's for a waitress at that Dining Rooms quite near the station. Apparently they do a good trade from men about to catch trains, so they need someone to wait on between six and eight. They close then but I'd take a bet that they'll expect me to stay on at least until nine to help with the clearing up.'

Molly pulled a face. 'You'll be on your feet the whole time and wore to a bone after a week,' she prophesied. 'Still, no harm in trying it, I suppose.' She indicated one of the silver dishes with a jerk of her thumb. 'Take that up to the breakfast parlour for us, there's a dear.'

Daisy got the job in the Dining Rooms, for which there was virtually no competition, and though she did indeed spend all her time on her feet, she told Molly stoutly that it was a good deal better for her than sitting for long periods, as she did during the day. Daisy worked hard and enjoyed her new job, but her time there was destined to be of short duration. War was declared on 3 September, and fired by a natural desire to take part she gave in her notice at both the surgery and the Dining Rooms, but was told that there was a waiting list to join any of the women's forces. Needing to earn, she went along to a munitions factory and applied for a job there.

Friends were astonished – munitions were generally agreed to be dirty and unpleasant work – but the money was good and Daisy was still very conscious of her family's need. Cynthia, who had abandoned the idea of finishing school and joined the WAAF, was aghast, though Daisy assured her that she still intended to become a Waaf too, but needed a well-paid job whilst her application was processed.

To her initial dismay, however, she received a letter from the WAAF telling her curtly that her job in munitions was considered essential war work and therefore her application to join the WAAF had been refused.

Christmas came; Daisy and Jake had agreed to spend the holiday at Ty Gwyn as Jake was between courses and Daisy had three days off. She arrived at Abergele station at eight o'clock, Christmas Eve. She had packed a small bag with her night things, her best dress and a pair of dancing pumps, but she wore her stout walking boots, her thickest jersey, a tweed skirt and her one and only overcoat. These garments, she felt, would cover all eventualities, but as she descended from the train she found herself hoping that she might catch a taxi back to the farm for it was an icy cold night, with a strong wind blowing off the sea, and the thought of a lengthy drive in the pony trap was not a pleasant one.

However, a surprise awaited her. When she emerged from the small station a figure, well muffled, approached her. It was Jake, though she could barely recognise him for he wore a leather helmet on his head, a thick dark scarf wound closely about the lower half of his face and some sort of coat fastened tightly up to his chin.

'Oh, Jake, I'm so glad you've met me, but why are you in disguise?' Daisy asked, handing him her bag and seizing one of his gauntleted hands to give it a shake. 'If I hadn't known you all my life I'd never have known you . . .' She giggled. 'That wasn't very well put but you know what I mean.'

Jake laughed too and pulled his scarf down to reveal his grin and the square determined chin she knew so well. 'I'm not in disguise; this is my motor-cycle gear,' he said rather reproachfully. 'Didn't you guess from the goggles?' He had pushed them up above his forehead but now he snapped them down over his eyes. 'I've bought an AER; they're made in Liverpool, you know. Grand bikes, the best in fact. I call mine the Chariot. I've brought a spare pair of gloves and a scarf for you because I'm telling you it's bloody cold on a motorcycle, for the driver at any rate. You can crouch down and keep out of the worst of the wind, or I suppose you can. I've never ridden pillion so I can't speak from personal experience.'

'What does AER stand for?' Daisy asked. 'And what about my bag? Can you hang it on the handlebars? I've never ridden on a motorcycle so I don't know what's possible and what isn't. And when did you get this bike anyway?'

'I've had it two weeks; bought it off a chap in the village near where I'm stationed,' Jake said. 'And fancy you, a Liverpudlian, not knowing what AER stands for! It's the maker's name, of course – A. E. Reynolds. As for your bag, we'll have to wedge it between us, because I imagine hanging it on the handlebars would unbalance the whole works. By the way, if you're wondering whether I've come into a fortune, I fear not. I borrowed the money off my pa and I mean to pay him back, though it may take me a while.' They had been walking along the road as they talked and now Jake pointed to a motorcycle parked by a lamp post. 'Isn't she just grand? I can tell you, we'll be at the farm in a tenth of the time it would take in the pony cart. I'll get on first to hold her steady, then you can nip aboard and wedge your bag down between us and then, love of my life, you can jolly well put both arms round my waist and hang on for all you're worth. In fact, when we reach the lane, I'll have to slow down quite a bit. It was muddy but this frost has turned it to iron, so unless I slow the ridges could tip the bike over sideways.'

He had kicked back the stand and climbed aboard the bike as he spoke, but Daisy hesitated.

'Isn't there a taxi?' she asked plaintively. 'Honestly, Jake, I'd feel a lot safer in a taxi. I've never been on a motorbike in my life and I don't want to spend Christmas nursing a broken head or a fractured leg.'

'How dare you!' Jake said indignantly. 'I may not have had her long but you'll be safe as houses, I promise you, because already I'm pretty expert. For God's sake, girl, stop quibbling and climb aboard.'

Hesitantly, Daisy obeyed, and promptly realised that her tweed skirt had now ridden up, leaving a great deal of stockinged leg and bare thigh at the mercy of the bitter wind. She informed Jake of this unwelcome fact at the top of her voice but since he had started the engine she doubted that he could have heard her, and before she could voice any more doubts the engine gave a maniacal scream, the machine leapt forward like a hare from its form, and they were off.

It was a nightmare ride. Despite Jake's extra scarf wound round her head, Daisy's nose and ears were ice cold, and the way the wind treated her nether regions was ungentlemanly to say the least. Within minutes of leaving the station she was longing for old-fashioned drawers, preferably sheepskin lined, and thought bitterly that she would tell Jake a thing or two when – or if – they reached the farm.

Through chattering teeth she was rehearsing

what she would say when her opportunity to deliver the lecture came sooner than either of them expected. They had reached the lane, and despite the fact that they had not seen another vehicle for miles, Jake detached his right hand from the handlebar and stuck it out to indicate that he meant to turn. Daisy imagined that as he slowed and slewed the wheel round it must have hit a patch of ice, and because he was driving one-handed whilst, presumably, applying his brakes, the bike tilted, roared and tipped sideways, though Jake hastily stuck a foot down to prevent it from crashing to the ground. Daisy, however, flew through the air in a graceful arc, landing in a huge pile of frosted leaves which at least were a good deal softer than the iron-hard ground. Jake, supporting the wildly revving bike with one leg whilst trying to kick the stand into position, uttered a few highly coloured curses before wedging it upright and hurrying over to where Daisy was struggling to her feet. 'You poor girl! I'm so sorry,' he panted. 'Are you all right? I meant to tell you to lean to the right for a right turn but I'm pretty sure you leaned to the left, which was how I lost control. Good thing them leaves were there; at least you had a soft landing.'

'A soft landing?' Daisy shouted. 'That's what you think! Oh, I *knew* I should have got a taxi . . . even walking would have been better. Let me tell you, Jake Elgin, that I'm so cold I wouldn't even know if I'd broke both me legs. And as for your

357

bloody motorbike, I never want to see the damned thing again, far less have a ride on it. It's dangerous and hateful and I've split my only tweed skirt and laddered my stockings and I hate you . . .'

'Oh, but Daisy, my darling, I'm really sorry . . .' Jake began, putting an arm round her waist, but Daisy pushed him off and swept on regardless.

'Don't you dare try to put the blame on me! If you'd told me to lean to the right then I'd probably have done so, but since you didn't tell me you can scarcely blame me for doing what I did. Anyway, it was all your fault and I'll never ever get on your beastly bike again, because you're neither of you to be trusted. You can jolly well take my bag and tootle off to the farm, but I'm walking.'

'You can't possibly walk. It must be almost two miles, and you might turn your ankle on one of these ruts, or slip on the ice, or – or do a thousand and one other things,' Jake said wildly. 'Please, please, please, Daisy, me darling, don't let me down. Auntie and my pa worry about me quite enough without you telling them I tipped you off. Not that I did, of course,' he added slightly resentfully. 'If you'd leaned to the right . . .'

'Shut up!' Daisy screamed. 'If I walk up at least I shan't get hurled across the road again. And remember, your pride may be hurt but it's my perishin' body that sailed through the air and landed with a pretty hard bump.'

'Yes I know, and I've said I'm sorry over and

358

over,' Jake said rather sulkily. 'Be a sport, Daisy: give me another chance. You were always full of guts; once you'd have laughed like anything and climbed straight back aboard. So what's changed you?'

By now, however, Daisy's blazing indignation was giving way to cooler reason. The accident really wasn't entirely Jake's fault and to tell Auntie Jane and Uncle Bob what had happened would not only let her old friend down, it would also give the Elgins something more to worry about. So she heaved a deep and dramatic sigh, picked up her bag and jerked her thumb at the motorbike. 'Get on then, and I'll climb on to the pillion,' she said resignedly. 'But mind you go really slowly, then I won't tell anyone you tipped me off, I'll just say I don't have the right sort of clothes for motorbike riding, which is true, and in future I'll stick to the pony cart if you don't mind, or even if you do.' She giggled suddenly. 'I'm sure I'll have chilblains tomorrow in most unusual places. And now let's get moving or my aunt and your father will imagine you've killed the pair of us.'

'You're a sport, Daisy Kildare,' Jake said fervently, climbing aboard the bike and revving the engine as Daisy's arms crept around his waist. 'I planned to take you on a sightseeing tour tomorrow – ever visited the Isle of Anglesey? – but only if the frost lifts, of course.'

Daisy sighed. 'Tomorrow's Christmas Day, you owl, and nobody will be going anywhere,' she said firmly, and would have elaborated on this theme except that Jake started the engine once more and speech between them became impossible. True to his promise, he drove sedately and carefully up the lane and presently turned into the farmyard. He kicked the stand into position and climbed off, then helped Daisy to alight, which she did somewhat stiffly, remarking: 'I'm going to have some lovely bruises tomorrow.'

'But not anywhere that will show,' Jake said hopefully. 'Your bum may be black and blue but you're scarcely likely to be asked to strip before Aunt Jane gives you your breakfast, so your secret will be safe with me.' He glanced at her sideways as they approached the house, a wicked gleam in his dark eyes. 'And if you want someone to apply embrocation, I'm your man.'

Then, laughing and scuffling like a couple of kids, they entered the warmth of the farmhouse kitchen.

Despite the motorcycle incident, the Christmas break would have been a happy one had Daisy and Jake not had a serious misunderstanding on Boxing Day. Christmas Day itself had been everything such a day should be with an excellent lunch, crackers beside each plate and small presents piled beneath the Christmas tree. Jake had bought Daisy a beautiful fountain pen, a thick pad of cream-coloured writing paper and some envelopes. Across the card which accompanied it, he had written *To keep in touch with your pals in the forces as well as everyone at Benmacraig*, and she had been touched by the thought that must have gone into the gift as well as by the fact that the fountain pen was an expensive one, with just the sort of nib she most liked, and the paper smooth and rich, positively enticing one to write upon it. It must be admitted that she had not put the same amount of thought into her present for Jake, buying him a pair of thick woollen socks and a small diary in which she told him he must record the events of each day so that his letters home would be more interesting.

She had gone to bed that night happy, and had awoken to winter sunshine and the mildest of breezes, in fact to a day so tempting that when Jake had suggested that they take a trip on the motorbike as far as Llandudno, where they could walk on the shore and explore the charms of the seaside, the Great Orme and Happy Valley, she had actually consented to do so.

Everything had gone well at first. Although the day had been mild, the sea had been freezing cold, but they had paddled nevertheless, shrieking and kicking spray at each other and generally behaving like a couple of kids. Rather to Daisy's surprise, they had found a small café open and thronged with visitors, where they had had a meal of sandwiches and coffee before returning to the motorbike, for Jake had said firmly that they would ride up to the top of the Orme. 'With a bit of luck we'll be in time to see the sunset,' he had told her. 'It's a remarkable sight and one I wouldn't want you to miss.'

Daisy had felt doubtful that the motorcycle would manage the steep climb but Jake had assured her that on his previous visit his beloved vehicle had flown up the steep inclines like a bird. 'Yes, but she only had one person to carry,' Daisy had pointed out. 'Well, if she can't make it we'll just have to turn round and watch the sunset from the prom.'

Jake had scoffed at this, however. 'You're such a little thing, you're a featherweight. The Chariot won't even notice there's someone on the pillion. Ready? Then off we go!'

Jake had been right: the Chariot had taken the steep slopes of the Orme in its stride and presently they had reached the summit, parked the motorcycle and made their way through a flock of inquisitive sheep to the edge of the cliff. 'Just in time,' Jake had breathed and they had both watched in awed and reverent silence as the scarlet ball of the sun sank beneath the horizon.

Dusk comes early on winter evenings but for a while neither could have torn themselves away from the beauty of the scene before them. Stars had pricked out and a frail moon floated, insubstantial as a bubble, in the sky and presently Daisy had heaved a deep sigh and said that they had better be getting back before it became too dark to see the road. In silence they had returned to the Chariot but then Jake had seized her by the shoulders and swung her round to face him. 'Daisy, we've got to talk,' he had said urgently. 'Now I'm in the air force I can't pop home whenever I feel like it. I might easily be posted abroad – lots of chaps do their training in America or South Africa – but wherever I go, getting leave will be a problem. I know last time I asked you to be my girl we were probably too young, but that was ages ago. Please, Daisy, just say you won't go with anyone else, you'll wait for me . . .'

'Oh, Jake, I've told you over and over that I don't want to get involved with anyone,' Daisy had said distractedly. 'I'm your friend and always will be but it wouldn't be fair to you to pretend I'll ever marry you, because I shan't. I expect you'll meet lots of nice girls once you're in uniform and you'll probably fall really in love with one of them. The only reason you think you're in love with me is because we've known one another for ever. So please, dear Jake, let's just remain good friends.'

'I don't want a nice girl, I want you,' Jake had said wildly, and before Daisy had guessed what he meant to do he had swept her into his arms. A brief struggle had ensued before Daisy could tear herself free, but then she had set off at a run and had been quite halfway down the descent before Jake and the Chariot had caught her up. He had apologised, of course; had said he would try to understand her feelings, had even agreed he would not lay a finger on her until she gave him the go ahead, a remark which had her bristling.

'It isn't until, it's never,' she had said crossly, climbing gingerly on to the pillion. 'I can't help it, Jake. Loving someone seems to me to end in unbearable pain and I've had enough of it. Can't you understand that?'

But Jake, it seemed, could not, and Daisy had returned to the farm positively glad that she would be going back to Liverpool at the crack of dawn the following day.

Jake waved Daisy off, and as the train disappeared into the distance he told himself that he had acted too precipitately. In some ways, despite the troubles which had rained down upon her – or perhaps because of them – Daisy was still very young for her age. Jake was pretty sure that it had never crossed her mind to consider him, or anyone else for that matter, as a boyfriend. He would have to proceed very much more slowly and with considerable caution if he was to persuade her that they could be more than just friends. He thought about Cynthia, who was not even a year older than Daisy, but was already talking and thinking about marrying her young man one of these days. He wished Daisy would follow her example, then hastily changed his mind; he did not want his girl getting involved with anyone else, for he realised, as he had said to Daisy, that they might easily be parted for long periods.

Perhaps it was best to follow his first plan, which was *Softlee, softlee, catchee monkee.*

Since Daisy had firmly refused his offer of a lift on the motorbike, they had come down from the farm in a taxicab, so now Jake headed for the town centre. He would be leaving himself tomorrow morning and meant to buy Aunt Jane a small present, something pretty yet useful, to say thank you for all her hard work during his stay. Resolutely, he made for the shops.

Daisy returned home to Rodney Street to be greeted by a truly horrible shock. She had walked up from the station and went round to the side door to let herself in with her own key, and was met halfway across the hall by Mrs Venables. Daisy began to greet her cheerfully, then took in the older woman's white strained face and shaking hands. 'What's happened?' she said anxiously. 'Oh, Auntie Ven, don't say you've had bad news. Is Cynthia all right?'

Her aunt stared at her blankly for a moment. 'Cynthia? Oh yes, Cynthia's fine. I had a letter this morning but I've not had time to read it yet, I just skimmed it to make sure she needed nothing. No, my dear, it's the doctor. He's had a slight heart attack, and though the doctors at the Royal assure me that he has every chance of making a full recovery, we've been advised that the attack was largely due to overwork and he has decided to retire and go somewhere really quiet for rest and recuperation. He hopes to work part time once he

365

recovers, so we've decided on Cornwall. He was born there, you know, and the climate is milder than up here in the north.'

'Oh, Aunt Venables, what a dreadful thing to happen,' Daisy gasped. 'And when you were by yourself too, with neither Cynthia nor me to give you support. But why on earth didn't you send me a telegram? I'd have come at once and I'm sure Auntie would have come as well. Oh, goodness, do you think the doctor's attack had anything to do with driving the car? I know he found it difficult sometimes to find his patients in the suburbs.'

Daisy had taken Mrs Venables's hands in her own but now she dropped one of them and led the older woman into the small breakfast parlour where a good fire blazed. She sat Mrs Venables down in a comfortable chair before slinging her bag on to the floor and struggling out of her coat and hat. 'Have you written to Cynthia? I could do that for you, and anything else that may be necessary. I'm sure the munitions factory will give me compassionate leave of absence for a couple of days when they hear what has happened.'

Mrs Venables had returned the pressure of Daisy's hand but now she shook her head and leaned back in her chair. 'No, I've not written because I don't want Cynthia worried. There's really nothing she can do, so I shall wait until Dr Venables is out of hospital and well enough to make the move to Cornwall.' She turned to gaze at Daisy. 'But what will you do, my dear? I know how important it is for you to give all the financial help you can afford to your brother and sister, so you won't want to come to Cornwall with us. We shall have to sell this house, but my husband suggests that you move into the coachman's quarters; we can make it a condition of sale that you, as a sitting tenant, may remain there for as long as you wish, paying a minimal rent which will be decided between us.'

'Auntie Venables, you must be the most generous person in this world,' Daisy said, her voice breaking. 'To think about me when you have so many real worries on your mind! But of course the coachman's quarters would be ideal. Why, when Cynthia comes back to Liverpool on leave, we could share the place.' She chuckled. 'She could even pay me rent since she's always saying when her allowance comes due every quarter that she scarcely knows how to spend the half of it. And now how can I make your life a little more comfortable? I'll do anything within my power, you know that. You and the doctor couldn't have treated me better had I been your own child.'

Mrs Venables had closed her eyes as though too weary to look about her, but now she opened them and smiled with real affection at Daisy, who had knelt by her side and was still holding her hand. 'You've no idea what a comfort it is just to have you back,' she said. 'And if you really think Miss

Dalton – I mean Mrs Elgin – would come back for a while, it would help immeasurably. She is such a wonderful organiser and so hard working that her mere presence would be an enormous help. As for yourself, my dear, you are doing important war work and are highly valued. Naturally, I'd be grateful for your assistance at weekends, but you must not jeopardise your future. You are young and have your life before you. Do you really think your Aunt Jane would come to our rescue?'

In bed that night Daisy reflected that the Venables' news had turned her life upside down. Naturally she had known things would change dramatically when war came, but she had always considered Dr Venables and his wife to be as solid and immovable as a couple of rocks. Why, she could not remember the doctor ever suffering from so much as a head cold! It was Mrs Venables who occasionally spent a week in bed, fighting a tendency to bronchitis, and it was he who had sometimes said, worriedly, that she would do better in a milder and more equable climate. He had talked of the south of France for their retirement, but Daisy had always secretly considered this to be what Dr Venables himself referred to as a pipe dream, and had thought in her heart that her kindly host and hostess would end their days in Rodney Street.

Pulling the covers up to her ears, for it was a cold night, she told herself that nobody's life ever

368

proceeded along predictable lines, so why should she be different? And it was wonderfully generous of the Venables to let her move into the coachman's quarters. For many years now, they had been like parents to her . . . like parents . . . parents . . . and Daisy slept.

Within moments of falling asleep, she was back in the nursery-tale land of which she had dreamed so often. The other dreams had grown to seem fuzzy and unreal, yet this one was as sharp and clear as though it were really happening. There was the fat old woman in her scarlet dress and billowing white pinafore, her hair done up in a fat black bun on the nape of her neck. And there were the balloons, a huge colourful bunch. And Daisy looked around her, half expecting to see her parents and her brothers and sisters smiling and waving from various balloons. But this time it was Dr and Mrs Venables whose balloons were breaking free from the bunch and floating upwards, and Cynthia as well as Daisy who turned their eyes heavenwards to watch the slow ascent. But on this occasion Daisy understood the message and had no desire for her own balloon to break from the bunch. And nor, she saw, did Cynthia, whose balloon also remained earthbound. And from somewhere in the air around her, she could hear voices: *Every chick must fly the nest*, the voices sang; *every child grows up and turns to tread its own path, so why should you be different?*

She was struggling to answer, to say that she

understood, that she too meant to leave the nest, when she awoke to find snowflakes tapping against her window pane and knew, in the odd way one sometimes does, that nursery-tale land had gone for ever, and she was ready to enter the adult world at last.

Chapter Eleven

May 1941

Cynthia had managed to get a lift into Liverpool from her air force station and now she thanked the driver and climbed down, looking around her with wide apprehensive eyes. She had heard wireless reports of the raids on Liverpool and had been desperately worried for Daisy, knowing that her friend was still both living and working in the city, though her factory was on the outskirts and, Daisy had assured her, extremely well hidden and unlikely to be targeted by the Luftwaffe. She and Daisy exchanged both letters and telephone calls and despite their very different lives were closer now than they ever had been, so Cynthia tried to tell herself that her friend would be safe.

Only bombs do not always fall on target and here on the Scotland Road, with the docks so close, the city was barely recognisable. The air was thick with dust and smoke, and everywhere she looked Cynthia saw more destruction, more desolation. The lorry which had dropped her off drove away and Cynthia began to walk towards Rodney Street, for Daisy still lived in the coachman's quarters, though she shared her accommodation with three other girls. Cynthia felt a cold wave of panic at the thought that the coachman's quarters might be no more, then scolded herself. If Daisy had not been at work during the raid last night, she would have gone to a shelter; foolish to panic simply because this particular part of the city had been pretty well razed to the ground. Daisy would be all right; she had to be!

As she walked, her feet crunching on broken glass, Cynthia reflected on the strangeness of life in general. Daisy had been determined to join the WAAF when war broke out, but had taken a job in a factory making munitions. She had done so because the girls doing the dirty and dangerous work were well paid and Daisy had thought it only fair to continue to help her family as much as she could. Cynthia knew she had still intended to join the WAAF, but her application had been turned down since she was in a reserved occupation. Cynthia had been indignant on her friend's behalf but to her astonishment Daisy had laughed and shaken her head. The two girls had met for a quick meal at Lyon's Corner House on Church Street and Daisy, pink-cheeked and bright-eyed, had assured Cynthia that she had no regrets. 'I'm happier than I've been for years and years,' she had said contentedly. 'I never thought I would be, but the enthusiasm and friendliness amongst us girls is wonderful, truly it is. Everyone helps everyone else and though shift work can be pretty exhausting, we know we're making a real difference to the war. At first I was slow, because I was afraid of making a mistake, but once you get into the work and begin to understand what you're doing, you can speed up. Why, our production rates have trebled in the past few months, and that has to be good news.'

'Well I still think it's a waste of your intelligence,' Cynthia had said obstinately. 'Here am I, translating, taking notes at important conferences and having uniform, food and travel paid for by the government, and all you have are those tatty overalls, endless hard and dirty work, and not even a canteen meal to make life easier.'

'Yes, your uniform is lovely and ours is horrid,' Daisy had admitted. 'I don't know that I can explain it, Cyn, but within a month of starting work I felt that, for the first time since Benmacraig, I fitted in. Oh, I tried to do so at school and at the Venables', but I was always a round peg in a square hole and in my heart I knew it. Now I'm a round peg in a round hole and I like it, honest to God I do. When I first came to Rodney Street, you said I was common – amongst other things – and you were right. But kids will always try to conform so of course I spent years trying to be like you, and now I'm not trying to be anyone but myself and I'm telling you, it's grand.'

Cynthia had felt her cheeks grow hot. She remembered how she had resented Daisy, always trying to belittle her and cut her down to size. But that hadn't lasted, she told herself defensively. Daisy had proved her worth and Cynthia had grown to admire not only her scholastic achievements, but also the courage her friend had shown when everything seemed to be against her. She had said as much and Daisy had laughed. 'Oh, you!' she had said affectionately. 'What changed the way you felt about me was meeting Clive and falling in love. And now you can tell me all about your glamorous job and I'll try not to be envious since I wouldn't leave my factory now for double my wages.'

'Watch out, miss!'

Cynthia jerked her mind back to the present, realising she had nearly walked straight into a bomb crater. She stepped back hastily, grinning at the delivery boy who had shouted the warning.

'Thanks very much; I think I must be half asleep,' she said. 'I'm heading for Rodney Street; have you been in that direction this morning? My pal lives there and I'm a bit worried . . .'

'I come down there earlier,' the boy said, his face clouding. 'That there church – St Andrew's ain't it? – took a packet and some of the houses is cordoned off. But your pal will have gone to a shelter, I don't doubt.'

Cynthia thanked him and hurried on, and presently found herself on Rodney Street. She heaved a great sigh of relief when she saw No. 39 still looking exactly as it had looked on her last visit. The new owner had changed the house so that it accommodated as many people as possible, and now Cynthia hurried down Mount Street and

374

turned into Pilgrim, her heart thumping out an uneven rhythm as she crossed her fingers that the coachman's quarters had not been affected by the bombing. She turned in through the well-remembered gate, crossed the garden, noticing that it had all been put down to potatoes, and entered the cobbled courtyard. And there was the garage, empty now of course, with the coachman's quarters above it.

Cynthia felt a smile break out and ran across the cobbles, ascending the stairs two at a time and banging impetuously upon the door before she remembered that the girls might well be sleeping. Hesitantly, she turned the knob, knowing that it led directly into the small kitchen, for the living room was now used as a bedroom where two or three girls slept whilst Daisy, as the original inhabitant, had taken over the bedroom.

The kitchen seemed full of people but Daisy shot across the room and enveloped her friend in a hard hug. 'Cynthia! It's grand to see you and the last thing I expected. Honest to God, wharra night we've had! Molly – do you remember Molly? – and I were fire-watching, and the other two were on nights. But I've gorra introduce you; that's Grace eatin' porridge and Hilda is the little dark one. Girls, meet me pal Cynthia.'

Cynthia registered that Daisy was now speaking with the local accent but guessed this was a form of protective coloration; she would not wish to sound posh when with her workmates.

The girls exchanged murmured greetings and then Daisy plied Cynthia with questions; what was she doing in Liverpool? Had she got leave? A forty-eight perhaps? Why hadn't she gone to visit Clive? Daisy knew he was in command of a searchlight battery somewhere in Cheshire, and could not imagine Cynthia failing to visit him if she'd managed to get some leave.

'Daisy Kildare, how you do gabble,' Cynthia said reprovingly. 'To tell you the truth, I got compassionate leave because of the bombing. I told them you were my sister, working in munitions, and they gave me a forty-eight so I could check that you were all right. Telephone lines are down all over the city . . . I tried to ring your factory but couldn't get a reply, so they let me come.'

'Have you had breakfast?' the girl called Hilda asked. 'I could make you some porridge . . .'

'It's awright, queen, WAAF officers are fed and watered three times a day and don't have to pay a penny, or hand over a perishin' coupon,' Daisy reminded her friend. 'Go off to bed, the three of you. Cynthia and me will have a bit of a crack and then I'll have to go to bed meself, or I'll never get to work this evening.'

As soon as the other girls had disappeared into the living room, Daisy cut two wedges off the loaf, spread them thinly with margarine, and then added jam which, she explained, had been made by Aunt Jane and delivered on her aunt's last visit to the coach house. 'She's awful good to us and sends us real eggs, bags of potatoes, anything she can spare, in fact,' Daisy explained. 'I miss her something dreadful but we're so busy at the factory now that I'm too tired to trek out to the farm, even when I get a day off, which ain't often.'

'Look, you'd best get to bed for a few hours too,' Cynthia said, noting her friend's pallor and dark-rimmed eyes. 'I'll go off and take a look around and come back here about four o'clock. I'll find a café which still has some grub and treat you to a meal before your night shift starts; how's that?'

'You're an angel, queen,' Daisy said gratefully. 'I'm damned nearly asleep on my feet. You can stay here if you'd rather, have a bit of a kip yourself. There's an old sleeping bag and a pillow in the cupboard under the sink which we keep for when pals drop in. Or there's books . . .'

'No, it's all right, Daisy, I'd rather take a look at what's left of the city,' Cynthia said grimly. 'See you at four.'

It was a sunny day, but Cynthia's wander around the city could not have been described as a pleasant experience; far otherwise in fact. The destruction seemed to have touched everywhere. Very soon she was lost, unable to recognise places she had known well. Lewis's, Blacklers's and many other big stores, where she had enjoyed shopping and hours of browsing, were now smoking shells. The library on William Brown Street had gone, and she kept her eyes resolutely turned away from the docks, knowing the devastation there would be terrible.

At four o'clock she returned to the flat and found her friend looking very much better for her sleep. They made their way to a small café on London Road, ordered sausages, mash and baked beans, to be followed by apple pie and custard, and then settled down to catch up on each other's news.

'Do you realise we've not had a chance to really talk for the best part of a year . . . maybe more,' Cynthia said as the waitress delivered two thick white plates, piled with food, put a bottle of Flag sauce between them and left. 'Oh, I know we write and even telephone sometimes, but it's not the same.'

'You're right, it's not. In fact there's an awful lot I haven't told you and I expect there's an awful lot you haven't told me,' Daisy agreed. 'You always tell me when you and Clive meet up for instance, but you never go into any sort of detail.'

'And you used to tell me when Jake put in an appearance, but you've not so much as mentioned him for ages . . . nor anyone else for that matter,' Cynthia observed. 'You talk about dancing at the Grafton, going to see a flick or visiting the theatre, but you never say who you went with or what happened afterwards.' She smiled affectionately at her friend. 'And don't pretend you don't go out with fellows because you're far too pretty to be a wallflower.'

Daisy smiled and popped a piece of sausage into

378

her mouth. 'These aren't bad, these sausages,' she said approvingly. 'And you're right, of course. There is someone . . . but I'd better go right back to the beginning and tell you how I met up with Sean O'Grady . . .'

Daisy's mind flew back to a certain summer evening, almost a year ago. She remembered everything about it, for she and the girls in the factory had had a rare treat. They had been taken by bus to a Royal Air Force station where a dance was being held and had accordingly dressed in their best. Daisy had worn the locket Jake had given her and had borrowed a pair of earrings shaped like daisies, which went well with it. She wore black dancing pumps with diamante buckles and felt she was looking her best. For days beforehand, the girls had been begging, borrowing or stealing the prettiest clothing they could lay their hands on, for the dance included a supper, and was being held to celebrate the successful evacuation of the BEF from Dunkirk. Daisy had heard the evacuation described in many less complimentary ways, as a retreat, a rout or even an escape, but now it was pretty generally agreed that living to fight another day was what really mattered, so the girls had been pleased to be asked to the dance. None of the munitions workers had ever visited an RAF station before, and they were impressed. The dance was held in the NAAFI, where the chairs and tables had been pushed back against the walls and the floor cleared for dancing, whilst a band played from a stage at one end of the large room.

Daisy stared ahead of her, seeing that evening from the very first moment she had entered the NAAFI . . .

'I say, may I have the pleasure . . . ?'

Daisy, amongst her friends, had been feeling, if the truth were told, both shy and a little out of her depth. So many young men, all in uniform, of course, and all staring at the girls as though they were . . . well, something delicious. And now one of the young men was standing in front of her as though he had picked her out . . . he had picked her out . . . as a suitable partner! Daisy stared up at him, then frowned, puzzled. There was something . . . had they met before? But surely she would not have forgotten, for he was exceptionally good-looking, and – and – yes, he was grinning at her as though the two of them shared a private joke. 'Do – do I know you?' she asked uncertainly. 'Only I'm sure, if I did, I'd not have forgotten you, and . . .'

'Daisy Kildare, you can't have forgot me,' he said reproachfully, and she heard the Irish in his voice and stared up at him even harder. 'Now come along, t'ink, alanna!'

'Were you at school with me?' Daisy asked doubtfully. 'Only I was hardly ever in school, back in Connemara. Oh, do tell me, because I'm an awful bad guesser, so I am.'

He smiled, cocking a dark eyebrow. 'Keep

guessing! And remember, I'm only asking you to dance,' he said reproachfully. 'You can waltz with a feller wit'out knowing where you saw him last!'

Daisy got slowly to her feet and slid into his arms. 'It'll come to me in a minute,' she said as they took to the floor. 'Sure and what's a nice feller like you doing over here when Ireland is a neutral country?'

The young man smiled down at her. 'I'm what they call a career officer,' he told her. 'Now do you know who I am? Didn't Brendan tell you that I'd been and gone and left the old country? I'm sure he must have mentioned it in his letters, though we didn't see so much of each other once your family had left the croft and gone to Roundstone.'

Daisy stopped dead, causing havoc amongst the other dancers. 'You're Sean O'Grady!' she said. 'Of course I remember you now. I've still got the seagull you made for me when I left Benmacraig. Well I never did! But Brendan never said ... his letters are always short, and after ... oh, well, he never said,' she ended lamely.

Sean gave her a squeeze. 'I'm so sorry about your parents,' he said quietly. 'My mam wrote and told me ... what a terrible tragedy. Poor little Daisy, you've had more than your share of sadness, what wit' being whisked off to live in England when that crook took possession of your croft. But Brendan does write to me a couple of times a year, and the last time I got a letter he said his baby sister was working in munitions somewhere in

381

Liverpool, said I might like to look her up if I was ever in the neighbourhood . . .'

'And you did,' Daisy said wonderingly. 'Only how did you find out that I was here?'

'Didn't. Oh, I meant to take the gharry into Liverpool some time in the next few days and find you – Brendan said you lived in Rodney Street – but I came along to the dance without any idea that you'd be here. Talk about lucky coincidences . . . oh, Daisy, you were always a pretty kid but now you're a lovely young woman and I'm t'rilled, so I am, that we've met up again.'

'So am I,' Daisy said dreamily. 'And now I come to think of it, Brendan did mention in one of his letters that you'd joined up and were flying fighters – Hurricanes I think he said. He was real fed up because he'd give almost anything to be able to get into one of the services, but of course he dare not abandon Benmacraig when it needs him so badly.'

'I know. He told me a while back that Amanda's husband had come over and joined the army, so he couldn't look for help from that quarter. But Brendan's a resourceful feller and the hardest worker I know. He'll be all right, you mark my words. I say, we dance well together, don't we?' he added as the music ended and he led her off the floor. 'I t'ink I shall keep you as my partner; us Irish should stick together.'

'Well, I don't know about that,' Daisy said, giving a chirrup of laughter. 'You said it was a waltz and that was probably what you were doing, but I *think* it was a quickstep; still, I don't believe anyone noticed.'

'Was it?' Sean said. He beamed at her, settling her in a chair and taking the seat beside her. 'Well now, that's remarkable, so it is, since I've never learned to dance. I just put me arms round me partner, pull her as close as she'll permit, and shuffle. And now, Miss Kildare, tell me how you like living in Liverpool and working in munitions.'

Daisy was only too pleased to tell him. Whilst she did so, she studied him closely, deciding that he was easily the best-looking man in the room. She felt quite ashamed of not having recognised him, but reflected that he had changed a lot from the rather gangly lad she had known. He was tall and broad-shouldered with a square, determined chin, deeply cleft, and when he smiled, showing very white teeth, a dimple appeared in his right cheek. True to his avowed intention, he spent the whole evening with her and at supper time produced a piece of paper from his pocket and made a note of Daisy's address and the telephone number of her factory. Then he gave her the telephone number of his mess, so that she might ring him whenever the opportunity occurred. 'Only don't forget that I shan't always be available, not when we're on ops,' he said, only half joking. 'Did I tell you I share an old banger – an Austin Twelve actually – with some other chaps in my squadron, so when we're not flying we can sometimes get off the station and visit pals.' He gazed at her, cocking his head on one side and giving her a charming, lop-sided smile. 'Can I come and visit you, alanna? We could see a show, go dancing, have a meal out . . .'

'That would be lovely,' Daisy breathed. She had had a great many invitations from young men since the war started, but had never felt inclined to accept any of them until now. Oh, she had gone around with Jake, to be sure, but that had been simply as a friend, on her side at least. This, she told herself, was entirely different. She and Sean had known each other for ever, though they had not actually met for . . . gracious, it must be eleven years . . . but he was nevertheless an old friend, and Irish as well. Dancing with him had been a blissful experience and when, presently, he took her outside to get aboard the bus which would take her home and kissed her in the shadow of a nearby hut, she felt her stomach clench with excitement and melted into his arms, telling herself that at last she knew why Cynthia meant to marry Clive, and also what made girls like bad Betty, who worked on the same bench as she at the munitions factory, behave the way they did.

After that heavenly night, she and Sean met as often as they possibly could. She telephoned his mess, wrote many letters and longed for their next meeting. Yet she had hesitated to tell Jake of this new and wonderful relationship, for two good reasons. The first was that Jake still insisted he was in love with her and that she, in the fullness of time, would realise she shared his feelings. The second reason was that Sean had come successfully through his pilot training and wore the coveted double wings upon the breast of his tunic. Jake, on the other hand, though he was aircrew, was a tail gunner and would never fly a fighter, despite the fact that it had been his greatest ambition. She knew that if she admitted to Jake that she was going out with a pilot he would take it doubly hard, and Daisy felt she could not do such a thing to her old friend.

But of course Jake had found out in the end, and in the worst possible way. He had got a forty-eight and had come hurrying back to Liverpool intending to take her out, and had been told by Hilda, the only girl at home in the coachman's quarters at the time, that Daisy had gone dancing with her boyfriend.

'Her boyfriend!' Jake had squeaked. 'She hasn't got one . . . I mean *I'm* her boyfriend!'

Hilda had smiled placatingly at him, wishing, she told Daisy later, that she had kept her big mouth shut. 'It don't mean nothing, it's just an expression,' she had said. 'He's just some feller she met, I dare say, but if you want to find her I believe they've gone to the Grafton. Or were they going to see a fillum? I ain't certain.'

In actual fact, Hilda had thought that they had gone to the theatre and then out for a meal, but as luck would have it, they really *had* gone to the

Grafton. Jake had walked into the ballroom and spotted them at once. Sean's dancing had improved considerably and the two of them had been circling the floor dreamily, Daisy with her head pillowed in the hollow of Sean's shoulder, and this had been too much for Jake's hot temper to stand. He had stormed across the floor, dragged Daisy away from Sean, and then started a fight with the other man. They were both in uniform and other RAF personnel had managed to separate them, but not before Jake had split Sean's lip and Sean had blacked both Jake's eyes. Daisy, trying to explain, absolutely furious with Jake and wishing that she could be as horrid to him as he had been to Sean, had wished the floor would swallow her up.

Of course Jake had not known at the time that Sean was an old friend from way back, that they had been close neighbours when she had lived at Benmacraig, but Daisy had intended telling him just as soon as she could do so. She had realised that it was partly her own fault for not being straight with Jake, but when he had followed them out of the dance hall she had lost her temper and told him he had behaved disgracefully, and then stormed off, cuddling up to Sean in what she realised later must have been a very provocative fashion.

Sean had been understandably very angry over the whole affair, saying he had no idea that Daisy was involved with anyone else, and Daisy had had to assure him that she was not involved with Jake,

386

that he was merely an old pal from her childhood who imagined that he had some sort of hold on her because of their long friendship. She had placated Sean in the end, but he had been seriously ruffled. 'I don't mean to share you,' he had said impressively, as they had stood in the courtyard below the coachman's quarters. 'If you're my girl – and I believe you are – then I want you to promise you won't see that chap again.'

That had rocked Daisy back on her heels, for she had never thought of Sean as being possessive. But a moment's thought convinced her that he had a point. They had talked of marriage when the war was over. He had made it plain that he would like to have a more intimate relationship but had never tried to persuade her into bed with him because he said he respected her too much. Now he had simply been asking her to be faithful, and what was wrong with that? Daisy knew Sean could have any girl he wanted, but she was the lucky one; the least she could do was promise him that she would see Jake just once more, to explain the situation, and then put him out of her heart and mind for ever.

She had done so, though she had been surprised by the pain it had given her, especially since Jake had not taken it well. He had shouted and raged and then, when she had proved adamant, had wept, and it had taken all Daisy's resolution to keep to her promise and tell Jake that she would no longer exchange letters with him, would put the telephone down if he rang her, and would make sure, before visiting the Elgins, that there was no chance of his arriving at the farm.

Now, telling Cynthia everything, she saw her friend's eyes widen, saw the look of dismay cross the other girl's face. 'You're horrified that I could treat anyone so harshly,' Daisy said guiltily. 'You think I was cruel to cut Jake completely out of my life. But you don't know Sean; he's not only the best-looking bloke I've ever met, but he's really kind, and – and dammit, I love him. I couldn't risk losing him, particularly after the way Jake behaved. Anyway, you'd better let me tell you the rest, then maybe you'll change your mind.'

'Go on then,' Cynthia said. 'And I do see your point; no one can have two boyfriends at the same time, and although you say you saw Jake just as a friend, he saw you as his girl.' She hesitated, looking across the table at Daisy, and then dropped her eyes to stare down at her now empty plate. 'Daisy, when you truly love someone, you – you want to be theirs, to belong to them completely. I know, because Clive and I . . . what I'm trying to say is, if you truly love Sean . . .'

'Oh but I do, and I know what you mean,' Daisy said, feeling her cheeks go hot. 'But we've only known one another nine months . . . maybe ten . . . and we've not had much opportunity . . .'

Cynthia laughed. 'No. Well, I don't mean to encourage you to live a life of sin and I know you Irish aren't anywhere near as free and easy on the moral front as us English. But I interrupted you; you were going to tell me what happened next.'

'Well, one night a few weeks later – I'm not sure how long it was but I suppose it was the next time he could wangle a forty-eight – Jake was waiting for me when I got home after my shift. He flung his arms round me and started saying he was sorry and that I didn't understand, and when I tried to struggle he got really rough. To be honest, Cyn, he – he frightened me. I – I thought he was going to do something really awful – you know – so I screamed and punched him on the nose. The girls came thundering down the stairs; I was covered in blood from Jake's nose, and so was he of course, and I just bolted up the stairs and slammed the kitchen door. The girls said he kept apologising and begging them to fetch me down but they wouldn't. Apparently he hung around for ages, but he was gone by morning, so I wrote him a – a rather nasty letter. Then, a week later, when I knew he would have got it, I telephoned him. I meant to apologise and to explain that Sean was now my steady boyfriend and had insisted on the conditions I had laid down about not seeing him again, but before I could do more than say I was sorry he cut in. He said not to worry, he had accepted defeat and wouldn't be bothering me any more. Then he said if I ever changed my mind I knew how to find him, but that he wouldn't be holding his breath. And then he simply hung up.'

There was a long silence, during which the waitress took their empty plates away and brought their pudding. Finally, Cynthia spoke. 'I'm sure you did the only thing, the right thing,' she said. 'I never thought Jake was good enough for you, even though he was so clever. That hot temper made him a great many enemies and I often felt he was sneering at me. When can I meet your Sean?'

As Daisy made her way to work that evening, she thought that telling Cynthia all about the break-up with Jake had brought it back to mind, which was a nuisance, because it was an episode she was still trying very hard to forget. It was the second time in their relationship that she had punched Jake on the nose, though of course Cynthia did not know that.

Despite the fact that she no longer saw Jake, she kept in regular touch with Aunt Jane, and meant to visit the farm when she had a few days off in order to explain to the Elgins just why it would be awkward for her to find herself in Jake's company. She reflected, crossly, that it shouldn't be; Jake had never been more than a friend so far as she was concerned. Life had been so pleasant and uncomplicated when the two of them had squabbled their way to and from school, argued over whose turn it was to give Roddy a hand with some small task, or played cricket or football in the jigger. Why could they not simply remain pals, she wondered; when had it suddenly changed?

She could remember the first time he had put his arm round her; that had been in Clayton Square, because of her distress over the balloon seller, but they had been kids at the time, so it didn't count. Had things changed when Aunt Jane and Uncle Bob had taken them to New Brighton? No, she was sure things had been perfectly normal then. Perhaps it was the May ball. Perhaps she should never have agreed to go as Jake's partner because he had shown more than a friendly interest on that occasion. Yes, that was definitely the first time. And it had not been her fault; she was positive she had never given him any sort of encouragement, and even after the episode at the May ball she had stubbornly persisted in thinking of him as her best friend, a brother figure who could be relied upon to take her side, and to back her up when difficulties arose between herself and Cynthia, or some other member of the household.

But now everything had changed. She and Sean were in love and going to get married, though because of the war they had not attempted to set a date. She no longer corresponded with Jake but Aunt Jane persisted in telling her how he was getting along and what he was doing and she supposed, rather bitterly, that the same thing was happening in reverse; either Aunt Jane or Uncle Bob was sure to be telling Jake how she, Daisy, was coping with life in a city ravaged by the bombing. It was annoying, of course it was, but she supposed it was inevitable. Naturally, she had told Aunt Jane that she had met up with Sean O'Grady from her old life in Ireland, adding that he and she were 'going steady'. Aunt Jane had said placidly, in her reply, that it was always nice to meet old friends, and that was why Daisy intended to visit the farm and break the news in person that she and Sean were serious about one another.

How her aunt and Jake's father would react to the news she did not know, but she saw no reason for them to object. After all, she had made no secret of the fact that Jake was just a friend and Sean very much more, and though she had no idea what Jake might have told them she thought he would not have said too much, since he had never been one to wear his heart on his sleeve. Besides, time had passed and by now he had probably sought consolation with a pretty Waaf or someone else who could appreciate his good qualities and did not see him as a brother.

The bus jolting to a stop outside the factory brought her mind abruptly back to the present, and she found herself wishing that she could take Sean with her the next time she visited the farm. When she reached her bench and was beginning to pour TNT powder into the first shell case and to smooth it off at exactly the right level, she said as much to Lilly, who worked next to her and had become a good friend.

Lilly was a pretty girl, engaged to a soldier who was at present in India. She missed him sadly but often accompanied the other girls to dances and social events, though she always wore her engagement ring, and told the young men who invited her out, that she was 'spoken for'. Now, she turned to Daisy, her fair eyebrows rising. 'Well, why don't you? You keep saying you think of Jake as a brother, that you've never given him the slightest encouragement to think of you as anything but a sister, and you want your aunt and uncle to understand that Sean is your feller, so why not take him to the farm when he next has a forty-eight? The supervisors all know you've taken scarcely any time off since you started here back in '39, so I can't see they'll turn you down. I'm telling you, queen, it's better to be straight with people; God knows you were straight enough with Jake, from what you've told me.'

Daisy winced. She still felt a little stab of guilt whenever she remembered how she had treated her old pal, yet what else could she have done? Sean was right: a clean break meant they could both get on with their lives. 'Jake's probably got a girl of his own by now,' he had pointed out, the last time she had fretted aloud about what to tell the Elgins. 'I can't say I noticed what he looked like particularly – I dare say he weren't looking his best anyhow – but he's bound to have met someone else, someone who appreciates him, I mean.'

'Daisy? Did you listen to what I were saying?' Lilly asked. 'Take Sean back to the farm with you and one sight of his beautiful curly black hair and blue eyes will convince your aunt and uncle that you're serious about him.'

'He is good-looking, isn't he?' Daisy said, reaching for the next shell case. 'And I think you're right. I'll ring him as soon as I get back from work this evening and suggest it.'

Daisy was as good as her word, but when she telephoned Sean's mess, he had news of his own which he was eager to impart. 'Thank God you rang; the squadron has been ordered abroad so I've a bit of embarkation leave,' he said. 'It'll be grand to see your Aunt Jane again . . . I dare say she won't remember me because I were only a kid at the time, but when I came over to visit Brendan at Benmacraig and your mam was out selling fish, your Aunt Jane gave meself and Brendan a cut of soda bread and some of her home-made lemonade.' He chuckled. 'Didn't I just love that lemonade! I reckon she brought the lemons with her from Liverpool, because I don't recall anyone else makin' it and it was delicious.'

'Well I never did! But of course I should have guessed, because when you and Brendan were in school, Daddy used to say he seldom saw one without t'other. Right then, do you want to pick me up at the flat, or shall we travel separate?'

Sean blew a raspberry into the telephone, making Daisy giggle. 'Travel separate, indeed, when we could be together? Besides, I wouldn't know how to find Ty Gwyn. No, I'll call at the flat, real early in the morning, and you can make us a carry-out to eat on the train. The cookhouse will give me what they call a packed lunch, but it's never up to much. Stale Spam sandwiches, a tiny bar of chocolate and a piece of cookhouse cake you'd break your teeth on. Still, the Elgins keep pigs, don't they? Pigs will eat anything, even stale Spam.'

'Right you are; I'll find us something tasty and make a flask of hot coffee. I wish I could make lemonade like Aunt Jane's, but I've not seen a lemon for two years,' Daisy said, wondering where on earth she could find 'something tasty' which wasn't either rationed or impossible to buy unless you knew a black marketeer and had a great deal of money.

'So when do you want to set out? Remember, although I'm getting embarkation leave, I may only be able to manage a couple of days.'

Jane and Bob had just finished their breakfast when the back door rattled and shot open, revealing an old and very wrinkled brown face, adorned by a wide, toothless grin and topped by an ancient navy-blue peaked cap. '*Bore da*, missus, *bore da*, Mr Elgin,' the ancient said. He produced a bundle of letters from the satchel hanging on one shoulder and hobbled across the room to lay them carefully in the middle of the table. 'One iss from your son, Mr Elgin, one – no two – are from the Ministry, one iss from your gal, Mrs Elgin, and the other iss from someone livin' in Ireland, judgin' by the postmark.'

'And you are a nosy old beggar, Mr Jones,' Bob said cheerfully as the postman, without asking, pulled out a chair, sat down on it and glanced meaningfully at the teapot. 'Well I guess you deserve a cuppa, having toiled all the way up the lane, pushin' that rusty old bike.'

'Aye, I reckon a cup of tea would go down right well,' Mr Jones agreed. He turned to Jane. 'Made any more of that sody bread you give me last time, luv? Now that I'm workin' reg'lar for the Post Office, I leaves home before my Blodwen is up, so I don't get no breakfast till I've finished me round. Ta, missus,' he added, as Jane placed a cup of tea and a triangle of bread, well buttered, before him. He sipped the tea noisily, then took a big bite of bread and spoke rather thickly through it. 'You must be longin' to open your letters; don't let me stop you,' he said. 'It's a while since young Jake were home; mebbe the letter will say he's got leave.'

'Oh, Mr Jones, were you so rushed this morning that you didn't have time to steam all the letters open?' Bob said innocently. 'I am so sorry; but of course, I'll open the letters immediately, or at least the one from Jake. I'll let my wife have the one from her niece.'

'Ah, niece is it? I always think of her as your daughter,' Mr Jones said, apparently unruffled by Bob's remark. 'And I'll have you know, Mr Elgin, that I've no use for nosy folk. What I do have is – is me fair share of neighbourly interest, that's all.'

He spoke a little haughtily, but Jane saw the

twinkle in his eye and saw, also, how eagerly he leaned forward as Bob slit open the envelope and produced two closely written sheets. He read them to himself, then turned to his wife. 'Jake's squadron is being moved again; further away this time,' he said resignedly. 'He's hoping to get home for a few days at the end of the month.' Bob put the letter down. 'He says he'd be obliged if we'd ring either this evening or tomorrow, to let him know that we'll not be entertaining anyone else at that time.'

'Entertainin' anyone else?' Mr Jones said incredulously, before Jane could open her mouth. 'What on earth do the feller mean? It ain't as if you've a tribe of youngsters, all wantin' to come home for a few days.'

Jane had opened her letter and scanned it quickly, and now she turned to smile at the postman. 'I expect Jake means to bring a friend home – a lady friend – and knows we've only the two spare bedrooms,' she said tactfully. 'Is that right, Bob?'

'That's right,' Bob said briefly. He eyed the letter in his wife's hand. 'Is our Daisy coming home? At the end of the month, I mean, when Jake – oh, and his friend – are due?'

'No, she's coming the day after tomorrow, and bringing somebody she knew years ago in Ireland, an old pal of Brendan's,' Jane said rather guardedly. 'She's on nights at the factory and wants me to ring and leave a message at the office if it's all right for them to come.' She glanced meaningfully at the postman, who had just drained his mug and

397

was struggling to his feet. 'Thanks very much, Mr Jones. See you tomorrow.'

'You've not opened the other letter yet,' Mr Jones said reproachfully. 'Better do so in case the king and queen want to stay at Ty Gwyn next week, so popular you are, man!'

Jane and Bob both laughed, but Jane picked up the envelope and slit it open, shaking her head at the old man as she did so. 'Curiosity killed the cat, Mr Jones,' she remarked. 'It's from my nephew, Brendan, who most certainly won't be visiting anyone since he has a farm to run, same as us. I wouldn't say his letters were dull, but they're full of details about the potato crop, the price of fish, or the number of bonaveens his sow has produced.'

'Ah now, you'll be able to compare prices, then,' Mr Jones said, and for a moment Jane feared he was about to turn back and resume his seat. But after a few desultory remarks concerning the two fatteners he kept, he left them.

Bob and Jane exchanged rueful smiles before beginning to discuss the subject now uppermost in their minds, which was the rift between Jake and Daisy. They had learned of it months earlier, for Jake had visited them quite soon after the debacle at the Grafton. Jane was sure he had not meant to say a word, but it had been impossible not to see his distress, and though he had tried to deny that anything was wrong their concern was such that, in the end, he had told them everything.

'But dearest Jake, your father and myself have

always thought of you and Daisy as being like brother and sister,' Jane had said, and had been shocked by Jake's furious reaction.

'Brother and sister?' he had shouted, the colour darkening in his cheeks. 'Bloody brother and sister? Aunt Jane, how can you have been so blind? I've loved the horrible kid almost from the first, though of course I didn't realise it. Kids don't, do they? But as we began to grow up . . . oh, dammit, I knew I wanted to spend the rest of my life with her, and if that ain't love, I don't know what is.'

Now, across the breakfast table, Jane looked thoughtfully at her husband. 'I sometimes wonder if it might be better for Daisy and Jake if they did meet up,' she said. 'Seeing Daisy starry-eyed over another man might make Jake realise that things aren't going to alter and he must get on with his own life and stop hoping that Daisy will change her mind. Do you agree?'

Bob considered, a frown etched between his brows, but when he spoke, it was with decision. 'I'm afraid I disagree completely, love,' he said. 'For one thing, I believe Jake has accepted that Daisy is lost to him, and for another, forcing them to meet when it's plainly the last thing they want would be downright cruel. Remember, the only occasion on which they came face to face – the boys I mean – they fought like a couple of jealous dogs. Do you want that sort of confrontation? But I know you don't – you just haven't thought it through.'

Jane got up and went round the table. She

squeezed her husband's broad shoulders, then kissed the side of his neck. 'You're right, of course: the last thing I want to do is to hurt either Jake or Daisy,' she said. 'But Jake hasn't really suggested bringing a girlfriend home, has he? I just said it on the spur of the moment because I didn't want Mr Jones finding out that Jake and Daisy weren't on the best of terms.'

Bob laughed and pushed back his chair, then stood up and gave his wife a hug. 'No, he'll be coming home alone,' he admitted. 'But that doesn't worry me because I'd rather he didn't rush into a relationship on the rebound from Daisy, so to speak.'

'Jake's always struck me as being very level-headed so I don't think you need fear that he'll act impetuously,' Jane said. 'And now we'd better get to work; if you're going into Abergele market, I'll come with you. I mean to buy a few tomato plants, pot them up and see if I can bring them on by standing the pots in our bedroom. The windowsill is in the full sun until mid-afternoon so I reckon it will be almost like a greenhouse and it would be nice to grow our own tomatoes, wouldn't it?'

Daisy had always thought of Sean as being self-confident, but in the taxi approaching Ty Gwyn she realised that he was actually nervous. He had tried to engage the driver in conversation, but the man answered in monosyllables and Daisy guessed that his first language was Welsh, which probably meant he found Sean's Irish accent difficult to follow. They had set off very early that morning, through drizzling rain, and Daisy had moaned, as they got aboard the train, that it was just her luck to be taking Sean to Ty Gwyn for the first time in such bad weather. Sean, however, had laughed at that. 'Why on earth should a bit of rain matter?' he had said cheerfully. 'Sure and doesn't it rain cats and dogs most days in Connemara? A bit of rain won't melt a pair of sturdy Irish peasants like me and yourself.'

'What a cheek you've got callin' me a peasant, Sean O'Grady,' Daisy had said, giving him a playful punch in the ribs. 'Still, it surely won't rain for three whole days! There's so much I want you to see; not just Ty Gwyn itself, but the surrounding countryside. Uncle Bob, being a farmer, is an essential user so he takes the car out from time to time. I thought we might borrow it one day and go a bit further afield, but if it rains all the time . . .'

They had been alone in the compartment, for the train had not been crowded. 'It won't, Daisy me love, it wouldn't dare,' Sean had said, giving her hand a squeeze.

Now however, comfortably settled on the cracked leather seat in the back of the old taxicab, Daisy remarked that Sean had been right. The weather had already begun to clear and through the cab window the sun shone, lighting up the beautiful hill country and causing the distant sea to sparkle like sapphires.

'Told you so,' Sean said complacently. 'It's always finer on the coast than inland. I say, is that your aunt's place?'

It was, and as the taxi drew up outside the front gate Daisy, glancing at her companion, saw a fine dew of perspiration break out on his brow and marvelled that he should be so nervous. It was not as if he had never met Aunt Jane before – or perhaps, she thought with an inward smile, it was because he had met Aunt Jane before. Being so much younger than Sean and Brendan, Daisy had no idea whether, as small boys, they had plagued her aunt or teased her by bringing worms into the kitchen – Aunt Jane hated worms – or cajoling her into crossing an apparently empty meadow when they knew perfectly well that when she was halfway across the grass a herd of young bullocks would come galloping over, skidding to a halt a bare couple of feet before the newcomer, curious as always to know what was going on.

As they descended from the taxi and Sean paid their fare, she voiced the thought aloud. 'Were you a bad little boy, Sean? Only you do seem somewhat nervous and I can assure you that neither Aunt Jane nor Uncle Bob eats young flying officers for breakfast.'

Sean bent to pick up their two holdalls, then smiled sheepishly as Daisy swung open the gate and headed, not for the front door which was seldom used, but for the path which led round to the farmyard and the back door. 'I wouldn't say Brendan and me were angels and we did get Aunt Jane going a couple of times,' he admitted. 'But we were only real bad to her once, that I can recall. We had persuaded her to climb aboard Tina, said it were the quickest way to get up to the peat bog, which was true, and then we gave the donkey a cut across the rump and she set off at a gallop. Your aunt weren't expecting it, of course, but she hung on like a limpet. It were only when Tina stopped to help herself to a fine thistle plant that she and Aunt Jane parted company.' He grinned guiltily down at his companion. 'She landed on her bum with her legs in the air and her skirt up round her waist and my, wasn't she mad wit' us! If she'd caught us we would have been scalpt, but we ran like a couple of hares and by teatime we were in my mam's kitchen. Next time I saw your aunt, she were in the donkey cart wit' Mr Kildare, going back to the station. She give me a grim look but that was all. And I do remember Brendan saying she'd not split on him, though she gave him a thundering scold. D'you reckon she'll remember?'

Daisy, much amused by this tale, chuckled. 'We all played tricks on her because she wasn't a countrywoman and was scared of all sorts, so she was,' she said, as they crossed the cobbled yard. 'It's a miracle, now I come to think of it, that she's taken to farming life the way she has, but I suppose it's different when it's your own place and when farming is your husband's dream. Is it yours, Sean? I've never asked, but do you want to farm when the war's over?'

She was putting out her hand towards the doorknob as she spoke, but before she could reach it the door shot open and Aunt Jane pounced on her, giving her a hug. 'You're early!' she said joyfully. 'We didn't think you could possibly reach us before teatime, and here you are, just as I'm preparing the midday meal. I scrubbed some extra potatoes, just in case, and there's a tray of Cornish pasties in the oven, so no one's going to go short.' She turned to Sean, holding out a hand. 'How d'you do, Mr O'Grady? I dare say you'll remember me; I certainly remember you!'

Sean stood the holdalls down on the quarry tiles, shook his hostess's hand and groaned dramatically, removing his cap as he did so. 'I was hopin' to God you'd forgot, Miss Dal . . . I mean Mrs Elgin,' he said, and Daisy could hear the suppressed laughter in his voice and how embarrassment had thickened his accent. ''Tis sorry I am that I played tricks on you, but I were only a lad, after all.'

'So you were,' Aunt Jane said placidly. 'And I dare say the sight of me lyin' on me back in the lane, with me drawers on display and me skirt round me ears, was a sight you'll remember to your dying day. But I'm a farmer's wife now. I feed the pigs and milk the cow, and Bob's taught me to drive the pony cart, though I've never ridden a horse in me life and don't mean to start now. But what am I thinking of? Daisy will show you to your room while I pour us all a nice cup of tea. My husband will be in, wanting his grub, in ten or fifteen minutes, and then we can start our meal.'

As Aunt Jane waved them off at the end of their stay, Daisy reflected that the visit had been successful beyond her wildest dreams. Aunt Jane had told her niece that she thought Sean delightful, and Uncle Bob had admitted he was a grand chap, though he was rather disappointed when Sean had made it plain that he had no intention of returning to Ireland when the war was over. 'I've two brothers, both older than meself, who have remained on the farm, and it's not big enough to support any more members of the family. No, I've other plans. I want to fly civil aircraft and I'm told the place to do that is the United States of America,' Sean had said. He had grinned at Daisy. 'A new life in a new country for both of us. How does that appeal? If you hate the idea I could try for work in England, but I couldn't stand a desk job, and I'm not cut out for farming.'

'Nor me,' Daisy had said, though she thought, rather sadly, that in truth she had imagined that when peace came she would return to the countryside, if not actually to Connemara. But it would scarcely do to say so; and anyway, nothing mattered but being with Sean, doing what he wanted to do. Silly to imagine that he would long for country life once more. 'And I'd love to go to the States, Sean.'

'Good,' Sean had said, smiling lovingly down at her. 'There's an Australian in my squadron and he says there'll be a great many jobs for pilots in his country when the war's over, but I'd like to try the States first, if you agree.'

'I do, I do,' Daisy had said eagerly. 'Just as long as we're together.'

The family had been sitting round the kitchen table, topping and tailing gooseberries. There were four old bushes right at the back of the home pasture, which Bob had threatened to dig out since they were straggly and, he thought, no longer productive. It was almost as though the gooseberry bushes had heard him, however, for this year the crop had been so heavy that the branches had bowed beneath the weight of the fruit and Aunt Jane had announced that she would bottle most of them and sell any they themselves could not use at the market.

Uncle Bob had been reading the evening paper whilst he worked and had looked up at this point, to give first Sean and then Daisy a penetrating glance. Sean appeared to have noticed nothing but Daisy, meeting Bob's eyes, had remembered that he was Jake's father and that father and son had always been close. She had felt a stab of guilt, but had shaken it off. Why, in heaven's name, should she feel guilty because she was in love and had announced that she would follow the man in her life wherever he might go? Abruptly, she had remembered those royal lovers, the Duke of Windsor, who might still have been king, and Wallis Simpson, who had undoubtedly set her sights on one day becoming queen. What was it the duke had said in his abdication speech? 'I cannot discharge my duties as king without the help and support of the woman I love' – or something like that, anyway. Well, that was just how she felt; if she did not have the help and support which Sean was offering her, she could not imagine what her life would be like. Satisfied on that score, she had returned Uncle Bob's gaze, then had impulsively leaned across the table and squeezed his hand. 'I love the farm, and I love you and Auntie Jane, but America isn't the other end of the world,' she had said. 'I shall always think of Ty Gwyn as my home . . . and you know, once Jake meets the girl that he will one day marry, we'll be friends again, and we'll be able to meet each other on our old terms.'

Bob had smiled and returned the pressure of her hand. 'Of course you will,' he had said heartily. 'My boy isn't one to bear a grudge; oh aye, things will come right between you.' Then he had turned to Sean. 'You've got yourself a grand little girl in young Daisy here,' he had said gruffly. 'Mind you take good care of her, or I shan't be the only one after your blood.'

Daisy had thought it had been generous of Uncle Bob to say what he had but Sean, once they were on the train bound for Liverpool, said that he thought Mr Elgin still harboured hopes that Daisy might change her mind.

'Rubbish!' Daisy said robustly. 'He was talking quite happily about Jake meeting someone else and the two of us – no, the four of us – becoming friends. What fault can you find with that, pray?'

Sean's brows came together and he began to speak, then appeared to change his mind and shut his lips firmly on whatever he had been about to say. Daisy, however, did not mean to let him think that Uncle Bob was not sincere. 'When he said he was not the only one who would be after your blood if you were unkind to me, he meant Aunt Jane,' she said, though in her heart she thought he had probably meant Jake. 'Now stop being foolish and tell me what you were going to say.'

There was a short silence, then Sean looked at her from under his lashes. 'Flying fighters is a risky game,' he mumbled. 'If I were to die . . .'

'Oh, Sean, don't say such things,' Daisy said, her heart lurching. 'Everyone's at risk during wartime. Why, I've never told you but we've had fatalities in the munitions factory; girls have been killed in the room I work in and in other sections as well. So please don't even think about what might occur; think about all the good times we've had together, and all the good times still to come.'

Sean gave a reluctant smile and squeezed her hand. They had been talking in low tones, for the carriage was full, and now he leaned even closer so that he could whisper into her ear. 'You're right, of course, and I suppose I should be generous and say that if anything happened to me, your happiness would be what mattered. Only . . .'

'Only I couldn't be happy without you,' Daisy whispered. 'And now let's change the subject or you'll have me in tears.'

Jake sat in his little swivel seat in the tail of his Wellington bomber. They had taken off an hour previously, having done all their checks, and as they crossed the North Sea he had fired a burst into the cold grey water below to test his guns. It had been a pleasant enough night on the ground but now, as they gained height, it grew colder and Jake shivered, fishing in his pocket for the mints which the skipper had handed round earlier, and telling himself to think cheerful thoughts. The trouble was, of course, that his mood had been one of black depression ever since Daisy's rejection. Oh, he had managed to hide it a good deal of the time, but whenever he was alone the black thoughts came swarming. It wasn't so bad when he was on the ground. He went to dances in the NAAFI, sometimes even flirted with a pretty girl, took the gharry into the nearest town to see a film or have a meal, and of course he and his pals enjoyed a drink at the local inn. When they were over Germany with searchlights, enemy fighters and bursts of flak to dodge, the depression left him completely; then, his whole mind was fixed on his guns and the tasks he had to perform. His depression would lift one day, he told himself. He would meet someone else or simply start thinking of Daisy not as the only girl he could ever love, but as an old friend. In the meantime, his life and the lives of the rest of the crew depended upon each one concentrating on getting them to and from the target without untoward incident. Indeed, if it had not been for the long, cold, boring flights to and from their objectives, Jake honestly believed that he would have begun to beat the depression by now.

He knew the rest of the crew would be as bored, cold and cramped as he was himself, and having taken a good look round, began quietly to stretch his arms and legs. He was friendly with all the crew but Tubby, the waist gunner, had suggested that the two of them might take off on their first free evening and see Humphrey Bogart in *The Maltese Falcon*, which was being shown in the nearest town. Concentrate on that, he told himself fiercely. Think about the little Waaf who cuddled up to you the last time you danced with her in the NAAFI. He actually thought he was succeeding as he recreated the scene until he realised that the tune to which they were dancing was an old favourite: *Daisy, Daisy, give me your answer do . . .*

He wrenched his mind away from the NAAFI and instead, despite his resolve, the evening of the May ball came into his head. He saw again the lazily winding river, the willows leaning over it and the great silver moon above, casting long shadows whilst Daisy, with her drenched frock in her hand, had glanced wickedly up at him, her dark curls dancing, her mouth curved into the adorable smile he loved so well. He tried to banish the image, then gave up; what the hell? If remembering the good times got rid of the depression, then why not enjoy his memories? Everyone's life was all sunshine and shadows; why should his be any different? Satisfied that he was doing the right thing, he gave memory full rein and immediately felt warmth invade his mind.

Chapter Twelve

Summer 1943

It was a fine summer afternoon and Daisy lay on her stomach on the ragged and unkempt lawn which fronted the old manor house in which she, and a great many other girls, were billeted. She was very nearly asleep, for she had worked a double shift the day before which meant, thank heaven, that she would now have a couple of days off.

Her job had changed from making munitions to making aeroplanes when she had become allergic to the explosive with which the shells she had made were filled. It had started innocently enough. Whenever she began work, she would begin to sneeze and mop her reddened eyes, which ran with tears. 'A summer cold,' her supervisor had said and had advised her to take a couple of days off. She had done so and the sneezing miraculously stopped, but when she had returned to work at her bench, not only had she begun to sneeze helplessly once more, but strange blotches had appeared all over the skin of her hands and forearms. The blotches had begun to split and weep and Miss Murphy, the supervisor, had told her she must put in for a transfer.

Excited by the thought of change, Daisy had decided to apply for one of the services, only to be told that no further volunteers were to be accepted since the most urgent need, now, was for more aircraft. Even the Land Army was no longer recruiting and God knew that food was wanted pretty urgently, so since the need for girls to make planes was even greater than the need for crops, Daisy had been happy to take a job at an aircraft factory, even though it was twenty miles from Liverpool, and meant she could no longer live in the coachman's quarters.

The factory was in what were, to Daisy, delight-fully rural surroundings. She shared a long attic room with nine other workers in the old manor, originally requisitioned by the army for the use of soldiers guarding both the factory and the nearby airfield. Those troops, however, had moved on, presumably into Nissen huts, leaving the old house to be occupied by the girls who had taken over the men's jobs at the aircraft factory.

Daisy had only been working here for a few months, but within days she had known that the change was for the better. The skin of all the girls working in munitions went yellow, as a result of the material they handled. It was not possible to wash the colour off, but it faded with time and now Daisy was her rosy-cheeked self. Since she was not allergic to any of the materials used in aircraft manufacture, the other symptoms from which she had suffered had gone completely. The work,

413

though demanding, was more congenial and needed a far more skilful approach. Then of course she was living in the country again, and the girls who shared the manor house took turns with all the cooking, cleaning and housework, and had even begun to cultivate a vegetable garden, despite the fact that they worked ten-hour shifts around the clock. 'But we know we're doing truly important work for the war effort,' Daisy's friend, Suzie, had said. Her boyfriend was in the air force, a bomb aimer in a Wellington stationed many miles away in Norfolk, and the two exchanged telephone calls a couple of times a week, and spent their leaves together whenever they could.

Sean had been in the Middle East for two years, so telephone calls had not been possible. But only the previous week Daisy had received a letter from him announcing that he had now done sufficient tours to enable him to return home to Britain, where he would spend at least six months training other fighter pilots. The letter had been a long time in transit, which meant that he would be home any day, and he had promised that as soon as he landed he would get in touch.

You must get time off. I'm sure there'll be no objection to your taking some leave if you explain that we've been parted for so long he had written. *Darling Daisy, I can't wait to hold you in my arms again. I don't see why we shouldn't marry, then we can get digs near whatever airfield I'm*

sent to, and at least be together for six months,
though of course I'm hoping for a home posting
when my stint as an instructor finishes.

Daisy had had no opportunity to write back,
explaining that she was doing essential war work
and did not think she would be allowed to move
away from her factory, though of course no one
could prevent their marrying. However, such
explanations would be better made face to face
and she was pretty sure that in one thing at least,
Sean was right: she would be given a couple of
days' leave at least, once he had returned to Britain.

Daisy had put the point to her supervisor that
she had taken no leave since she had moved into
aircraft manufacturing. Although her supervisor
had pulled a doubtful face, Daisy was sure he
would agree when the time came. Frank Walker
had been a sergeant pilot in the RAF but had lost
an arm during a raid over Germany and was now
in charge of some of the girls. He had told Daisy
that she always did a good job, never complained
over double shifts and ought to get the time off,
even though she had only worked with his team
for a relatively short while. So now Daisy was
waiting for the wonderful call which would
announce that Sean was 'somewhere in Britain'.

She was on the very verge of sleep when
someone dug her in the back, then flopped down
beside her. Daisy gave a muffled squawk and
turned her head to see Suzie, still clad in their

uniform of dungarees and regulation shirt, pulling the densely crocheted net from her head and running her hands through her thick mouse-coloured curls. 'Phew!' she said. 'Ain't it a grand day? I were goin' to bike into the village 'cos I've got some sweet coupons, and I thought Mrs Bagshot might have some of them acid drops what Lucy got last time she went shoppin'. Only it's so hot and you looked so comfortable lyin' on the grass that I thought mebbe I'd leave it for now.'

'You'd have to walk to the village because I looked into the bike shed earlier and it was empty,' Daisy observed. She sat up, then gave an enormous yawn. 'Crumbs, you didn't half startle me when you jabbed me in the back! I was almost asleep.'

'If you drop off now you won't sleep tonight, and that would never do,' Suzie said smugly. 'Tell you what, let's make a daisy chain. God knows there are enough daisies to make one a mile long. Then we can walk down to the Sullivans' cottage and give it to baby Beryl. It 'ud be a thank you for the plums.'

The Sullivans' cottage had once been the lodge and Mr Sullivan the gatekeeper. But that had been long before the war and now Mr Sullivan worked on the land and his wife looked after baby Beryl for her daughter and kept their small garden in full production. The gates themselves, of course, great wrought iron things, had gone long since to be melted down and used in the war effort.

Daisy surveyed her surroundings, thinking guiltily that what they should really be doing was getting the mower out of the shed and cutting the grass, the daisies, the clover and all the other intruders which had turned the once immaculate lawn into what amounted to a small meadow. But the mower was old and blunt and she thought the three-year-old Beryl could very well make her own daisy chains and would infinitely prefer a few sweets from the village shop if thanks for the plums were to be rendered. She said as much to Suzie, who laughed and agreed but said that a trip into the village would have to wait until there was a bicycle free. As for mowing the lawn, why on earth should anyone do such a thing? 'It's real pretty, with all them wild flowers,' she observed, 'and besides, Mr Sullivan's old pony and them two goats mowed it flatter'n any machine last year, so I dare say they'll do it again.'

'Oh? But how did they stop the goats – and the pony for that matter – hopping round the back and guzzlin' our vegetables?' Daisy asked rather suspiciously. 'And then there's the washing on the line; goats will eat anything, including my best knickers. We had goats at Benmacraig when I was little, and I remember how furious Amanda was when one of 'em ate her pink blouse!'

Suzie laughed. 'They can't wander wherever they want, they're tethered, you idiot! You know, they tie one end of the rope round the animal and the other end round a wooden peg which they bash into the ground. Honest, queen, no one would take you for a country girl.'

'I didn't think,' Daisy admitted, getting reluctantly to her feet. 'Look, how about if I come with you into the village? It won't seem half such a long way if there are two of us and I'm pretty sure that if we take Beryl a few sweets Mrs Sullivan will give us some more plums – or let us pick them rather – because the weight of the crop is beginning to break some of the thinner branches.'

Suzie looked doubtful. She was a city girl through and through, having been born and brought up in a court off the Scotland Road, and had never walked for pleasure in her life. She began to say as much now but Daisy interrupted. 'Suzie Smith, think of the times you've told me how you and your pals would go off to Seaforth for the day. Kids never had any money so I don't suppose you caught the Overhead Railway, or hopped aboard a passing bus. If you walked when you were a kid, why can't you walk now?'

Suzie giggled. 'We skipped a lecky to get to Seaforth Sands, and that don't cost nothin',' she pointed out. 'Then Mam would give us a penny or two for doin' her messages, and when the schools were out there were a special ticket for kids. But if you're set on it, I suppose I could walk. Only aren't you tired, queen? I don't want you collapsin' on me after a couple of miles!'

'I won't,' Daisy said stoutly, heading for the house. They reached the enormous kitchen and were halfway across it when Daisy suddenly stopped short and grabbed her friend by the arm. 'I've had a better idea,' she said excitedly. 'My brother sent me a parcel a few days ago – he's awful good like that – and yesterday I baked ginger biscuits. We had some of 'em at teatime, but I put the rest in a tin and took 'em up to our room. We could give them to baby Beryl, and if Mrs Sullivan does give us some more plums we could make a pie; I've enough ingredients left for some pastry.'

'Good idea,' Suzie said, beaming. 'Anything to avoid a walk!'

The girls toiled up the stairs to their dormitory – for that, in effect, was what it was – and Daisy produced her tin of biscuits, found a crumpled brown paper bag and tipped the contents into it. The two girls were halfway down the stairs again when the telephone in the hall below began to ring. Daisy squeaked and began to hurry, but the door of the big living room, where the girls congregated in the evenings when they were not working, shot open and a large figure emerged. Daisy recognised Daphne Bullock and slowed her pace, for Daphne was engaged to a soldier on an ack-ack battery; probably they had arranged that he should phone at this particular time, which was why Daphne had emerged so promptly. The two girls headed for the kitchen but before they could leave the hall Daphne turned, holding out the receiver. 'It's for you, Kildare,' she said rather grudgingly. 'Don't be all day; me feller promised to ring between two and three, and it's ten past the hour already.'

Daisy had hard work not to snatch the receiver, but took it from the other girl with attempted nonchalance and held it to her ear. 'Hello?' she said, and heard her own voice higher than usual and more than a little breathless. 'Hello? Daisy Kildare speaking.'

'Daisy, me darlin', I'm back!' Sean's voice said in her ear. 'Ah, God, I can't wait to see you! I've had my debriefing session and shan't be needed for the best part of a week. What shift are you on? What about leave? Any chance? I'd give anything to see you . . . can't wait. Is there a pub in the village where I could stay for a couple of days? Even if they won't give you leave you surely must have some time to yourself!'

'Oh, Sean, it's just so marvellous to hear your voice,' Daisy said breathlessly. 'I'm sure I can get some leave; my supervisor thinks it can be managed. But if you're free, and can come here, it would be wonderful.'

'Right. I'll look up the trains and so on. But, me darlin', could you get me a room at the pub? I reckon I'll set out by the first train tomorrow and probably be with you by evening. What station am I to ask for? And what's the name of the pub? Any chance of you meeting me off the train?'

Daisy gave a gurgle of amusement. 'Since I don't know what train you'll be arriving by, I can't possibly meet it,' she said regretfully. 'And besides, trains don't always run according to plan in wartime . . . the pub's called the Green Man. If you get a ticket to Chester you can get a bus out to the village. I'll make my way to the pub around opening time and stay there until you arrive. Oh, Sean, I don't know how I shall wait until then!'

Next day, Daisy worked the early shift in order to have the following day off and was free from four o'clock. She and Suzie returned to Lacey Manor and went up to their room where Daisy borrowed Suzie's best buttercup-yellow blouse and Enid's nice brown pleated skirt, for the girls always rallied round and swapped clothing for important dates. 'Ain't you lucky to have natural curls though?' Suzie said, rooting in her bag for a length of yellow ribbon. 'Are you going to tie it back? If so, this ribbon should suit.'

Daisy tried the ribbon but decided to leave her hair loose. Then she brushed her eyelashes with a tiny smear of Vaseline and borrowed Joan's lipstick, then decided it was the wrong colour and rubbed it off again. 'Wrong colour? You're very fussy all of a sudden,' Joan said, reclaiming her lipstick. 'Want a dab of powder? Only you've got so tanned that it might look a bit odd. Still, it would cover them 'orrible freckles.'

'Don't listen to her, she's just jealous,' Suzie said as Daisy dived at the mirror and anxiously surveyed the half-dozen or so freckles on her small nose. 'You look grand, queen, honest to God you does. And if you're going to go into the village, you'd best bag a bike before they're all taken, otherwise you'll have to walk and you'll never get there by opening time.'

'Oh lor', you're right, I'll have to go,' Daisy said. She snatched up her brown cardigan and her gas mask case, and headed for the door. 'I'll be back here later tonight but since I've got a few days off I thought Sean and I might catch a train down to Abergele tomorrow and spend a day or two with Aunt Jane and Uncle Bob; if Sean would like it, I mean. See you later!'

Daisy felt foolish going into the public bar by herself for the girls were usually there in groups, but the landlord greeted her pleasantly, asking her whether her gentleman friend was likely to want a meal when he arrived. Daisy, who had booked a room for Sean over the telephone, admitted that she had no idea whether her friend would be able to get himself a meal or whether he would be famished. Indeed, she had no idea at what time he might arrive and said so.

'Never you mind, my dear; there's always bread 'n' cheese 'n' pickles, and a nice piece of plum pie,' the landlord said comfortably. 'Provided he's here before closing time, though, my wife will get him a hot meal.'

'That's awfully good of you,' Daisy said gratefully. 'I hope you don't mind if I wait for him in here, at least until the bar begins to fill up. Later,

I might take a walk along the street but it would look rather odd if I hang about the village.'

The landlord suggested that she might prefer to sit in the snug just as the door opened and two farmhands entered, both elderly men whom the landlord obviously knew well since he greeted them by name and began to pull a pint of beer without waiting for them to order. Daisy decided that she had better buy a drink before taking herself off to the snug, but before she could do so the door opened again and a noisy group of airmen from the nearby airfield came in. Daisy knew several of them and they exchanged greetings, for despite being almost engaged to Sean she had attended dances and social events and was on friendly terms with several of the personnel. Toby, one of the ground crew mechanics, was a frequent visitor to the manor and knew all about Daisy's young man. 'It's not like you to be in the pub alone at opening time,' he said, smiling. 'I bet your feller's landed at last and you're meeting him here.'

Daisy nodded vigorously. 'That's it. Only I don't know when he'll arrive,' she said. 'I've got a few days' leave and so has he, so we'll be together until he gets his new posting.'

'Well I hope you don't intend to hang around here,' Toby said, leering at her. 'What you want is a nice dirty weekend. If I were your feller I'd whisk you off to somewhere on the coast, a nice little hotel, or a guest house, where they'll take Mr and Mrs Smith in their stride. You can't do that here because everyone knows you're not married to anyone, not yet.'

'How dare you!' Daisy said with mock indignation, for Toby was always teasing. 'I'm not that sort of girl. No, I thought I'd take Sean down to my aunt's place. It's a farm in the hills behind Abergele, so we could spend time at the seaside, if the weather was right.' She knew Toby had a slight crush on her and was always interested in her comings and goings. 'I've told you about my aunt before; she's a real sport, and of course, though we'll give her our ration cards, staying with her won't cost us anything like what a hotel would.'

Toby stared. 'But I remember you telling me that Uncle Bob isn't your real uncle because your aunt is his second wife,' he said. 'You said he was Jimmy's father . . . was it Jimmy or Johnny? . . . so how can you possibly take Sean to your old boyfriend's place?'

'Oh, Toby, what a memory you've got, except Bob's son is called Jake, not Jimmy or Johnny. But I've not seen him for . . . gracious, it must be nearly three years, and since he's stationed absolutely miles away it would be the most frightful coincidence if he turned up at the farm whilst Sean and I were there. Still, I'm glad you mentioned it because when I give Aunt Jane a ring to tell her we plan to visit, I'll ask her whether Jake will be coming home during the course of our stay. Although three years is a long time and I do know that Jake's got a girlfriend now, so I suppose it wouldn't really matter if our visits did coincide.'

'Course it would matter,' Toby said. He had bright ginger hair and white eyebrows, and now the eyebrows climbed almost to his hairline, then descended into a deep frown. 'You're not a very sensitive soul, are you, Daisy? Even if he's got over you, and you've obviously got over him, there is Sean to consider. I remember you saying he was possessive – most men are – so he wouldn't exactly hang out the flags if he found himself sharing a house with your ex.'

'He is *not* my ex,' Daisy shouted, then lowered her voice as several heads turned in her direction. 'We were big pals as kids but that's because we were brought up in the same household. I was really fond of Jake as a friend, but nothing more, and to tell you the truth I can scarcely remember what he looks like.'

As she said the words, a picture of Jake formed in her mind: dark spiky hair, thick brows which nearly met across the top of his nose, eyes so dark they looked almost black and a narrow but determined chin. Guiltily, she tried to banish the picture, realising with some dismay that it was clearer in her mind than her image of Sean, for whenever she thought of him she saw the photograph which he had given her before leaving the country, and could not conjure up anything else.

'All right, all right, have it your own way,' Toby said. 'Well at least your Jake has got some sense;

you say he's got himself a girl, which is more than I've managed to do. I say, Daisy, suppose you find Sean isn't the feller for you after all? How would you like to go steady with a red-haired mechanic who's crazy about you?'

'I wouldn't, though I'm sure there are plenty of girls who would,' Daisy said, causing Toby to give a crack of laughter and poke her in the ribs.

'Plenty of girls who would what?' he enquired. 'Girls can be divided into two groups, those who will and those who won't, and it's my misfortune that I always fall for girls who won't. I suppose your Jake has got himself a pretty little Waaf? Wish I was so lucky . . . only of course my heart's been given to a riveter up at the aircraft factory.'

Daisy, who was a riveter, snorted. 'There must be a hundred of us, so that gives you a good wide field,' she said. 'I think I'll just take a stroll outside; it'll get awfully smoky in here as the evening wears on and I've no idea when Sean will turn up.'

'Oh, don't go, Daisy; let me buy you a drink,' Toby urged. 'I've not seen you for weeks. What's the gossip up at the manor?'

'I can't think of anything interesting,' Daisy admitted. 'I won't have a drink though, thanks, or not yet at any rate. To tell you the truth, I'm beginning to feel really nervous. I think I'd be better by myself for a while.'

Toby guffawed. 'You're going to rehearse your first speech,' he said mockingly. 'You won't have to say a word, you daft girl. You'll fly into each

426

other's arms like they do in all the war films. I think I'll come out with you; it'll be an education to see you hurl yourself at a bloke and start kissing and cuddling.'

This, however, was not at all what Daisy wanted and she said so with a firmness which even Toby could not fail to recognise. 'I won't stay out for long, and when I come back you can treat me to a ginger beer,' she promised him. 'But please, Toby, don't spy on me. I've looked forward to this moment for so long and it has suddenly occurred to me that it isn't going to be easy. Don't make it harder for me, there's a dear.'

Toby patted her arm. 'Sorry, Daisy, love, I wasn't thinking,' he said gruffly. 'Off you go and when you come back I'll buy you that ginger beer.'

'Thanks,' Daisy said huskily and headed for the street. Outside, the air smelt sweet and fresh, and after the noise in the pub it seemed wonderfully peaceful. She wandered up the street, gazed into the window of the small general shop, then went and leaned on the churchyard wall, contemplating the ancient gravestones and the tall limes which flanked the path leading to the church door. Overhead, the rooks which nested in the tops of the trees squabbled and cawed.

Daisy was just thinking that she might use the pennies in her pocket to phone Aunt Jane when it occurred to her that Sean might have other ideas. Suppose he thought as Toby did and suggested a weekend down on the coast as Mr and Mrs Smith?

427

What would she say? It would seem awfully cruel to deny him if she really meant to marry him one day. She knew that Cynthia and Clive had spent several weekends as Mr and Mrs Beamish, but it was different for them. They knew each other as well as any husband and wife, thought of each other in that way, and intended to marry as soon as the war was over. Both held important jobs two hundred miles apart, which would mean that even if they married now they could not be together. It was different for herself and Sean, for they had been going together for less than a year when he had been sent abroad, and now they would seem like strangers after two years apart.

She was still contemplating the old churchyard and wondering what she should do if Sean did not want to visit Ty Gwyn when she heard the sound of a vehicle approaching. Instantly, her heart jumped into her mouth. She swung round in time to see an ancient taxi coming along the road. It drew to a halt beside her and a figure in crumpled air force uniform emerged, hauling a holdall after him. 'Daisy!' he said, half held out his arms, then dropped his luggage and instead of hugging her turned to the cab driver. 'What's the damage?' he asked briskly. The man told him, money was handed over, the driver tried to give him change but was told, brusquely, to keep it and then Sean, for it was he, turned to Daisy and scooped her into a tight embrace. He tried to kiss her mouth but Daisy, horribly embarrassed, turned her head away at the crucial moment so that their noses bumped. Sean continued to hold her as the taxi drove off, though she saw he was looking down at her with puzzlement in his blue eyes. Blue! She had somehow imagined him to be dark-eyed, though she could not think why. 'Daisy?' His voice sounded suddenly young and uncertain. 'Oh, Daisy darling, is something the matter? Have I changed so much? You're taller than I remember, and your hair's different . . . look, we can't stand here in the street. If we go to the pub will they let you come up to my room? Then we can talk.'

He released her but slung a careless arm across her shoulders and Daisy, horribly ashamed of her initial reaction, put her own arm round his waist and gave him a tentative squeeze. 'You are different,' she said shyly. 'You're thinner and browner, though I'm sure you haven't changed that much. Oh, Sean, isn't this awkward? I thought you'd be exactly the same, I'm sure I am, but I feel a bit – just a tiny bit – as though I – I'd never met you before.'

'Oh, my darling girl, two years is a long time and letters aren't like telephone calls,' Sean said as they began to walk towards the Green Man. Because he was so much taller than she, their progress was awkward and uncomfortable, until Sean obviously realised and slowed down, matching his pace to hers.

'Well, we've got three whole days to get to know each other again, but as for my coming up to your room, I'm afraid that really isn't on,' Daisy said. 'But there's a little room called the snug, off the main bar. The landlord said we can go in there, and his wife's making you a hot meal too, provided you arrived before closing time.'

In the event, however, the landlord conducted them round the bar and into his own parlour, telling them with an avuncular smile that this would give them complete privacy and that his wife would serve both of them with rabbit stew and dumplings, as well as what he described as 'a mess of garden peas'.

In the quiet little parlour, eating the excellent food which the landlord's wife had provided, Daisy began to feel a little less stressed. She got Sean to tell her about his journey home, then regaled him with stories of life in the factory whilst covertly examining him, because he still seemed almost a stranger. It was not his physical appearance, she decided at last, though he was both thinner and browner as she had said; it was something else, something which she could not immediately identify.

By the time they had finished their meal, however, she felt sufficiently at ease with him to discuss what they should do over the next few days. 'I thought we might visit Aunt Jane and Uncle Bob at Ty Gwyn,' she said rather shyly. 'It won't cost anything – well, not very much, anyway.'

Sean looked at her, then dropped his eyes to

examine his own hands. 'Go to your aunt's place?' he asked. 'But Daisy, I want to be with you. I know they're delightful people and of course Ty Gwyn is in beautiful countryside but, as you said earlier, I think we need to get to know one another all over again. I thought we might book ourselves into a small hotel or boarding house, and . . .'

'And call ourselves Mr and Mrs Smith?' Daisy said baldly. 'I thought you respected me too much. Or at least that's what you said before you were sent abroad, if you remember.'

Sean's colour darkened but Daisy thought he looked more annoyed than embarrassed. 'I've not asked you to share a bed with me, only a small hotel or a boarding house,' he said stiffly. 'Naturally I meant that we would have single rooms. Is that so terrible? Can you not bear the thought of being under the same roof as me for three days without your aunt to act as chaperon?'

Daisy looked doubtfully across at him. She had never heard of a man suggesting that he might take a girl off for a weekend at the seaside or in the country whilst not expecting her to share both his room and his bed. But then she scolded herself for her naivety because the truth was, she had absolutely no personal experience in that line. But now was the time to put things right, to stop shilly-shallying. She took a deep breath and leaned across the small table which separated them, taking both Sean's hands in hers and meeting the gaze of his dark blue eyes unflinchingly. 'I'm sorry if I spoke out of turn,' she said quietly. 'I do understand that visiting Ty Gwyn might not be a very good idea, so if you want to book us into a hotel or a boarding house in somewhere like Rhyl, then that will be fine. And if you want us to share a room – to call ourselves Mr and Mrs O'Grady – then I'm sure that will be fine too, only – only I've never done anything like that in my life and I don't know if I'll be very good at it.'

He began to answer her, spluttered, and then laughed so loudly that she released his hands to clap a palm over his mouth. 'Shut up!' she hissed. 'Shut up, Sean, or you can bloody well go to Rhyl by yourself.' And then, because she was so keyed up, half ashamed and half proud that she had actually offered herself to him, she burst into tears.

Although at the time Daisy had been deeply ashamed of her tears, she thought afterwards, as she made her way back to Lacey Manor, that her show of emotion had not been a bad thing after all. Sean had jumped to his feet, taken her in his arms and then sat down again with her perched on his lap. He had cuddled and caressed her, apologising over and over for his tactlessness in appearing to laugh at her. He had told her that the only reason he had laughed was at the thought that he could ever have doubted her innocence. 'Of course you've never done anything like that before,' he had said, tenderly wiping her tear-wet cheeks with the palms of his hands. 'I know you

432

would never break your word, so I won't even ask if you've met up with Jake whilst I've been away, because I know you haven't.'

Daisy had straightened indignantly and pulled herself out of Sean's embrace. Going round the table, she had sat down in the chair she had just vacated, propped her chin in her hand and gazed steadily at Sean. 'As it happens, I've not so much as spoken to him on the telephone, far less met up with him,' she had said stiffly. 'But now that you've brought the subject up, I think a bit of frankness might not come amiss. It was very wrong of you, Sean, to make me promise not to see or speak to such an old friend. You never allowed for the fact that Jake might have turned up at Ty Gwyn at the same time as I did. It's complicated every visit I've made to the farm and I'm sure Uncle Bob and Aunt Jane must have wondered why I never visited them without telephoning first. They never said anything, but in the end I had to explain to Aunt Jane and I'm pretty sure she felt you were being over-possessive. I mean, it's not as though Jake had ever been a boyfriend in the accepted sense of the word. He was just an old pal.'

Sean had flushed darkly and reached across the table to take her hand. 'You make me feel ashamed,' he had said quietly. 'The truth is, I am possessive. But I agree that it was wrong of me. However, whatever your feelings, you can't deny that Jake was in love with you. Dammit, he was quite prepared to fight me simply because I danced with

433

you. A man doesn't behave like that unless he's . . .
well, let's say deeply involved.'

Daisy had gently disengaged her hand and stood
up. 'Well, I never did believe in crying over spilt
milk; as I said, I've not so much as spoken to Jake
since you left,' she said. 'Maybe it was the best
thing though, because Jake has a girlfriend now
so even if he was in love with me, which I don't
believe – I think it was just a sort of crush – then
he isn't any more, so you've no need to worry.
And now I'd better be getting back to the manor.
What time should we meet in the morning? If we're
off to Rhyl early, we'd better order a taxi now.'

'Then you've not changed your mind, Daisy?
Even knowing what a possessive, jealous bloke I
am?' Sean had said, sounding light-hearted and
also rather pleased with himself. 'You're a girl in
a million so you are, and don't worry, alanna, I
promise not to do anything you wouldn't like.'

He had offered to walk her back to the manor
but Daisy had scoffed at the idea, for he had been
travelling all day and she knew he was very weary.
Besides, she felt she needed some quiet time on
her own before facing the barrage of questions with
which she would be bombarded as soon as she
entered Lacey Manor.

It was a mild night with a full moon shining in
the dark sky and only a gentle breeze to waft the
night sounds of a country lane to listening ears.
Daisy heard the rustle of a bird, disturbed from its
sleep by her passing, saw an owl float by on silent

wings, and, when she reached a mossy gate, stopped for a moment to peer over it at the humped shapes of the dairy herd as they lay in the lee of the hedge. Despite herself, she could not help wondering how she would feel next day when she and Sean arrived at whatever hotel or guesthouse he had booked. She feared that when he signed the register, pretending they were married, she would go as red as any beetroot, thus giving away the truth as surely as if she had shouted it aloud. But probably even newly-weds blush when they both walk into the same bedroom, she told herself bracingly, and from what she knew of human nature, she thought it was very unlikely that in these hard times a landlord or landlady would turn away prospective customers.

Having reassured herself on this point, Daisy quickened her pace. I'm twenty-three years old, the same age that my mother was when she married my father, she told herself. At least half the girls I work with know more about men than I do, so it's high time I caught up. Besides, Sean has made it as obvious as he can that he isn't going to rush me. Why, I dare say we'll get twin beds and not share anything other than the room for the whole of the three days. And nights, of course. For some reason, the thought made her giggle. How foolish she was being, to agree to what Toby had called a dirty weekend and then to spend all her time planning how to turn it into a sort of girl guide and boy scout affair in which both parties would quell their natural desires and behave like brother and sister. This made her laugh again; she was being quite absurd! She could tell herself that she could change her mind, back down, but she had no real intention of being such a wimp. One did not, after all, when offering so much as a peppermint humbug to someone, hold it out and at the last moment snatch it back, and that, she felt, would be the equivalent of agreeing to go to bed with Sean and then changing her mind.

By this time she had reached the drive which led to Lacey Manor, and she began to hurry. When she reached the door of the sitting room, she could hear the subdued hum of voices behind it, and threw it open. Suzie looked up, smiled, and gestured her to join them where they sat in a row on the sofa, each girl doing some small task or other. Suzie was knitting a pair of socks for her boyfriend and the others were engaged in similar ploys.

'How did it go?' Suzie asked eagerly as Daisy sat down beside her. 'I take it he's arrived? Are you going to your aunt's?'

'Yes, he's arrived. He was pretty early, actually, so we had most of the evening together,' Daisy said. The girl next to her, Patty, was stoning plums, the very ones, Daisy guessed, that she and Suzie had picked the day before. She helped herself to one of the un-stoned fruit and spoke through her mouthful. 'The landlady of the Green Man made us supper, rabbit stew and dumplings followed by plum pie. I'm going to ring my aunt tomorrow morning, before we set out.'

Suzie gave an incredulous squeak. 'D'you mean to say he agreed to your going to Ty Gwyn?' she asked. 'The man's a saint!'

Daisy giggled. 'Actually I think we shall probably be going down to Rhyl,' she admitted. 'I was just having you on. But it will all be perfectly proper, of course; single rooms and all that. He said so, as soon as he suggested Rhyl.'

This of course was perfectly true but she saw by the expression on Suzie's face that her friend was sceptical to say the least, and as soon as she was unobserved she gave Suzie a wink and then stood up. 'Well, girls, since I shall be off first thing in the morning, I think I'd best get an early night,' she said. 'Are you coming up, Suzie?'

'Sure am,' Suzie said breezily, and the two girls left the room and clattered up the stairs. As soon as they reached their attic dormitory, however, Suzie turned to her friend. 'Did he honestly say single rooms?' she asked. 'I'm your pal, Daisy; surely you don't expect me to swallow that one?'

Daisy laughed, feeling her cheeks grow warm. 'He did say it, honest to God he did,' she protested. 'And I think he would have stuck to it, only . . . well, the truth is I said the "Mr and Mrs Smith" bit. I'd been talking to Toby – you know, the red-headed one – whilst I waited for Sean to arrive, and he asked me if Sean and I were going to be Mr and Mrs Smith. I laughed it off, but then, when

Sean got all holier than thou, I realised that he was embarrassed and wouldn't say straight out that he wanted to . . . well, do the Mr and Mrs Smith I suppose. So I said it would be all right and he was pleased as Punch.' She looked rather apprehensively at Suzie. 'It will be all right, won't it, Sue?'

'Of course it will be all right, if you're sure that you and Sean are made for each other,' Suzie said. 'The fact is, queen, that Mr and Mrs Smithing, as you call it, is one way to find out whether you really are right for each other. Oh, I know it isn't what your Aunt Jane would call "acceptable behaviour", but older folk don't realise that peacetime morals don't work in wartime. Our generation knows there may not be a tomorrow so we have to take what we can, when we can, particularly the men.' She leaned across, for by now they were both sitting on the end of their respective beds, and squeezed Daisy's hand. 'Don't look so glum and worried, chuck. I don't mind admitting to you, though I wouldn't tell no one else, that the first time I slept wi' Bert I was just about as terrified as a mouse what finds itself in bed wi' a cat. But he were real kind and gentle and it sort of sealed the way we feel about each other. If anything happens to my Bert, which God forbid, I don't reckon I'd want to look at another feller, lerralone sleep with him.'

'Well, that's very nice I must say!' Daisy said. 'So it's either Sean for ever, or eternal spinsterhood! But I reckon we'd best get some sleep now, having told everyone we were getting an early night. What shift are you on tomorrow?'

Suzie pulled a face. 'Nights, so I shan't need to set my alarm clock, but I expect I'll wake around seven; I usually do now the mornin's are so light. Tell you what, I'll wake you when I wake, and we'll chuck some clothes on and go and bag a bike and I'll ride it while you sit on the carrier, though we'll both have to walk the uphill bits. Then you can introduce me to this Sean of yours before you go off for your wicked weekend.'

'Would you? Oh, that would be absolutely wonderful,' Daisy said gratefully. 'I can't cycle down by myself, of course, because of getting the bike back here, but if you really wouldn't mind . . .'

'Course I wouldn't. I'm dying to meet this paragon,' Suzie assured her friend. 'And now let's get some sleep.'

Next morning, the sun woke the girls and Daisy threw some clothing into a bag and dressed in her own skirt and blouse, having returned the borrowed clothing the night before. 'Pity you haven't got a pretty nightie,' Suzie said as they hurried downstairs. 'Still, people don't expect smart clothes in wartime. Now let's get some breakfast.'

The kitchen was already occupied by a couple of girls who were clearly on the day shift. They had finished their breakfast – porridge and tea – and were clattering their crockery into the big stone sink, preparatory to leaving. Suzie fished a loaf out of the bread bin and cut two hefty slices. 'Since we don't know what time your train leaves, I think we'd better give porridge a miss,' she said, as the girls on the day shift left by the back door, calling a cheery goodbye as they went. 'Put the kettle on the stove, there's a dear. It'll still be hot and a nice cup of tea will help to make up for no porridge.'

'Right you are,' Daisy said. 'Fancy, if we're in a hotel or a boarding house, we'll probably get a cooked breakfast. Imagine, bacon and eggs for three whole days!'

'Lucky blighter,' Suzie said absently, scraping margarine on to the bread and adding home-made marmalade. This concoction owed a good deal to the presence of grated carrot, since oranges were unobtainable unless you had a blue ration book, and even then they were as rare as hen's teeth. 'Tell you what, just in case you have a lot of hanging about to do, I'll make you a couple of sandwiches. You can have Marmite in one and plum jam in the other, and I dare say you'll be glad of them before you arrive in Rhyl.'

'Thanks, Suzie, you're a pal,' Daisy said gratefully, pushing an enamel mug of tea across the table. 'Good thing we've both learned to drink our tea hot.' She drained her mug, gobbled her bread and marmalade, and then wrapped the substantial sandwiches which Suzie had made in greaseproof paper and shoved them into her bag. Then the two girls headed for the back door and

440

the shed where the bicycles were kept. As they selected their steed, for with two aboard they wanted the sturdiest machine available, Daisy said casually: 'Any more news from your Bert? I know you said, last time he rang, that they hadn't been able to make it to their own airfield but had had to send out a darky call and land somewhere nearer the coast, but I reckon he should be back home by now.'

A darky call was made by a pilot who was lost and needed to land urgently for one reason or another, as both girls well knew. 'Yes, he's back on his own airfield, safe and sound. He phoned me yesterday morning; he was rather upset to tell you the truth. The skip got the Wimpy down all right, but there was damage to the undercarriage, so of course they couldn't fly until it was put right. There was an enormous raid planned which they couldn't go on. He said it involved some sort of secret weapon, though he couldn't say what it was, and apparently it was a big success. He said he was sick as a dog to be left out of it, but two of his crew did go – as substitutes, you know – in an aircraft which would otherwise have been a couple of crew short. The plane they were in was quite badly shot up, and part of the fuselage caught fire. Bert said the pilot was a first class fellow and got down all right, but one of his chaps, who was acting as waist gunner, told him that the tail gunner had been pretty badly burned round the face and neck. They were going to visit him in hospital today,

I think. Of course his girlfriend – she's a Waaf, Belinda something or other – has been sneaking in most days even though she isn't officially allowed. She told the fellers that if you carry a clipboard and walk briskly, no one seems to query your presence.'

'Gosh, that's awful,' Daisy said. 'But it wasn't one of Bert's chaps, was it?'

'No, thank the Lord,' Suzie said. 'This saddle's too low; hang on a minute whilst I adjust it. Chuck us a spanner, will you? They're hidden away on that shelf.'

Daisy stood on tiptoe, found the appropriate spanner and handed it to her friend. 'It's nice of Bert to go and visit someone who isn't actually a member of his crew,' she said. 'Who is he, do you know?'

'I don't know his real name – you know what the fellers are – but they called him Marbles,' Suzie said. 'He was probably a whizz with the ollies at school . . . Daisy? What's the matter?'

Daisy had been holding the bike whilst Suzie fitted the spanner over the nut which controlled the height of the saddle, but she felt the blood drain from her face, leaving her cold as death, and her suddenly nerveless fingers lost their grip on the bike so that as Suzie spoke, but for her friend's quick grab, it would have crashed to the ground. Hastily, she took hold of it again, her heart hammering and her breath coming short. 'Marbles? Did – did you say burned? Oh, my God!'

'What the devil's the matter?' Suzie asked blankly. 'Don't say you know someone called Marbles? It's an odd sort of name; if you'd ever mentioned it I'm sure I'd remember . . . Daisy, what are you doing?'

Daisy had jerked the bicycle out of her friend's hold and was strapping her bag to the carrier. Her legs wanted to buckle beneath her, but she forced herself to walk slowly as she wheeled the bicycle out of the shed. 'Where did you say the airfield was?' she enquired, trying to keep her voice steady. 'Suzie, I've got to go to him. We had the most God-awful row last time we met and I said some terrible things. He's my oldest friend and I can't let him go on believing that I meant them. I've got to go to him!'

She was pushing the bicycle across the paved courtyard as she spoke, and Suzie was trotting alongside, one hand on her friend's sleeve. 'But *Jake's* the one you insulted; Jake's your oldest friend, you've said so about a million times,' Suzie said breathlessly. 'And you're supposed to be meeting Sean down at the Green Man and going off to Rhyl with him, remember?'

'Yes; but that's not important,' Daisy said impatiently. 'Marbles *is* Jake; they called him that at school because his surname is Elgin. Look, Suzie, would you mind going down to the Green Man for me? Tell Sean I've been called away, tell him I've gone to my grandmother's funeral . . . tell him anything you like so long as he understands I shan't be around for a few days.'

'I can't tell him that; he won't believe me for a start,' Suzie said, catching hold of the bicycle. 'And I don't understand why your Jake should have been called Marbles just because his surname is Elgin. Come to that, how d'you know there aren't other people nicknamed Marbles in the Royal Air Force? Look, queen, you've said over and over that Jake is only a pal. Are you sure you're not simply using this as an excuse not to spend the next three days in Rhyl?'

'It doesn't matter why I'm doing it, but perhaps you're right and it would be better to tell Sean the truth,' Daisy said. She mounted the bicycle, then jumped off it again. 'Suzie, can you lend me some money? I don't know what it will cost to cross the country . . . where did you say the airfield was?'

Suzie told her again, adding that her friend's best bet would be to hitchhike. 'I've only got a couple of bob on me, so getting lifts would be best. And don't take chances; try to get respectable-looking drivers to pick you up, preferably someone in the services,' she advised. 'An' I'll tell Sean the truth, only I'll do it diplomatically. I'll say you've gone to see an old friend what's been badly injured, and I'll do my best to make it sound as though the old friend's a woman, but I don't mean to lie, queen, not even for you. For one thing, I never could tell a whopper without going as red as a beetroot, and for another thing, I guess he'll have to know some time.'

Daisy turned to stare. 'Why do you say that?' she demanded. 'Jake's got a girlfriend, you know, and it's ages since we've met. I'll – I'll probably just tell him I didn't mean the things I said and apologise for hurting him so. Then I'll come back here.'

Suzie gave an indulgent little laugh and shook her head. 'You may fool yourself but you can't fool me,' she shouted as Daisy began to walk down the drive. 'You will have cooked your goose with Sean and I can see you don't give a damn.'

'You're right,' she called over her shoulder. Even now her voice trembled oddly whenever she thought of Jake in trouble. 'You ride the bike down to the village and tell Sean what's happened. I'll – I'll phone the manor some time, let you know what's going on.'

Suzie retrieved the bicycle, and turned it to face the village, for her friend was already heading in the opposite direction, towards the main road. 'You won't; you'll ring the manor this very evening so that I'll know you're all right,' she shouted. 'Then I'll tell you how Sean reacted . . . not that there's much doubt of that! Good luck, Daisy, and I pray you'll find that this Marbles chap isn't your Jake at all, but an injured tail gunner.'

Daisy nodded and waved, but she had no doubt whatsoever that it would be Jake. She thought she would have known it even without the old nickname. Some instinct, older than time itself, had made her ask Suzie who the injured man was. And now, inside her head, she was saying a prayer, chanting a litany which, though she did not know it, she would continue to chant throughout her journey. *Let him be all right*, she prayed to whichever God kept his eye on injured tail gunners. *Please God, let him be alive and get him better. Let me arrive in time!*

Chapter Thirteen

Jake lay flat in his bed, gazing up at the ceiling above him, or rather gazing at what he assumed must be the ceiling, for his sight was now almost non-existent. He could see shapes, could tell day from night, but recognised other patients and visitors chiefly by their voices. He had been on the ward for ten days and though the doctors had assured him that his sight would improve, he privately thought that was doubtful. When the fuselage had started to flame, he had thought it was the end, and indeed even before they landed he had passed out, but someone – he rather thought it was Ronnie, the waist gunner – had somehow managed to get him out before the plane had become a raging inferno. He had a vague memory of voices, hands on him, his clothing being torn off . . . and of course, though he tried not to, he could remember the pain.

The journey to the hospital had been a nightmare of plunging in and out of consciousness and the first few days had been hell. He was still rarely out of pain but he did know that it must be easier because he was managing to sleep at nights, though only with the help of the tablets the doctors prescribed. At first he had been forbidden visitors, but the ban had been lifted the day before and the aircrew with whom he had been flying when the accident had occurred had come tiptoeing up the ward. They had stayed for twenty minutes, despite being told that only ten were allowed, and Jake had been exhausted by the time they had left.

He had been going steady with a Waaf on his station and she had come visiting even before the fellows had managed to gain admittance. She had been very sweet, sitting on the edge of his bed and holding his hand, feeding him delicious lemonade in one of the teapot-like feeding cups the hospital provided. He had asked her to tell him the extent of the injuries to his face and she had said, lightly, that he was lucky it was not worse. 'You've got no eyebrows or eyelashes, no hair, and bad burns to the left-hand side of your face,' she had said, trying to keep her voice steady, but he could hear the tremor in it. 'They can do wonders with plastic surgery, you know; by the time you get out of here you'll be good as new.'

He had tried to grin at her but knew it must be a fairly feeble effort when she squeezed his hand and asked if he would like her to read to him. Jake had bitten his lip; he knew there were girls who came into the hospital to read to men who could no longer read for themselves and it made him feel like a useless old hulk who would, in future, need help to cut his finger and toenails, or to read the simplest notice warning of an obstruction on the pavement ahead. Her offer, therefore, convinced him that he must seem pretty far gone.

'I'd rather just talk,' he had said tiredly. 'Tell me how you got here, Daisy.'

'I'm not Daisy, I'm Belinda,' she had reminded him quietly and Jake had told her, as he had told her many times before, that it was an easy mistake for him to make.

He supposed now that he had first made a dead set at Belinda because she was so like Daisy: small with dark hair and eyes and a neat figure. Apart from the physical resemblance, however, the two girls were totally different. But of course, now that he could no longer see her, he had no excuse for using the wrong name since Daisy's voice still held, he supposed, a soft Irish burr and Belinda spoke, though she tried to suppress it, with a slight cockney accent. Also, Daisy's enthusiasms had been many; she was courageous and quick-tempered, seldom showing a sulky or discontented face. He had only ever known her cry once in front of him, though when her parents had died he knew she must have spent many nights weeping for her loss. She could never have been described as a quiet girl, for she was no such thing. The cook at 39 Rodney Street had likened her to a well-shaken bottle of ginger beer, always fizzing with some new plan, always laughing, joking, or chattering.

Belinda, on the other hand, smiled rarely and did not often laugh either. She was sensible, serious and what he would have called a career Waaf. So far, she had only reached the rank of corporal but was being encouraged to seek officer status as soon as it was offered her. Jake knew that she would excel as an officer for she was a natural leader, managing to persuade others to obey her without appearing bossy or dictatorial. Yet despite her seriousness, he liked her well enough to continue their friendship and had planned to suggest that they should marry when the war was over. Had he managed to become a pilot he, too, would have remained in the RAF; he pulled a wry face at the recollection, remembering his present near-blindness. Still, he had hoped that with the peace Belinda would accompany him to civvy street, where they could both seek congenial work.

Now everything would change; he was pretty sure that Belinda would not want to give up the possibility of a good career in the WAAF to cope with someone whose disabilities might well mean he could not work at all. His mind shivered away from the sheer dreadfulness of the thought and his hand went instinctively up to the bandages which covered his head and his left eye. The doctors kept telling him how lucky he was to still have his right eye, which meant, he supposed, that his left eye was either no longer there at all, or completely useless. But the medical staff had been immensely cheered when, on his third day in hospital, he had told them that not only could he tell day from night, but he was also beginning to make out fuzzy shapes when someone loomed up beside his bed.

Now, he heard the crash as the doors at the end of the ward were pushed open, and raised his head a little. Folk said that when one sense let a man down, other senses sharpened in response. He had never believed it, regarding such a thing as an impossibility, but now he had to acknowledge that there was something in it, for he could often tell who had come on to the ward even though, for all he knew, the trolley they were pushing might contain food, a tea urn or even medication. On this occasion he recognised that the incomer was big, flat-footed Nellie, the tea lady from the canteen. She flapped along in shoes comfortably too big for her and he knew she had a sizeable bosom because when she had leaned across him on one occasion to pick up his empty cup, which he had put on the windowsill instead of his locker, it had brushed against his chest.

'Wake up, lads, if any of youse is asleep! Who's goin' to give Nellie a big "ta ever so" for two ginger biscuits or a bit of Victoria sponge, along o' his cuppa?'

Jake gave himself a congratulatory pat on the back. He had been right: it was Nellie. The nurses who dispensed medication wore flat, rubber-soled shoes which made little noise on the linoleumed floor, and the canteen workers who brought round the meal trolleys clacked their way along the wards in shoes with hard heels. Only the tea trolley rattled and bounced, causing its load of cups to do likewise.

The trolley came to a crashing halt by his bed. 'Afternoon, sunshine! Fancy ginger biscuits or a bit of me Victoria sponge? An' is it just one sugar?'

'That's it, Nellie, and I'll go for the ginger biscuits, please,' Jake said. If he was reasonably careful he could cope with ginger biscuits, but sponge cake created crumbs and being unable to see them he was also unable to brush them away. The nurses would do so before he settled down for the night, of course, but he would have to endure them until then. Besides, he preferred ginger biscuits. He thought longingly of the ones Aunt Jane baked in the Ty Gwyn kitchen. The hospital biscuits were shop bought, hard as nails, but Aunt Jane's were softer somehow. His father and Aunt Jane had promised to visit him just as soon as it could be arranged, though Jake suspected that the hospital had probably dissuaded them from coming while he was at his worst, not knowing if he would ever see again.

'There you are, lad.' Jake felt two, no three, ginger biscuits pressed into his hand and heard Nellie crash a mug down on his bedside locker. Then she took his free hand and guided it to the mug. At first, he had been forced to use the spouted feeder, but now he could cope with a mug provided it was not over-filled and Nellie, bless her kind heart, always made sure that he had touched it before she moved on to the next bed. Once he knew its precise location, he told himself that he managed very well, though eating from a plate was still a bit of a nightmare.

The main meal was lunch, delivered at noon – the evening meal was sandwiches and ice cream, easier to deal with – and the previous day's offering had been mutton, mashed potatoes and peas. He had thought he had done extremely well until he had had cause to ask for a bedpan. Little Nurse Robbins, who had brought it, had swished the curtains around him and pulled back his covers, only to collapse with mirth. She was young, he could tell from her voice, and he knew she was pretty because Charlie, in the next bed, had remarked upon it. So he had said: 'What's so bloody funny?' knowing that she would tell him, whereas the older and more experienced staff tended to hesitate before replying to his questions.

Nurse Robbins had giggled again. 'You wanted a pee . . . and the bed's full of 'em,' she had said. 'Oh dear, oh dear, what a good thing Sister or Staff ain't on the ward. They'd tear me bloody ears off for laughing at a patient.'

Jake had laughed, too, acknowledging that it was funny, but he had felt foolish. How had he managed to spill so many? He had refused the spoon the girl had offered, thinking he could squash the peas on to his fork with his knife. Telling himself that in future he would take all the help he could get, he had climbed out of the bed and let the still giggling nurse guide him to a chair so that she might clean up. It turned out, however, that she had had to change the sheet and get him new pyjamas as well, which was by no means so amusing. Sister had come fussing up the ward and read him a short lecture on independence being a fine thing, but had reminded him that he must learn not to run before he could walk, and must also remember that there was a war on, and linen cupboards no longer bulged with spare bedding the way they once had.

Naturally enough, the other patients had pounced on the whole episode, dropping the name of Marbles in favour of Peabody, and oddly enough this had cheered Jake up a lot. He knew that if he was really about to become a blind and useless hulk, the men – and the nursing staff – would not have thought it right to tease him and continually remind him of an episode which could have been interpreted as humiliating.

So he let fat Nellie curl his fingers round the mug, made a mental note of the way his hand had travelled to reach it, and began to crunch the first ginger biscuit.

He went to sleep that night feeling more optimistic than he had done since the accident and next morning, when Sister came to his bedside, he was able to greet her almost cheerfully. Changing his dressings was a horrible, painful business, frequently conducted by Sister herself, but as soon as she spoke his name he knew that this was a social visit of some description. 'Sister Edwards here, Flight Sergeant Elgin,' she said formally. 'There is a letter for you; would you like me to read it or would you prefer one of the other patients to do so?'

454

'I'd be very grateful if you would read it, Sister,' Jake said at once. 'One of the nurses told me my father had telephoned – has done so every day, I understand – but Dad did say he'd write when he and my stepmother could get away from the farm for two or three days and come to see me. My dad isn't much of a one for letter-writing, and of course this is the busiest time of year for all farmers, but naturally I'm longing to see them.' He stopped short, realising the inaptness of the remark. 'Perhaps I should say I'm longing for them to see me,' he ended, feeling foolish.

Sister, opening the envelope – he could hear the paper tear – said reprovingly: 'Now, now, Flight Sergeant, you know what the doctors say: you'll be good as new in a few weeks. We've men in a far worse state than you, who will still recover, believe me.'

'I do, Sister . . . believe you I mean,' Jake said quickly. 'I'm sure the eye I've got left will get stronger, as you all keep telling me, but for the moment at any rate I won't be able to see my parents in the accepted sense of the word.'

Sister sniffed, then said grudgingly: 'Very true. So you've accepted the loss of your left eye? You're a sensible young man.'

Jake cringed inwardly; he had known, of course he had, but until this very moment no one had officially admitted it. He supposed he had hoped . . . but what did it matter, after all? He would probably have to resign himself to losing

455

Belinda, but that had always been on the cards. She was ambitious and he was not; she was serious and he was not. He realised that if she broke off their friendship he would take it philosophically and move on, which must mean that his fondness for her was only skin deep. Poor Belinda! It occurred to him that cool, calm and collected as she was, she would probably never know the dizzy heights of being in love. Oh well, the fact that she would never know the ghastly depths of losing one's love was the other side of the coin and one he thought her fortunate to have missed.

But Sister was beginning to read, so he dragged his attention back to the present.

My dear old boy,

How are you? Either Jane or I have phoned every evening and the nurses think you are getting better and will make a full recovery, or as full a recovery as is possible. As you know, summer is a busy time on the farm but we have worked like the devils in hell to get ahead of ourselves so that we can come and visit you. We've managed to get old Grimshaw and his grandson to come over and feed the stock and see to things generally for three whole days, and Jane has found a boarding house very near the hospital. We'll be travelling by train of course since we've not enough petrol, even as essential users, for more than one trip into Abergele every other week and I don't think the pony cart would be suitable (ha, ha!). Since it's a cross-

country journey, it will mean a number of changes, so don't expect to see us before six or seven o'clock on Tuesday, but you may be sure we'll come up to the hospital the moment we arrive.

Jane wanted to tell Daisy you were in hospital but when we received the letter you had dictated to a pal, you expressly said you'd prefer that we told nobody, and I insisted that that meant Daisy, too. She'll have to know, of course, but maybe later, when you're up and about. It's about time that old quarrel between the two of you was forgotten.

Reading this over, I see I've put it badly, but I'm sure you'll understand what I really mean. You've got Belinda now, and Daisy has that Sean fellow, so I guess you could meet again as friends.

I'm no good at letter-writing, always put my foot in and say the wrong thing, but Jane is up to her eyes in baking (most of her cooking will be coming your way, so mind you don't overeat on Tuesday!) and she's all over flour, otherwise she would have added a line to tell you how much we love you, but a man can't say that outright, even to his own son. You know we're thinking of you and saying many a prayer.

Your affec father.

There was a short pause whilst Jake turned his head blindly towards the window to hide what he knew was a tear trickling down his cheek. His dear old dad! He could just see Aunt Jane rolling out pastry, running a floury hand through her thick

457

blonde hair and telling Bob that he must write the letter because, fond though he was of herself, her stepson would doubly appreciate a letter from his beloved father.

'Well, Flight Sergeant? I've read many letters from fathers to sons, but this one just about says it all. I trust you're pleased? It takes a strong man to reveal emotions, so I take it your father is such a one?'

Jake turned back towards her and grinned, tears no longer threatening. 'Yes, my dad's a grand chap,' he said quietly, and held out a hand. 'Thank you, Sister. I shall keep this letter, and I'm sure that one day I'll be able to read it for myself.'

It took Daisy very much longer than either she or Suzie had supposed to cross the country by hitch-hiking. This was mainly because, after one rather unnerving experience, she had been forced to spend the night actually sleeping rather than journeying on. Her chief difficulty was, of course, that there were few private vehicles on the roads and it was private drivers, on the whole, who offered lifts. Military convoys, and there were many of these, could scarcely halt the whole column to pick up one small bedraggled girl, and Daisy had soon realised, as she trudged through the mud and the pouring rain which had begun to fall within an hour of her leaving Lacey Manor, that she could not be a very prepossessing sight. Believing that she was going to travel by train to Rhyl, she had not brought her waterproofs and so had speedily got drenched.

Her first lift had been in an ancient blue van driven by a plumber, a taciturn individual, who had told her that he could take her twenty miles to a town where he had to pick up several lengths of lead piping. Daisy, a natural chatterer, had asked him a few questions about his work, but when he had replied in monosyllables, or with grunts, she had given up and retreated into her own thoughts.

As promised, the plumber had dropped her off just before the town was reached and Daisy had plodded along in the wet, a hopeful thumb held out whenever she heard a vehicle approaching from behind. Her next lift had been a luckier one, in that it had taken her quite thirty miles on her way. She had found an army lorry, with a couple of men in the cab, drawn up beside the road. The men had been eating their midday snack and when Daisy had asked them if they were heading east the elder of the two, a hefty red-faced corporal, had said that they were and had offered to take her on the next leg of her journey. The army lorry had been old and not good on hills. Every time a steep incline had been encountered, they had had to stop at the top to let the engine cool down, which had meant that it was quite late before they had reached their destination.

By that time, Daisy had been both tired and hungry, Suzie's sandwiches a mere memory, but after walking a couple of miles she had been overtaken by a furniture van, which had pulled up at the sight of her hopefully uplifted thumb. The driver had lowered the passenger window and peered across at her.

'Are you travelling east?' Daisy had asked eagerly. Her legs had been aching, her stomach rumbling, and this had been the first vehicle to have passed her for miles.

'That's right,' the driver had said laconically. 'I'm goin' to King's Lynn; any use to you?'

Daisy's knowledge of geography was not great but she did know that King's Lynn was somewhere in East Anglia, so she had said eagerly that that would be fine and had popped into the passenger seat, apologising for the fact that she had brought a good deal of mud and wet into the cab with her. The driver had been a small gingery man with a long, rather lugubrious face, wearing stained dungarees and lace-up leather boots. He had asked Daisy where she was bound, and Daisy had told him that she would be visiting her fiancé in hospital. He had then told her that he was doing a removal for a family moving from Cheshire to Norfolk. He had explained that his mate, who usually travelled in the van with him, had been taken ill, which had left Mick, the driver, in the lurch. 'The back of this 'ere van is crammed wi' furniture, includin' a damned great double bed. And how I'm expected to get them out of the back, let alone into the family's new house, is more than I can imagine.'

'I'll give you a hand in return for the lift,' Daisy had suggested. She had opened her bag and produced a thin towel which she had packed earlier, and had begun to rub her hair vigorously. 'I'm a lot stronger than I look. Or maybe you'll find the man of the family waiting to give you a hand when you reach King's Lynn,' she had added hopefully, for she had not wanted to delay her journey if she could possibly avoid it.

Her companion had shot her a curious glance from under half-lowered lids. It had been a sly look, but Daisy had told herself that she was reading too much into what was probably just plain old-fashioned curiosity. 'I may take you up on that,' her companion had said. 'Now why don't you take off them drippin' clothes and change into the dry stuff what's in your bag? I won't look.'

Since this remark had been accompanied by a suggestive laugh and what could only be described as a leer, Daisy had shaken her head decisively. 'No, I shan't bother. I only brought one change of clothing and I'll need that when I reach the hospital,' she had said.

Outside, the rain had seemed to be easing off a trifle but Daisy had still been grateful for the shelter afforded by the van and had chattered away with her usual freedom, though she had wished that the driver would not keep eyeing her from top to toe, almost as though he could see through her wet clothing to the cold and shivering Daisy beneath.

After a couple of hours, during which Mick had told her all about his marital troubles, his children and his intention, when the war was over, to start his own removal business, the furniture van had swung off the main road and Daisy, immediately suspicious, had edged a little nearer to the door. 'Where are you going?' she had asked, trying to sound casually interested, though her voice had come out rather high and squeaky. 'Is this a short cut?'

The man had given a bark of laughter but had shaken his head. 'No, I'm headin' for a little transport café what me an' my mate often stop at. They're open all hours and do a grand sausage and chips for a bob. Then I'll lay up for a few hours 'cos it's no joke drivin' cross-country in the dark.' He had leered at her again and this time had licked his lips with a pointed red tongue. 'If you really want to pay me for giving me a lift, then there's that big double bed in the back and a heap o' blankets. We could keep each other warm.'

Daisy had laughed uneasily. 'I told you I was on my way to visit my fiancé; but I'm sure you were only joking, weren't you?'

'Course I was,' the man had said, as he had manoeuvred the van into a large car park and drawn up beside a low wooden hut, with the words *Dolly's Transport Café* in red letters on the fascia board. 'C'mon, you'll feel better after a hot meal. I'll treat you to sausage and chips.'

'It's quite all right, thank you. I've got some

money and I prefer not to be beholden,' Daisy had said frostily, climbing down from the furniture van and heading for the door into the café. She had thought, rather guiltily, that the suggestions Mick had made might have been partly her own fault. She had chatted away in her usual inconsequential style, telling him all about work in the munitions factory and her move to become a riveter after her allergy had made itself felt. She had encouraged him to talk about his own work, had listened to his complaints about his wife's behaviour with feigned sympathy, and had pretended amusement when he had started telling smutty stories. She had not liked to snub him so possibly she could not blame him for assuming she was a bad girl.

No doubt because of the lateness of the hour, there had only been half a dozen customers seated at the wooden tables, but the room had been beautifully warm and the smell of cooking irresistible. Daisy had gone straight to the counter, ordered and paid for a couple of large mugs of tea and sausage and chips for two, then had turned to her companion. 'I hope that pays you in some small way for giving me a lift,' she had said coolly. 'But I shan't be coming with you any further. I'm sure I'll have no difficulty in getting another lift from someone heading my way.'

Mick, looking hangdog, had taken the tea and the food to a table by the wall, and though Daisy would have liked to sit far away from him she had

463

felt that such a move would have been all too obvious and might have led to awkward questions from the fat proprietress. So she had settled herself in the seat opposite Mick and had taken a long drink from her mug of tea. He had done the same, then had leaned forward, lowering his voice to a confidential hiss. 'Look, miss, I see I got the wrong idea about you an' I'm real sorry. Only you seemed . . . oh well, I got the wrong idea. I did mean to lie up for a few hours an' I reckon I still will, but I'll climb into the back of the van an' leave you to stretch out in the cab. You can lock the doors from the inside an' I'll give you the key so you won't have to worry. Then, when we wakes up tomorrer, we can have a cup of tea and a butty afore startin' the rest of the journey.'

Daisy had given him a long hard stare. How could she know if he was genuinely sorry? How could she know, for that matter, that he did not have a spare key to the van? She had begun to shake her head, to tell him that it was not on, when he had broken into speech once more. 'Look, m'dear, at least you an' me knows where we stand. If you go for another lift at this time of night, you could pick someone a lot worse'n me. An' think on; Dolly and her husband sleep in a caravan pulled up along-side the café, and most of these fellers' – he had jerked a thumb at the half-dozen customers – 'will be in their lorries, snoozin' till it's light. One shriek from you and I'd be cold meat. So what d'you say?'

Daisy had heaved a deep sigh. 'OK, but one wrong word or move from you and I'm warning you, I'll not only shriek the place down, I'll brain you with the starting handle,' she had said bluntly. 'Is there a pillow in the back of your van?'

Mick had given a relieved grin and had said that he would find her a pillow and a blanket, then had suggested that Daisy might like to make use of the facilities before they settled down for the night. Daisy had taken advantage of his suggestion to go over to the counter. She had asked Dolly where she could find the lady's room but was not surprised when Dolly said they only had a gents. 'Still 'n all, gal, you can use me own little lavvy,' she had said generously. 'Come round behind the counter and I'll show you.'

As soon as they had gone out of Mick's sight, Daisy had put a hand on the fat woman's arm. 'I – I thumbed a lift off the feller I'm with, not realising he meant to spend the night parked up,' she had said urgently. 'He – he made a suggestion which I didn't – didn't care for, but now he says I can sleep in the cab and he'll bed down in the van itself. He says I can lock the doors and keep the key, but – well, would you hear me if I screamed? I spotted the starting handle on the floor of the cab and I've told him I'll brain him with it if he somehow manages to sneak in during the night, but I'd be a lot happier to know you'd come running if I yelled.'

Dolly had chuckled comfortably. 'Mick's all talk

and no do, I reckon,' she had said. 'His wife ran off with a sailor – I expect he told you – but there's no real harm in him. As for yellin', you'd have half a dozen fellers rushin' to your aid at the first peep and most of 'em's twice Mick's size. I'd offer you a bed in me caravan but my old man does the early shift and we don't have so much as a spare blanket, let alone a spare bed. Tell you what, just to be on the safe side, you warn old Mick that if there's any trouble, Dolly'll never serve him so much as a round of bread or a sip of tea in future.' She had chuckled again. 'That'll fix him. We're the only decent pull-in for lorry drivers for fifty mile; he won't risk being banned, I'm tellin' you.'

By now they had made their way out of the back door and Dolly had jerked her thumb at a small hut which stood against an ancient caravan. 'There you are, luv; I won't wait in this perishin' rain 'cos I dare say you can find your way back to the caff without needin' a road map!'

Daisy had thanked her sincerely and presently she and Mick had returned to the furniture van and had made their arrangements for the night. Mick had handed her a pillow, a blanket and the key to the van, then had left her, and Daisy had curled up, feeling that she had done everything possible to ensure an undisturbed night's sleep. She had woken once, at around five o'clock, when the van had bounced and she had heard one of the back doors cautiously open, but she had guessed that Mick was answering a call of nature and had fallen asleep again within moments.

It had been seven o'clock before Mick had rapped on the windscreen and by then Daisy had been fully awake. She had folded her blanket, unlocked both doors and combed her hair, and had felt very much happier than she had done the previous day. She was on her way, she had managed a good night's sleep, and would presently have a hot cup of tea and some sort of breakfast. She had grinned at Mick, opened the passenger door and jumped down, running round the van with her bedding to return it to its rightful place. Then she and Mick had gone into the café where a positively enormous man, bald as an egg and clad in a brown overall, had greeted them with a wide and toothless grin. He had thrust two mugs of tea across the counter before they had said a word, and had suggested corned beef sandwiches since he knew they would not want to linger but would rather get going before convoys began to creep along the main roads. He had also suggested that Daisy might like to pop into the gents before his other customers began to arrive. 'There's a jug of water and a basin; you'll feel better if you have a bit of a splash,' he had said tactfully, and presently Daisy, feeling very much more the thing, was sitting in the van, eating a sandwich and chattering away as they bowled along the empty early-morning roads.

The anxieties of yesterday were pushed to the

back of her mind. Very soon now, she would be seeing Jake; that there would be difficult explanations she had no doubt, but that was only to be expected. For the first time, it occurred to her that for all she knew he might actually have married his Waaf, though she did not think this likely; Aunt Jane would have told her, thinking that such news would ease Daisy's mind. That it would most certainly not have done so had not even occurred to Daisy herself until she had heard of his accident and had realised, in a flash, how much he meant to her; much, much more than Sean ever had.

But at this moment there was no point in dwelling on mistakes or asking herself unanswerable questions; all that seemed to matter was that Jake should be alive and able to accept that she had been terribly wrong to cast him off. She had not understood the true meaning of love, had confused it with infatuation, for she realised now that she had been dazzled by Sean's handsome face and obvious admiration of herself. She had never looked beneath the surface, never wondered why her picture of Jake had remained crystal clear, whereas she had found it difficult to visualise Sean during their two years apart.

She reached the hospital, tired after her long journey but still certain that she was doing the right thing. She had been lucky and had got a lift from King's Lynn in a bakery van, so had arrived bright and early. Despite her longing to see Jake as soon as possible, Daisy had gone first into a ladies' lavatory and changed her bedraggled clothing and lace-up brogues for a clean print dress and sandals. Fortunately the rain had ceased and it was a brilliantly sunny day, the sort of August day one imagines but seldom sees, and she entered the hospital grounds confident that she was looking, if not her best, at least as presentable as one could expect.

She knew Jake had suffered severe burns to his face and neck, and she grew increasingly nervous as she walked up the hospital's short drive. Would he be able to recognise her? More important, would he welcome her visit? If he and his Waaf were serious, she might be sitting by his bedside at this very moment, holding his hand! Daisy was tempted to wait a little, to hang around and see how things stood, but she shook off the unworthy thought, trod resolutely up to the revolving doors, and went boldly over to the reception desk.

She feared that she might have to undergo a catechism as to who she was and what right she had to visit a man who might be seriously ill, but told herself that since Suzie had said his girlfriend had seen him and Bert's crew planned to, then other visitors would surely be allowed. So she smiled brightly at the receptionist, an elderly woman, and explained that she was an old friend of Flight Sergeant Jacob Elgin and had come to visit him. She was cast down when the woman shook her head. 'I'm afraid that's not possible,' she said firmly. 'Visiting is between three and four in the afternoon, but that is at Sister's discretion only, and six to seven in the evening. Of course, we make special arrangements for relatives who have had to travel a long way, or for members of the armed forces who can only visit when they're not on duty, but I'm afraid civilian visitors have to come at the prescribed times.'

'I – I'm a relative,' Daisy said wildly. 'And I've come miles and miles and miles, right across the country in fact. I'm sure it would do him good to see me.'

The receptionist's eyebrows shot up. 'You said you were a friend just now,' she remarked reprovingly. 'And you clearly aren't a member of the armed forces. However, if you would come back at six o'clock this evening . . .'

'Oh! But I understand he's very ill . . . and I know it would make him feel better to see me,' Daisy pleaded. 'We had a quarrel, which was all my fault. I – I want to tell him how sorry I am, to put things right . . .'

'I'm sure you do, dear,' the woman said blandly. 'Will it help if I tell you that Flight Sergeant Elgin is making good progress and will still be here at six o'clock? Just you go off and get yourself some lunch. Then you could try ringing the ward – he's on Fleming – and ask Sister if you can visit between three and four.'

'Thank you; I'll do that,' Daisy said, heading for

the revolving doors once more. Outside, however, she decided she had no intention of letting herself be turned away. When the woman had said Fleming Ward, she had glanced towards one of the three corridors leading off the reception area, and now Daisy watched through the glass as nurses and doctors and patients in pyjamas, many of the last-mentioned wielding two sticks, came and went, some of them leaving the hospital through the revolving doors whilst others remained within.

At last came the moment for which Daisy was waiting. A doctor in a white coat, a stethoscope round his neck, approached the receptionist and handed her a pile of papers. The woman took them from him and, to Daisy's delight, disappeared into the office behind her. Quick as a flash, Daisy shot into the foyer and walking briskly, head bent as though in deep thought, made for the corridor the receptionist had inadvertently indicated and headed for Fleming Ward.

Jake sat up in his bed feeling anticipation growing within him. His father and Aunt Jane were coming next day, so there was really no point in his getting excited just yet, or not over their arrival at any rate. But Belinda was coming in to see him today and would be bringing letters from his fellow crew members, which she would read to him. He told himself that this was a good enough reason for feeling cheerful and optimistic, for in truth he felt happier than he had done since the accident.

That morning, Sister had come round and promised him that when members of staff had the time, they would take him along to the bathroom and give him a real bath, not the blanket sort. He was lucky, Sister had told him severely, that the burns were only on his face and neck; the rest of him could be immersed in water provided he was careful not to splash, and since everyone knew that only four inches of water were allowable, no matter how one might long for more, he was unlikely to splash very much. Besides, he would be accompanied into the bathroom by at least two nurses. The girls Sister chose for the task would be fine, strapping wenches, he had no doubt of that, capable of helping him into the tub and then of heaving him out. One thing you could say for being almost blind, he told himself, was that embarrassment over being seen in the buff by a woman did not long endure. They were all sensible, kindly girls who seemed to enjoy their work, even when it involved unpleasant duties such as changing dressings and lifting heavy – and helpless – patients.

The doors at the bottom of the ward crashed open and rubber-soled shoes squeaked towards him. A nurse stopped by his bed – he knew it was a nurse because of the rubber-soled shoes – and a hand reached out for his, even as a voice began to speak. 'Mornin', Flight Sergeant! Sister told me and Nurse Roberts to bag one of the bathrooms. If you can just swing your legs out of bed, I'll help you into your dressing gown and slippers, and you can have that bath Sister promised you.'

Jake felt her pull the covers back and obediently swung his legs out of bed and felt for his slippers. Undoubtedly the bath was the reason why he felt so unaccountably cheerful, so strangely optimistic. Of course it would be lovely to talk to Belinda, but even lovelier to get into hot water. Everything was scarce in wartime, but a fellow sufferer further down the ward had spoken of decent toilet soap and a sprinkling of Johnson's baby powder before you replaced your pyjamas. Little things become important when you're bed-bound, Jake told himself ruefully, standing up and letting Nurse Jones fumble him into his dressing gown. He tied the cord and was shuffling towards the doors at the end of the ward when Nurse Roberts joined them. In the corridor, the nurses took up their positions on either side of him, linked their arms in his, and began to lead him towards the bathrooms. Presently, Jake was in the tub with a good bar of what felt and smelt like Pear's toilet soap in his hand, vigorously washing himself and singing; *'We'll meet again, don't know where don't know when, but I know we'll meet again some sunny day.'*

Laughing, the nurses joined in, Nurse Roberts breaking off to exclaim: 'Dear old Vera; what would we do without her? And now, young man, brace yourself, because Evans and I are about to bring you on to dry land.'

Though he had enjoyed it immensely, the bath

tired Jake out. The nurses returned him to his bed, tucked him up and left him to fall immediately into a deep sleep. He woke, still with that delightful feeling of anticipation, and glanced towards the window against which his bed stood. When the day was sunny, as it was today, he was often able to tell the approximate time by the place where the sunlight fell on his counterpane. He patted the warm patch, then moved his hand across to find the cool shadow, and realised, from the position of the border between the two, that he had missed the tea trolley which came round with elevenses, but would shortly hear the dinner trolley rattling up the corridor. With some difficulty he sat himself up, feeling thirsty as well as hungry and telling himself that, having missed his mid-morning cup of char, he would ask if someone would fetch him a drink of some description.

He heard one of the swing doors at the end of the ward – only one – slowly open, as though the person about to enter was unsure whether he or she had found the right room. Soft footsteps advanced and the door swung closed. Not a nurse; the footfall was all wrong for a nurse. Could it be Belinda? Yet she had visited him perhaps a dozen times, and he could not recall that her footfall was ever tentative, and her shoes were sturdy lace-ups. He smiled to himself. She knew her worth, Belinda, but whoever it was, he was pretty sure it was a woman. She was moving towards him, at first slowly, and then with increasing speed. He guessed that most of the other occupants of the ward had gone to the day room, where they could play cards, smoke and listen to the wireless. He would have gone himself just for the company, had he not fallen asleep.

The footsteps came on down the ward.

Daisy found Fleming Ward and hesitated for a moment, suddenly uncertain. When she peered through the glass, the beds nearest the door all looked empty and she was suddenly aware that she was trespassing. She had been told not to visit that morning and had ignored the prohibition. If she came back at six, she would go into the ward with a great many other visitors, and if Jake was not pleased to see her she could get away almost unnoticed. She half turned back towards the foyer, then scolded herself for stupidity as well as cowardice. If he had other visitors that evening, she and Jake would be unable to talk with any freedom; she must be brave. At least, as she gently pushed the door open, she could see down the whole length of the room and knew that no one else was visiting. Indeed, almost all the beds were empty and for a moment she thought her visit was to be pointless. The beds were arranged in two long rows with a wide stretch of linoleum between them. To her right, against the wall, three beds were occupied. One held a man with both legs in traction. He was reading a paperback book but she could see his face and knew at once that it was not Jake. The other two patients were right down the far end of the ward. One was simply a hump under the covers, apparently fast asleep, and the other had so many tubes emanating from him that he looked like a hedgehog. All three men were on the right-hand side of the ward, opposite the long windows. There was only one man on the left, and when she looked at him, though she could scarcely see his face for bandages, Daisy knew at once that it was Jake.

Hesitantly, she began to move forward. He looked terrible. One eye, and most of his head, were completely covered by a thick wad of bandage and his face and neck were deeply scarred; the wounds, which were puckered and scarlet, were covered in some sort of emollient cream which probably made them look worse. He was thin, too; as she drew nearer the bed she could see his hollow cheeks and the way his collarbones stood out, and the bones of his wrists. She had always thought of him as sturdy but that word could not possibly apply to the gaunt figure in the bed.

Slowly, she continued to approach him. He had looked up, his expression uncertain, and she realised that his gaze was not on her face but over her shoulder, as though someone stood behind her. She said: 'Jake?' and suddenly he was grinning, a flash of white teeth in that drawn and sallowed face. He leaned forward and then his smile spread until it lit up all the space between them, and he held out his arms. She stumbled towards him and knew, without another word spoken, that he could not see her; that he had recognised her solely by the one word she had uttered.

With a sob she ran the last couple of steps towards him and fell into those welcoming arms, hearing the muttered words: 'Daisy, oh, my little darling, oh, Daisy, you don't know how I've missed you! Don't let's ever lose each other again 'cos I think it would kill me.'

She opened her mouth to tell him how sorry she was, how horribly she had missed him, how she longed for his forgiveness, and said none of those things. Instead, she simply repeated his name, over and over, adding that she had always loved him, would always love him, and would never, never let anything or anyone come between them again.

Clasping her closely in his arms, Jake tucked his bandaged head into the soft hollow between her neck and shoulder, and she crooned love words against the bandages as his hot tears flowed.

Jake's grip round Daisy tightened as he felt wave after wave of sheer undiluted happiness roll over him. He knew there would have to be explanations; he would want to hear what had happened to Sean as she must need to know all about Belinda, but that was for later. Now all he had to do was convince her that she was the only person who truly mattered to him, and that she loved him too. He heard her sigh, felt her finger run down the side of his face and across his lips. Yes, there must be explanations, but for now it was enough to simply reiterate the words which had been burning in his mind for so long. 'I love you, Daisy Kildare,' he murmured. 'Oh, my darling, what a mess we've made of things! But we'll put it right now. No more shilly-shallying, no more saying one thing when we mean another. Love, true love, is too precious.'

Daisy felt Jake's arms tighten about her and wave after wave of sheer, undiluted happiness rolled over her. She knew there would have to be explanations; he would want to know what had happened to Sean, and she needed to be told about his girlfriend, but that was for later. Now all she had to do was convince him that he was the only person who truly mattered to her in the whole wide world, the only person she would ever love. She sighed and changed her position slightly so that she could look into his face. She noted the bandages swathing his head and covering his left eye, and reached out a tentative finger to run it along the side of his face and across his lips. Yes, there must be explanations, but for now it was enough to simply reiterate the words that had been burning in her mind for two whole days. 'I love you,' she murmured. 'Oh, Jake, what a fool I've been not to realise . . .'

'Hey, hey, hey, what's all this? Mr Elgin, you know full well you aren't supposed to go cuddlin' young ladies at dinnertime. What'll you have, eh? There's a lovely mince stew or a nice braised heart.

Come along now, make up your mind, or you'll get nowt.' It was Ethel, the dinner lady, and he had not even heard the crash as she pushed her trolley through the swing doors, or the clatter of her approach. Love, it appeared, was not only blind but deaf, too!

They turned Daisy out, of course they did, but though Sister scolded her, it was indulgently. And since she said Daisy could return at three, Daisy was not too dismayed. She walked into town, had a sandwich and a cup of coffee in a milk bar and then returned to the ward, delighted to see Jake beaming at her. She knew he could not see her, and had recognised her by the sound of her sandals as she hurried up the ward. They talked non-stop, often picking on the very same topic, as they had done so often as children, sometimes using the very same words. Then, it had seemed natural, though others had sometimes teased them, and now it seemed natural again though Jake said, contentedly, that she had been a fool not to realise it had meant they were made for each other. Explanations regarding Sean and Belinda proved to be brief, for what interested them most was how long Jake would have to be in hospital, how soon some measure of sight would return to his right eye, and when they could get married.

'Because I'm not going to let you go again, not for one moment,' Jake said firmly. 'You're such a silly little thing that you'd probably go and fall for

479

some feller with two good eyes and a handsome face. Maybe even someone with no scars.'

Daisy scoffed at such a ridiculous suggestion. 'The scars will give your face character,' she assured him. 'And when they take the bandages off, Sister says you'll have a black eye patch, just like pirates do in the fillums. You'll be fighting off the girls, so I guess you're right and we'd best get hitched as soon as possible.'

'I reckon it 'ud be best to tie the knot,' Jake agreed. 'I didn't bargain on marrying anyone whose face I couldn't see, but I suppose I'll have to take your word for it that you're as pretty as ever.' He reached for her hand and began to play with her fingers. 'I never thought I'd ask anyone to marry me whilst I was still so useless, but I guess it's that or wait months, and we've waited long enough, so how about it, Miss Kildare? Are you going to make me the happiest man on earth?'

Daisy laughed, then kissed him lightly on the unscarred side of his chin. 'Of course I will,' she murmured. 'Just wait till we tell Aunt Jane and your father. Won't they be surprised!'

Chapter Fourteen
September 1943

'I'm not surprised,' Aunt Jane said stoutly, grating carrot into her cake mixture with a prodigal hand. 'I've always known that Jake and Daisy were made for each other. I'm just relieved that they realised the truth before either of them had made the sort of mistake that is followed by a lifetime of regret.'

Bob, peeling the carrots at the sink, turned and gave his wife an indulgent glance. 'Oh no, you weren't surprised,' he said sarcastically. 'Your mouth was one big round O and your eyes two more when we walked into that ward and found Daisy sitting on Jake's bed, close as two peas in a pod. But I mustn't tease you because when Sean came to the farm you had to tell him that it was all over between him and Daisy. It must have been horrid, my dear, but I know you coped well.'

'I didn't have to tell him anything, not really,' Jane observed. 'Daisy's friend Suzie seemed to have done a pretty convincing job already. I *told* you, I got the definite impression that it was Sean's self-esteem which had taken a knock and not his heart.'

'And Jake, bless him, did his own dirty work and told Belinda that he meant to marry someone else,' Bob put in. 'How's that cake coming along?'

Jane stirred some more grated carrot into her mixing bowl, regarded it critically for a moment, then added a shake of mixed spice from a small drum and stirred it carefully into the creamy mixture. 'It's a poor sort of wedding cake, with not so much as a single currant or sultana, and no icing or decorations, but it's the best I can manage at such short notice,' she said ruefully. 'If only they'd agreed to wait a little longer . . . but you can't blame them. With Jake being released from hospital in a few days, it's natural they should want to be together.'

'True,' Bob said. 'The only thing is that they said they wanted a small quiet wedding only it's turning out to be a very large one indeed. Don't tell me it's not their fault because I know it, but it's made things awfully difficult for you.'

'Oh, I don't know; all their pals will come to the church but I've warned them that the reception will be an austerity affair,' Jane said quickly. 'I know I said I'd make the wedding cake and do a pile of little cakes and as many sausage rolls as I could manage, but think of all the help I'm getting! Just about everyone who's ever worked with Daisy is contributing something, her family in Ireland have been sending food parcels, and even Jake's old school friends and the chaps from his station have promised to bring any food they can lay their hands on. It'll be all right, honest to God it will.'

'If only they could have got married here in the village church, it would have been simpler,' Bob observed, dipping a finger into the cake mix and getting his wrist slapped. 'But it was difficult when neither of them was ever resident in the parish, so you can understand them wanting to go back to Liverpool, to the church they attended as youngsters. And the Reverend is letting them use the church hall for the reception free of charge.'

'Well, everyone is doing their best to make it a memorable occasion,' Jane said. As she spoke, she tipped the cake mixture into a greased tin and carried it across to the oven. 'Oh, Bob, after all the uncertainties and misery that poor Jake has undergone ever since Daisy abandoned him, he must feel he's on the right road at last.'

'I know. He's extremely happy, though he wanted to get his sight back before they wed so that he wouldn't be a burden to anyone,' Bob said. 'But I think he manages pretty well, one way and another. He trusts Daisy completely, you know; they walk along arm in arm at a good speed and she warns him of uneven paving stones, or steep kerbs, or low shop doorways, so that to a casual observer he must seem completely normal. I think they'll go on very well.'

'Ye-es, but it's a shame he won't be able to see dear little Daisy in that pretty dress Amanda has sent,' Jane said regretfully. 'It was Amanda's own wedding dress and I didn't think it would fit Daisy, so I put a couple of darts at the waist and turned the hem up four inches, and she looks like a little princess. But clothes aren't important; I dare say

Jake would be just as happy if she turned up in her old dungarees. Not that he'd know what she looks like, poor lad. If only . . . but the surgeon says he may well recover some degree of sight in time; we must just be patient, as Jake is.'

The church was full, with many members of the congregation in air force uniform. The Reverend John Porlock checked that everything was in order. The groom and his tall, red-haired best man stood waiting, the groom perhaps a little nervous though he never glanced behind him but stared straight ahead. Presently, there was a stir and a rustle and the bride, all in white, with one hand tucked into the arm of the man who was to give her away – the Reverend John understood he was her Uncle Bob – began to walk down the aisle as the organ music swelled into the wedding march. The Reverend John, robes swishing, his prayer book in his hand though he knew his part by heart, began the service. 'Dearly beloved, we are gathered together here in the sight of God, and in the face of this congregation, to join together this man and this woman in holy matrimony . . .'

Without really looking up from the page, the Reverend John saw the girl reach out a small hand and take that of her bridegroom, and as she did so the young man turned towards her. The priest noticed that his thick dark hair had been flattened down with Brylcreem and that his air force uniform, with his aircrew brevet on the chest, was impeccable. He thought what a nice couple they made and how good it was that they should marry, for he remembered now, vaguely, that the boy had been in some sort of accident. No doubt that was the reason for the piratical eye patch and for the scars across the left-hand side of his face.

She was a pretty girl, this little bride, dark-haired, dark-eyed, and with a most appealing smile; yes, he told himself, this was no rushed affair, for now that he thought back he could remember them, first as children and then as young people, always together, arguing and fighting sometimes, but mostly up to some mischief and thick as thieves. A relationship of long standing then . . . but he must not allow his mind to become distracted; he continued with the service: 'It was ordained for the mutual society, help and comfort that the one ought to have of the other, both in prosperity and adversity.'

He was opening his mouth to continue when the boy in front of him burst into speech. 'You're wearing that old tin locket I gave you when you came to the May ball,' he said. 'I thought you'd have chucked it away years since! Oh, Daisy, fancy you keeping . . .'

The Reverend John glared at the bridegroom. Now he thought about it, the lad had been a right little terror, fidgeting his way through services, laughing when he should have been serious. He was wagging a reproving finger when pandemonium broke out in the pews on both sides of the

485

church. The congregation surged into the aisle and rushed up to the young couple. The uncle who was to give the girl away was hugging the groom, the best man was pumping his hand up and down, and everyone else was laughing, crying, or exclaiming. Only the bride and groom said nothing, but both were beaming, and the Reverend John saw with amazement that tears were trickling down their cheeks; tears of joy, he was pretty sure, though he still could not understand the sudden change from the quiet solemnity of the marriage service to what was rapidly becoming something altogether different.

Abruptly, he decided to take control. He clapped his hands sharply. 'Please return to your seats,' he said, with all the authority he could muster. 'Explanations are obviously called for, but there will be plenty of time for that later.' He waited until the church was quiet again and then began to speak once more. 'Into which holy estate these two persons present come now to be joined. Therefore, if any man can show any just cause why they may not lawfully be joined together, let him now speak or else hereafter for ever hold his peace.'

To find out more about Katie Flynn why not join the Katie Flynn Readers' Club and receive a twice-yearly newsletter.

To join our mailing list to receive the newsletter and other information* write with your name and address to:

Katie Flynn Readers' Club
Arrow Books Marketing Department
Random House
20 Vauxhall Bridge Road
London
SW1V 2SA

Please state whether or not you would like to receive information about other Arrow saga authors.

*Your details will be held on a database so we can send you the newsletter(s) and information on other Arrow authors that you have indicated you wish to receive. Your details will not be passed to any third party. If you would to receive information on other Random House authors please do let us know. If at any stage you wish to be deleted from our Katie Flynn Readers' Club mailing list please let us know.

arrow books

Forgotten Dreams

Katie Flynn

Lottie Lacey and her mother, Louella, share a house in Victoria Court with Mr Magic and his son Baz. Lottie is a child star, dancing and singing at the Gaiety Theatre to an enraptured audience, whilst Louella acts as Max Magic's assistant. But Lottie was in hospital for weeks after a road accident and has lost her memory. Louella tries to help but the white mist remains. Until Lottie meets a boy with golden-brown eyes who calls her "Sassy" and accuses her of running away.

It is after this meeting that the dreams start, dreams of another life, almost another world, and Lottie, sharing them with Baz, begins to believe he knows more than he chooses to tell. But then Merle joins the act and Lottie feels Baz and Merle, both older than she, are in league against her.

Then the dreams begin to grow clearer and Lottie realises she must find her past, at no matter what cost.

arrow books

ALSO AVAILABLE IN ARROW

Beyond the Blue Hills

Katie Flynn

Laura Collins, a widow, is struggling to make a good life for her daughters, Tess and Tina. They are living with Laura's sister Millie and her seven children so when Laura is offered a good job, with accommodation, she is delighted.

Life is very different for the Brewsters, living on Manor Farm in Herefordshire. Danny and his girlfriend, Sophie, intend to marry one day so that they can run Manor Farm together but his cousin and best friend, Phil Ryland, feels differently. He longs to get away from farming and intends to escape as soon as he can.

Then war comes and changes everything. Tina is evacuated and Tess joins the Land Army. She means to be true to her boyfriend, Mike, but he is far away. Danny and Phil join the RAF, Danny to pilot bombers and Phil as navigator. They end up on the same airfield and fall in love with the same girl. But Phil has a secret which could end his chance of happiness, and Danny is the only person who knows what that secret is . . .

arrow books